It's That Time Again!

It's That Time Again!
The New Stories of Old-Time Radio

Edited by Ben Ohmart

It's That Time Again!
The New Stories of Old-Time Radio
All Rights Reserved © 2002 Ben Ohmart

Thanks go to the authors for their permission to use the following stories in this collection: "One Principal Too Many, One Principal Too Meanie" © 2002 Clair Schulz; "Tom Mix and the Mystery of the Bodiless Horseman" © 2002 Jim Harmon; "The Japanese Sandman" © 2002 Jack French; "Perils of the Tiger Barn" © 2002 Roger Smith; "The Case of the Bashful Spider" © 2002 Bob Martin; "A Call From the Storm" © 2002 Jim Nixon; "The Cradle of Peace" © 2002 Martin Grams Jr.; "A Matter of Ethics" © 2002 Carol Tiffany; "The Vanishing Ruby" © 2002 Stephen A. Kallis Jr.; "You've Got Me, John" © 2002 Ben Ohmart; "The Letter From John" © 2002 John Leasure; "The Ticket Stub" © 2002 Michael Leannah; "Attack of the Crawling Things From Outer Space" © 2002 Justin Felix; "Willoughby Goes and Gets It" © 2002 Joe Bevilacqua & Robert J. Cirasa; "A Pine Ridge Christmas Carol" © 2002 Donnie Pitchford; "One Card Draw" © 2002 Michael Giorgio; "A Poole of Blood" © 2002 Stephen Jansen; "The Paddy Rose Matter" © 2002 Patrick W. Picciarelli; "The Case of the Missing Bandleader" © 2002 Bryan Powell; "Concerto in Death Major" © 2002 Christopher Conlon.

For information, address:

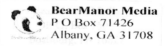

BearManor Media
P O Box 71426
Albany, GA 31708

bearmanormedia.com

Cover design and *Black Museum* illustration by Lloyd W. Meek
Typesetting and layout by John Teehan

Published in the USA by BearManor Media
ISBN - 0-9714570-2-6

The show is about to begin...

Table of Contents

A Word From Your Sponsor

Radio is not dead. Not even dying. Old-time radio isn't even ill. The spirit of OTR lives on in ever-increasing audience numbers, in respect and in admiration. The fact that little fiction is being produced for the wireless these days (in the United States, anyway) does not take away from the power of this cult, if indeed 'cult' is the right term. The economy is partly to blame. So is that evil, glowing box called television which does it all for you. Nothing left to the imagination there.

But for those of us who still like to think while being entertained, we certainly miss the breadth of choice and material that made the 1930's and 1940's "The Golden Age." We hanker for new adventures with our old heroes. Hence, this book.

While I myself was not old enough to enjoy the magic that was live radio, I did get hooked on the sport from an early age, often frequenting Waldenbooks or any other book/gift shops that dared to stock box sets of my beloved *Bickersons*, *Fibber McGee* or *Duffy's Tavern*. From there, my tastes grew up and outward and, like the many radio lovers gathered together in this book, I seized every opportunity to increase my collection, my knowledge, my mind's eye.

As you are about to see, our favorite characters are not gone. Not only do they remain on a vast amount of cassettes, CDs and reels, but they inhabit the fertile minds of many good people, fine writers and great collectors who know more about old radio shows than - well, I don't know what. And that is the point of what you now hold in your hands.

I had the idea earlier this year (2002) to solicit new adventures of old-time radio shows from those who know the form or characters best. I wanted to "hear" something new, to experience not only new adventures, but finally put to paper new scripts in a different way. Fiction. Luckily, the idea met with support, from some very able minds, and soon the project was under way. I was not seeking major writers, nor celebrities, but I wanted the fans themselves and OTR club people to have a go at something like this. Not forgetting the nostalgia writers who had shown support for our medium in various magazines.

1

Fan fiction, you may call it. You're right. And you will be surprised. There are some strong stories in this collection. You might be puzzled by the choices of shows (yes, I'll admit, there are some odd picks here), but I tried to let authors go with their instincts, as long as no two submissions were on the same show. Indeed, even anthology series, like *Dimension X* and *Inner Sanctum*, which had no sustaining characters or plot, are fair game in this book. Authors were allowed to write their own bio and show introduction too. Any faults or inconsistencies in this book are mine. All praise must be directed at the authors.

A few people have worried about the soundness of this book idea. Could "scriptwritten" events and casts be simulated properly or successfully in a fiction format? And, how do we disassociate ourselves from the modern world completely? Well, the only real criteria I had for this collection was to keep to the original sense and age of the story: no time machine stuff, no shows that did not originate with radio (i.e no *Superman*, *The Thin Man*, etc.), no language that doesn't fit the era. For the most part, I think we got it right. Please pardon any slips. This is the first collection of its kind—and I hope not the last—so there is always room for improvement. In fact, we'd love to hear from you, dear readers. Tell us your thoughts, concerns, praises, and what you'd like to see for a second volume. Remember: there may *be* no second volume without your support. If you like what you read, tell your friends!

The writers worked very hard to assemble this collection for your appraisal. There were more submissions than there was room. So there is already almost enough stories for another volume. We hope you like. We know you will remember…

— *Ben Ohmart*
October 2002

The Shows

THE BICKERSONS became a household word for marital "realism" when it usurped the usual Ozzie and Harriet kind of goody-goody humor in the mid-1940s. Appearing on *Drene Time* then *The Old Gold Show*, Don Ameche and Frances Langford as John and Blanche Bickerson were often quoted as "arguably" the freshest thing on radio. Trying to come up with a new situation that would still give rise to the snores, the cat and the usual Bickerson formula was difficult. They'd already been on vacation, on a second honeymoon, on a train, on a boat, and in bed. All that seemed left was a plane, and a bowling ball salesman convention.

THE BLACK MUSEUM, Scotland Yard's "mausoleum of murder," featured everyday objects—a matchbook, a cuff link, a bent and rusty nail—each playing a critical role in a story of murder. Narrator Orson Welles would guide his radio listeners down the aisles of the cavernous museum, stop to observe an item on display, and, with great authority, tell its chilling tale. In "The Ticket Stub," we hear the final account from that grisly chamber of horrors.

CANDY MATSON, YUKON 2-8209 was the best among about a dozen lady crime-fighter series that appeared on network radio. Created, written, and directed by Monty Masters, it starred his wife, Natalie Parks, in the title role. This weekly series ran from June 1949 to May 1951. A San Francisco based show, it took pride in incorporating Bay area geography into every episode. The series was transcribed, but only 14 episodes (including the audition show and a reprise) are currently available.

CAPTAIN MIDNIGHT first aired in 1938 as a syndicated 15-minute aviation adventure serial. In the fall of 1940, Ovaltine took over sponsorship and the program was broadcast over the Mutual network. With that change, Captain Midnight, a skilled aviator, became the leader of a paramilitary organization, the Secret Squadron. With a basic team of Chief Mechanic Ichabod Mudd, and two teens, Chuck Ramsay and Joyce Ryan, Captain Midnight contended with wartime foes and peacetime criminals. The program was highly popular and rather than being aimed at children, was written so that adults would enjoy it as well (just under half the audience was over 21, according to Ovaltine). It was a *special* show growing up, and listening to the relatively few surviving Ovaltine recordings as an adult, I still appreciate it as a *special* program. After writing *Radio's Captain Midnight*, which chronicles his adventures through World War II, I decided to create a story involving Captain Midnight's adventures after the show went off the air, and the following is the result.

THE CLYDE BEATTY SHOW. The world's greatest wild animal trainer, Clyde Beatty, and an exciting adventure from his brilliant career! The circus means thrills, excitement and snarling jungle beasts. The circus means fun for the young folks and old. But under the Big Top, you only see a part of the story. The real drama comes behind the scenes, where 500 people live as one family, where Clyde Beatty constantly risks death in the most dangerous act on earth. This master of the big cats has journeyed to Africa and India, hunting down his beasts in their native jungle. All of this is part of the Clyde Beatty story!

As a 4-year old crippled kid, I was carried into the Big Top of the Clyde Beatty Railroad Circus, during a visit to relatives in Tyler, Texas. Seeing the man in person was my epiphany. I knew exactly what I wanted to be. I listened to his radio show on Mondays, Wednesdays, and Fridays over the Mutual Network. He was sponsored by Kellogg's. When I saw Ben Ohmart's request for chapters for his Old Time Radio book, I jumped through flaming hoops for the Clyde Beatty assignment.

DIMENSION X. Considered to be the first serious radio science fiction series, *Dimension X* aired on NBC from 1950 to 1951 and featured stories by Ray Bradbury, Isaac Asimov, and Kurt Vonnegut. It was the forerunner to such TV series as *The Twilight Zone* and *The Outer Limits*. In writing a short story in the style of *Dimension X*, we tried to be true to the original, while using characters from our own current radio series, "The Whithering of Willoughby and the Professor." The result is both a post-modern tribute and a story that holds up on its own merits.

FRONTIER GENTLEMAN, personified by John Dehner as *London Times* reporter J.B. Kendall, was one of the last network dramatic shows to premiere during radio's golden age, riding in on the coattails of TV's western craze in 1958. Introduced in the program opening as "a man with a gun who lives and becomes part of the violent years in the new territories," Kendall faces something more dangerous than a mere gun: a marriage-minded woman and two over-eager bachelors.

THE GREEN LAMA was a detective show with a twist—the hero was a wealthy young American who developed mystical powers during his many years of study in Tibet. (Author Bob Martin notes that his short story is based on fictional characters portrayed in the original radio program, and does not represent actual beliefs or practices of Buddhists and the Tibetan people.) The radio show was most notable for its talented cast, with the incomparable Paul Frees in the starring role and veteran radio actor Ben Wright as his sidekick, Tulku. Paul Frees would later become famous for his voice-over work in commercials and cartoons, creating unforgettable characters such as Boris Badenov in *The Rocky and Bullwinkle Show*, and Professor Ludwig Von Drake for Disney.

The short-lived *Lama* was heard on CBS during the summer of 1949. Only four episodes are known to exist today, and are highly sought after by Paul Frees fans.

THE HALLS OF IVY was one of my favorite shows during the early 1950s. This show was a highly unusual type of situation comedy representative of its time in its emphasis on morals and ethics. Series creator Don Quinn, writer of *Fibber McGee and Molly*, wanted to try a more literate comedy and worked on the idea for several years before the show emerged in its final form. The show revolves around Ivy College president Dr. William Todhunter Hall (Ronald Colman) and his British musical-comedy star wife, Victoria (Benita {Hume} Colman). The characters complemented each other beautifully. The intellectual Dr. Hall would seem stuffy without the warm witticisms exchanged with his more down-to-earth wife.

Although this series was at heart a comedy, many of the scripts tackled serious issues of the times presented as student and/or faculty problems to be solved by the Halls. For me, at least, the lyrics of the theme song say it all, "we love the halls of Ivy, that are here with us today, and we will not forget though we be far, far away…"

HONEST HAROLD was a light, whimsical series that ran for one year in the early 1950s on CBS and starred the legendary Harold Peary of *The Great Gildersleeve* fame. Indeed, the show was sometimes introduced as *The Harold Peary Show*. In many respects, Harold is a lot like Gildy. He is an amorous bachelor and quite connected with the people of his hometown (many of whom were suspiciously similar to characters in *The Great Gildersleeve*, which was still being concurrently produced on NBC without Peary).

One of the challenges of writing an *Honest Harold* story is that the cast of characters would change periodically. On several occasions, key characters would just completely disappear in the next week's episode—with no explanation. Despite this, *Honest Harold* had a fair share of funny episodes, and I thought it would be fun to do a story that used Harold Peary's self-caricature. This story takes place some time before the Thanksgiving episode of *Honest Harold*.

INNER SANCTUM MYSTERIES, which survived on various networks from 1941 to 1952, is perhaps best remembered not for any of its individual stories, but for the eerie creaking door heard at the beginning and end of each broadcast. The program's delightfully lurid organ music also helped set the mood, as did The Host's gruesome sense of humor in introducing the tales. The plays themselves were generally slight, and campy: insanely fast-paced stories of apparent supernatural doom, usually frittered away at the end with a (sort of) "logical" explanation. This new "Inner Sanctum" piece, "Concerto in Death Major," imagines The Host as he might be living now, today, on the afternoon he receives a final visit from his old sponsor—Mary, the Lipton Tea Lady—to whom he tells one final macabre story.

LUM AND ABNER, radio's long-running rural comedy, premiered in 1931 and signed off in 1954. Though there were brief gaps during those years, the program nonetheless built loyal fans and inspired a series of seven motion pictures. *Lum and Abner* starred Chet (Lum) Lauck and Norris (Abner) Goff, boyhood friends from Mena, Arkansas, who based the dialects, locale and characters on the people and places they knew so well. Since 1984, the National Lum and Abner Society has thrived to keep their memories alive. "A Pine Ridge Christmas Carol" was written by NLAS President "Uncle Donnie" Pitchford in 1987 for the publication *The Jot 'Em Down Journal*, being patterned after the characters and situations in the original programs.

MA PERKINS resided in Rushville Center and on the network airways for some 27 years from 1933 through the infamous "The Day Radio Died" in November, 1960 when CBS cancelled the last hour of network radio soap opera. *Ma Perkins* revolved around the wisdom and common sense of the title character and the dilemmas of her children, grandchildren and close friends. The hallmark of the show was the performance of Virginia Payne as Ma, who conveyed the gentle, loving soul of her character in a timeless fashion. Listen to the show today, and it still resonates with a quality of quiet truth. The story in this collection remembers the only war death of a major character in a radio soap opera. The death of John Perkins stirred heartfelt and angry protests from listeners because the characters of "Ma Perkins" were both written and acted with a certain reality.

OUR MISS BROOKS is probably radio's best comedy program whose debut occurred after the end of World War II. Week after week the same combatants, perky Connie Brooks and crafty Osgood Conklin, were tossed into the same academic ring where they circled each other relentlessly, looking for openings to land pungent punch lines.

As the years go by, the marvelous performances of Eve Arden and Gale Gordon on the show increase in stature. Teachers of speech or acting would be well-advised to play tapes of Our Miss Brooks to students to demonstrate how, when two polished actors deliver lines with just the right nuances of intonation, an amusing program can be elevated to the heights of sublime comedy.

What is sometimes overlooked when people recall the series is the bittersweet flavor of the story lines. By the end of most episodes Connie was frustrated in her pursuit of Boynton and battered by her exchanges with Conklin. When the bell rang for the next round or class, we know our Miss Brooks would come out swinging even though she probably felt more like throwing in the towel or crying in it. It is that undercurrent of "smile though your heart is breaking" that I tried to capture in "One Principal Too Many, One Principal Too Meanie."

PAT NOVAK, FOR HIRE was unlike any other radio show. Not quite a detective series, and not quite a comedy, it catapulted its main star, Jack Webb, to stardom. The plots tended to run as thin as the metaphor-laden dialogue ran thick. Listeners tuned in mainly for the snappy, overdone, smart-mouthed patter. In virtually every episode, Novak gets knocked out cold in a fight, then awakens next to a recently-murdered body. Inspector Hellman is always nearby to accuse Novak of the murder, until Novak uncovers a few more clues that prove who really did it.

Those who enjoy the *Pat Novak* series should also search out the later 1947 Mutual series *Johnny Modero: Pier 23*, a carbon copy of *Pat Novak*. They might also like *Pete Kelly's Blues* from 1951, a slightly lighter version of *Pat Novak* with a 1920's jazz speakeasy background. Of course, Webb also did the enormously successful *Dragnet* series, but it's a little harder to dredge up such hearty belly laughs from that one.

I dropped in tidbits from all of these series in my *Pat Novak* pastiche, along with some OTR inside jokes, for some added depth.

QUIET PLEASE. From 1947 to 1949, an underrated program entitled *Quiet, Please* introduced listeners to the true origins of fantasy. The dividing lines between horror, science-fiction, and fantasy have become as controversial today as the themes they represented. Yet Willis Cooper, the brain behind all of the scripts, seemed to have an endless imagination when it came to plots so intriguing as to experiment with any themes that bordered these topics. The proverbial corner cobwebs were dusted away, illuminating the way to fantasy untold and unsung. Always told in the first person, each story dealt with human interests and versatile themes, ending with a comment leaving the audience to ponder thoughts outside our Universe. One such broadcast introduced listeners to the ghost of a twelve-year old girl who sang and played the piano in the attic. Others showed us the world seen from the insects' point of view, and their plans for world domination; war-torn and weary soldiers routed for a Christmas dinner instead of gunplay, only to receive a dinner guest celebrating his birthday; lovers on a grass knoll philosophized the meaning of life, while admiring the stars, heavens, and a distant planet named Earth; a robot forced to come up with a defense after being accused of killing its creator. And so the stories went...drama after drama.

Due to judgments no doubt initiated by the broadcast "powers that be," *Quiet, Please* was bumped into different time slots throughout the two years, never allowing a stable following of listeners. Ultimately, the program was canceled—against the wishes of Cooper, who threw his best feet forward into the projects. Thankfully, most of these performances survive on tape and their recordings can be enjoyed by a younger generation. What follows is an original short story, in memory of the program that inspired the author, in the same stylistic themes of *Quiet, Please*.

ROGUE'S GALLERY, which debuted in 1945, was a satirical detective vehicle for actor Dick Powell. Powell was fresh from his triumph as Philip Marlowe in the film, *Murder, My Sweet*, which was based on the Raymond Chandler novel, *Farewell, My Lovely*. *Rogue's Gallery* featured Powell as Richard Rogue, a wise-cracking, hardboiled detective who offered listeners "a personally conducted tour through Rogue's Gallery." In almost every episode, Rogue got whacked on the head, knocked unconscious, and floated up to "Cloud Eight" to talk with "Eugor" ("Rogue" spelled backward), a cackling, smart-mouthed sprite who nonetheless usually offered Rogue valuable perspective on the case in question. After Rogue, Dick Powell appeared as a radio gumshoe in the audition episode of *Yours Truly, Johnny Dollar* in 1948 before beginning a stint as *Richard Diamond, Private Detective* in 1949. Diamond and Rogue had much in common, although Diamond had a less painful gimmick: he sang a song at the end of each episode.

SGT. PRESTON OF THE YUKON was created in 1938 by Tom Dougall, a writer working at WXYZ in Detroit, when station owner George W. Trendle decided to add a new adventure program to complement *The Lone Ranger* and the *Green Hornet*, already big hits. Dougall was a fan of the poems of Robert Service, and so decided to cast his hero as a Mountie during the years of the great northern gold rush. Featuring an intelligent Husky named King, its human hero roamed the "snow-covered reaches" of the early Yukon Territory in his "relentless pursuit of lawbreakers." When the stories were set in summer, Preston rode a horse named Rex, but it was King who fulfilled the role of the intelligent animal getting the Sergeant out of tight situations. Many of the scripts conveniently ignored the long Arctic nights and bitterness of the weather, so I wanted to create a story that would incorporate both elements and pit Preston and King against them while coming to the aid of someone unfamiliar to the territory.

Tom Mix and his Ralston Straight Shooters was on the air from 1933 to 1950, with the year 1943 not doing broadcasts because the sponsor feared wartime daylight saving time would put the show on too early for kids to come in from their play. The first year the show came from New York and had Tom Mix impersonated by Artells "Art" Dickson who went on to join the original Tom Mix on the screen in the smallest way, with Western musical short subjects. The show then went to Chicago where Tom was played by Russell Thorson (later "Jack" on *I Love a Mystery*). After 1943, radio's Tom Mix was Curley Bradley. In 1975, I finally was able to locate Curley and we worked to revive the series. Curley Bradley's *Trail of Mystery* was a short series we tried that year. In 1982-83, Ralston executive Steve Kendall offered new Tom Mix premiums including cereal bowls, a watch, a comic book (edited by myself) and a few new radio episodes with Curley Bradley, written and produced by me (and I played Pecos).

This story is new, but it contains elements from many of the old episodes arranged in a new manner. The forest fire and Tony's broken leg are from separate serials from around 1939. Sam Hawk is actually from my 1975 Curley Bradley series, there played by my dear old friend, Kirk Alyn. The Bodiless Horseman or invisible rider is from one of the last half-hour shows in 1950, scripted by George Lowther.

Yours Truly, Johnny Dollar was the last detective drama to leave the airwaves. It completed its run in 1962 after fourteen years and over 900 shows. Arguably the best of the Dollars was Bob Bailey who captured the spirit of the freelance insurance investigator in hundreds of dramas, most notably the 5-parters (considered the best of the series).

I listened to Johnny Dollar as a 14-year old during the last year of its run. Although a child of television, I was fascinated by the Dollar radio dramas and would lay on my bed in my room with the lights out and a transistor radio plastered up against my ear every Sunday night at six. Thirty years later, when I began to collect OTR, I sought out all the Johnny Dollar shows. I own over 600 and my collection is growing.

OUR MISS BROOKS

One Principal Too Many,
One Principal Too Meanie

by Clair Schulz

During my years of teaching English at Madison High School I have stood over the wishing well in the nearby park many times tossing in coins and hoping that Mr. Boynton would make his move and that Mr. Conklin would just move. If what happened recently is any indication of how efficacious my wishing efforts have been, the next time I visit that well I am going to keep my purse closed and throw myself in.

If someone had told me that Madison's beloved (by his wife and daughter…sometimes) but autocratic principal, Osgood Conklin, was going to be replaced, I would have been pleasantly surprised. Surprised? I would have helped him move his chair out of his office while he was still in it.

But, as the ancient Greeks said, there's many a slip between the cup and the lip. Or, as they say in my crowd, somebody kiboshed the caboose before it got out of the station.

It all started when Mr. Conklin summoned (or let's say ordered because "Be here or be gone" does seem to have a marching orders flavor to it) Philip Boynton and myself to his office after lunch last Friday. Technically, the few minutes we teachers have after eating should be our own time and I do so look forward to sharing a table with the bashful biologist, even if it's only to flip a quarter to see who pays for the meal, but Mr. Conklin has always insisted that "For devoted teachers there is no such thing as 'free' time. They should always be vigilant, ready to serve when duty calls." The foreign legion lost a great commandant when Osgood Conklin decided on a career in education.

When I opened the door on that fateful day, Philip was already sitting in the chair next to the walnut desk behind which sat Mr. Conklin with his hands on the arms of his brown leather chair that members of the faculty referred to as "the Throne." Hanging on the wall behind that chair is a faded and cracked oil portrait of Madison's revered founder, Yodar Kritch, in some of his mutton-chopped glory. Whenever I look up at Kritch's stern visage, I imagine him pitching right in and helping the students of his day with some of his pet projects like cutting hickory switches, building pillories and stocks, and doing their stretching exercises on the rack.

Mr. Conklin graciously offered me a seat (i.e. he pointed emphatically to the chair directly in front of his desk that I called the hot seat). Before I could adjust it to medium-well he said, "I'll come right to the point, Miss Brooks. I have asked you and Mr. Boynton here to apprise you of an educational initiative that I believe will be beneficial to all parties involved. As you know, there is an opening on the school district's administrative team and I am being considered for that position. As chief assistant to the superintendent I will be reaching the heights of my ambition and soaring with the big boys. It would be quite a feather in my cap to join that team. You understand what this means to me, Miss Brooks?"

"Yes," I replied. "It means that you'll not only win your letter but they'll also put a band on one of your legs."

For a moment Mr. Conklin said nothing. He just flicked his salt-and-pepper mustache (he had just finished lunch, too) and stared at me with cold gray eyes. Then, without losing eye contact, he lowered his head like a bull preparing to attack, affording me a view of the receding hairline along his temples and the bald spot at the crown of his head, and calmly noted, "Miss Brooks, there are those who would claim that I am seeking this promotion for financial gain. They are wrong. There are those who would say that I am a status seeker who wants to impress my peers. They also are wrong. But if someone accuses me of trying to find some way to avoiding any further contact with you, well, I would have to take the Fifth."

"Fine," I said, putting my foot next to my molars. "You pour and I'll get the glasses."

His eyes rolled heavenward and, finding no consolation there, came down to me and my colleague. Still in a prayerful mood, his fingers formed a steeple first under his nose and then under his chin.

"Miss Brooks," he said after his black mood had passed and his ebony one had set in, "I'd like to continue bandying words with you but I don't so I won't. I will be brief. I intend to demonstrate to Mr. Stone, head of the board of education, that I am the best person for this job in the superintendent's office by doing something bold and innovative. I believe Mr. Stone has been somewhat reluctant to promote me because of the shortage of principals. I think he also considers me, shall we say, somewhat of a yes man who kowtows to him and who has no ideas of my own."

"If I may insert a comment here," Mr. Boynton said. "I would like to state unequivocally that you certainly are a fine principal and that you would be difficult to replace."

"All that's missing is *si, ja,* and *oui* and he's in the yes man hall of fame," I said *sotto voce*. Apparently I put too much *sotto* in my *voce* for Mr. Conklin shot a very dry gimlet of a glare at me before continuing.

"My plan is to address all of these matters in one sweeping initiative. As you know, Boynton has taken coursework in school administration. My intention is to allow him, as it were, to assume the position of principal for a week under my gentle tutelage. Perhaps, with additional courses this summer, he could acquire the necessary credentials to be hired full-time next fall after I move, shall we say, onward and upward."

Before he started flapping his wings again I tried to form an objection but all that came out was "But—But—But—"

"We can dispense with the imitation of a motorboat, Miss Brooks. Now if—"

"But I don't understand," I continued, steering for the nearest rocks. "Mr. Boynton can't be here acting as principal and in his class teaching biology at the same time."

"That is true," he said, nodding his head. "Even you, despite your regular sprints between your room and Mr. Boynton's lab, cannot be in two places at once, although, in some of my more fanciful moments, I have pictured you in another, shall we say, warmer place."

And happy pitchforks to you, I said, this time to myself.

"I, Osgood Conklin," he said, sitting up in his chair and puffing out his chest, "will take charge of the school and assume a role which will demonstrate that I am a multi-faceted, ingenious dynamo who will be a shining beacon on the educational horizon."

That would make a swell movie, I thought: *Osgood Conklin is a Many-Splendored Thing.*

"Mr. Stone has sometimes intimated that I am too removed from the student body and therefore out of touch with today's youth, a baseless claim that I will disprove during the time next week when I temporarily turn the reins of this office over to Boynton for part of the day while I demonstrate my versatility as an educator by taking over some of his biology classes."

"But you—But he—But how—"

"Push down on the throttle, Miss Brooks," he said, leaning forward like a fisherman with gaff in hand. "What are you trying to say?"

I turned to Mr. Boynton, hoping that he would say what I was thinking, but why should he start now? If he said what I was thinking, we would have been married five years ago.

"Mr. Boynton," I pleaded. "You have the certification to teach biology. Mr. Conklin doesn't. Is this fair to the students?"

"It's only for a couple classes in the morning for just a week, Miss Brooks," he said. "Mr. Conklin wanted you to be here today because you're so popular with the students and teachers he knows you could handle any objections they may have.

Besides, this will be a good test to let me know if I'm cut out to be a principal. And who knows," he added with a small laugh, the only kind he ever gave or earned, "maybe Mr. Conklin will like teaching biology so much he'll become the next Luther Burbank."

He's doing a good job as the most recent Simon Legree, I thought before turning back to Mr. Conklin whose smug expression I hoped to erase with my next objection.

"But what does Mr. Stone think of this idea?"

"Mr. Stone is currently on vacation and will return one week from today. At that time I will be able to present to him ample evidence that I can handle any situation, that I am a bold innovator, a highly competent educator, a take-charge administrator, and—"

Mr. Conklin might have added anything from a prince of a fellow to the father of our country had not the bell rung, signaling the end of the lunch period. He dismissed us with a wave of his hand as if to say, "Begone," so we bewent. The last glimpse I had of Conklin before the door closed was of him gazing up at the portrait, chuckling warmly as if he and Yodar were sharing some private joke about the Inquisition.

I didn't see Mr. Boynton again until after school when we met at our usual rendezvous in front of the primate cages at the zoo. You haven't lived until, after getting paid peanuts, you spend a date flipping peanuts to monkeys and their kin with a dreamboat who is more concerned with his feeding than with the woman alongside him who is eating her heart out and, believe me, I haven't lived.

But, even though he's a square who can be obtuse when it comes to things romantic, I still love all four corners of him. There is something about the tender way he offers a tidbit through the bars that makes me say to myself, "This is the man I'd like to be the father of my chimps, er, children."

The conversation, which had consisted of sweet nothings between Mr. Boynton and his gibbering pals and real nothings between Mr. Boynton and myself, turned naturally to Mr. Conklin's plan. Philip had apparently given the matter much thought because he had a ready response to my question as to why Conklin had gone to so much trouble trying to earn his promotion.

"Maybe he doesn't want to be principal the rest of his life."

"Well, he's been the principal most of my life, or so it seems. Now he just arbitrarily changes schedules solely to suit his own goals so he can move 'onward and upward.' He isn't concerned at all with the fact that by finding a principal right here to take his place it would leave Madison short one biology teacher. And he's not qualified to teach biology even for a few days. He hasn't taught a class in at least ten years."

Mr. Boynton raised a forefinger as if testing the wind direction or sending a message to the creatures behind him and said, "You forget, Miss Brooks, that he has a lifetime certificate to teach. He's been grandfathered in."

I waved that objection off with a gesture which may have sent the chimpanzees behind us scurrying in another direction and replied, "I don't care if he's got a notarized letter from his great-aunt. It's not fair to the students. He taught penmanship. What's he going to say when they're dissecting a crawfish? Tell them to put dots over the eyes and ask them to make certain the abdominal incision reads 'Open Sesame' in cursive letters?"

He threw a handful of peanuts into the penetralia of the cage and said, "Oh, there won't be anything like that next week. Besides, I'll be right down the hall. That's the nice thing about this arrangement. Mr. Conklin and I have each other to fall back on."

"And when you're both sprawled there on the floor, who's going to pick you up?" I angrily flung a peanut past a monkey who first looked at the missile and then at me as if asking what he had done wrong before scampering after his treat. "I wonder if it ever occurred to Mr. Conklin that his scheme could backfire and he could be demoted instead of promoted."

"I don't think there's much chance of that. You see, the way he explained it to me, the teaching is just part of his grand plan. He wants to prove to Mr. Stone that he's a Renaissance man who can do it all: handle the faculty, communicate to the board, instruct students, write curriculum…"

"Leap tall buildings, climb mountains, do laundry on Saturdays… But even if he can do all those things, what gets me is the sneaky way he usurps authority. He waits until Mr. Stone is on vacation and then sets the rules."

"Well, you know the old saying, 'When the cat's away, the mice will play.'"

"There's another saying I'm making up right now: 'When the rat sets the trap, he better make sure his tail is out of the way.'"

At that Philip's blue eyes sparkled, he flashed a smile, the cleft on his chin seemed to wink, my knees buckled and, if they had known the tune, my heartstrings would have gone zing.

"I know you're joking," he said, leaning against the railing like me and turning his back to the animals. "But you haven't said anything about me taking over his job for a few mornings. How do you think I'll look behind a principal's desk?"

"Like a dreamboat in dry dock," I muttered. "But it takes a special kind of person to be a principal. Do you think that's the right job for you?"

He turned to me and said, "That's what I want to find out. I've taken some classes, but I need to get in there and see if I've got what it takes."

Since his face was only inches from mine I leaned closer and whispered, "I've got what it takes if you're one who takes what somebody who's willing to give something for the taking, and if you'll stop this merry-go-round I'll get off at the next funhouse."

He put his left arm behind me on the railing and painted a lovely picture with his right hand. On the painting he pointed to the additional income he would be making as principal, the house he could afford with that money, and the wife and family who would live in that house with him. When I artfully asked him if he would like to sign and date that work, he shyly said that at present he would have to borrow a card from one of the serials titled "To Be Continued" to hang on the piece. I left it at that, though I realized that "To Get Started" would have been a more appropriate sign.

Project Osgood, as I liked to call it, began on Monday and, after three days, all I had to say was that if Thomas Edison's experiments had been as successful his life story would have been called *The Light That Failed*. Word had come to me through the grapevine (Walter Denton being the juiciest grape on that vine) that Mr. Conklin usually deflected questions as if they were pitches to be batted back into the faces of students. During a discussion of trees belonging to the poplar family, for example, Walter asked about the marginal teeth of the quaking aspen, only to be told that anyone whose grades are marginal should be quaking at the prospect of failing and should therefore sink his teeth into his book where the answer quite obviously was if only he had the determination to find it.

Meanwhile, in the principal's office, Mr. Boynton was taking the time to listen to concerns with his usual thoughtfulness and courtesy. The problem was that he had left all his solutions in bottles back in the biology lab. Tuesday morning when I informed him that when I went to the stock room and discovered that we were nearly out of notebook paper, he proceeded to start a lecture about how paper came from secondary xylem which I stopped with the comment that I didn't care if it came from Upper Sandusky and that if we didn't requisition an order soon all of us would be writing on slate which brought forth a diatribe about metamorphic rock which I never heard the end of because I needed to get to my next class. Trying to get a concise, pertinent answer from Boynton as principal was like working on a book of crossword puzzles and finding that the answers in the back had come from an algebra text.

I was discussing the difficulties we had been having at school with my landlady, Mrs. Davis, on Thursday during breakfast. I am reluctant to say *over* breakfast for, considering her penchant for creating exotic combinations like rutabaga muffins and shrimpballs marinated in kumquat wine, I don't want to bring up the inevitable. (I guess I just did that anyway.)

Mrs. Davis sat across from me in her plaid robe, gazing over her spectacles as she attempted to read my fortune in tea leaves. Upon finding a pleasing omen in her cup she exclaimed, "Oh, Connie! I see a handsome man in your future."

"I'd settle for a homely one in my past. But right now I need to get the two men in my present back to where they belong."

"I've always said that Osgood doesn't belong in a classroom. He doesn't have the patience to be a teacher. He's like a fish out of water."

"And in biology especially. Walter told me that yesterday when a student asked Mr. Conklin to explain the difference between the monocots and the dicots, he said he couldn't tell one of those singing groups from another."

Mrs. Davis reached a consoling hand across the table, patted my arm, and said, "Neither can I, dear. I draw the line at Perry Como. He sends me."

I decided to leave unwell enough alone and move on. Mrs. Davis is a dear soul, a sweetheart who rarely asks for the rent money I have owed her since Bette Davis was doing Jezebel, but her mind wanders so often I have to put out an All Points Bulletin to bring it back.

"Mr. Boynton is in over his head, too," I said. "He can't give a straight answer. He just cites some analogue from science. Yesterday before school I told him that we needed to get out more publicity about our clean-up-the-parks campaign so that our students will be recognized for their citizenship, and instead of taking notes or calling the newspaper, he said, 'Speaking of being recognized, did you know that over 3,000 species of trilobites have been identified?' Imagine that! He wanted to talk about trilobites."

I could tell by her glazed eyes that she had been doing the mambo with Perry because her head vacillated between the licorice waffles and the watermelon omelet on the table as she asked, "Try a bite of what?"

"Trilobites, Mrs. Davis. They're fossils from 200 million years ago."

"Well, in that case, I wouldn't want any. I don't even keep hard rolls longer than a week or two."

"Good idea," I said. I threw the switch to prevent another derailment. "But at least in the afternoon when Mr. Boynton is back in the lab and Mr. Conklin is in his office life goes on somewhat normally. If you call this normal and if you call this living. Although he's a dictator at times, say between 7:00 a.m. and 6:00 p.m., at least Mr. Conklin can make a decision even if that decision is that he rules the world."

Mrs. Davis punctuated her agreement by raising her cup and declaring, "Once a martinet, always a martinet."

I clinked my cup with hers and offered a toast: "To the only man who would demand to play both leads in *The King and I*."

The horn that sounded then was not that of Triton beckoning me to a frolic in the sea but rather an invitation to put my life in Walter Denton's hands which emanated from under the partial hood of his jalopy. I bid good-bye to Mrs. Davis, who might well have spent the day trying to decide whether to send some of her recipes to Betty Crocker or Robert Ripley, and hurried out to join Walter in a vehicle that looks like it either left the assembly line an hour too soon or three decades too late.

You could call it a two-door except there were no doors and you could call it a hardtop except there was no top. There were no fenders and the license plate in front appeared to be the only thing holding that bumper on. When Walter told me one day that he had been thinking about selling the car for parts I asked, "You mean you haven't been already?"

He gunned the engine which threw a plume of black smoke out the muffler and into our lungs, then touched the accelerator with all the gentleness of a Mexican hat dancer who had a grudge against sombreros. By the time we were three blocks away and I had peeled the back of my head off the cushion I asked Walter if he was ready for his first-period class which just happened to be biology.

"Yes and no," he said, glancing at me with determination in his eyes.

"Well, that makes it clear. At the next corner turn left *and* right."

"What I mean, Miss Brooks, is that I am not ready to answer questions related to today's lesson, but, boy oh boy, am I prepared for what's going to happen in a few minutes."

Without any coaxing he explained that was tired of being humiliated in class by what he considered to be Mr. Conklin's deliberate attempts to embarrass him. He cited as one example that after Harriet, Mr. Conklin's daughter and Walter's girl-friend, had described a fluke as a parasite noted for its stickers which it attaches to its host, Mr. Conklin told the class that it would be a fluke if Walter was ever invited to dinner again so he could stick his host for another meal.

The final blow to his dignity occurred Wednesday morning when Mr. Conklin noted that Cro-Magnon man, despite limited intelligence, created admirable wall paintings, and then remarked, "That might explain your passing marks in art, Denton."

"I took umbrage at that, Miss Brooks."

"So would I, Walter. So would Umbrage. That's taking unfair advantage of his role as tyrant, er, teacher."

"Ah, but today the worm will turn. In fact, the worm turned yesterday when I said out loud that the earthworm has five hearts which is five more than someone I know and for that, even though I didn't mention his name, Mr. Conklin made me stay after school to clean up the lab. So while Mr. Boynton and Mr. Conklin were up in the office after school, that's when I hatched the plot of all plots."

What emerged next from Walter's throat was a combination snicker, cackle, and giggle that could only be generated by adolescent adenoids. When I convinced him to stop rubbing his hands like John Barrymore's Mr. Hyde and return them to the steering wheel, he revealed his course of action.

After inveigling from Harriet a phone number where Mr. Stone could be reached at an upstate resort, he had placed a call to the head of the board after supper and, by using a disguised voice, pretended to be Mr. Conklin with a cold, hinting about an emergency which had arisen that he could not handle and insisting that it was imperative Mr. Stone be at school early the next morning to deal with "a matter of life and death."

Knowing which one of those two options would be his fate if his scheme was discovered, Walter asked me to bring Mr. Stone to the lab as soon as he came to school. Because I do not have a class during the first period this term, I told him I would do my best but also expressed displeasure at such a deception.

"It's for the good of the school, Miss Brooks. Old Marblehead, er, Mr. Conklin is a crab who needs to be swimming in his own pool, away from the students most of the time. And, although I know you're fond of Mr. Boynton, I wish he was back in his lab because he's lost in the office. Yesterday when I complained to him about the stale food in the cafeteria and demanded that he do something about it, he spent about three minutes telling me about the spores of black bread mold which spread with amazing rapidity. Gee, Miss Brooks, as editor of *The Madison Monitor,* I'd hate to have to tell the students in the school paper that if the vegetables in the lunchroom make you sick, Mr. Boynton says you should try the penicillin in the moldy bread."

After we agreed that we were better off, to use Walter's ungrammatical but felicitous expression, "when our status was quoed," he unleashed his most fiendish crow before revealing the measures he had taken to assure the success of his stratagem.

"You know the pull-down diagrams above Mr. Boynton's blackboard? Well, when Mr. Conklin pulls them down today, the class will get an anatomy lesson they'll never forget."

Before I could object, Walter explained that he had also borrowed a prop from the school stage to replace the flashlight in one of the drawers that Mr. Conklin had used in the lab to shine in the eyes of students when asking them his version of *Twenty Questions* which the students considered a form of the third degree. Finally, to assure the triumph of his revenge, he had taken liberties with some of the labels in the lab. I refrained from asking him when we could expect the sneezing power to appear for fear that he might produce a full bag of it from under his seat.

By that time we had reached Madison High School, an austere, three-story red brick building whose architecture can aptly be described as early medieval dungeon. Forbidding gothic archways open into fusty sepulchral hallways which harbor bleak classrooms, which, if one spends enough time in them, lead to abject poverty for teachers and severe depression for students. Guests at other high schools seek out trophy cases displaying cups and medals or plaques listing the names of honored scholars; visitors to Madison wonder where is the graffiti that reads "Ygor crept here."

There was no sign of Messrs. Boynton, Conklin, or Stone in the office. In fact, the only creature stirring besides the secretary was McDougall, Mr. Boynton's pet frog, who was croaking softly (pardon the oxymoron) in his cage just outside Mr. Conklin's door. I suspect that at times during the week, like the hapless brooder in "The Raven" who had turned to a bird for solace, Mr. Boynton had been consulting McDougall to answer administrative questions, and I am certain that "Glug" shed as much light on educational matters for Philip as "Nevermore" had brightened the nocturnal reader's Plutonian shore.

It was my curiosity and not just my matutinal habit of visiting the lab that drew me to that room. By opening the door a couple inches I could see what was going on inside and still have a commanding view of anyone going into the principal's office down the hall just by leaning my head back.

I heard and saw Conklin tap for attention with the mandible of some has-being which happened to be on the black counter top of the long oak desk that served as a demonstration table in the front of the class. *Alas, Poor Yorick,* I thought, *I knew you before you became a gavel.*

The class had been studying aquatic life and Mr. Conklin was talking about the whoppers he had caught at Crystal Lake which were nothing compared with the whoppers he was telling. When Walter, who was sitting near the back of the room under Conklin edict because Harriet had been placed front row center, asked if he had ever caught a coelacanth in Crystal Lake, Mr. Conklin sensed a dodge and, after consulting a reference book, made a comment about one that really got away that only he and Harriet (out of familial devotion and fear of flying jawbones) honored with a laugh.

After a couple minutes of the driest sea discourse since the ancient mariner couldn't swallow a drop of the stuff, Walter glanced back at me and, after I had given him the "no luck" sign, attempted to stall by asking if eating the cartilage of sharks was good for the bones.

The corners of Mr. Conklin's mouth almost formed a smile but instead settled into what might be termed a benign grimace. Then in carefully measured tones he said, "Denton, as to that I cannot say, but I will state quite emphatically that the sight of a shark nibbling on your bones would be very good for me."

The remark prompted some tittering from a few girls but more significantly spurred Walter into action. After another look back at me, he nudged the boy in front of him who asked if Mr. Conklin could again show them the difference between caudal and dorsal fins.

"Of course," he said, pulling the ring that brought down the charts and diagrams above the blackboard and reaching for his pointer simultaneously. He would have been better off reaching for the pills to control his high blood pressure because the figure displayed behind him was not a slithering fish but a curvaceous Marilyn Monroe in an outfit that could stop a bus.

"Notice first the fishnet stockings and shapely legs. Now, if you compare these with—FISHNET STOCKINGS AND SHAPELY LEGS?!!"

With that he snapped the pointer like a matchstick and his head pivoted back and forth like a scarecrow's in a windstorm as if he could not believe what he was seeing. His normal complexion, which could be described as mortician gray, had turned crimson as his lips uttered unintelligible imprecations. He silenced the laughter with a resounding "Quiet!" and moved his left leg up and down like he was pawing for a charge or auditioning for a "Slowly I turned" tryout. With an off-on gesture he adjusted the corners of his mustache as he seemed to be debating between sending the whole class through the sawmill or tying them to the nearest railroad tracks.

"Someone will pay for this act of sabotage," he promised, opening a drawer under the counter and once again leaping before he looked. "I'm going to go down each row and shine the light of this stick of dynamite in the eyes of each one of you and when I find the culprit who—THIS STICK OF DYNAMITE?!!"

With that he tossed the stick away from him like it had bitten him, which prompted squeals and screams from girls who either climbed on chairs or sought refuge in the arms of nearby boys.

"Mind if I look too, Miss Brooks?"

Like the boy on the burning deck I was on duty but I also got a hotfoot because I had become so preoccupied with the springing of Walter's trap that I had been asleep at the switch and had let down my rear guard. From the upcoming production, *How Mixed Was My Metaphor.*

Before I could stammer out an explanation Mr. Stone said, "You know, you don't have to look through a keyhole. Everyone gets in free. Say, what game is going on in there?"

"Ah...Mr. Conklin is teaching biology."

"So I heard. I just came from the principal's office where Mr. Boynton seems to be in charge. I mentioned to Boynton that I saw a hot rodder speeding though the parking lot and, when I asked him if anything is being done about that, I was told that the squid also travels quickly by a form of jet propulsion due to stringent contractions. When I left him just a minute ago, he was talking to a frog who, for all I know, is now head of the music department. Shall we go inside?"

He followed me into the classroom where Harriet was applying a damp towel to her father's forehead. When he saw my companion, Mr. Conklin's eyes got even wider than they were when appraising Marilyn's knees.

"Mr. Stone! You're early."

"Mr. Conklin. You're late. Or rather you're about to become the late. Whether it's the late principal or the late Mr. Conklin depends on what I hear from you. And what is the meaning of this disgraceful photograph being displayed here?"

"I can explain everything, Mr. Stone," Mr. Conklin asserted. "But first, I need some water." He poured a glass for himself, drained it, looked at the label on the pitcher he had used and said, "Ah, there's nothing like a cool glass of formaldehyde to settle one's nerves. Now, why don't we go back to my office where we can–A COOL GLASS OF FORMALDEHYDE?!! Quick, Harriet! Mr. Stone! I've been poisoned! Call a doctor! Get me to my office!"

The bell rang and, while the sniggering students filed out, Harriet tried to calm her father whose mouth was opening and closing like a beached flounder gasping for breath. Mr. Stone sniffed the contents of the pitcher with his aquiline nose and said, "I think you'll live." He examined the phony explosive whose fuse appeared to be a piece of clothesline, then nodded as if confirming a suspicion. "But perhaps you're right. We better discuss this in your office. If it still is your office."

Harriet assisted her father down the hall to his office where he pleaded his case. After much groveling from Mr. Conklin, Mr. Stone pronounced his verdict: Conklin needed to learn humility as principal before he would be considered for advancement and he was specifically instructed to leave teaching to those who can; Mr. Boynton was advised to gather up his amphibious friend and to take a lesson from the passenger pigeon by flying back to his classroom before his job at Madison became extinct; and I was told to mind my own business by keeping my eyes on my own students and out of drafty places.

Although Walter can secretly gloat that vengeance is his, the scandalous pinup is not because to claim ownership would be to admit that he contrived the artifice. Mr. Stone said he was going to keep the photograph to remind Conklin if he ever got too big for his britches again, although I suspect that he has it rolled up somewhere as a reminder to himself of what women look like without britches.

So nothing really has changed. Mr. Conklin is still my nemesis, the man I can't get rid of and Mr. Boynton is my heartache, the man I can't get. If I ever meet that Robert Browning, I am going to ask him just one question: If all's right with the world, what planet am I living on?

TOM MIX

Tom Mix and the Mystery of the Bodiless Horseman

by Jim Harmon

Tom Mix and Wrangler were riding back to the TM Bar from the grange meeting in Dobie. Tom was on his sorrel mount, Tony, his broad brimmed "Tom Mix model" Stetson shadowing his hawklike features from the bright moonlight, wearing his red-Heldorado shirt with its oval of pearl buttons, his fitted riding britches, and tooled leather boots. The Old Wrangler rode beside him on his yellow palomino, Comanche, in his brown hat, white shirt, black vest, and faded Levis.

There was a cool wind off the desert as they started the turn around the Last Chance Rock. A soft whinny came from the other side of the rock.

"Somebody waiting for us, Tom?" Wrangler's hand went to his six-gun.

"The horse is standing," Tom said. "Could be the rider is just rolling a smoke."

The older man sniffed. "He ain't lit it yet."

"Let's see if he needs a match."

Tom touched Tony's flanks and they moved through the shadow of the rock to make the turn.

Both men reined up their mounts. The scene before them was certainly nothing they expected to see.

"I see him, Tom, but...but I *don't* see him!"

There was a rider on a black horse. Or at least *part* of a rider.

A pearl-gray Stetson hung in the air above empty space, and two light tan gloves held the reins, resting on the saddle horn.

"Good evening, Gentlemen," said the voice coming from above the black horse. "Wonderful moonlit night, isn't it?"

23

"Is this appearance of yours some kind of elaborate joke?" Tom asked.

"I'm not joking," the voice said. "I'm very serious. I want you and all your friends and ranch hands to get off the TM Bar. I intend to take it over and make it mine."

"And who is making this demand?" Tom asked.

"Oh, I suppose you might call me the Headless Horseman. No, I am more than that, aren't I? I am the Bodiless Horseman, and I am as real as death in what I tell you."

"We don't take threats quiet-like, Mister!" Wrangler said, drawing his six-gun and firing a shot between the floating hat and the gloves. The horse startled a bit, but the hat continued to hang in the air.

A soft laughter built up from the direction of the horse. "You don't kill a ghost with a bullet, Wrangler."

"Easy, Wrangler—he's done nothing to deserve being shot for. But he's asked for a little personal contact."

"Turn, Midnight!" The horse obeyed the voice. "Go, Midnight, Go! We've delivered the message." The horse took off, and went into a gallop. "You might be interested in what is happening at your ranch house, Mr. Mix," the voice called back, and laughed again.

"Look at that horse travel, Tom. It's like he was carrying no rider at all."

"Yes, Wrangler. I guess ghosts don't weigh much."

Wrangler wiped the sweat from his forehead. "But you could catch him on Tony, Tom."

"Yes, but I think we better see what he meant about the ranch house."

Wash opened the front door of the ranch house in answer to the unrelenting knocking.

The thin-faced man in the Eastern business suit said, "This is the ranch house of the TM Bar Ranch, owned by Tom Mix?"

Wash flashed his usual friendly smile, his even black features cordial.

"Yes, sir, it is the home of Mistah Tom Mix. He is not here just at the moment, and I might say it is a bit late for calling."

"This is an urgent matter. Do you expect Mix back soon? Can I wait?"

Wash considered the situation. "Why, yes, sir. Step in. I expect he will be back from the grange meeting right soon. While you wait can I show you the latest card trick of the Wonderful Wash, Master Magician?"

The visitor darted inside, glanced around nervously. "Just so long as I can get inside and see how you saw a woman in half."

"Oh, that's for the big stage show. Right now, pick a card."

With a grunt the man selected a card from the fanned deck Wash presented to him. Wash shuffled the deck, and drew forth a card. "Queen of Spades! Is that your card?"

"Yes, yes, it is…careful!"

The cards spilled from Wash's hands to the floor. The man bent over them.

"Hey—these are *all* Queen of Spades! You couldn't miss! You—what's this?"

The visitor found himself staring into the twin barrels of a shotgun.

Wash continued to smile. "Sometimes I act the clown some. It fools the enemy. Tom's got a private detective friend in San Francisco and he sometimes acts like a crook to fool the enemy too. But I got your number, Mister."

Outside, two horses rode up and two men dismounted, walking into the ranch house.

Tom Mix said, "I suppose you have a good reason for holding that shotgun on this man, Wash?"

"I sure do. A good cook has to have a good nose, and this feller just reeks of gunpowder."

Wrangler searched the man. "Here it is, Tom. Some kind of bomb in his side pocket."

Tom nodded. "Not big enough to blow up the place, but big enough to start a fire to burn down the ranch house. Wash, phone Sheriff Mike Shaw at the Dobie Jail to come get this fellow. Mike's sleeping in back on a cot until we get that room for him here fixed up. You can put the shot gun down."

"Yes, sir."

Tom smiled his knife blade-thin smile. "And next time, Wash, you better put some shells in that gun."

"Oh, shells. Yes, sir. I'll phone."

The visitor smiled without humor. "That little fire here might have worried you a little bit. But the fire up on Magic Mesa is going to be a whole lot bigger problem for you, Mix."

Wrangler went to the window. "Tom, he's right. You can see a big fire along the timberline up there on the Mesa."

"Great Guns! That fire will spread quickly onto the Ravenhead reservation. Those light lumber cabins of theirs won't last long in a blaze like that."

The man smiled.

Rangler gasped. "Tom, they planned it that way, this sidewinder and others that must have been working with him. But why would they want to endanger those harmless Indians?"

"Because that's the way the Horseman wants it," the intruder said.

"This is the first time I ever heard of a gang of crooks taking orders from a ghost," Tom Mix said.

"Well, take my word, this isn't the last time you've heard of the Bodiless Horseman!"

Tom Mix reined Tony in sharply as they came onto the tarmac of the Dobie Flying Field.

The tall brown-skinned man in the Stetson waved to him. "Tom! I've got the cargo plane all loaded with the fire fighting chemicals you ordered."

"We've got to drop those chemicals on the Mesa fire," Tom said, as he dismounted. "We've got to stop it before it hits the Ravenhead Reservation."

"Okay, but I don't know why you asked me along. You can fly a plane as well as me."

"Sam Hawk, you do the flying. It will take the two of us. I'll push the chemicals out the cabin door, drop 'em onto the fire. Someday they will have bombers that drop chemicals onto fires through bomb-bays. But we aren't there yet."

A smile split Sam Hawk's Native American features. "Okay, you drop 'em, I'll fly 'em."

The air rushed through the open cockpit door, almost drowning out the roar of the airplane engine, as Tom Mix shoved the opened boxes of fire-retarding chemicals out into emptiness.

"Can you get any lower, Sam?" Tom shouted. "I want to hit the hot spots square on."

"I'm doing my best, Tom. We're practically giving those trees a haircut right now."

Almost as if in answer to Sam Hawk's image of the propeller trimming the leaves as if it were a razor, the propeller struck a thin branch climbing high out of the forest. Instantly violent vibrations shook the plane.

"Feels like we're inside one of those mixers making a malted down at the Dobie drug store," Tom managed.

"The plane won't take it long," Sam said. "Neither will the engine. We've got to land fast or crash."

"Where can you land your plane in a forest on fire?"

"We can land in the area that has already burned," Sam said, "and I think I see just the place."

Tom wiped at his eyes, the smoke now pouring through the open door. "Still be a lot of burned tree stumps."

"Not where there was just brush and light saplings. Here we go!"

Tom strapped himself quickly into the copilots seat.

The tree tops seemed to form a deceptive carpet beneath the plane for a moment, but then they burst through the layer of smoke and there was a blackened field below. In an instant their wheels touched down and there was a bumpy ride into the center of the tree-encircled area.

Sam Hawk let his pent-up breath escape. "We're down. But look at that splintered propeller. We can never take off with that. At least we're safe for the moment."

The face of Tom Mix was grim. "But not safe for long. We're surrounded by trees that haven't burned yet. I think we've stopped the fire from advancing on the Ravenhead nation. But even though there is nothing left to burn here, when those surrounding trees go they will create a firestorm that will suck all the air out of here and leave us in the middle of an inferno of heat."

The white-mustached face of big, burly Sheriff Mike Shaw was grim as he turned away from the radio, from which he had heard Tom Mix tell of their situation from the plane's radio.

Mike's expression was mirrored in the face of the tall, rangy blond cowboy who stood behind the chair of the lawman.

Pecos said, "Sheriff Mike, we can't just leave Tom and Sam there to die in the plane."

"What can we do, Pecos? Airplanes ain't as common as tumbleweeds in these parts. Sam had the only plane in a hundred miles of Dobie. And anyway, no plane could get in there now that the fire is worse."

Pecos looked thoughtful. He usually left the hard thinking to Tom, but now he had to try to be like Tom, to think it through the way he would. "Maybe a plane couldn't, but maybe a horse could."

Sheriff Mike shook his gray head. "No, no, Pecos, no horse could sashay through that."

"One horse could. Tom's horse, Tony. Tony will let me ride him. He knows Tom's my partner."

"Tom's as much my partner as yore'n."

"Mike, Tom Mix is the partner of everybody on this earth who believes in giving the other fellow an even break, who believes in being a Straight Shooter. But we got no time to argue about that."

Mike shook his head. "No, no, you're dead center on the mark, Pecos. But what good could you do riding Tony in there? You'd just get your own self stuck."

"I'm trying to think like Tom," Pecos said. "What's wrong with their airplane? A busted propeller. I've seen them things over at Sam's flying field. If I could get one of those things, strap it onto Tony, and ride in there…"

Sheriff Mike Shaw's face remained sober. "Tom would never ask you to do such a thing. He also might not want to risk Tony, but if Tony himself knew he was helping save Tom's life, he would take cards on the deal. I'm going to get back on the radio and try to work out some of the details with Tom…"

Fire!

Fire everywhere—burning trees, burning limbs, burning shrubs.

A tall cowboy rode the sorrel cow pony with white stocking legs through the fire and smoke, a red neckerchief tied over the horse's eyes.

"You wouldn't want to see this anyway, Tony. But we got to get this wooden thing strapped to your side to Tom. It's mighty important, Tony. Tom's life depends on it. Can you savvy that, Tony old boy?"

A familiar whinny rose above the roar of the fire.

"I think you do savvy it. Come on, Tony! We got to get through!"

Tom Mix and Sam Hawk stood beside the downed plane, covered by an ever deepening cloud of smoke.

"You got your tools ready, Sam? You think you can change propellers if Pecos can actually get through?"

"Sure, Tom," Sam said. "I got the broken propeller off, didn't I? I also got the rest of the stuff out of the cargo compartment. We can fit Tony in there."

Tom nodded. "We should be able to do it. I heard on the radio that Gene Autry got his Champion on board a plane to fly back to Madison Square Garden in New York. I know Gene from when we were both in Hollywood making movies, and he has a lot of progressive ideas. I know if Champ can do it, Tony can do it too."

"Those horses look so much alike, they could be the same horse if I didn't know—*Tom, look!* Here come Pecos and Tony through the smoke!"

Tom saw the horse and rider. And he saw something was wrong. The sure steady gait of Tony was missing. He was lame.

Helping Pecos from the saddle, Tom said, "Thank God you didn't get yourself killed, Pecos. But Tony, there's something wrong with his leg."

Pecos turned away, working on the ropes around Tom's Wonder Horse.

"Let me get the weight of this propeller off of Tony…Tom, you don't think Tony's leg could be…broke?"

Wrangler paced the living room of the TM Bar ranch house, as Tom Mix's young ward, Jane, sat in a chair near the console radio that played faintly in the background with moody Western music of the plains and desert.

"Tom is out there in the stable with Tony, and he's just sunk into the ground with sorrow. Maybe I should be with him, Janey."

"No, Wrangler," Jane said, "he wants to be alone with Tony now."

"It ain't fair, Janey. After Tony saves the lives of everybody down in that forest fire by bringing in that propeller, he breaks his leg and… Well, there's only one thing we know to do for a hoss with a broken leg."

"Yes, Wrangler, I may be a young one but even I know that."

"It just ain't fair. Pecos can rest in the bunkhouse, recovering from them burns, with Sheriff Mike and Wash looking after him, but Tony…"

The music on the radio stopped. "We interrupt our afternoon concert to bring you a live broadcast from the Texas Derby. An interesting sidebar to the story is that one of the entrants will be Wildrange, a horse that suffered a broken leg…"

"Let's turn that radio off, Janey," Wrangler said. "I don't reckon we're in the mood for a lot of palaver…"

"Wait, Wrangler," Jane said sharply. "Listen!"

The radio announcer continued. "It was the brilliant young Dr. Jacob Lester whose innovative techniques were able to restore the broken leg of Wildfire to race again…"

"Wrangler, didn't you hear? There's a doctor who can restore the broken leg of a horse. We've got to tell Tom!"

The old cowpuncher's eyes widened. "Yeah, yeah, we got to get down there to tell Tom, and we got no time to waste putting on fancy saddles, considering what Tom thinks he has to do to Tony. Let's get goin'!"

Tom Mix stood beside Tony, who lay on his side and whinnied softly as Tom patted his neck. "Doc Green is a people doctor, Tony, but he gave you something to kill the pain for awhile."

Tom took something from his pocket.

"Remember this, Tony? A silver bullet given us for first prize at the Dobie Rodeo by our friend, the Masked Man. He's been fighting for law and order since before the turn of the century, but thirty years later he is still a fine looking man. You can see enough of his face to know he is kind and strong. He may not be here with us at the TM Bar, but he's a real Straight Shooter. Nice of him to give us one of his silver bullets, huh, Tony."

The injured horse snorted quietly.

"It was you who deserved the prize, Tony," Tom went on. "It was you who rode down the steers, let me get a rope on them, and then stopped on a dime to let me haul 'em down. It was you who won the race, it was you... But it's always been you, Tony. You warned me in time when Bull Haggerty was fixing to ambush me from that stand of rocks. I was able to wing him just in time. And that time we got caught out on the desert...any other horse or man would have given up when our water ran out. I was about blind and crazy but you got us to the waterhole. Now what can I do to repay you..."

Tony looked up at his partner, his eyes filled with pain but somehow clear and steady.

"This sure isn't much to repay you, partner, but it's all I can do, what I have to do even though it will be like putting this silver bullet through my own heart..."

The old cowpuncher and the young girl ran along the path to the stable.

"Oh, Wrangler, we just have to get there in time," Jane gasped.

"Maybe Tom can hear us from here, Janey. Let's give him a holler..."

At that moment, a gunshot split the early evening air.

"Oh, no, oh, no," Jane said.

"Let's get on down there, Janey."

The two no longer hurried, but went on grimly.

When they entered the stable, Tony lifted his head and gave them a friendly whinny.

"Tom, Tom, you didn't..." Jane began.

"I tried, Janey," Tom said. "I tried to aim true, but...I couldn't see him so clear..."

Wrangler pushed his Stetson back on his head. "Thunderation! The first shot I ever knew Tom Mix to miss!"

Jane grabbed Tom's arm. "Tom, you've got to listen. We just heard on the radio—there's a doctor who can fix a horse's broken leg, make him well enough to race again. We can get that doctor. We can pay him. I can sell that gold mine I inherited..."

"Don't worry," Tom said. "We'll talk to him. We'll get him. We'll pay him. Tony will race over this range again!"

The slight form of gray haired Doc Green came out of the stable.

"Don't worry, Tom," the medical man said. "I can keep Tony quiet, out of pain until Dr. Lester gets here. You say you arranged everything by phone."

"That's right, Doc," Tom said. "Lester said he would be here in the morning.

His treatment will take about six weeks but after that, Tony will be good as new."

"Well, that's fine," Doc said. "Now I had better get over to the bunkhouse and see how Pecos Williams is getting along. Oh, it looks like Wrangler is coming back from there."

Wrangler came up to join them. "I just told Pecos the good news about Tony. That perked him right up."

The three men looked up at the clatter of hoof beats, and two of them saw again the fantastic sight of the Bodiless Horseman, and Doc Green got his first look at the horse carrying only a hat floating in the air and two gloved hands on the saddle horn.

"Whoa, Midnight," came the voice. "Have you made arrangements to leave the TM Bar yet, Tom Mix? Something worse could happen to that horse of yours, to your friends."

"Not if I stop you first, hombre." Tom pulled one of his guns.

"Wrangler was not very effective with gunfire against a ghost," the voice boomed. "Maybe he didn't shoot you enough!"

Tom blazed away, laying six shoots in a row across the empty saddle beneath the floating hat. Suddenly, the hat no longer floated. It fell to the ground.

Wrangler let out a yippee. "You did it, Tom. You shot that invisible man right out of his saddle. But his hands are still on the saddle horn, holding the reins."

"At least his empty gloves are there," Tom said. "Check that hat. I think you'll find a stiff wire attached to it, holding it above the saddle. One shot wouldn't get it, except by chance. But I fired enough that one bullet cut the wire."

"Turn, Midnight, go, go!" came the voice of the Horseman.

"He's still speaking, Tom," Doc Green observed.

"That's the two-way radio in the horse's saddlebags, Doc," Tom explained. "He could talk to us, and give orders to the horse. That's one of the first things I noticed, how he told the horse what to do."

Wrangler looked around. "He's got to be close by, I reckon. To see what's going on. Down there, Tom—there's a panel truck."

Tom pulled the Winchester from the scabbard of Wrangler's horse, Comanche. He aimed carefully, and fired twice.

"That truck isn't going anywhere with two shot out tires. Let's get over there!"

The man who was the voice of the invisible horseman gave up without a fight. He was an old enemy. At one time he had simply called himself the Big Boss.

"Why did you want the TM Bar, Arthur Hern?" Tom asked, giving him his real name.

"I had a deal. This place would be perfect to make films for something new coming in—television."

Wrangler snorted. "That gadget will never catch on. Who's going to stop listening to Fibber McGee and Molly to look at some little figures in a box?"

"Be that as it may," said Tom, "all Hern or the Big Boss or the Bodiless Horseman, call him what you will, has proved is what I have always told Janey—lawbreakers always lose, Straight Shooters always win. It pays to shoot straight!"

CANDY MATSON, YUKON 2-8209

The Japanese Sandman

by Jack A. French

An attractive blonde, attired in a tangerine-hued robe and comfortable slippers, sipped her morning coffee in her penthouse apartment on Telegraph Hill. Her blue eyes scanned the headlines in the *San Francisco Chronicle*: "President Truman Signs Farm Bill," "U.S. Forces Capture Seoul," and "Alger Hiss Appeals His Conviction."

Just as she reached for the sports section to begin an article on the Forty-Niners' upcoming game with the Browns in Kezar Stadium, the telephone began ringing on her antique maple desk. In a deft motion, she removed her left earring and placed the telephone to her ear.

"Hello, YUkon 2-8209," she purred into the receiver.

A man's anxious voice on the other end asked, "Is this Miss Matson?"

"Yes, this is Candy Matson," she replied.

"Good," he said, "I need the services of a detective to handle an urgent matter."

"I'm your gal—you tell me your problem and I'll tell you my fee, Mister...ah?"

"Actually, it's Doctor...Doctor Dabney Essex. I'm a dermatologist. The Japanese Sandman has been stolen from my wife's gallery."

"Hold on, Doctor, not so fast. Let's review the bidding... what's the Japanese Sandman?"

"Miss Matson, it's a Nippon urn of enormous value that was taken by thieves last night. I will pay handsomely for its speedy return."

"I certainly love the sound of that, Doctor. A girl has to make a living, you know. Where is your wife's gallery...and have you notified the police?"

"Yes, we've notified the law enforcement authorities. That is required by our insurance company. And her gallery is called Asian Dreams. It's located at the corner of Stockton and O'Farrell Streets. Can you meet me there in a half hour?"

"Make that one hour. I'm drying some unmentionables now in the delicate cycle."

"Very well, Miss Matson, let's say ten-thirty."

"Let's," she replied as she returned the telephone to its cradle.

Candy scribbled a few lines in her notebook, glanced at the Crimebeat section of the *Chronicle*, and then took a shower. After, she dressed quickly, selecting her outfit from a walk-in closet full of attractive, elegant clothing. As a former model and film actress, she had developed a keen eye for fashion. She chose a mint-green angora sweater and a tan skirt and jacket, with complimentary high heels and purse.

The lady detective took the elevator to the basement garage, got into her automobile, and sped away into the autumn sunshine of San Francisco. She drove smoothly through North Beach and Chinatown to her first destination, about nine blocks away. It was a combination apartment and photo studio on California Street, just off St. Mary's Square. Candy rapped sharply on the door as she called out, "Wake up, Rembrandt, it's Candy Matson."

Rembrandt Watson, a short, slightly overweight man with a mustache, attired in a lavender dressing gown, opened the door with a wry smile. "Candy, you little dove, what brings you to me humble lodgings at the crack of dawn?"

The blonde detective brushed by him and strode into the apartment. "Guess again, Rembrandt, it's almost 9:45. I thought good photographers could tell time just by looking at the sun." She perched on his faux-velvet sofa and helped herself to the candy dish.

"I'm sure you'll love those chocolates; they're Belgian. A gift from an admirer. But tell me why you're here, please? You didn't come over here just to sample me sweets," Rembrandt said.

"I need some info, duckie, what do you know about the Japanese Sandman?"

"Gracious, you do have good taste! The Japanese Sandman is the nickname ascribed to an exquisite bolted urn of Nippon porcelain which dates back to the turn of the century. Japan manufactured thousands of Nippon porcelain of all kinds from approximately 1891 to 1921, primarily during the Meiji Period, me thinks."

"So why is this one urn so valuable?" Candy asked with an arched eyebrow.

"My darling, the value of any artistic piece is strongly influenced by beauty and rarity. Japan exported thousands of Nippon items to our shores before World War I and they came in dozens of different shapes, decorated with hundreds of various scenes. Nearly all of them have increased in value. But the Japanese Sandman is a one of a kind and its current price tag probably exceeds $12,000. And that's a lot of cabbage, my little lamb," he replied.

"Laddie-boy, the depth of your knowledge delights my girlish heart. How did it get the nickname of Japanese Sandman?" she asked, crossing her shapely legs.

"Well, luvie, the scene painted on the front of the urn is an elderly Japanese spirit-man, clutching a staff in one hand, and a small lamp, or perhaps an hourglass, in the other. So me thinks it was whimsy to give it the title of that 1930 pop-blues song."

"Oops, strike one for Rembrandt! 'Japanese Sandman' was composed in 1920, not 1930. Dick Whiting and Ray Egan wrote it; I remember because that song was in one of my movies."

"Verily now? I stand corrected, O Goddess of Detection," he replied with more humor than sarcasm. "But I am sure that one can view this lovely piece of Nippon at a local downtown gallery."

"Strike two! It was stolen from there last night," Candy chuckled as she arose from the sofa and started for the door. "But don't worry, Rembrandt, I'm on the case!"

With her chum sputtering behind her, she opened the door and left him with a cheery: "I'd better leave now, before you strike out."

She walked briskly back to her parked car, spun it away from the curb, and wove her way through increasing traffic, up Pine Street to Powell, then past Union Square, to O'Farrell Street and eventually found a parking spot in front of Mon T. Masterz Book Store, about a half-block from the Asian Dreams Gallery. Her high heels clicked a staccato on the sidewalk as she walked to the gallery and opened the etched-glass front door. About a half-dozen people were milling about inside and she announced herself to them: "I'm Candy Matson; is there a doctor in the house?"

A tall man with a florid face and pencil-thin mustache, dressed in a dark gray suit with a red silk tie walked toward her, saying, "Hello, Miss Matson, I'm Doctor Essex. You are prompt. I like that."

"Oh, you'll like me even better when you get to know me, Doctor. Now about my fee…"

His right hand reached into his breast pocket and extracted a check, which he offered to her. "Here's a retainer of $500; I'll put more in your hands when the Japanese Sandman is in mine."

"You are most gallant, kind sir. Let me put this negotiable instrument in my purse, just to keep it warm and cozy," Candy said. " Have all the police left?"

"Yes, they have, Miss Matson," the doctor answered, waving his arm in a sweeping circle. "An insurance adjuster is over there by that counter, talking to Gloria Neilson, my wife's assistant manager, and Felix Quirk, one of her sales clerks. My wife, Phyllis, has taken this very hard, I'm afraid; she's in her office in the back. The man by the cash register is our plainclothes security guard, I think his name is James or Jay…something, I forget. There are no customers in the store at present."

Candy scribbled a few lines in her notebook as she said, "Am I to understand that this gallery is operated by your wife, without your assistance?"

"That is correct. She runs this establishment, and has for eight years. While I certainly give her moral support, I'm far too busy with my professional duties in my medical practice to have anything to do with her gallery. My office is in Regent's Professional Building, on Sutter, just off Van Ness."

"That being the case, let's go talk to your Missus," Candy said as she suddenly started for the back office, with Dr. Essex following closely behind. By the time they reached the curtain of the back office, Essex barged ahead of Candy, announcing loudly, "Phyllis, that detective I hired is here and wants to speak to you."

Phyllis Essex, a short, dumpy woman with red hair, turned around slowly from her work-strewn desk. She wore a black polka-dot suit and a sullen, disinterested expression.

"How do you do, er, Miss Batson, isn't it?" she said, extending a hand with five brightly painted fingernails.

Candy shook the offered hand, saying, "No, it isn't. It's Matson, Candy Matson. But thanks for the Captain Marvel reference. Now please tell me what you know of the theft of the Japanese Sandman."

"It's a tragic loss...the most valuable Nippon piece in my gallery, and now it's gone! Jay Rendon, my security man, discovered the theft when he arrived this morning at 6:30 a.m."

"Mrs. Essex, how did the thief gain entry?"

"Oh dear, that's the strangest part. The police could find no evidence of forced entry, so they suspect someone had a duplicate key."

Candy glanced about the office. "How many of your employees have a key to the gallery?"

"They all do," said Phyllis Essex. "That would be Gloria, Felix, Jay, and one other clerk, Betsy Simms, who's sick today. And of course, my husband and myself each have one, so that makes five."

"No, that makes six," Candy replied, "but who's counting? Tell me, did your security alarm go off during the theft?"

"It did not. That dreadful thing is located on the outside of the building, near the alley. The police told me it had recently been rendered inactive by cutting some wires or something."

"Well, Mrs. Essex, I'm going to do my best to find the Japanese Sandman and I'll need the help of you and your staff. I need to interview each, separately. May I use your office for that?"

After getting the grudging acceptance of Phyllis Essex, the blonde detective spent the next two hours interviewing the owner and her staff. Mrs. Essex, who was alternatively anxious and aloof, was the type of person who volunteers answers to questions she was never asked. She told Candy she had no children, had owned the gallery eight years, never learned to swim, did not do background checks on any of her employees, extended credit liberally to good customers, hated all smokers, and had experienced only minor thefts in the past.

Gloria Neilson and Felix Quirk had good alibis, had no idea of how the theft was accomplished, and they were having an affair, although neither seemed very enthusiastic about it. Both thought it was strange the thief took only one piece, especially since the Japanese Sandman was so distinctive no pawn shop would touch it.

Security guard Julian "Jay" Rendon was sure the alarm system was working when he locked up at 9 p.m. last night so it must have been tampered with later. He had not seen any suspicious persons recently and he knew most of the regular customers on sight. Betsy Simms was his niece and she'd been sick with the flu for the last three days.

Candy finished all her interviews and crime scene search, packed the notes in her purse, next to the $500 check. She told Dr. and Mrs. Essex that she would keep them advised and then she walked back to her car and headed south in the direction of the Hall of Justice. She deposited her check *en route*, parked in a pay lot on Bryant, and walked into the Hall of Justice, pausing only at the newsstand to get the first edition of the *San Francisco Daily News*. She was not surprised to find the theft of the Japanese Sandman to be on the front page, just below the fold.

She quickly found her way to the Homicide Unit and greeted the Sergeant at the desk. "Hi, Callahan, is Mallard in, asleep on his desk as usual?"

Callahan, a husky policeman with bushy eyebrows, laughed. "Don't let him hear you say that, Miss Matson, he's working on the quarterly report for the Commissioner."

Candy breezed past Murphy's desk toward the office door of Lt. Ray Mallard. "Well, we taxpayers certainly appreciate that."

From the inside of Mallard's office, the sound of his voice reached the outer office. "Murphy, if that's Miss Matson talking about my sleeping habits, please tell her to get on her tricycle and go back to her detective's correspondence school."

"Why don't you tell her yourself, you big lug?" Candy retorted as she strode into Mallard's office.

"Candy, my little cupcake, what a pleasant surprise! Did crime take a holiday so that San Francisco's best detective has time on her hands to visit auld acquaintances who may be forgot?"

"Nice try, Mallard, but I am on a case...and a big one too. Look at this article," she said, slapping the *Daily News* down on his desk, pointing to the headline of the Nippon disappearance.

Ray Mallard, a handsome man with dark curly hair and a lithe body, glanced at the piece in the paper and chuckled, "Somebody stole an empty jar? And that's your big case? Nobody was murdered?"

"Yes, this is my big case. And when I recover that stolen urn, Mr. Homicide-Solver, I'll be happy to let the San Francisco police exactly know how I did it."

"Don't count your chickens before they hatch, I always say...what do you always say?"

"I always say, you can't teach an old dog new tricks, but in your case, I'll be glad to make an exception. Can you break away for a late lunch, Mallard dear?"

"Sorry, Candy, I'm only half way through this homicide report to the Commissioner. I should be done by seven tonight. How's about dinner and a Tex Acuff movie? There's a new one at the Royal Theater, *Song of Six-Gun Justice*. Doesn't that sound great?"

"Wal, podner, sounds like it has Academy Award branded on it," Candy drawled. "But Ah cain't make it. Me and Rembrandt will be rounding up some strays tonight…stray facts, that is."

"Suit yourself, Kitten. Want to take a rain check on the movie?"

Candy started out the door, "Tell you what, Mallard…you sit here and hold your breath until I call you with my decision in a few days."

"Did I mention that I'll also spring for the large popcorn?"

"G'bye, Mallard…your sweet talk is making my girlish heart go pitty-pat." She blew him a kiss, walked past Callahan, down the hall, and out of the Hall of Justice.

She spent the next two hours in the morgues of the *Chronicle* and the *Examiner*, reviewing clippings about antique thefts, and then stopped at the Better Business Bureau to check out the two businesses of Dabney and Phyllis Essex. Back at her penthouse apartment, she telephoned Rembrandt and got him to agree to accompany her to an evening appointment in a bar near Chinatown.

It was 9:30 p.m. when Candy and Rembrandt entered The Green Gull, a tavern on Clay Street, just off Kearny, on the edge of Chinatown. A young, pleasant-faced Asian-American, dressed in slacks and a not-too subtle plaid jacket, waved them over to his booth. Jimmie Loo was a part-time hustler and full-time flirt.

Candy introduced the two men as a buck-toothed barmaid sauntered over for the drinks order, a notepad in one hand and a chewed pencil in the other.

"I'd like an Old-Fashioned," said Candy.

"A Martini, with two olives, please," said Rembrandt.

"Gimme another beer," said Jimmie.

"Comin' up," said the barmaid, shoving the pencil into her dishwater-blonde hair, as she returned to the bar.

"Doll-Face, I gotta tell you. You're still broad where a broad should be broad," Jimmie began.

Rembrandt seemed impressed. "He's quoting Oscar Hammerstein. How delovely! Jimmie, did I tell you that your big shoulders look like they belong on a Pacific beach?"

"Boys, don't turn this into some enchanted evening," Candy warned. "We're here to talk about the theft of the Japanese Sandman." The blonde detective gave the two a summary of her crime scene search and her interviews at the gallery, but stopped when the drinks arrived. After the barmaid had left, Candy asked Jimmie, "Any chance the Japanese Sandman will show up in a Chinatown pawnshop?"

"Not in Chinese New Year, sweetie, hocking that piece of Nippon is like dragging a Mona Lisa around. If it's a fake, it's worth nothing. If it's real, it's still worth nothing, because no pawn shop can display it or resell it."

Candy took a sip of her Old-Fashioned. "So what did the thief have in mind in snatching it?"

"Beats me, Gorgeous," Jimmie replied, "but if I had to guess, I'd say some private collector was behind this. He could hire some mug to steal it for him and then put it in his private collection for his personal enjoyment. But he can't risk showing it to friends, because anyone would recognize it as stolen."

Rembrandt sucked the gin out of one olive and waved his toothpick around. "Candy, you said this was an inside job. Why don't you make all the gallery staff produce their keys?"

"Elementary, my dear Watson, we don't know who among them made a duplicate and then passed it to an unsavory confederate," replied Candy. Then she nodded to Jimmie. "What have you heard about the Essex folks?"

"About her, almost nothing, except that Asian Dreams gallery is barely breaking even. About him, more. Dear ol' Dabney loves the ponies, or at least loves placing wagers on them. Skin doctors don't necessarily know good horseflesh, and Doc Essex is losing money fast. How much, I don't know, but from what I hear, we're talking serious sums."

"But there are no race tracks in San Francisco," Rembrandt pointed out.

"Nope," Jimmie replied, "But there's some nearby, Bay Meadows in San Mateo and Golden Gate Fields in Richmond. And Bay people can find a bookie on almost any street corner and get some action. Some bookies are legit; most are not, and that kind can be dangerous to your health."

The barmaid returned, "Wanna 'nother round?"

"Just the check, please," Candy said. "And give it to me, I'm treating my two favorite uncles tonight."

Outside, after bidding Jimmie Loo farewell, Candy turned to Rembrandt. "You know, duckie, there is this one more tiny favor you can do for me…"

"Not if it involves a loss of me beauty sleep," he replied.

"Nope, this is an easy as pie. I want you to have that mole on the back of your neck checked out by a dermatologist tomorrow."

"Let me guess, Nancy Drew, I should choose the services of Dr. Essex."

"Correct, old chum. He's never met you and I need a set of eyes and ears to check out his office practice. Will you do it?"

"Gladly. I've got a photo shoot tomorrow afternoon, in Natalie Park on Fulton Street, near the Art Museum. So I can pop in on Dr. Essex in the morning and then meet you for lunch. And do bring extra cash, my dove, because I'll probably be very hungry.

"Should I make an appointment first with the good doctor?"

"No, Rembrandt, that way when you just show up, you'll be stuck in the waiting room and the longer, the better. Just remember…what big eyes you have, Grandma."

"The better to see the clues, my dear," the photographer replied. "But please tell me I don't actually have to have this mole removed."

"Of course not. Think of this as Operation Big-Stall. You just absorb all the details about the Doctor and his office and, no matter what he recommends about your mole removal, you say you'd like to think about it for a few weeks."

"Can't I just tell him I'm saving it for a collar-button in me old age?"

"I leave it to your good judgment. Now, c'mon, I'll drive you home."

The next day, Candy ran credit report checks on both Dr. and Mrs. Essex and made a few telephone calls to some friends on the Burglary Squad to share notes. Thirty minutes after high noon, she arrived at The Franciscan Deli on Golden Gate Avenue; she was dressed in a navy suit and butternut yellow blouse. She had barely been seated when Rembrandt joined her at the small, round table.

"Candy-dear, I bear glad tidings of great joy!" he gushed as soon as the waitress left them alone.

"Spill it, Rembrandt, I'm all ears."

"Well, luvie, first of all, I know you're dying to hear all about me mole. Doctor Essex examined it carefully and was a little concerned about both its size and color and he recommends that—"

Candy interrupted. "Don't toy with me, Shutter-Bug, just tell me what you learned about Dr. Essex and his office practice. If you don't, then you have to buy our lunch."

"Heavens, I was just having a little fun..." Rembrandt apologized. "Let me dispense some factual information. First of all, his is a modest practice at best. It's a small office with what appears to be a middle-class clientele, some of it walk-in business. A lot of room for improvement, me thinks."

A slender waiter with a crewcut took their drinks-and-lunch order efficiently and then disappeared behind the counter.

"How many assistants in his office?" she asked.

"The doctor is in practice by himself, with only one nurse, Miss Monet, who doubles as the receptionist. Her first name is Yvette and her French accent is real."

"And let me guess," Candy smiled. "You're not going to tell me she's fat and forty."

"No dearie, more like trim and twenty. And our dermatologist obviously enjoys watching her skin, and as much of it as possible. The feeling is noticeably mutual. She and the Doc have one of those heterosexual attractions that I've heard about now and then."

"Are you trying to tell me the good doctor prefers French cuisine to home-cooking?"

"Ah, may the gods grant us all your insightful grasp of the obvious," Rembrandt teased.

"Good work, Rembrandt, now we have to figure out why an expensive Nippon urn would be stolen from a woman whose husband is cheating on her and running up gambling debts..."

That night Candy slept fitfully, tossing about, her mind sorting out dozens of facts and clues about the theft of the Japanese Sandman. Finally, about 3 a.m., she was sleeping soundly, with just the teeniest snore coming from her lovely nose, when the loud ringing of her telephone shattered her slumber. On the third ring, she managed to pull the phone to her ear on the pillow, and say, "YUkon 2-89, no, I mean, 2-82, oh, who is this ?...and it better be important!"

"Oops, did your handsome prince awaken Sleeping Beauty?" Lt. Mallard said in mock innocence.

"Mallard! Are you suffering from insomnia? Why are you calling me in the middle of the night?"

"Candy, honey, I am sorry. I can just imagine you there in bed, your beautiful blonde tresses cascading across the pillow, your lovely arms wrapped around your Little Orphan Annie doll, your funny little snore..."

"That's it, Mallard, talk sense or I yank this phone out of the wall."

"Agreed...I've got some good news and some bad news. The good news is that you can eliminate one of your suspects on the Japanese Sandman theft. The bad news is that Phyllis Essex is being fished out of the bay and she's as dead as a mackerel."

Candy bolted up from her pillow, now fully awake. "How did it happen?"

"Suicide. She drove her brand new 1950 Cadillac Fleetwood right off a commercial pier near Berry Street into the China Basin a little after midnight."

"Where are you now, Mallard?"

"I'm still at the pier. Our divers finally got the Caddy attached to a crane and they pulled it up on the pier about thirty minutes ago. The crime lab boys are about finished. Her body will be *en route* to the coroner's office to confirm the cause of death. Then our forensics team will take the vehicle to the impound lot over on Hooper Street."

"This so-called suicide sounds all wrong to me. Maybe she was murdered."

"Are you running for the coroner's office now? Look, tell you what...meet me in my office in, say, three hours, and I'll buy you breakfast and furnish you with the preliminary results, which your San Francisco police will be gathering while you finish your beauty sleep."

"It's a deal, Mallard, I like plain bagels with cream cheese—"

"And black coffee, no cream, two sugars."

"Your memory is improving...good night now," she said drowsily as her head sunk into the pillow.

Candy arrived at the Hall of Justice by cab a few minutes after 6 a.m. Most of the fog had disappeared from her blue eyes, despite her hectic night, and she walked eagerly toward Mallard's office in the Homicide Section. He was waiting with a bag of bagels, cream cheese, two coffee containers, and a handful of sugar cubes.

"There will be cookies for you, and sugar for the brain, dear," he said, paraphrasing every child's traditional letter to Santa.

"Please, Lieutenant, just pass me my breakfast and start filling me in on Phyllis Essex's untimely departure."

"Can do," he smiled, "and I know you'll be delighted that I was right...once again. It's suicide. Coroner reports lungs filled with unsanitary Bay water, no marks or bruises, alcohol content minimal, perhaps one glasses of wine with dinner. Cause of death: Drowned, probable suicide."

"Oh, so the coroner said 'probable?'"

"Yes, he did, but he'll delete that adjective when he sees the suicide note."

"You didn't tell me on the phone that she had left a suicide note."

"I didn't have it then. Dr. Essex gave it to the investigators when they contacted him with the sad news about 1 a.m. Poor fellow was all broken up. He said he had a late dinner with two doctors from Mary's Help Hospital. He got home about 11:30. She wasn't home but he did not worry because she had told him she was visiting friends in Broadmoor and he was not to wait up. He was sound asleep when our detectives woke him up. They searched the house together for any suicide note and found one on the fireplace mantle. But they couldn't reach me on the pier to tell me about it."

"I see…and the note said what?"

"Cupcake, be patient, I'm coming to that. Basically the note said she had been depressed for several months, she felt responsible for losing the most expensive piece in her gallery, and she wanted to end it all."

"Mallard, I spent some time with this woman right after the theft. She wasn't depressed and she didn't feel responsible. If anything she hovered between uncon-cern and arrogance. I think that letter is a phony."

"I'll bet it isn't," he replied. "The Lab boys are examining it now, and odds are it was typed on her typewriter, signed by her, and has her fingerprints on it."

"OK, I'll bet. If that suicide letter is really hers, I'll take you to that Tex Acuff movie. But if it's fake, you have to treat me to a moonlight dinner on Fisherman's Wharf."

"It's a bet, sweetheart, and I know you're gonna love Tex's film. I'll have the lab report by noon at the latest. Where can I call you?"

"Why, I'll be at Fisherman's Wharf, making dinner reservations," she laughed, planted a peck on his cheek, and walked out of his office with a bagel in one hand and her coffee in the other.

Returning to Telegraph Hill via cable car, she later tried to contact Dr. Essex by telephone at his home and office, but could get no answer. She combed the newspa-pers for additional details; the death of Phyllis Essex, occurring right after the theft of the Japanese Sandman, had given rise to a great deal of newspaper ink. The Exam-iner quoted one of the divers who recovered the Cadillac as saying that there were three shoes in the vehicle, two worn by the victim and a third wedged under the brake pedal.

About 11:30 a.m., she telephoned Mallard. "Does the lab report say we're going to dinner at Fisherman's Wharf?"

"No, Cupcake, the suicide note was genuine. Lab confirmed it was typed on her office typewriter on her stationery. The signature is hers, not a forgery. And here's the best part: they found seven latent fingerprints, full and partial, on the letter. All of them are those of Phyllis Essex and there are no other fingerprints on the note or envelope."

"OK, so she wrote the letter. What about that extra shoe in the car? Does that bother you?"

"It does not. The forensics report also shows two purses, both belonging to the victim, were recovered from her Cadillac. Maybe she just wanted to take everything with her."

"Mallard, you mean she goes to meet her Maker carrying three shoes and two purses? What woman would do that?"

"C'mon, Candy, people who commit suicide are not in a normal state of mind. Who cares about the extra shoe? Maybe it was in the car for days. Maybe she had picked it up from a shoe repair place and forgot to take it out. And two purses is not significant either. Anyway, you've lost the bet…the suicide note is legit so you can pick me up at 7 p.m. tonight for that Tex Acuff movie."

That night, as Candy drove Ray Mallard to the movie theater, she continued to try to convince him that the suicide of Phyllis Essex was not necessarily so. "Tell me about the third shoe, Mallard, that is very suspicious."

"What's to tell?" he asked. "The two shoes on her feet were ordinary black pumps. The third one was a beige high heel shoe that was probably a gift since it had her initials imprinted in it."

"And there were two purses in the car…what about the contents of each?"

"Cupcake, don't worry your pretty little head about every detail. The contents were nearly identical: comb, compact, lipstick, cough drops, fingernail file, etc. Only difference was one purse had her driver's license and credit cards in it, but the second one didn't."

"That is very interesting, don't you think? What about insurance? Did Mrs. Essex carry life insurance?"

"Yes, she did. She had a policy in the amount of one million dollars, with her husband as the sole beneficiary."

"Now we're getting somewhere, Lieutenant…don't most life insurance policies have an anti-suicide clause?"

She turned the car north on Larkin, heading for the Royal Theater on Polk Street, as Mallard answered her question. "Yes, they do, and this one did also. But they usually expire two or three years after the policy is issued. In this case, her policy was obtained in 1947 and the anti-suicide clause expired six months ago. So Essex will collect a cool million."

"How convenient for Dr. Jekyll and his Mrs. Hyde…does your brilliant detective mind not find that coincidence a bit uncomfortable?" she asked.

"Look, sweetie, not every sudden death is neat, tidy, and free of loose ends. I've got sixteen pending homicide cases now, and I don't need to turn an ordinary suicide into a murder because of an extra shoe, purse, or routine insurance payoff."

"Look here, Mallard, I'm not saying it was murder…I'm just a mighty suspicious gal. Did you know Dr. Essex was romancing his nurse, Yvette Monet?"

"Who cares, sweetie? Last time I checked it was not a violation of the California Penal Code for a doctor to kiss his nurse?"

"You're missing the point, Mallard dear. Yvette could be his motive for sending dear Phyllis to the great beyond."

Mallard scratched his ear. "Why is it," he asked, "that every time we're on a date, we end up sounding like Nick and Nora Charles?"

"Actually, they're on a different network," she replied and pulled into an underground lot, one-half block from the Royal. Its bright marquee lights proclaimed, "Tex Acuff and his horse, Mustard, in *Song of Six-Gun Justice*...Two Cartoons...Plus Selected Shorts."

Candy bought the tickets and popcorn and they found seats in the second row of the balcony. The Acuff movie saga contained all the ingredients of Hollywood's "Real West": a stampede, a foiled lynching, a stagecoach plunging into a watery ravine, an avalanche, interspersed with plenty of songs and gunplay with blazing six-shooters that each fired 25 shots. Mallard thoroughly enjoyed everything on the screen. Candy enjoyed the popcorn.

The next afternoon Candy was in her penthouse apartment, attired in an ice-blue jacket and skirt with a single strand of pearls. A visitor she was expecting arrived promptly at 2 p.m. "Good afternoon, Dr. Essex, thank you for coming."

Essex entered, removing his hat. "Your telegram only advised me to meet you here since you had solved the case. Please tell me what you've learned."

She took his hat, placed it on a small table which was in front of a large Colonial screen by her door, and then led him to an easy chair which faced her sectional. "I shall," she said, "but first, may I fix you a drink?"

He smiled, with just a trace of nervousness. "Yes, please, bourbon and soda."

"I'll join you, with the same," she replied and crossed to her wet-bar to fill two small tumblers. She returned to him, handed him his drink with a small green-tile coaster, and sat it on the settee. "May I get you anything else?"

"No, but I'm very anxious to hear about your solution of the case. Have you recovered the Japanese Sandman?"

"Almost," Candy replied. "You see, it all ties in with your wife's murder—"

"You mean suicide," he interjected.

"Well, it was supposed to look like a suicide, but—" She was interrupted by the ringing of her telephone. "Excuse me, Doctor." She picked up the receiver and said, "YUkon 2-8209...this is Candy Matson."

The voice on the other end of the line was Rembrandt Watson. "Hello, dearie, you told me to ring you up at 2:10 precisely, and here I am, punctual as Peter Pan."

"Yes, Lt. Mallard, I understand..." Candy said, without looking at Essex.

"No, you don't understand," Watson replied, slightly annoyed. "It's not that stuffy policeman, Candy, it is me self, Rembrandt."

Candy nodded her head and said, "Of course it's all right, Lieutenant. Were you able to confirm my theory on the Essex case?"

The voice on the line was more cheerful now. "Oh, so that's it! You're bluffing someone on your end of the line, so it doesn't matter what I say. Fine, here goes…Candy was a little lamb whose face was white as snow."

Candy arched an eyebrow as she said, "That's good. So you have Yvette in your custody?"

Essex tried to assume an air of unconcern about Candy's side of the phone conversation by pretending to watch the soaring seagulls outside her penthouse windows.

Rembrandt, not knowing the seriousness of what was transpiring in Candy's apartment, enjoyed the ruse more with each moment, so he kept talking. "A focal-plane shutter incorporates a black shade with a movable, variable-sized slit which moves across the exposed film, don't you agree?"

Candy's next reply was, "And she's confessed to his whole plot of killing Mrs. Essex in that fake suicide?"

Her jovial chum responded on the phone by beginning to recite his favorite spicy limerick. "There was a saucy wench from Nantucket—" but Candy cut in with, "Then Yvette told you the location of the Japanese Sandman?"

Essex squirmed out of his easy chair, his thin mustache appearing to grow darker as the color slowly drained from his face. He stood up, his nervous smile dissolving into an evil grimace, and he produced a small automatic from his suit pocket and aimed it at the blonde detective.

"That's enough, Matson, say goodbye to that meddling cop and hang up the phone—Now!"

Candy appeared to have no choice but to comply. "Goodbye, Lieutenant," she said into the phone, but the unsuspecting Rembrandt got in the last words before the connection ended. "Well, Happy Trails, my little buckaroo…"

"Matson, it appears you have solved your last case. The two of us are now going on a long ride, but only one of us is coming back."

Candy was grim, but calm. "Why not just throw me off my balcony? It's fifteen stories down. That would give you time to write my suicide note, like you did your wife's."

"Actually Phyllis wrote her own note, the stupid cow. She was in on my plot to fake her death and take the proceeds from the Japanese Sandman and the million dollars in her insurance. She actually thought I would be joining her in Costa Rica as soon as the insurance company paid off."

"Only she didn't know that you were really going to send her to the bottom of China Basin, and after a suitable grief period, fly off with Yvette, to Paris, I'm guessing?"

"No, we'll be going to Normandy. We can rent a small cottage there and start converting our million dollars to Francs. But we're wasting time, Matson, let's go…"

"Oh, look behind you, Doctor, there's a handsome policeman standing there."

"You disappoint me, Matson, that's the oldest trick in the book, and I—"

Suddenly the burly arms of Lt. Mallard wrapped around Essex, stripping the automatic from his hand, and twisting his wrists behind him, as he was slammed up against the wall. Mallard adroitly snapped handcuffs on the doctor, and turned him over to two uniformed policemen who had entered from the hallway.

"Take him down to the Hall of Justice, boys," Mallard said and turned to Candy. "I gotta hand it to you, Cupcake, you promised me that if I hid behind your screen this afternoon, Essex would appear and confess to the whole thing. Who was that on the telephone? Watson, I'm guessing?"

"Yes, it was…and I'll tell you all the rest of the details tonight during our moonlight dinner at Fisherman's Wharf."

That evening they were sipping their after-dinner drinks on the wharf terrace of DiMaggio's Restaurant, enjoying the comfortable breeze blowing in from the Bay.

"So what made you first suspect Dr. Essex?" Mallard asked, loosening his tie.

"Just a gal's instinct at the beginning, I guess. He and his wife were such a mismatched pair. He even feigned more concern for the Japanese Sandman than she was able to muster. When I found out he was interested in his nurse, and he had serious gambling debts, I figured he might have been trying to kill two birds with one suicide. The Japanese Sandman was valuable, but not worth killing anyone, so I assumed it was meant to cover another crime more lucrative, like getting his wife's insurance money."

Mallard continued for her, "And Essex gets his wife to believe they are going to fake her suicide, collect the big bucks, and sunbathe on a beach in Costa Rica in their old age. They disconnect their alarm, steal the Japanese Sandman, and then stage their bogus suicide…only it's not a rehearsal for her, it's the final curtain!"

"Right you are, Mallard, old chum. But to fake the suicide with no body, they had to make it look like she was definitely in the Cadillac. So they planted her purse and a shoe with her initials to be found when her vehicle was recovered. When he met her at the pier in his car, he probably couldn't think of a way to retrieve the extra purse and shoe without arousing her suspicions. I suppose he got her in the car on a ruse, maybe with last minute instructions to get fresh fingerprints on the steering wheel while the engine was running, and then he reached over and shifted the gears, sending the Cadillac straight into China Basin. She couldn't swim a stroke so she was a goner the minute she hit the water."

"What tipped you to the significance of the extra shoe and purse?" he asked.

"I hate to admit it, but it was your Tex Acuff movie. You remember when they decided that the old prospector must have been in the stagecoach that went into the river ravine, even when they couldn't find his body. Why? Because they found his pouch of gold nuggets in the stagecoach. So what better proof that Phyllis was in the car than finding her purse and a shoe with her initials?"

"You think the Doc wedged the shoe behind the brake pedal?"

"Probably not, that was just dumb luck. Don't forget he would have preferred to get that extra shoe and purse out of the car since they were extraneous, with her dead body in the vehicle. Oh by the way, Mallard, was the Japanese Sandman where I guessed?"

"Yes, Kitten, you hit a home run on that one too. Yvette had it stashed in her apartment. The Doc couldn't take a chance on having it in his home with an anticipated visit from the police after his wife's death."

"They were going to double their take on that urn: first collect the insurance money on the fake theft and then sell it when they got to France."

"But soon they're both going to be long-term guests of the California Prison Administration. Ah, Margo, the weed of crime bears bitter fruit," he chuckled softly.

"You're right, Lamont," she replied, joining in his levity. Then, taking his hand, she led him over to the terrace railing, saying, "But now it's just me and my shadow…"

They gazed into the darkness of San Francisco Bay and quietly watched the outline of an ocean liner, slowly heading west toward the Golden Gate Bridge, a necklace of lights adorning its upper decks.

After a few minutes, he broke the silence. "Cupcake, this is a wonderful evening."

"Mallard dear," she replied, her head snuggling up to his shoulder, "it's always a wonderful evening when I end up in the long arm of the law."

———◆———

THE CLYDE BEATTY RADIO SHOW

Perils of the Tiger Barn

by Roger Smith

The stark Depression year of 1935 dawned through threatening snows at the Rochester Winterquarters of the Cole Bros. and Clyde Beatty Circus.

Barrel fires warmed the training barn early in January's bitter Indiana morning. The barn was tense with concentrated quiet around the barred circle of steel as Clyde Beatty silently, tediously cued the deadly Sumatran tigress, Sleika, down the stair-step pyramid seats and onto the rollover platform just above the sawdust floor. Gathering herself, cutting her eyes quickly about, stealing noiselessly into position, either she would fling her striped fury fully at Clyde, or allow one velvet, taloned foot to touch the tanbark beneath her, and take her cue for the feature trick Clyde needed, the coveted rollover.

Clyde had backed off across the arena, keeping her attention, drawing her to him, giving her time to respond to his hand cues, and space to calculate her decisions. A coursing sweat dripped from his face. He was down on one knee, his whip slung across his shoulder, his kitchen chair out front in his left hand, his gloved right hand waving before her, touching the sawdust, cueing her down, working her into the draw. Her descent slowed. Her head dropped below her hackles. On the floor seat, she stopped and fixed her eyes onto Clyde's.

Sleika, primed to attack, was darkly beauteous as an adult Sumatran. Her sleek, burnt-orange basecoat gleamed even as cold gray light strained winter's day through scattered panes. Her broad, black stripes shuddered, shadowing primitive power. Sleika was tensing, her cross-patterned head lowering in a slow tilt, fangs dripping, pupils dilating to pools of black, ears laying back, her slowly twitching tail steadying to a standstill. Clyde saw her haunches constrict tightly beneath her.

"She ain't rollin'," Cap Bernardi, muttered to himself. The veteran trainer, stationed on the Safety Cage, re-gripped his hickory pole and blank revolver. "She's gonna go."

Her leap was striped lightning, four hundred pounds streaking in mid-air over twenty feet. Clyde shot to one side, into the open forty-foot arena, needing space to reposition for the promised second spring. Sleika missed, landing a yard from Clyde, and instantly spun and leapt again. Clyde caught the weight of her on his chair and began to push her back, but she shot the claws of one paw into the flesh below his elbow and tore back only at the three reports of his .38 blanks. His arm was ripped, and Sleika turned hard for another onslaught. Clyde dodged her again, relying on instinct to betray her position. She missed narrowly, and clawed the chair into her mouth, splintering its legs.

Seeing Clyde maneuvering to counter-positions, Sleika recoiled in anger. She scented the flowing blood. Confused that her attack had not brought Clyde down, she retreated to calculate the killing assault. With this needed advantage, Clyde bore in on Sleika. Cracking his whip for her attention, wielding his chair with his damaged left arm, he drove her hard across the steel-barred cage, back onto the seat from whence she'd leapt.

Sleika spun hard on the seat, roaring furiously at Clyde, extending unsheathed claws to the fullness of her reach as Clyde came in close, less than an inch from her swinging hooks. She brought down her patterned face and expelled primordial rage in deafening force. Clyde faced her down, cueing her to come square on her seat, tapping his whipstock to place her feet, compelling the volume of her murderous voice. Sleika was within a foot of Clyde's face.

Clyde slowly backed away, repeating his hand cues to bring the tigress down. She cautiously set a paw on the sawdust, staring hard at Clyde, but this time taking her cue. Blood drained from his forearm, but he focused on the advancing Sumatran. She was coming down now, responding to Clyde's tedious ten days of training.

Viciously, Sleika charged Clyde, roaring and flashing her claws. Clyde gave her space, then stepped into her. Sleika halted. Clyde dropped to one knee and cued her down. Slowly, she lowered herself in grudging response to his will. With his three-foot twisted-willow whipstock, he coaxed her onto her side. He gently stroked her with the whipstock across her head, behind her ears, along her side.

In a sweeping gesture, he flung the lash of the whip over his shoulder, and hand-cued her into an initial roll to her other side. Completing the roll, she bounded from the floor and charged Clyde. He fired a single blank, and intensely signalled her down again. Curiously, she allowed the cue, and lay in readiness for another roll. Deep in Sleika's consciousness, repetitive schooling was reaching her. Clyde sensed his training had taken hold. He allowed her to remain prone and quiet for scant seconds. Then he brought her into a series of flawless rollovers that swept across the front of the cage into a wide arc back across the arena in front of the heavy pedestals where soon lions would be added.

At Clyde's nod, an assistant shoved in the long wooden hurdle between the bars. Clyde drove Sleika around to the hurdle for a fast series of over-and-back leaps that were the conclusion of the Sumatran's featured spot in the act. With her last vault, Clyde glanced at his tunnel-door man, Charlie Gorr.

"Take her home!" he shouted, as Sleika sped for the door. Her gleaming stripes vanished through the animal gate and down the chutes to her assigned cage.

Harriett Beatty was too seasoned to distract her husband when he was training, even to seek his exit from the cage when injured. But she was also his wife. When Clyde stepped from the Safety Cage, he had taken a look at the four long rips down his forearm. He knew he'd been infected the instant he was clawed. Harriett quickly brought him his robe and wrapped a towel around his arm. She embraced him in silence. She turned her eyes to Cap Bernardi.

"I'll bring the car around," Cap whispered.

"Curses!" exclaimed Zack Terrell. "I should've been in the barn! *Blast it!* How bad is it?" he demanded.

"We don't know yet, Zack. The cageboys are pretty worked up, but everybody gets excited when a trainer gets nailed," replied Terrell's partner, the fabled circus manager, Jess Adkins. "Clyde'll be all right. These won't be his first scars, you know. Take it easy, Zack."

"Easy? Take it easy?" Terrell exploded. "Our one and only asset of value subject to losing an arm, and I get 'Take it easy?' Blast it, I knew it. I didn't like it when Clyde bought that Sumatran, and I said so. I should've been in the barn!"

"What were you gonna do, Zack?" needled Adkins. "Jump in there and bite the tiger?"

"Aw, Hell's afire, Jess, you know what I mean," surrendered Terrell. "My God, Clyde's like a son to me."

"And to me," Adkins said quietly. "Harriett's gonna need us. Let's get to the hospital."

Jess Adkins and Zack Terrell were renowned veterans in outdoor show business. Both were gifted as managers of America's major railroad circuses. Bold and forward thinking, even in the very midst of the Great Depression, the men committed to a partnership to create an all-new circus and to field their prospectus for backing. Financing any circus in business history has been less than attractive, and the winter of 1934 could not have been a more formidable time to ask for money. But Adkins and Terrell held an ace that Ringling Bros. had relinquished when that circus embittered Beatty with low pay and cavalier treatment, at a time when the trainer of the world's only forty-animal lion and tiger act was already an author, a film star in Universal's *The Big Cage*, and a household name. After talks with the young trainer, the partners came away with a contract bearing the signature of Clyde Beatty. On the strength of Beatty's name in ink, the Depression notwithstanding, Adkins and Terrell got their loan.

But the partners had reason for concern. They knew a tiger's convex claws carried virulent infection, and Clyde's injuries came at a crucial time. Adkins and Terrell had not only to open a spanking new railroad circus in the Spring of 1935, but had contracted acts from their fledgling enterprise as a package for a series of lucrative winter dates. Clyde didn't have the customary luxury of four months in Winterquarters to break out his second act of forty animals—his training time was cut in half by the off-season commitments. The two new impresarios solemnly strode the confines of the waiting room.

"They saved his arm," Harriett announced quietly, as she entered the room. "The doctor debrided the cuts and closed with drain tubes. One claw had scraped to the bone." Her stoic posture dissolved. She sank to a chair and wept.

Adkins knelt before her. "Every resource Zack and I have is at your disposal, Harriett. We'll spare no expense to get Clyde through this."

Terrell sat down beside her. It took him a moment, but he turned to her. "Harriett," he said, struggling with emotion, "We're the only ones who know what we mean when we say, 'we're circus.' This is family for us. Like Jess said, every asset…"

"You can see Mr. Beatty now," interrupted the Charge Nurse.

"Clyde feels…I don't know," Harriett paused. "An odd sense of letting everyone down. They say that's part of recovery." Her beauteous blue eyes welled. "When he sees both of you here, maybe he'll snap out of it. Let's go in."

There was no end of consternation among the hospital staff when Clyde left the next morning, calmly explaining he had work to do. His doctors warned him to continue his antibiotics or suffer secondary infection and loss of the arm, as Clyde thanked them very much and drove off with Harriett, who was livid with anger at him, and in an absolute huff.

Once home, Harriett, devotedly protective of her husband, slammed shut their front door. Shucking her purse and jacket, she lit into him with operatic protests over dismissing himself from the hospital too early. She dreaded he might slide on his antibiotic doses, and further subject himself to re-infection in the septic conditions of any animal barn, be taken back in OR, be anesthetized, and…

Clyde was stirred by her passionate entreatments. He embraced her, and hushed her, and kissed her, and honored her rare beauty, and in the privacy of their darkened home, he loved his wife.

Cap Bernardi wasn't surprised when Clyde entered the barn the next morning. He'd had his own scars as a past master trainer, and frankly, Cap would have been a little curious if Clyde had taken off another day.

No man can assemble a forty-animal mixed lion-and-tiger act alone. When Adkins and Terrell signed Clyde, they promised him the best animal men to assist the gifted young trainer to produce the act. Clyde had known the best of the trainers from the old American Circus Corporation shows, once owned by John Ringling, and his pick of them were in Winterquarters, in Rochester, Indiana.

Clyde entered the Cat Barn with the left sleeve of his jacket swollen with bandages. Harriett clung to his good arm, sick with fear of his returning to the cage so soon. Clyde kissed her and turned to his men.

"We're mixing Sleika and the other tigers with lions today," Clyde began. "Cap, send in those dozen lions we got from Frank Buck, and I'll run 'em up on the wall. Once I got 'em seated, let me have those five Louie Goebel lions, from Thousand Oaks, and I'll spot 'em along the front. Then," Clyde directed steadily, "send me Sleika."

Theatre and movie production call it rehearsal. Circus calls it practice, and Clyde called his commands. If the director of a film is considered the ultimate word, circus men consider the directives of the man in the cage abreast of religion.

Cap Bernardi sectioned off the Frank Buck lions, and sent them down the tunnel to await their entrance. The maned cats, accumulated by now from the first dozen to more than twenty-five, were lined up in sections of the tunnel. Cap allowed himself a smile remembering Clyde's nickname around circuses. "Ten tons of props and a hundred miles of tunnel—here comes 'Scrap-iron Shorty!'"

Next followed the fifteen tigers, led by Sleika. In a circus wild-animal act, it was animal management that placed Sleika as lead tiger. With her in first for the stripes, she affected the dramatic descent to the rollover platform that conclusively sold the trick. In a circus, it is one thing to perform your act, or a given trick within it, but entirely another to put it across to a ticket-buying audience. Drawing the work of his intensified performance into the consciousness of his audience, selling the act was Beatty's gift. No other trainer compared.

Sleika was skittish during her acclimation time, getting accustomed to the other thirty-nine animals. She'd had weeks to see them in the Cat Barn, and accept their presence. But now, in a circle forty-feet in diameter, she learned what trainers themselves must adjust to—once the cats are in, the arena shrinks dramatically, if only in the imagination. She wasn't the only inexperienced animal in the act. Others had it all to learn too, and the learning was coming quick.

Clyde sped his twenty-five lions to their seats amidst ear-splitting roars. The pace of the act seemed unbelievable to the other trainers. His call for fifteen tigers seemed suicidal.

One by one, the tigers were sectioned through the tunnel door. Sleika led. Clyde knew Sleika was a side-drive, and moved in quickly on her right flank. She kept her eyes on his as she stalked across the floor. At her seat, she spun left and ran up the seats to her own, and turned and bared her claws at Clyde, but he was by then seating other tigers. Old Charlie Gorr, Clyde's tunnel-door man for the previous season, was sweating blood over the entrances and exits of this many cats.

They were in. All forty were seated. The awed faces of his supporters broke into broad smiles. The sustained applause was begun by the owners, whose faces seemed relieved, if a little pale.

Clyde worked the early routines smoothly, and began now to approach Sleika for the rollover. She'd never rolled with so many lions behind her, but she needed to catch on. Time for the circus was running short.

Clyde tapped his whipstock on each of the seats Sleika would come down on, reminding her gently of her prescribed path. She seemed anxious to gain some distance from the challenging lions, and her descent was more rapid than dramatic. Drama and suspense would be honed in time, but now Sleika was on the floor. She moved into her spot and took the cue for the lay-down. She didn't like looking up at twenty-five lions, and charged Clyde hard in her excitement. A single .38 blank backed her up and brought her attention fully to Clyde. She lowered again, tediously, firing glances at her co-stars. Clyde stroked her calmingly with the supple whipstock. She sank to the sawdust and lay on her side. Clyde immediately turned and challenged hard each of the lions on the pyramided seats, "bouncing his wall," drawing every lion to lean from the seat, roar threateningly and swing their claws too closely. With their attention on his back, he returned to the prone Sleika, knowing this was a make-or-break moment in her training. Cap Bernardi saw Sleika slowly turn her head, taking the cue. Clyde had his rollover tiger.

Sleika completed her furious rolling back around to the hurdle cagehand Dave shoved in. She was over and back for eight jumps, and Clyde signaled Charlie Gorr to take her home. Sleika *bounded* past the sweating Charlie and vanished down the tunnel.

Clyde worked the lions in the massive laydown, sent them home over the hurdle and, after encouraging Big Pharoah to chase him into the Safety Cage, Clyde slammed out of the arena, perspiring profusely, heart pounding, smiling, triumphant.

Harriett wilted in relief, but allowed herself a small smile of pride for her husband. She gathered herself and walked over with his heavy, blue robe and towel.

Beatty remains the only man to assemble two mixed lion-and-tiger acts of forty animals. When the Ringling interests refused to sell him a single animal, he replicated what circus folk called The Big Act in record time for Cole Bros. and Clyde Beatty, the first of every circus thereafter to feature his name in the title. The circus, revered as "The Miracle Show" rolled on time out of Rochester, and into legend.

⊰•◊•⊱

THE GREEN LAMA

The Case of the Bashful Spider

by Bob Martin

Two men stood talking in the parking lot of the Mountain Whisper Motel. "I am Tulku," said the young Asian gentleman with a polite smile to the newspaper reporter. "Jethro Dumont studied in my homeland of Tibet for ten years, and upon his return to the United States, it was my duty and honor to serve him. His great wisdom and powers of concentration earned him the title of Lama. As a crime fighter, my Lama chose the color green, the symbol for justice among the six sacred Tibetan colors. Now he is widely known as the Green Lama, and travels the world to solve puzzling crimes."

"And what brings you here, Tulku?" questioned the reporter.

"Last night, my Lama and I traveled here from New York to assist the Deerfield County Sheriff in his investigation of the mysterious death of a visiting university student. The sheriff is the son-in-law of my Lama's old friend, Sergeant Waylon of the New York Police. My Lama agreed to this trip to central Colorado as a favor to the Sergeant. We are scheduled to meet Sheriff Grayson at the morgue this morning. That's all I can tell you about the case at this time."

Tulku excused himself from the interview as he spotted a taxicab turning into the lot.

"Our taxi is here, my Lama," shouted Tulku.

Dumont exited his motel room carrying a small duffel bag, and joined Tulku as the cab rolled to a stop. The reporter shoved his pen and small notepad into his shirt pocket and headed for his car. He would conduct additional interviews before returning to the office to write his front-page news story for the Deerfield Gazette. He already had a news headline in mind, "Green Lama Assists Sheriff In Mysterious Death."

A short taxi ride transported the pair from the rustic motel to the modern, two-story county building downtown.

"Let's go inside, Tulku," said Dumont as he handed cash to the taxi driver. Tulku exited the cab and gave him a quick nod. Dumont at first glance appeared to be a confident, well-dressed gentleman of obvious wealth, while upon closer inspection his inner calm and unwavering focus revealed he was more complex and interesting than your average "Joe."

Jethro Dumont was a tall, handsome man in his 30's, with a muscular build. The features of his face were sharply defined, with high cheekbones, a fine nose, strong jaw and chiseled chin. He was clean-shaven with a full head of straight, black hair and thick eyebrows. His deep blue eyes twinkled when he smiled, and he had an infectious laugh. When at home in New York City, he would spend countless hours reading books on science, anthropology, philosophy, history and the arts to broaden his knowledge and enhance his investigative skills. As far as a social life was concerned, he enjoyed going to the theatre or to a fine restaurant with a woman on his arm, but his frequent travels didn't allow him to maintain a serious relationship.

The two entered the back of the building through a heavy metal door. Lettering on the wire-reinforced window read "Deerfield County Morgue." A group moved toward them as they proceeded down the hallway. The sheriff was first to reach them and extended his hand.

"You must be Jethro Dumont, the Green Lama! And his assistant, Tulku. Welcome, I'm Sheriff John Grayson," he said as he eagerly greeted Dumont and his companion. "This is Dr. Herbert Lang, our Coroner and his assistant, Susan Brooks." As Grayson continued the introductions, the group shook hands and exchanged hellos. "And this is Dr. Carl Stoller, lead member in his science department's expedition from the University of Kentucky. Dr. Stoller and his team are here to study some kind of rare spider living in our nearby cave."

"That's correct," said Stoller, "our primary subject is an unusual species of *Mundochthonius* that is *cavernicolous*, meaning it's a cave-dweller. Our mission is to study and document the behavior of this new species. We have already collected several samples for dissection and cataloging. We are currently observing its feeding and mating habits, its predators and prey. We're interested in learning how this spider survives in a cave environment, and its role in the local ecosystem." Satisfied he had explained the purpose for his expedition, Stoller turned to his partners and said, "Oh, and allow me to introduce my associate, Dr. Michael Mullins, and Miss Brenda Massey, one of our graduate students on the expedition." The group extended its greetings to Stoller's associates.

"Now that we've all been properly introduced, shall we proceed into the examination area, ladies and gentlemen?" Grayson posed to the group.

"Yes," said Dumont, "I'm anxious to study the evidence in this case."

The group moved through tall swinging doors into a large, bright room. Reflective surfaces of stainless steel tables and equipment projected irregular, white streaks of light on the walls. Dr. Lang took the lead and moved the mob to a body lying on a table covered with a white sheet. As Lang pulled back the cover, Stoller explained, "This is Stewart Biggs, a student member of our expedition team." The outstretched body was that of a young man, apparently in his early 20's. Members of the group repositioned themselves to get a better look.

Dr. Lang and Miss Brooks were both wearing white lab coats and rubber gloves. Lang began describing his findings, "The subject was pronounced dead at the scene late yesterday afternoon. Upon my initial examination, I determined the time of death was approximately 4:00 p.m. The deceased appears to have been in good health, and there are no obvious signs of external trauma." Lang lifted the victim's head with both hands, turned it to one side and pointed to an area on the neck. "Except this, two small puncture marks located here, below the right ear. The surrounding area exhibits swelling, a purplish discoloration and dead tissue. The puncture marks measure seven millimeters apart, consistent with a fang bite from a spider or small reptile."

"Excuse me, Exalted One," Tulku whispered privately to Dumont, "may I humbly suggest this death is easily solved. The student was bitten by a poisonous spider and died from its effects."

"I'm not so sure, Tulku," responded Dumont, "there may be more to this case than first meets the eye."

Stoller, hearing their conversation spoke up, "Yes, that's correct, Mr. Dumont! Stu had separated from our group to explore a new section deeper in the cave, and was only alone for a couple of hours. Although a bite from a spider can be deadly on rare occasions, it would take considerably more time than that to kill a person. Besides, the subject of our expedition is a species of spider that is not poisonous to humans."

"I see," said Dumont.

Tulku had been closely listening and acknowledged this new evidence with several nods of his head.

Lang continued with his report, "We'll conduct a full autopsy later this morning. Body fluid samples were collected and sent to the lab last night."

"We should have the lab results back by tonight," added Miss Brooks.

"Yes," said Lang, "we hope the autopsy and lab tests will shed some light on the cause of death. At this time, we just don't know."

Dr. Lang was appointed as coroner in Deerfield County twelve years ago. He and his family decided to move to rural Colorado for a better quality of life. He had seen just about everything in his previous position as medical examiner in a large, urban region of Illinois. Thankfully, Lang's memory of the aftermath of violent, inner-city crime had faded with the passing years. He and his wife and children were now deeply rooted in the local community and thoroughly enjoyed country living.

Dumont turned to his companion and said, "Tulku, I think it's time for us to investigate the death scene."

"Yes, my Lama," whispered Tulku, "it is written, *talk doesn't cook rice.*"

Dumont laughed and replied, "That's true, Tulku, but it is also written, *to know the road ahead, ask those coming back.*"

Following the friendly exchange of proverbs, Dumont and his sidekick led the group out of the room into the hallway.

Tulku had served with Dumont for the past three years. He was a slender man of average height, and a few years younger than Dumont. He wasn't particularly good looking, but he had an engaging personality. His smile revealed a hint of mischief, and he enjoyed making Dumont laugh at every opportunity. He dressed casually on most occasions, in contrast to Dumont, who wore fine, tailored suits whenever he was out in public. Indeed, the two seemed an unlikely pair, but those who observed their relationship came to understand they were an effective team and good friends.

Dr. Lang and Miss Brooks returned to their work as the others exited the building and climbed into the expedition's two, open-top Jeeps. Sheriff Grayson followed in his patrol vehicle, a four-wheel drive Ford Bronco. The cave was a kidney-jolting forty-five minute drive from town. The asphalt gave way to unimproved dirt roads after the first ten miles. Deep ruts caused by heavy runoff during the wet season were difficult to negotiate and required four-wheel drive to maintain forward motion.

Grayson was a big man, standing six-foot, four inches tall with a heavy, muscular build. He was elected Deerfield County Sheriff ten years ago. Prior to his election, he had worked five years as a deputy for an inept county sheriff with dubious law enforcement methods. Grayson vowed to turn things around when he entered the elected office, to restore staff morale and build public confidence. Through hard work and perseverance, he accomplished his goal, creating a pleasant work environment for his staff and gaining the local community's respect. He and his wife had two, grammar school-aged children and lived on an acre of land just outside of town.

Dumont studied the landscape as they motored into camp. The team members had been in camp for three days, and were scheduled to stay another week. The camp was set up seventy-five yards from the mouth of the cave. Several olive-drab tents encircled a large fire pit. Empty wooden crates, which had transported the expedition team's equipment and provisions on the trip from Kentucky, were stacked neatly inside a small trailer. Ropes strung between mature trees had blankets and fresh laundry folded over them to dry. Tubs filled with pots, pans and silverware were placed on a large picnic table, along with lanterns, a three-burner stove and other camping gear.

The passengers brushed the thick dust off their clothing as they climbed out of the Jeeps. It took them a few moments to get back their "land legs" after the long, jarring ride from town. Two young men jumped from their chairs and moved quickly forward to greet them.

"Here are two more members of our team," said Stoller, "graduate students, Jeremy Poole and Angelo Pazzi. The only team member you haven't met is Judy Carter.

"Oh, there she is," he added as he caught sight of her exiting a tent. Carter was visibly shaken—she was weeping uncontrollably and unable to speak. When she saw Stoller, she quickly turned her head away and dashed back into the tent.

"Judy was hardest hit by Stu's death," explained Stoller. "They were close friends."

Brenda Massey, Angelo Pazzi and Judy Carter were second-year graduate students. Massey was the well-scrubbed, athletic type. She rarely wore makeup or lipstick, and usually pulled back her black, curly hair into a ponytail to keep it out of the way. Gym shorts and a sports bra under a tank top was her outfit of choice. In camp, she wore faded blue jeans, a khaki, long-sleeved shirt and hiking boots.

Judy Carter was decidedly more feminine with a slender, curvy frame. She spent time on her appearance in camp, brushing her mid-length, fine brown hair each morning and reapplying her subtle shade of lipstick throughout the day. Her camp attire included designer jeans, a long-sleeved blouse and name-brand chukka boots.

The expedition team members settled into cloth folding chairs around the fire pit and invited the visitors to sit down and "rest their bones."

"So you study spiders, huh?" questioned Grayson.

"Yes, spiders are fascinating subjects," replied Pazzi with enthusiasm. "Did you know a Black Widow Spider's bite is 15 times more toxic than a rattlesnake's bite? Luckily, the amount of venom received in a typical bite only causes illness in human beings. In its natural environment, a spider's venom is injected through fangs to kill or paralyze its prey. Following incapacitation, it uses digestive enzymes to liquefy its meal prior to ingestion."

Angelo Pazzi was an average looking young man of short stature, with dark features. He was the most animated member of the team, never remaining still for very long. His tattered jeans and faded t-shirt were practical attire for a field trip, if not fashionable.

Jeremy Poole was a first-year grad student, having entered the program only six months ago. He was a quiet, serious student with average looks. His body type was long and lean, like a long-distance runner, with dark, bushy hair that billowed out from under his favorite ball cap.

Stewart Biggs had entered the graduate program the same time as Poole. He was more outgoing than Poole, and less serious about his studies. He was tall with long, blonde hair, blue eyes and fine features. He was attractive, almost "pretty," and found it difficult sometimes to convince others he was a science grad student, not a male model or theatre arts major.

With the exception of Poole, the grad students frequently socialized together, attending nightclubs and parties on Friday and Saturday nights. Although Massey, Pazzi and Poole occasionally dated, none of them had a "steady." Stu Biggs and Judy Carter hit it off immediately and became good friends. What the others didn't know was that their friendship had blossomed in recent weeks into a serious relationship. The two had kept this a secret from the others for fear of compromising their positions in the department.

"What spiders are poisonous in this area?" asked Dumont.

"There are only four spiders known to be poisonous to humans in the United States," replied Dr. Mullins. "The Black Widow, Brown Recluse, Hobo Spider and Yellow Sac Spider. The Black Widow and Brown Recluse are the only dangerous spiders in Colorado."

"Would a bite from one of these poisonous spiders be fatal?" asked Dumont.

"There are several factors which determine how serious a bite will be to a person," replied Mullins. "including the age and general health of the subject, the depth and location of the bite, and the amount of venom injected."

"I see," said Dumont.

Mullins was single and in his mid-30's. He had been with the University only two years, specializing in medical entomology. He worked closely with pharmaceutical companies, providing them with venom from various sources for anti-venom serum production, DNA research, and the development of new "wonder drugs" derived from venom peptides. Knowing Mullins' long-standing affiliation with the drug companies, Stoller suspected his actions were not always in the best interest of the department. Occasionally, Stoller and Mullins argued about research priorities and departmental goals. On field expeditions, however, they worked well together as a team.

Although not "People Magazine" handsome, Dr. Mullins was well groomed and attractive. Uncharacteristic for a university professor, he was a party-goer, and frequented the same nightclubs and parties as the student team members. Intellectually, he was a brilliant man with many interests, including mechanical engineering and speleology, the study of caves. He spent many weekends each year exploring Kentucky's 350-mile long Mammoth Cave, the world's longest cave. His work history was less stellar, having bounced from university to university over the past ten years.

Their conversation about spiders was interrupted by a radio call from Dr. Lang at the morgue. Sheriff Grayson switched the call to the external speaker in his Bronco so the others could listen in.

Lang said, "Miss Brooks and I have completed our autopsy. We found extensive damage to the subdermal tissue and skeletal muscle in the area of the puncture wounds, and remarkable evidence of acute respiratory failure. There was also apparent swelling of the liver, and damage to the heart and kidney tissue. We continue to suspect the cause of death was due to envenomation, the introduction of a potent, toxic substance in the victim's body through a bite or sting, but we won't know for sure until the lab results are back."

"Thank you, Dr. Lang. Please keep us informed," Grayson said as he ended the call.

It was noon and Stoller suggested they eat lunch before venturing into the cave. Several volunteers joined in to make sandwiches and set out chips and beverages for the midday meal. Judy Carter decided to come out of her tent and eat lunch with the others. Her eyes were puffy and her nose was red from crying. Although she only spoke a couple of words during the meal, she was doing better than earlier in the day.

The subject of discussion at lunch centered around Dr. Lang's autopsy findings. Stoller continued to wonder how Biggs could have died so quickly, and sustained such serious internal injuries. Carter worked hard to ignore the details of the discussion, because she didn't want to think about Stu's death or how he may have suffered.

Dr. Stoller had been with the University for twenty-seven years. His primary focus during his tenure had been insect behavior and ecology. He was in his early 50's, married, with two grown children and three grandchildren. Stoller was comfortable in his position at the University, and was not interested in retiring any time soon.

When lunch was over and the discussion had run its course, Dumont suggested it was time to enter the cave and search for clues. The group agreed and each member grabbed a coat, boots and tools for the cave exploration. No one was surprised when Carter announced she would stay in camp. As they assembled at the outskirts of camp, Poole handed each person a powerful flashlight and an extra set of batteries. The cave was without electrical power, so flashlights were required to navigate its interior.

The entrance to the cave was an oblong slash in solid rock about six feet high and three feet wide. Tulku had imagined the opening would be much, much larger. A heavy, solid steel door was propped open with a boulder to the left side of the entrance. The door was used by the Park Service to close off the cave to visitors when the water table rose during the wet season and flooded most of the chambers and passageways.

The cave entrance was dark and foreboding. The group entered one at a time, crouching instinctively to protect their heads from bumping the rock ceiling. An odor of moist dirt and rock permeated the cool, damp air. Small streams of water ran down the sides of the walkway. Darkness quickly enveloped them as they walked a few paces inside the cave. Flashlight beams danced on the walls and crossed over each other, like the monstrous spotlights pointed into the night sky at a Hollywood premiere.

Dr. Stoller led the single-file group into the first large chamber, which was about 40 yards in from the entrance. The mob congealed again to listen to Stoller's words.

"The cave is actually a system of connected chambers, and runs approximately one mile long. The temperature in here, unaffected by outside weather conditions, maintains a near-constant 65 degrees Fahrenheit. We studied our subject primarily in this area the first two days, setting up cameras and recording time-lapse images of its habits. In about another 150 meters, the walkway will divide into two paths. This divide is commonly known as the Wishbone. We'll be taking the right leg of the Wishbone to reach the spot where we found Stu's body."

The group made slow progress as each member negotiated the uneven ground and stepped over fallen rocks in the inky black. Finally, they arrived at the Wishbone and veered to the right, continuing on the established path.

Ten minutes later, Stoller pointed to the ground and said, "We found Stu's body here, face down. His skin was cool to the touch."

"There was no apparent sign of struggle," added Grayson. "It's as if he had been struck by lightning and fell dead in his tracks. We looked around the body and found footprints going both directions in the cave, but nothing else. We considered the presence of footprints unimportant, since cave explorers travel this section of the cave all spring and summer. We took a number of photos of the scene and then removed the body for further examination."

"I'd like to see those photos, Sheriff," said Dumont.

"No problem, Mr. Dumont," replied Grayson, "the photos are in my vehicle."

Stu's body had been found in one of the many chambers of the cave. These chambers were wider, taller sections of the cave connected by narrow passageways. Some chamber ceilings were fifteen to twenty feet high or more. Mullins, the resident authority on caves, had previously explained in camp that the entire cave system was created by underground water seeping into limestone cracks over thousands of years. The water absorbed carbon dioxide to form carbonic acid, which gradually ate away the limestone, widening and lengthening the cave each successive year. Minerals had dyed the walls in colorful patterns and formed odd-shaped deposits on cave surfaces. Cave inhabitants included spiders, bats, crickets, beetles and salamanders.

Once everyone had examined the chamber where Stu's body was found, the group split off into smaller teams to explore other sections of the cave. Dumont and Tulku spent time exploring the nearby chambers and passageways, shining their flashlights slowly up and down, from floor to ceiling. They studied the water flow, rock formations and mineral deposits on the cave surfaces. They also paid close attention to the number and direction of the footprints in the cave.

When he was satisfied he had seen all there was to see, Dumont turned off his flashlight, placed his hands together in front of his face and settled into a trance-like state. Tulku turned off his flashlight too, and quietly sat down on the cave floor.

Dumont slowly chanted, "*Om! Mani padme Hum!*" repeating the chant several times to clear his mind and sharpen his powers of concentration.

After several minutes, it seemed to Tulku that Dumont was waking from his trance, so he quietly asked, "My Lama, have you learned anything new from your meditation?"

"What? Uh, yes, Tulku," he replied in a hoarse voice as he shook off the effects of his trance. "In focusing my mind's eye on the evidence we saw here in the cave today, I have begun to form a theory about the cause of Biggs' death. It is written, *beware of a man's shadow and a bee's sting.*"

Tulku didn't fully understand Dumont's meaning, but added his own proverb, "It is also written, *every path has its puddle.*"

Dumont burst out in laughter and patted Tulku on the shoulder. "How right you are, my friend. How right you are!"

Dumont and Tulku started their walk back to the Wishbone to join the others at the appointed time. When they entered a large chamber, Dumont sensed something was wrong.

"Look out Tulku!" he shouted, as he pulled Tulku away from the wall. Several large rocks came crashing down near them from high up on the cave wall.

"That was close," said Tulku.

"Too close, my friend," replied Dumont. They waited a couple of minutes to make sure the rockslide was over, and then resumed their walk out.

After a time, the teams arrived at the Wishbone and began to compare notes. The highlight of the afternoon had been when Poole found a foot-high pile of bat guano inside a large, vertical crack in the cave wall. The search teams reported no other findings. Dumont chose to keep his theory concerning the cause of Biggs' death, and their close call with the falling rocks to himself for the moment. The group exited the cave and returned to camp.

"I'd like to examine those photos now," Dumont said to Grayson as they walked into camp.

"Sure, Mr. Dumont, I'll get them for you." Grayson grabbed a number of photos from a folder on the front seat of his Bronco, and walked back to hand them to Dumont.

"Thank you, Sheriff," said Dumont as he settled into a chair and began leafing through the photos. His examination of the scene pictures went beyond observing the position of Biggs' body on the ground. He looked closely at the details of the cave walls within the chamber in each photo, brightly illuminated by the photographer's camera flash.

Grayson was called away to answer another radio call from Dr. Lang. As before, he switched the call to the external speaker in his patrol vehicle.

"Yes, go ahead Dr. Lang," said Grayson.

"We have received the lab results on the bodily fluids collected from the deceased," said Lang. "I've never seen anything like it. The results indicate the presence of several toxins, including neurotoxins, necrotoxins and batrachotoxins. In other words, the level and mix of poisons in this young man's body was enough to kill one hundred men. Sheriff, in my experience, I know of no creature with this lethal combination of toxins. I believe we are looking at something that has never been studied before."

"Okay, thank you, Dr. Lang," replied Grayson. "Please let us know if you find out anything else."

"Will do, Sheriff. Goodbye."

Dumont studied the faces of the other members of the group as the news sunk in—most displayed the look of shock or surprise.

"This is unprecedented!" exclaimed Stoller. "We need to go back into the cave and search for the source of these toxins."

"This is certainly a new one on me," said Mullins. "I think the country bumpkins at the lab don't know what they're talking about! It's absurd to suggest several different toxins were introduced through envenomation. Did they check Stu's stomach contents to see if he had ingested any poison?"

"I'm sure they did," replied Grayson. "I know this new development may seem farfetched, but I have every confidence in Dr. Lang's professional opinion."

"Hog wash!" shouted Mullins.

"Gentlemen, gentlemen!" exclaimed Stoller. "This is getting us nowhere."

"I think we need to take a break and consider this new evidence before reentering the cave," Dumont said calmly.

As the others continued their debate, Dumont turned to his companion and said, "Tulku, I think it's time to meditate about this mysterious death."

Tulku nodded his head as Dumont entered an unoccupied tent. Dumont settled into a relaxed sitting position on the floor. He pulled out a thin, green cape from his duffel bag and placed it over his head and shoulders. Tulku could hear Dumont's chants from inside the tent.

"*Makuno bakuraga—ameem lockeh—monivom por satoom—meega rah brontesongo. Oh Makaruka, lift the cloud of confusion so the Green Lama may travel the one, true road to justice.*"

After a time, Dumont exited the tent, shielding his eyes from the bright orange setting sun.

"My Lama," asked Tulku, "did your meditation allow you to see more clearly?"

"Yes, Tulku," replied Dumont in a hushed voice. "I saw a brief vision of the killer, and I have formulated a plan to coax our bashful spider out from its lair."

Long shadows crept into camp as the sun set behind the neighboring mountain range. Dumont decided it was time to set his trap, and announced to the group, "I discovered something odd in the cave this afternoon, and I believe I may have solved this mystery. To confirm my suspicions, I'm going back into the cave to take another look."

"Okay, we'll join you, Mr. Dumont," said Stoller. Sheriff Grayson, Stoller, Pazzi, and Judy Carter would accompany Dumont and Tulku this time. Dumont was both pleased and concerned that Carter was going into the cave with them—pleased that she had regained her determination, but concerned for her safety. Mullins handed each person a flashlight and a set of fresh batteries as they exited camp.

On the short walk to the cave entrance, Tulku whispered to Dumont, "It is written, *after dark all cats are leopards.*" Dumont nodded his head and smiled in acknowledgment of Tulku's insight.

When the team reached the first chamber, Dumont stopped and explained they were looking for unusual scrape marks on the cave wall, and where to look for them. He also said he wanted the group to split into two smaller search teams at the Wishbone. Following Dumont's request, Stoller, Pazzi and Grayson took the left path at the divide, while Dumont, Tulku and Carter went right. Their growing familiarity with the cave allowed them to walk at a faster pace this time.

Dumont was leading the way, when his flashlight suddenly flickered off. He shook it and replaced the batteries, but it wouldn't turn back on. Tulku suggested that perhaps the bulb had burned out or a wire had come loose. They decided to go on with the light from the two remaining flashlights, so Carter took the lead from Dumont.

Grayson's search team walked several minutes on their path, focusing on the cave floor for clues. At the point where they figured they were nearly parallel with the chamber on the opposite path where Stu's body was found, they began to thoroughly study the cave walls for evidence. They found an area with broken rock fragments at the base of the wall, with three-inch vertical scratches on the wall face. Grayson placed a piece of folded notepaper on the cave floor to mark the spot. The team resumed their search, walking deeper into the cave.

When Dumont's team reached the area just beyond the chamber where Stu's body was found, Dumont and Tulku briefly stopped to look for marks on the cave wall. Carter was anxious to look further inside the cave and went ahead, despite Dumont's objection. Minutes later, Dumont and Tulku heard Carter scream. They ran in the direction of the scream and found her lying unconscious on her back. Her flashlight was smashed to pieces at her side.

Dumont sensed someone lurking in the dark.

"Tulku, come back!" he shouted. Before Tulku could move, he was struck on his upper back and neck by a heavy object. His flashlight dropped to the ground and rolled several feet away.

Dumont stood motionless in the pitch-black chamber and chanted, "*Om! Mani padme Hum!*"

A man's voice from somewhere in the dark said, "I have something for you too, Mr. Dumont. Or, should I say, the Green Lama."

At that moment, a flashlight came on and was shined directly into Dumont's eyes. Through the light, Dumont could see a figure moving in his direction. It was a man with an extended arm.

"I was expecting you, Dr. Mullins," exclaimed Dumont. "It will do you no good to resist. *Om! Mani padme Hum! The Green Lama strikes for justice!*"

Dumont leapt forward and wrestled Mullins to the ground. Mullins rolled over on top of Dumont and tried to force his right hand to Dumont's throat. The Green Lama pushed Mullins' arm away and delivered a powerful blow to his chin. Mullins continued to fight, so Dumont struck him again, this time squarely on the jaw. Mullins went limp and rolled off Dumont onto his back.

Tulku slowly rose to his feet in the dark, rubbing his neck and shaking off the effects from the blow he had received. He recovered his flashlight and shined it on Mullins and Dumont as he walked in their direction.

"Are you all right, my Lama?"

"Yes, Tulku," replied Dumont. "But Dr. Mullins is in trouble."

In the struggle, Mullins had inadvertently injected himself in his side with the poisonous toxins intended for the Green Lama. Dumont and Tulku kneeled at his side to examine two bleeding puncture wounds under his shirt. The wounds appeared to be identical to those found on Biggs' body.

Judy Carter regained consciousness and joined Dumont and Tulku. Mullins was shuddering in pain.

"What happened?" questioned Carter.

"Dr. Mullins tried to kill me like he killed Stewart Biggs," said Dumont. "His effort failed, and he wounded himself in the struggle."

"That's right, Judy," said Mullins as he gasped for breath. "I did it for you."

"What do you mean?" demanded Carter. Mullins eyes rolled back in his head. He made one short gasp and collapsed.

Carter broke down and began sobbing deeply. "Is h-he, is he dead?" she asked.

"Yes, he's gone Miss Carter," said Tulku.

She bent over from the gut-wrenching impact of the moment and exclaimed, "What did h-he mean when said he did it for me? I loved Stu!"

"And Mullins was in love with you," explained Dumont. "When he attended social events with you and the other graduate students, he observed your growing relationship with Stewart. He decided he would stage an accident on this expedition, and eliminate his competition for your affection."

He saw that Carter was growing weak, and in no shape to listen to more details of Stewart Biggs' murder. He suggested they make their way out of the cave. Although their walk out was slow going, they eventually made it back to camp.

An hour later, the camp was overflowing with patrol vehicles with rotating red and blue emergency lights. Officers, county officials, reporters and others were pouring in and out of the cave, like industrious ants building a new colony. The coroner's van was backed up to the cave entrance, ready to transport Mullins' body. Expedition team members were slumped in their camp chairs, half-asleep. Carter was seated with a blanket wrapped around her shoulders, staring off into the distance. Movements appeared to be in slow motion to her as she watched the activity under the surreal, red and blue spinning lights. It reminded her of nightclubs back home, where she had danced in the dark under a flashing strobe light. The activity continued well into the night.

The next day, Dumont, Tulku and Sheriff Grayson visited the expedition party at their camp. Dumont had spoken with reporters earlier in the morning, and now took the opportunity to explain Mullins' criminal actions to his team.

"Mullins' experience in medical uses for venom and his access to various forms of toxins made him a prime suspect early on. When we investigated the cave, Tulku and I found evidence of dirt and scuff marks on a chamber wall adjacent to where Biggs' body was found. Sheriff Grayson and his team found similar evidence on the other side of the cave, walking down the left path of the Wishbone. I had observed scuffmarks and mineral residue on Mullins' boots when I first met him at the morgue, and made the connection later on. With his caving experience, Mullins had located a tunnel near the cave ceiling, which ran between the two main pathways. He took the left leg of the Wishbone on the day of the murder, climbed up to the tunnel and crawled across to ambush the unsuspecting Biggs. He made his escape using the same tunnel. Mullins later used this tunnel to stage a rockslide, and launch a surprise attack on Tulku, Judy Carter and me."

"Our bashful spider was actually a specially-designed ring," explained Dumont. He showed everyone a college ring with a large, oval stone set in white gold. Mullins, with his experience in mechanical design, had created this diabolical instrument. The top of the ring was hinged open, revealing two long needle-sharp pins. "These pins are hollow and positioned over a small spring-loaded reservoir. The reservoir contained a lethal, fast-acting mixture of toxins from sources available to Mullins. When the pins were pressed to the skin, they created two deep puncture wounds like those of a spider bite, and the compressed reservoir injected a large dose of poison into the victim."

Dumont looked around at the faces of the group and continued his explanation. "Mullins knew exactly where to inject the toxic mixture for maximum effect. He pressed his ring to Biggs' neck where the poison would quickly enter his blood stream through the many veins and arteries located there. When Mullins' attempts to cover-up his murderous act began to unravel, he tried to inject poison into my throat to keep me from disclosing my suspicions. Thankfully, I was able to foil his efforts. He never intended to hurt Judy Carter or Tulku."

Tulku began where Dumont had left off. "One big mistake made by Dr. Mullins was underestimating the level of professionalism in forensic science here in rural Colorado. He didn't think a rural county coroner would have the expertise and resources to distinguish the cause of Biggs' death from that of a poisonous spider bite. He was mistaken, for Dr. Lang had a wealth of experience from his previous position as a medical examiner, and utilized the services of a modern laboratory."

Sheriff Grayson jumped in next, "Dr. Mullins didn't think Stewart Biggs' body would be discovered as soon as it was. His plan was to kill Biggs four or five hours before his body was to be found. As it was, Biggs' apparent quick death made it seem unlikely that a common, poisonous spider was the cause of his death."

The expedition team members expressed their appreciation to Dumont, Tulku and Sheriff Grayson for taking the time to explain the terrible events of the past two days. They were exhausted from this ordeal, and decided to break camp and head for home as soon as they were finished packing.

Following handshakes and goodbye hugs, Grayson, Dumont and Tulku headed back to town in the Bronco. On the trip back, the three men continued to discuss the murder case. Grayson remarked about how the clues, in retrospect, all led back to Mullins.

Dumont was in a philosophical frame of mind and said, "Sheriff, it is written, *crime leaves a trail like a water beetle, and like a snail it leaves its shine.*"

Tulku added his proverb to the occasion, "Gentlemen, it is also written, *he who commits murder should remember to dig two graves!*"

"So true," said Grayson with a smile in his voice. "And I too have a saying. It is written, *all's well that ends well.*"

They all laughed out loud, the kind of lighthearted laugh that comes with the relief in knowing you have accomplished your mission. They spoke of lighter things during the remainder of their drive.

"Mystery Solved—Justice Served—Case Closed," that's how the Deerfield Gazette's front-page news headline would read in the evening edition. When they arrived in town, Dumont and Tulku exited the Bronco, bid farewell to Grayson and made their way back home. In a short time, they would be off on another adventure of mystery and intrigue. For now, a long nap on the plane would do just fine.

SGT. PRESTON OF THE YUKON

A Call From the Storm

by Jim Nixon

It was December in the Yukon. Though it was only five in the afternoon, the sun had long since set behind thick clouds that had rolled in over the mountains earlier in the day. The two men inside the wood-frame headquarters building of the NorthWest Mounted Police at Dawson City could hear the howl of another storm gathering over the snow-covered bleakness outside. The older man, who carried the rank of inspector, sat absorbed in the reports before him on his desk. The scarlet tunic worn by the other man bore the stripes of a sergeant. He sat near the large stone fireplace, his hands busy with the sled harness he was mending.

In a week it would be Christmas, he reflected as he deftly worked the leather needle. The first Christmas of the new century, a century of great change, he was certain. Already a man named Edison had figured out how to record and playback voices and music. Internal combustion engines powered automobiles that were slowly replacing the horse and buggy. The telephone, of which there were even a few in Dawson, would soon link businesses and families all over the world. But civilization would be slow to reach this far north, even though Dawson had more wealth per acre than most cities in Canada and was the largest city west of Winnipeg.

Dawson was changing, however. Most of the gold seekers that flooded into the town in 1897 seeking riches on the Klondike had moved on, lured by rumors of even bigger strikes in Alaska. Some remained, but the large mining companies were beginning to bring in dredges and heavy equipment to work the claims. There was still plenty to keep the Mounties busy, though, new strikes or not. The gold being extracted from the rich Klondike River and Bonanza Creek claims would easily last another decade.

The room was warm, though drafts from the rising wind could occasionally be felt through the mud chinking in the walls. The single-story structure, like most in Dawson, had been thrown together hastily, built on the boggy ground that never thawed, the permafrost that lay beneath the endless expanses of muskeg cut only by the few trails leading into and out of town. Behind it was attached the barracks where a dozen Mounties lived and worked, earning scarcely more than a dollar a day from the Queen's treasury. But there wasn't a more dedicated group of men between the rocks of Newfoundland and the forests of British Columbia. The sergeant already knew in a way few men come to know that he was meant for this life.

Standing an inch and half over six feet, the Mountie was powerfully built. The broadness of his shoulders and size of his hands suggested reserves of strength greater than ordinary men possessed. Unlike most of the other constables in Dawson, he was clean-shaven except for a thin, well-trimmed moustache. His dark brown eyes sparkled with friendliness and intelligence, traits that usually proved more useful than mere physical strength. But three years in the Yukon had left unmistakable signs, sunburn from the twenty-one hour days of summer and small white patches inflicted by the cruel winds of winter. His education in the United States interrupted by the murder of his father, he had returned north and joined the Mounties in order to have the authority to pursue his father's killer. With his request for assignment to Dawson immediately granted, the young constable soon earned the respect of his peers by bringing in the fugitive. Later, when the man escaped prison, he once again tracked and recaptured the killer. His promotion to sergeant had arrived two days before Spike Wilson was finally hanged.

At his feet a large gray Husky lay quietly, following his master's gaze into the flames. No ordinary animal, this dog stood almost two feet high and weighed nearly fifty-five pounds. He could outrun any sled dog in the Yukon, and could easily work twelve hours straight without fatigue. The Malamutes and mixed breeds that comprised most of the sled teams in the frozen north immediately sensed that this dog was their master. His intelligent blue eyes were a throwback to his Siberian ancestors that had crossed the Bering Sea some 10,000 years earlier. Yukon King was the dog's name, and a finer lead dog or friend to a Mountie did not exist in the northwest.

Both man and animal looked in unison as the wooden front door suddenly burst open and a figure stepped into the room. Clad in a thick fur parka that fell over his face and stomping new black hiking boots on the floor to shake off the fresh snow, it was impossible to judge the person's age or nationality. "For Heaven's sake, close the door, man," Inspector Conrad said crisply as his right hand shot forward to trap several papers that had started to find their way onto the floor.

"Sorry," the figure mumbled, turning to close the door. The sergeant stood as the dog scrambled to its feet. "What can we do for you?" he asked, watching the newcomer struggle from his coat. Then, with surprise, he noted that the new arrival was no more than a youth.

The visitor unbuttoned his parka and hung it on one of several vacant wooden pegs protruding from the wall. He appeared to be no more than seventeen or eighteen, with unshaven light stubble clinging to his face. His hair was disheveled and distinctly reddish. From his smooth complexion, the sergeant could see he had not been in the Yukon long. The husky stood patiently at the Mountie's side, also observing the man, trying to identify the scent and decide if the figure was friend or foe. The boy regarded him with a look of both awe and fear. "It's all right, King won't hurt you," the sergeant assured him in a voice low and mellow. "I'm Sergeant Bill Preston, and this is Inspector Conrad. What brings you to Dawson, son?"

Responding to the sergeant's greeting, the boy took a tentative step forward. "My name is George McDougall," he said, shaking the sergeant's offered hand. "How did you know I just got here?"

"Well, everything you're wearing looks new," Preston said, smiling. "And I don't hear a dog team hitched outside, which means someone dropped you off."

"Yes, I found a man in Whitehorse who offered to bring me here with him. His name was Mr. LaFarge. We've been on his sled for over two days straight."

Preston could not conceal a brief expression of astonishment. This boy had just come four hundred miles on dogsled in the middle of winter. "Pierre LaFarge, yes," he said, reassessing the young man. "A fine fellow. You were lucky to find him. It's not an easy trip from Whitehorse this time of year. I imagine he's glad to be back for Christmas."

"Uh, yes, he said to say hello," the boy added, unconsciously rubbing his hands together and moving toward the fire.

"You're from Whitehorse, then?" Preston could see he was dog-tired.

"No, Vancouver," the boy answered.

"Vancouver?" Across the room, Inspector Conrad stopped checking reports and began to listen with interest. Travel from British Columbia this time of year was extremely difficult. "How did you make it all the way to Whitehorse? And if I may ask, how old are you?" Preston asked, his interest now fully aroused.

"I'm almost eighteen," the boy replied with a defensive tone.

"When did you leave home, George?" Preston continued.

The boy thought for a moment. "Let's see, that would be eight days ago now."

"You got here in eight days?" Doubt crept into Preston's voice. Perhaps the lad had run away from home and was simply making up a story.

"I got a job as a deck hand on a steamer to Skagway. The captain said he needed extra help, so he let me go one-way with him. Then I caught a work train on the new railroad to Whitehorse. That's where I found Mr. LaFarge…at the general store. Don't you believe me?"

Preston studied the lad. He seldom misjudged a man's character, and his instincts told him the boy's was telling the truth. The new White Pass railroad *had* just been opened between Skagway and Whitehorse, so that much was possible. "All right, George, I do believe you. Suppose you sit down and have some hot tea, then tell us why you came all this way on your own?"

"It's getting worse out there," the youth replied, ignoring the offer. "Can you travel in this weather?" he added, a look of concern on his haggard face.

"King is the best lead dog in the Yukon," the sergeant said matter-of-factly. "But there had better be a good reason. Besides the inspector here, I'm the only one on duty right now."

"I've got to find my father," the youngster replied earnestly. "His name is James McDougall. Do either of you know him, by any chance?" He turned first to the inspector, then the sergeant, with a look of hope mingled with worry.

"James McDougall," Preston repeated slowly. "I don't recognize that name. Does he live in Dawson?"

"No, he's got a claim somewhere up the Klondike. It's urgent that I find him. You see, it's my ma. She...passed away ten days ago. We all thought she was getting better, then she just died, r—real sudden." Preston could see the boy's attempt to hide the tears that began to form as he stammered out the words.

"Most miners close up for the winter and move to town," Preston said. "Are you sure he's not in Dawson somewhere?"

"Pa promised he wouldn't stay this winter. We expected him three weeks ago. I gotta find him. He...doesn't know. We need him to come home."

"Couldn't someone in your family just have written to him or sent a telegram?" Preston asked.

"Pa got the gold fever two years ago. He said he wasn't gonna leave his claim until he brought it in. We're worried maybe something's happened to him. They're waitin' to bury Ma so Pa can be there." The boy sank into the vacant chair near the fire. The exhaustion of the long journey and the loss of his mother seemed to flood over him. He was no longer able to hold back the tears. Preston laid a hand on his shoulder. "Easy, lad. I know it's been hard for you. You can tell us more when you feel up to it. I'll get you that tea."

Taking a battered ladle off the wall, he dipped it into a wooden water barrel that sat near the door connecting the barracks and office, then filled a small iron pot and hung it over the fire. "It'll just be a few minutes."

There was no sound but the cracking of the fire and the wind outside punctuated by George McDougall's occasionally sniffing. Preston prepared two cups of tea and sat opposite the youngster. "Here, drink this." He handed one cup to the boy. The husky, sensing the boy's distress, moved beside him and young George unconsciously began to stroke his fur. The dog did not pull away.

"King is a very good judge of character, George," Preston said. "He likes you."

"I'm sorry to be such a baby. I promise I won't do that again."

"Why don't you tell me a little about yourself," the sergeant said encouragingly. "You said 'we.' Do you have brothers or sisters?"

"I have a younger brother fifteen and a sister who's eleven," the boy said, raising the steaming cup to his lips. "Thanks for the tea. It's very good."

"And who's looking after them while you're gone?"

"My Aunt Maggie. She's my pa's sister."

Preston could not help being impressed by the boy's spunk, travelling on his own all the way to the Yukon this time of year. "So your father did have a paying claim?" he asked.

"He and a partner bought part of a claim from a man who found gold and wanted to cash in. He sub…sub…"

"Subdivided?" Preston suggested.

"Yes, subdivided the claim and went back to the States. Pa's sent back some money, not much. He always thought the next week, he'd find the real gold."

"What about the man who went in with him?"

"Pa bought him out last winter. He went on to Nome to look for a bigger strike."

"Your father can't get much mail or we'd know him," Preston said thoughtfully. "But we do have records of who's on most claims here," he added. "What was the name of the man who sold him the claim?"

"Bradford, I think."

"Oh, of course, old Tom Bradford's claim," Preston said, nodding. "I know where that is."

"Then you can take me there?" the lad asked, his gaze imploring.

"Normally, we won't do that," Preston answered. "But this time of year, you'd have a hard time finding a team and driver that would leave town, no matter what you offered them."

"Oh," the youngster said dejectedly.

Preston smiled. "But it just so happens that we have a number of Christmas packages here that need to be delivered. King and I were going to wait out this storm, but as soon as Constable Holt returns from his rounds, I go off-duty. I think we'd be willing to take you up the Klondike. But don't you think you should get some rest first?"

"No, I'm ready now," young McDougall said emphatically.

"Well, I'd have to get the inspector's permission," Preston said slowly, glancing at his superior across the room and letting the last word hang in the air.

"Permission granted, Sergeant," Conrad snapped. Preston knew he was trying to sound gruff, but had also been impressed with the boy. "But see to it you're back here in three days," the inspector added brusquely, turning back to the reports on his desk and simultaneously concealing a wry smile.

"Yes sir," Preston replied obediently. "I'll have to provision the team and reinstall this harness," he added as he fished a coin out of his pocket and pressed it into the boy's hand. "Why don't you get a meal at the café across the street, then come back here. We should be ready to leave in two hours."

Though he had traveled through many winter storms, Preston was beginning to question the wisdom of his decision to start at once. It was one thing to take King and the dog team in pursuit of a criminal in weather like this, quite another to travel with a youth unused to the harshness of the Yukon winter. The temperature had registered five degrees below zero on the barracks thermometer when they had set out two hours earlier. But he knew that once the center of the storm passed, the wind would switch to the north and the temperature would begin to plunge. Then they would be tested. The dogs, seemingly oblivious to the cold, surged on ahead, the drifts on the well used trail up the Klondike still not high enough to impede their progress. In front, running free, was King, his keen nose keeping them on the trail. Occasionally he would circle back to nip at the lead dog or the one behind him, a reminder of just who was boss of the team.

They had packed as lightly as they could. For balance, Preston placed their lantern, axe, cooking gear and their food, carefully wrapped in oilskin, in front, behind the small folded tent and meat for the dogs that he had picked up at the butcher shop just before embarking. The dogs weren't fussy what they ate as long as they got enough protein to replace the enormous amount of calories they burned dragging the sled. The mail and packages were stowed in the middle and behind them the sleeping bags, Preston's and a borrowed spare for George. The boy sat just ahead of Preston, who stood on the runners at the back working the gee pole. It was as dark as the bottom of an arctic lake at midnight, and felt just about as cold, Preston thought.

His plan was to press on until they reached a cabin at the base of Bear Creek that often served travelers in the winter. He doubted anyone would be there this time of year. They could overnight out of the wind and strike out up the Klondike after eating some breakfast. The sun would not rise until nearly eleven, and would set again before two. But Preston doubted they would see anything more than a brief grayness.

The wind pushed the snow nearly directly into their faces, making it almost impossible to look straight ahead. The storm had not yet passed them. He did not want to alarm the boy who so desperately wanted to find his father, but he too was concerned after hearing the lad's story. It was not sensible to work a claim in the Yukon in winter unless a shaft had already been sunk through the overburden to pay gravel. But from young George's description of his father's claim, and his own memory of what Tom Bradford had done with it, Preston doubted such a reason existed. If James McDougall was supposed to quit and head home three weeks ago, it was possible some accident had befallen him that prevented him from leaving. There were few people up here now, and days could pass before anyone happened on a man stranded in the Yukon. In that event, he was counting on King's help when they arrived.

They found the empty cabin without difficulty thanks to King's unerring sense of smell. It contained four rough log bunks and a small iron stove. One of the unwritten laws of the trail was that travelers who used this refuge always left dry firewood inside for the next party. There was no shortage of dead trees in the forests, it was only necessary to locate, cut and stack the fuel before they left. When they had warmed themselves, Preston set George to that task as he unpacked the sled. "Stay with George, King," he commanded. King would not let the boy get lost. He was proving to be intelligent and strong, even though he lacked familiarity with the rough conditions.

When enough meat for the dogs had thawed, he fed them first. "Look after yer dogs and they'll never fail ya," an old prospector had once told him. It was good advice. The dogs had worked harder than either of them and human food took too long to prepare for hungry dogs to scent.

George stomped back into the cabin with an armload of wood just as Preston had their supper grilling on the stove. Despite his exertion, he could see the lad shivering with the cold. The snow continued relentlessly. "Gosh, it's cold out," the boy said, setting his burden down. "But that sure smells good."

They ate in silence until George asked, "Do we have many stops to make before we get there?"

"Tom Bradford's claim was another twenty miles up the river from here. I'm going to stop at two claims that are directly on route and see if there's any news of your father. We'll save the rest to deliver on our way back."

"Thanks. Uh, I was wondering, does King stay outside all night?"

"King is a sled dog. He sleeps with the team and stands guard. He's used to this weather, believe me."

"He's a marvelous dog. You must feel very lucky to have him."

"Without King, I would probably be dead by now," Preston said solemnly. "He's got an uncanny sense of danger and is very intelligent. Sometimes I even wonder if he can read my mind."

"Gosh," the boy said admiringly. "How did you come to find him?"

"When King was just a puppy, his owner was delivering him to me as a gift for a favor he felt he owed me. He had an accident with the sled, however, and we didn't find him until it was too late. King was nowhere to be seen. It turned out a crafty she-wolf the trappers in the area called 'Three-Toe' had found him and taken him away with her. King learned a lot from her before I found him again."

"Did you have to shoot the wolf to get him back?"

"No. King fought hard to try to save her from a huge lynx. I killed the lynx, but old 'Three-Toe' had been too badly hurt. She died a few minutes later."

"Did King try to run away?"

"No. He remembered me from when he was just a pup and I picked him up from the litter. We've been pals ever since. Now get some rest. From the look of this storm, you're going to learn how to use snowshoes tomorrow!"

Preston slept uneasily. The wind had lessened during the night, but he knew the snow would be deep even before he opened the door and saw it caked halfway up the opening. As he kicked the snow loose, the light from the lantern cut a reddish shaft into the dark drifts outside. It was brutally cold and still snowing.

Suddenly, a shape moved in the gloom, and King bounded up to the door. "King, old boy," the sergeant said, stroking the great dog's head with his mitten. "We've got a lot of work ahead of us today, fella," he said. "Go on, rouse the dogs. I'll be out with some food in a few minutes."

King bounded back into the darkness, leaping forward with his powerful hind legs, his chest breasting the new snow. Preston could hear his barks and the answering yelps of the sled dogs. If the trail was as badly drifted as he guessed, they were in for a very difficult run.

They passed over the mouth of Hunker Creek and managed to reach the first inhabited dwelling sometime around midday. It had gotten light enough to see the trail about two hours earlier, though parts of it were covered with snow four and five feet deep. At these points, there was no way even the great dog King could make any headway unless a man went first on snowshoes. Preston took the first turn, showing George how to walk on the awkward shoes. "We'll make a sled man of you before we reach your father!" he told the boy, sounding more cheerful than he felt. They made scant headway behind young McDougall, but it allowed Preston sufficient rest. He constantly monitored George for signs of frostbite. He could already see that parts of the lad's forehead would serve as lifelong reminders of this journey.

"Sure you and the boy can't rest awhile, Sergeant?" It was Inuit Charley who asked the question as they readied the team to push on. Charley had been one of the first up the Klondike and his claim was producing enough gold now to warrant a full-time winter operation. Preston had accepted Charley's offer of fresh dogs, since, with the exception of King, his were tiring rapidly. He would have loved to sit, sip tea and exchange gossip for an hour or two to ease the ache in his bones. But a growing sense of uneasiness had gripped him, and he wanted to get back on the trail.

"Maybe on the way back, Charley," he replied cheerfully, then with a wave, turned to the team. "On King, on you Huskies!" King barked sharply and the sled lurched forward into the half-light. Soon, the warmth of Charley's cabin was only a memory. All they could see was the faint outline of the trail through the blowing snow. Somewhere on their left lay the frozen river, clawing its way eastward and daring them to follow.

He had inquired about James McDougall, of course. Charley knew him, but not well. "Keeps mostly to heemself," he'd told them. "Ain't bin dis way since mebbe last September."

Preston wasn't sure if the snow or the cold was worse. Days like this in the Yukon weren't rare, but when it got this cold, men with any sense sought shelter, not the open trail. Darkness had fallen four hours before they reached the second cabin, this one owned by Cyril Catlett, a massive man with a huge black beard and hearty laugh. Like Charley, he offered them shelter and a hot meal, but Preston again refused. By some stroke of luck, the trail drifts had begun to diminish as they moved eastward, so King was able to resume breaking trail for the sled. If they kept going, they could make it before having to make camp. With Charley's fresh dogs on the sled, they had made better time. So after ten minutes of conversation and questions about George's father, they were back on the trail.

"Mr. Catlett didn't know any more than Inuit Charley, did he?" George shouted over his shoulder to the sergeant.

"No. Do you know if your father owned a dog team?"

"I don't think so. He never mentioned one."

"Your father evidently didn't travel much at all," Preston answered, his voice muffled by his scarf and lips already numbed. "He must have shipped his dust out and stayed close to his claim."

"When do you think we'll get there?"

"At this rate, about three more hours."

Preston had hoped they wouldn't have to find the claim in the storm. For the boy's sake, he desperately wanted to see a light in a window and find George's father safe and warm. But as they reached the area of Tom Bradford's former claim, they saw no signs of life. "King, here boy!" Preston shouted. With an answering bark, the great dog peeled back from the front of the sled.

"Find the cabin, King," he said. "Go on, boy, find the cabin!" King took off into the swirling snow.

"How can he do that?" George asked stiffly.

"King can smell people. If anyone is cooking anything, or has dumped garbage or left any trace of habitation around, he'll pick it up. See, he's turned off the trail already." King's barking now came from their right. Preston jerked the harness lead and shouted at the team. "Follow King!" he commanded, steering the sled away from the trail. They could hear King barking ahead. He steered toward the sound.

King stood in front of a dark structure nearly completely covered with snow. There was no light in a window or smoke from a fire. The place looked as if it hadn't been occupied for some time. "Where is he?" George said, the worry in his voice evident despite the thick scarf and ice that clung to his mouth and nose.

They left the sled and waded through the fresh snow to where the faint outlines of a door could be seen. Preston swatted the snow away and worked the latch. The door swung inward, carrying with it a load of snow that quickly fell to the wooden floor. The man and the boy entered the cabin. "Stay, King," Preston said. The dog took up station just outside the door, his eyes watching both the team of dogs now busy burrowing into the snow and the doorway through which his master had vanished.

Preston managed to get the matches out of his pocket and struck one. The smell of sulfur tickled their nostrils as it mingled with the staleness of the air inside of the cabin. In this cold, nothing could decay, but Preston would not have been surprised to find a dead man somewhere in the darkness. Instead, when he lit the lantern sitting on the table against the wall, they found an empty cabin.

George peeled the scarf away from his mouth and threw back the hood of his parka. "Where can he have gone?" he asked uncertainly. Preston was already inspecting the provisions stacked on a shelf and the contents of an iron pot that sat on the small stove in the corner. He opened the stove and looked inside, then removed his mitten and stuck his finger into the pot, withdrawing it and holding it to his nose.

"From the look of things, I'd say no one's been here for a least a week, maybe longer," he said. "The stove's had a fire within the last month, for certain. We can't do anything more tonight. We'll have to get warm, rest and start looking in the morning."

"But what if he's out there, hurt or something, freezing to death?" the boy said plaintively.

Preston moved to place an arm on the boy's shoulder. "Son, a man can't last in this cold for a day, much less a week. Either your father is safe somewhere, or we'll find what happened in the morning. Try to put the bad things out of your mind and help me with the team. We'll learn what we can tomorrow."

They both slept uneasily in the cold cabin. Preston gave the boy the single bunk and slept on the floor. They'd eaten a cold supper after he'd managed to find enough food to tide the dogs over to morning when they could cut some wood. He'd taken a liking to the resourceful lad who never complained and had performed each duty assigned to him on the arduous trip. Surely he deserved to find his father alive. But all the signs were bad.

He wasn't sure exactly what woke him, or how long he had slept, but Preston was suddenly alert. It could have been the distant howl of a wolf somehow tangled in with the dream he'd been having and could no longer remember. He heard King scratching at the door. Quietly he pulled down the sleeping bag and slipped out of it. The floor beneath his thick wool socks felt like the ice on the river.

Opening the door, he met the dim form of King. "What is it, boy?" he said in a low voice. The dog lowered his head, then turned away into the darkness. He made no move to run, but made a strange whimpering sound in his throat. "Is something wrong, boy? Here, let me see." Preston knelt and felt King's paws, then parted his fur, feeling carefully for some sign of injury. The cold was making his fingers numb. He could find nothing. Far away, the ice in the river cracked, sounding like a rifle echoing in the frozen wastes.

"Come inside, boy," Preston said. King followed and Preston lit the lamp. Across the room, George stirred and rubbed his eyes.

"Is it time to get up yet?" he mumbled.

"Something is wrong, but I don't know what," Preston replied, again parting King's fur to see if he'd been injured. King pulled free and went to the door. He made the strange whining noise again. "I've never seen him act like that before," the sergeant said wonderingly.

Suddenly King growled and the hair on the back of his neck rose up. Preston flung open the door and held the lantern out. There was nothing there.

"Is there someone out there? Could it be Pa?" George said, now fully awake and sitting on the bunk.

"King would bark," Preston replied. "No man or animal could get within a hundred yards of this place before he would give the alarm."

"He wants to go out, doesn't he?" the boy asked.

"Let's see," Preston said. King took two steps outside, then stopped, his head inclined upward toward the swirling snow. Then he barked, not savagely but as if to acknowledge someone. "He appears to be seeing or sensing something, but doesn't know what to make of it."

"Could it be some strange scent on the wind?" the boy asked.

"Possibly, but I just don't know. If he'd wanted me to follow, he'd bark at me. At any rate, there isn't any apparent danger, so I think we'd better go back to sleep. Maybe we can get to the bottom of this in the morning."

When Preston again lit the lantern, it was nearly eight a.m. by his watch, but still pitch dark. They found enough wood to start a fire, then he fed the dogs by the light of the lantern. King seemed to be his old self again, without a trace of the strange behavior they'd seen in the middle of the night. After eating, they set out on snowshoes to explore the area, hoping to find signs of James McDougall.

Despite the gloom, they quickly found an old wooden sluiceway leading down from the hill behind the claim. Working their way awkwardly up the snow-covered rocks, they traced the length of the contraption but found nothing. They spent another torturous hour exploring the hill, but there was no sign of recent digging. King bounded through the huge drifts, occasionally stopping to scent the air, but even the great dog's superior sense of smell turned up nothing.

Inside, they had found a small amount of gold dust in a small leather pouch. On a rough log table beside the stove, they found a crudely sharpened pencil and some blank writing paper. It was not until they sought the shelter of the cabin after their initial search that George thought to look under the pine needle mattress on the bed and found a small notebook. Eagerly, he flipped through the few pages of faint writing to the last entry. Preston stood beside him, looking over his shoulder as the boy read aloud.

"It says here that he wanted to get a shaft started before he left for the winter. That entry is dated November the fifth. The next entry is December second, and he says he thinks he's found 'it,' whatever 'it' is, but needs more firewood to thaw the ground. That's the last entry. What does it mean, Sergeant?"

"Evidently, he *did* sink a shaft. At least, he started to. But it takes a constant fire to keep the ground thawed, so he must have used all the wood he had on hand and set out to find more."

"Why didn't he leave when he said he would?"

"A few of the miners in this area have made excellent strikes below ground. He may have been convinced he'd found gold ore. We should locate the shaft without delay."

They donned their gear again, and the sergeant led the way farther into the hill behind the claim, this time holding the lantern. "Look for a snow-covered pile of rock. It won't look like the surrounding terrain."

The climbing was difficult. After several hours of scrambling over loose snow and rock, they came to the base of a small frozen creek bed that flowed downward toward the river. Preston stopped. "There," he said, pointing to a cone-shaped heap of snow. Using a shovel retrieved from in the cabin, they soon uncovered the beginnings of a shaft cut into the permafrost. Only ten feet deep, it had been covered with two planks and was partially filled with snow. Charred pieces of wood lay in the bottom. But there was still no sign of James McDougall.

"Firewood," Preston murmured as he gazed out from the shaft. "He went to get more wood. My guess is that he never returned."

"Which way would he go?"

"All of the claims around here are closed for the winter. He could have gone to borrow some wood, intending to replace it before spring. Or he could have gone through all of that and headed into the hills to cut more. We didn't find a sled or his axe." Preston produced an old handkerchief from his pocket. "Here, King," he called.

"What's that?"

"I found it in the cabin. I'm pretty sure this belonged to your father. Let's see if King can find the scent." The great dog sniffed the handkerchief, then began prowling the snow beside the hole. Then he barked and moved toward the creek. "He's found something. Let's follow," Preston said, holding the lantern and striking out behind the dog. The boy fell in behind him.

Two hours later, it was clear that King had lost the scent. They were standing in some thick fir trees nearly a half-mile up the narrow creek. The snow had lessened to light flakes. Mercifully, the wind had fallen as well. "There's too much new snow, and the scent's too old," Preston said. "We'd better head back and get warm before we get too tired."

George reluctantly agreed, and soon they were standing in front of the warm stove once again. Preston was trying to think of a way to break the news to the boy that they would have to abandon the search for now. "I'm expected back at headquarters soon," he said regretfully. "I'll arrange then to have another search organized, but I'm afraid we'll have to wait until after the holidays."

"By then, it'll be too late for Pa to be at Ma's funeral," the boy said. Preston could sense his reluctance to give up the idea that his father was still alive. He made a final offer.

"The weather is improving. We'll try again tomorrow morning. Maybe King can come up with something then."

The last thing Preston expected was for King to begin acting strangely again that night. But it was nearly three in the morning by his watch when he was again awakened by King scratching at the door. The intense cold of the previous two days had eased, but as the Mountie stood outside wrapped in a blanket and scanning the darkness, there was no indication of what his dog was trying to tell him. "What is it, fella?" he asked in a low voice. King bounded away, then stood looking upward as he had the previous night. Then he barked and bounded forward, only to stop again a few yards further. The sergeant did not need a further sign. He woke George. "King wants us to follow him," he said, hurriedly getting dressed.

"Has he got the scent back?" the boy asked, donning his own outer clothes.

"It's not a scent he's got," Preston said, "but something else. I've always believed animals can sense things people can't, and whatever King sensed last night has returned. We need to go where he takes us."

"Gosh, that sounds spooky," George said.

"The natives here believe that there are many things men can't explain," Preston said as they donned their snowshoes. "They even believe some animals can communicate with the spirits of their ancestors." He filled the lantern with coal oil, then lit it, holding it high. "All right, King, we're ready, boy. Lead on!"

The snow had stopped and the stars were out. A brilliant display of northern lights threw eerie green and blue light onto the new snow. King patiently led them back over the previous trail. Then he veered into a deeper part of the trees, making the going more arduous. The faint outlines of a trail snaked through the darkness. Then, ahead, King stopped before a fallen tree covered with fresh snow. Preston and the boy moved beside him. "Sergeant, do you smell that?" the boy asked, sniffing the frigid air.

"It smells like...flowers," Preston said, taken by surprise. "That's impossible. It's the middle of winter."

"Roses," George said. "They were Ma's favorite flower."

Preston sniffed again. "I don't smell it now. It must have been our imagination."

King barked and pawed at the snow. The light from the lantern revealed what looked like a wooden sled half-buried in the snow. A dead tree lay next to it, and a dark object protruding from a mound of snow next to it. It was a man's gloved hand. They knew before they began to clear the snow that they had at last found James McDougall.

"He bled to death," Preston said as young George sobbed softly beside him. "Evidently, his axe glanced off a branch and hit his leg. He must have tried to stop the bleeding, but it was too cold. I doubt he suffered. He just fell asleep."

"How long...has he been h-h-here?" the boy stammered, wiping tears before they could freeze to his cheeks.

"We had a fresh snow ten days ago, then the new storm. He's been covered by both. I'd guess no more than two weeks, maybe less."

"Just about the time Ma died," he said slowly. "Sergeant, you don't suppose..." He left the thought unspoken.

"Did you say your mother died rather suddenly?"

"Yes. She seemed to be recovering, then it was like she just gave up."

"Were your parents close?"

"They were married when they were real young. Until Pa came to the Yukon, they were inseparable. If he hadn't wanted to make a better life for us, he never would have come up here."

"My guess is that you and your brother and sister will do quite well, George. I got a look at the sides of that shaft your father dug and there's definitely gold there. He probably didn't want to come home before he'd uncovered a little more and could tell you the news."

King came up beside Preston and made a small noise in his throat, his eyes focused somewhere above where James McDougall lay. They both looked up, but could see nothing. "It was King who led us here, sergeant," George said, "but I think I know who brought King."

"I don't know, son," Preston replied thoughtfully. "But whoever or whatever led King here made it possible for your father and mother to rest together, side by side. All I can say for certain is, this case is closed."

QUIET PLEASE

The Cradle of Peace

by Martin Grams, Jr.

Have you ever lost someone so dear that you wished they could return from the dead and visit you? No, I don't mean the Lazarus effect. I'm not even referring to body possession. I mean those little thoughts that pass through your mind...the scientific methods of bringing loved ones back, even for a short period of time. Well, it's not too hard to believe. I mean—here we are on the verge of chemical and biological breakthroughs. Everyone knows someone who has had their image changed, or their body shaped to the contours of their physical pleasure. Think not? Well, I didn't think so at first, but my wife knows better. She started the whole ball rolling...

I was returning home from work one day, thinking about what would be on the picture tube worth watching. Infomercials advertising products are the verge of the future. Every company has something to sell you, something you can't do without, and so affordable that installments and payments can be made to adjust to your lifestyle. Why, last night there was one of those cloning programs that brought your loved ones back. "Clone your loved one and never cry again." That was the pitch they made. Some sharp-looking salesman in a cheap bow tie and black toupee who screamed his product over the screen. A crew would visit your house, extract DNA from objects your lost one owned, and two weeks later, you'll receive a visit from your loved one. It would be as if they never left.

"What's so funny?" my wife asked me.

"Cloning someone already gone?" I laughed. "As if there would be anyone gullible enough to pay for that service. Too many problems and complications."

"Such as what?" she defended.

"Well…well take life insurance policies. The beneficiary gets paid for his wife's death, has her cloned, and then gets the notice that he's to turn over the money they paid him. What if he used the insurance money to pay for the service? Then what?"

"Oh, you're just being morbid. You're saying you wouldn't want me back if I was in an accident?"

"I never said you would die—"

"But you thought it—"

"Look. I was only laughing at the fella on the tube. Suggesting that the owners would want the dog that chewed up the furniture again. Mother-in-laws unite."

"Now I know you're being stubborn. If you'd keep that mind of yours open to the positive things in life, you might not think the world is against you."

"Oh—I don't want to talk about it anymore." I wanted to change the subject. "It's just a stupid notion."

"You think so? What if I was to tell you that I was thinking of having Charity back."

"Now look. I miss her just as much as you do, but we are not having our daughter cloned."

"And why not? I miss the sound of someone moving around the house…"

"If you even consider that kind of service . . ."

"You'd what? Leave me? Take the check book?"

"It's against all principals. There's a reason why people still protest outside those clinics."

"Yeah, they can't afford to have themselves cloned. I'd bet if the opportunity arose, you'd hold back."

"Hey, it's not my fault she died. Don't blame me."

"But if we could have her back, would you?"

I stopped for a second. "Would I what?"

"Pay to have Charity returned. . ." she lowered her head like she was in some deep thought, but not wanting to face me. Then I made up my mind, but only for the sake of ending the conversation. "Yeah, I guess it wouldn't hurt much."

It wasn't worth arguing with her. Like talking to a brick wall. I could sit all night and discuss the values of human moralities and she'd still go off on me – like it was my fault. Two years ago our daughter left for the school prom and on route, some idiot went through the stop light and hit the passenger side of the vehicle she was riding in. Charity never made it to the hospital. We got the call after nine and rushed to meet the doctor. I could tell by his expression, before he even gave us the news, that it wasn't good.

"I'm very sorry for your loss," he told us. My wife cried hysterically on my shoulder. "As a doctor I am supposed to give the news as easy as I can, but somehow, I can never seem to find the words when the time comes. I really don't know what to say, other than the fact that she didn't suffer."

That was two years ago, and she still blames me for Charity's death. I read somewhere that everyone goes through multiple psychological stages after losing someone so close. First is disbelief, followed by shock and sorrow, anger, and even regret. Blaming me was her way of venting and I guess I still let her vent—even if it's towards me.

I suspected that she didn't listen to me last night, and I found my hunch right when I got home. Parked in the driveway was a large white truck with the letters "Cloning Incorporated" on the side. The same company that advertised on the picture tube last night. I rushed in to find my wife filling out papers.

"Oh—you're home!" She acted surprised.

"Care to tell me what's going on?" I threw my hat on the chair.

"Allow me to introduce myself," spoke the gentleman who was clearly the moderator of this scam. "I am Ben 245, and we represent Cloning Incorporated. Your wife has expressed your interest in a revisitation of your daughter, Charity."

"We?" I asked.

"A crew of two men are in your daughter's room right now, extracting surviving DNA samples from her lamp, books, anything she might have handled. I can assure you that nothing will be out of place when they are finished. DNA strands last many years before becoming dormant, and with such a short period of time since…your loss, we expect a 95% success variable."

"Get out."

"I'm sorry, I don't understand," he said, looking at my wife.

She rose from the sofa. "Dear, we need to talk."

"There is nothing to talk about. We will not enroll in this farce, and they won't get one penny." I turned toward the guest. "You can order your men out of this house before I phone the police."

"But dear—"

"I can assure you sir, that we are no farce. We have many satisfied customers and can supply you references at your request."

"And just how do you accomplish the task of playing God?"

Our guest shrugged. "I understand your viewpoint, sir. Every customer we have had was hesitant at first, but they realize soon after that their fears can be put to rest."

I ordered the men to leave and they did. I can't remember much else that afternoon. I recall threatening to break their legs if they didn't leave the house, my wife crying on the sofa, and I cried a little too—before falling asleep.

Two weeks later everything was back to normal. I finished cutting the grass. Sitting on the front porch, drinking a glass of lemonade and pondering where the sweat was going to roll from my face, the smell of freshly cut grass was bringing back memories. Maybe it was the heat, illusions conjured up by the summer sun. But I swear I could see Charity jumping rope with the other girls.

"Lizzie Borden took an ax, and gave her mother forty whacks…" Memories are a good thing, when you want to remember them. I could hear her voice clearly as she giggled with her friends. "778…779…780…781…" She missed the rope and fell on the pavement. She cried like she did many times when a bee stung her, but this was a skinned knee. Rising from the porch I walked over to take her inside the house.

"This isn't going to hurt," I told her.

"What is it?"

"General Carter's Elixir of life. I call it peroxide. Put your knee over the sink." She did and when the contents dribbled, she twitched.

"You said it wasn't going to hurt."

"From time to time, something will always hurt. Even if it's not involving blood."

"Is that a Dino the dinosaur Band-Aid?"

"Yes." I placed it over her knee and lowered her down to the floor. She eagerly rushed out to show her friends and skip rope again.

I walked out on the front porch again and watched her play with her friends, but minutes later, the illusion grew and a beautiful girl of sixteen stood in front of me.

"Poppa, what do you think of my new dress?" she asked. I remember her wearing a dress like that before she went to the prom. Flashes of lightning shivered my eyes, and she still stood there. "Poppa?"

Then I realized, this was no illusion. Charity had come back.

"Dalton, do you see her? She's exactly as she was!" My wife was thrilled. I had to admit, the clone was the same—not just the small unobserved features on the face or arms, but the voice, mannerisms…I was impressed—but not amused. "When did they let you out of your cage?"

"Poppa!" she exclaimed. "I wasn't in no cage. I was—grown—and then educated and released." Then she turned to my wife. "And I got to ride home in a limo."

"A real limo?" my wife asked.

"Yes! With tinted windows. Can I see my room?"

I let the women go to Charity's room. I don't know if I was angry because of what my wife committed to, or the fact that I have a total stranger living in my house, pretending to be my daughter. I wonder what the psychiatrists would say about losing someone and then getting them back again.

I woke up suddenly to find a young girl jumping on my bed. "Wake up Poppa!"

"Hmmm? Huh—oh, it's you. What do you want?"

"I was wondering if you wanted to go bowling. Remember when we would go bowling on Tuesday nights?" She was too energetic at seven in the morning.

"I don't remember *us* going bowling on Tuesday nights."

"What's wrong, Poppa? Something bothering you? I know, you're not feeling well. I'll go make you a hot bowl of soup."

"I don't want any soup. Leave me alone, you little—" I stopped and she realized I wasn't in the mood. Quietly she backed off the bed and walked out. Now I was upset. Because of this energetic child foolishness. I tore the covers off the bed and got dressed. Walking out to the living room, Charity sat in the chair, pretending to read a magazine.

"You don't love me anymore, do you?" she asked, keeping her head towards the magazine.

"All right, I don't like you. You're not really my daughter. You are some perversion of science that only lives here because my wife wishes for that, and I let her. That's the only reason I haven't thrown you out that door two weeks ago."

"Mother has accepted me."

"But that doesn't mean I have to." I poured myself a cup of coffee in the kitchen. Charity followed me. "But I am your daughter."

"You are not my daughter!"

"Yes I am. How blind are you? You telling me that you'd prefer a dead woman instead of living memories?"

I walked over and twisted her arm. Charity cried in pain. "Can you feel this? Will you bleed if I cut you? Heal if your blood clots? Now you get this straight and get this good. You are not my daughter. Charity died in an auto wreck two years ago coming back from her prom. I made the arrangements myself. I was a pallbearer. I spent weeks grieving. My tears fell into her grave and if I want to talk to my daughter, I'll revisit that cemetery anytime I wish. You are a clone, a copy of an original, not worth half the value of the original and you will never take the place of my daughter. You are nothing more than a plant, designed and created forth from a seed. You were manufactured in an assembly line program, born in a test tube, watered until you sprouted like a plant and to implicate that you are my daughter when that is for me to decide is of undo justification."

Charity cried as I twisted her arm harder. "Stop! You're hurting me!"

"How about when you die? Will you go to heaven? Will you have a soul?" She couldn't answer, she was crying. She broke free and started for the front door. She said something about true faith is blind faith. "Trees grow and weep and willow. Times change and so do perceptions and whether you accept it or not, technology will continue to advance. I think you're afraid of what I have in my heart." And with that, Charity slammed the door.

I turned to see my wife standing in the hallway. "You really are emotionless." I didn't want to hear it from her, but somehow I felt guilty enough to listen. "Dalton, you were either born too late or born too early. But before taking it out your daughter, think how it's destroying me." I sat on the sofa with the coffee in hand. My wife sat beside me. For a moment we had comfortable silence, but she broke all that.

"Remember when I first told you I was pregnant? You came home from work that night with a handful of roses in your hand and I kissed you and told you how much I loved you. Puppy love. You thought nothing of it at first, at least, that was the impression I got from you. But when things settled in, you thought I was joking. We got married to start a family and things changed after the vows. You didn't want a child cause you feared the baby would get between what we shared and us.

"But God granted us that miracle of birth and blessed us with a beautiful daughter for sixteen years. And you took your anger out on me little by little, as the months grew by until the day I gave birth. When you held that little girl in your hands, your eyes filled with tears of joy and the grouch in you left. You became a father. A cradle of peace. And you were no longer angry at me for getting pregnant, you just wanted to hold your daughter. Sixteen years you were the happiest man I knew. After Charity's death, I realized you were seeping back to the grouch in you, because you were no longer happy. I felt that if we had Charity back, you'd be willing to accept her for the way she is, and things would go back to normal. Things haven't changed much, Dalton. There's still time to make amends." She rose from the sofa and went down the hallway. I could hear the bedroom door close, and silence crept through the house.

I was walking through the park that afternoon, and the temperature was still cool enough to warrant a jacket. I walked over to the large rock concealed by the green shrubbery. The place Charity and I would always go and chat and laugh. Father-daughter things. I walked over to the rock and sat down. Charity was there. Wiping the tears from her face.

"I didn't think you remembered." We both stared at the lake, fixating on the motions of the water. We made no eye contact.

"Of course I remember," she remarked. "Did you think I had no memory of the last sixteen years? Where we liked to sit and chat when times were complicated?"

"But how?"

"Too detailed. It's assembly-line fashion. New trend of the century."

I took a deep breath. "I'm sorry for the way I acted this morning. I guess I'm still a little ignorant of the facts behind this cloning process. It was bound to happen, of course, I guess I just didn't want to accept it."

"Am I such a bad case of life imitating art?"

"No. I guess I got my pliers mixed up with my wrenches. It's just that I cannot see how a microscopic piece of dead tissue can be used to hatch…you. When you lose someone you love, it takes a long time to accept the loss. And then, breaking the chain of life, I was asked two years later to accept a return, fishing for a shark instead of a tuna."

"So what's the weather report now? Where do we go from here?"

"I don't know. I really want my wife to be happy. I want to be happy. But it's just going to take time to accept this."

"You can have all the time you need," she explained.

I tried to look at her, but the water was hypnotizing. "When your grandfather was in the service—and he told this to me before he passed away—he was in Leyte Island in the Philippines. They had a password, Lovely Lady, because the Japs couldn't pronounce the letter L. Well, that evening a perimeter was established and after dark, a figure came walking to the trenches. It was too dark to make out who, so your grandfather called out. 'Hey! What's the password?' Well, the figure kept coming, not saying anything, so he called out again. 'Hey there! What's the password?' Again, dead silence except the sound of boots tearing into the ground. Finally a few men get up to the East side and start shouting the same. Still no word. Finally the platoon lieutenant tells them, 'Spray him.' And they opened fire. When the sun rose the next day, they come to find one of their own men, hands tied behind his back. And there were two Jap bodies behind him. All dead. Their man wasn't gagged, he just kept his mouth quiet to prevent the Japs from coming in with him. When you grandfather told me this, I wondered for a long while why.

"You see," I explained, "he was unable to accept the task he performed, and felt bad about what he did. So bad that he had to tell others to make him feel good. It was his way of coping with something he couldn't accept. After he told me this story, many years ago, I too felt sick. Not a physical sickness, just a sickness inside. And right now, I feel that sickness inside. I honestly feel sorry for what I did, and I do feel bad for treating you like an eggplant this morning. I'm sorry."

She grabbed the trouser leg of her jeans and pulled it up. She stopped when she passed the knee. "See this?" I skinned my knee when I was six years old. I remember I was skipping rope on the front yard and I fell. You took me inside and washed it off. The peroxide stung a little, but I kept my knee over the sink while you tended my wound because I trusted you. And I still do. You came back to take me home and make me feel better, just as you did when I skinned my knee."

"And you still trust me, ever after I hurt you?" I asked.

Charity rubbed her knee. "Of course. You're my father."

———◆———

THE HALLS OF IVY

A Matter of Ethics

by Carol Tiffany

D r. William Todhunter Hall, President of Ivy College in the town of Ivy, USA, little resembled a dignified college president on this cold February evening. A cheerful log fire blazed in the library hearth at Number One Faculty Row and Dr. Hall, in shirtsleeves and stockinged feet, slouched in an armchair before the fire with a book lying open but unread in his lap. He was mentally reviewing the afternoon's extraordinarily satisfying board meeting and eagerly anticipating sharing his news with his wife, Victoria.

He smiled, as he often did when he thought about Victoria, a secret smile that hid the little bubble of warmth which rose inside him whenever he remembered that sabbatical year in England. He reflected upon the sheer chance that took him to the theater on that first special evening and the many trips thereafter until he finally gathered his courage and spoke to the play's leading actress, Victoria Cromwell. He recalled the weeks that followed, during which he and Vicky explored the beauties of England together as they realized their mutual love and commitment. He remembered the joy he felt when he brought Vicky home to Ivy and the fullness in his heart as he saw his wife accepted and then cherished by his friends and colleagues.

"Toddy? Toddy, are you awake?" Victoria's voice broke his pleasant reverie and he turned to see Vicky shedding coat, hat, muffler and boots. Rubbing her hands together, she settled into the chair opposite his and extended them to the fire. "My, but it's getting colder by the hour," she said.

91

"Of course I'm awake," he rumbled. "How went the second-to-the-last rehearsal of this year's edition of the Junior Follies?" he asked, thinking of his pride in her willingness to help the students in the thankless capacity of ex-officio advisor for the Follies and other student theatrical productions.

"It's actually coming together quite well," Victoria replied. "I shouldn't wonder if young Mr. Wilbour quite surpasses himself once he gets over his first night butterflies." She tilted her head thoughtfully to one side. "I wonder, Toddy, if the students' performances really do get better every year; or is it just my perception?"

Dr. Hall smiled indulgently. "Perhaps it is the quality of the coaching they receive that causes the improvement?" he ventured.

Pleased, Victoria smiled back at him. "Honestly, Toddy, that is a prejudiced viewpoint if ever I heard one."

Her expression turned pensive as she continued. "The strangest thing happened this evening. A group of men showed up at rehearsal, a camera crew I believe, along with several others. They were passing out soft drinks and taking pictures. They weren't from the student paper and definitely weren't from the Ivy weekly. The photographer had some photo release forms he wanted the students to sign. I asked several of the men, but I couldn't get a straight answer from them about where and how the pictures were to be used, so I refused to allow the students to sign the releases. The whole group packed up and walked out when I tried to get more information."

"That's strange," Dr. Hall began, but the strident ringing of the doorbell, accompanied by a frantic knocking on the front door interrupted him.

"Penny!" called Victoria, "Penny! Oh dear, this is her night out. I'll get it." Victoria rose and hurried to the front door where the urgent summons continued unabated. She opened the door.

"Why, Mr. Wellman," she began, as a somewhat disheveled Clarence Wellman literally charged into the house.

"Ruined, we're ruined! We've been sabotaged!" cried the head of Ivy's Board of Governors.

Dr. Hall rose from his chair, hands raised in a placating gesture. "Mr. Wellman, to what do we owe this pleasant surprise?" he asked while taking Wellman's arm to guide him to a chair.

"Pleasant? Pleasant? Decidedly *un*pleasant I would say!" exclaimed Mr. Wellman. "$250,000 could be gone…down the drain! And all because of that silly, interfering woman! Because of her!" Wellman sank into the chair as he pointed an accusing finger at an astonished Victoria, standing frozen in the doorway.

"Mr. Wellman!" thundered Dr. Hall. "This lady is my wife!" His voice dropped to a deceptively quiet tone. "You will explain yourself, sir. Immediately! And you will remember that when you accuse my wife, you accuse me."

Wide-eyed, Victoria crossed the room to stand beside her husband, who took her hand in his as they both faced the rather abashed Clarence Wellman. "What do you mean, Mr. Wellman? What have I done?" she asked.

Wellman looked at Dr. Hall. "Do you remember the gift Merriweather announced at the meeting this afternoon? The $250,000 that put the building fund drive over the top?"

"Yes, I remember. I was about to tell Mrs. Hall about it when you arrived so precipitously."

"Well," Mr. Wellman continued, "that gift was from an Ivy alumnus named Claude Markham. He is founder and owner of the Zipcola Soft Drink Co. Just now, Markham's son-in-law called to tell me that the gift will probably be withdrawn due to Mrs. Hall's uncooperative attitude."

Victoria looked bewildered. "I don't understand how I could have been uncooperative. I've never even met the man."

"Clarence," Dr. Hall said, "don't you think we should know all of the facts of the situation before you get so upset? Now, why do you think the gift will be rescinded?"

Somewhat calmer, Wellman looked down at his hands, which he had been literally wringing since he entered the room, and took a deep breath. "When I arrived back at my office after the meeting this afternoon, this fellow, Willy Peters, was waiting to see me. He introduced himself as Markham's son-in-law and head of Advertising for Zipcola. He said he had an idea for a Zipcola promotion featuring college students. He felt certain that Ivy would be the ideal place to shoot his ads because of his father-in-law's affection for and support of the school. I told him I thought it would be all right and even told him he could start at the Junior Follies rehearsal tonight.

"Tonight, Peters called me at home to tell me that Mrs. Hall had practically ordered him and his camera crew out of the rehearsal this evening and had advised the students not to sign his photo releases. He was extremely upset and said the school was being uncooperative and that they might have to reconsider some things."

"He actually *said* that Mr. Markham's gift was contingent upon the school's cooperation in an advertising campaign?" asked Dr. Hall.

Clearly taken aback, Mr. Wellman answered. "He didn't *say* that the gift would be withdrawn; only that they might have to reconsider. But he certainly seemed to imply that we would lose the $250,000 for the building fund."

"No one with the group who came to the rehearsal said a thing about advertising," Victoria put in. "Essentially, they just came in, passed out the soft drinks, set up their equipment, and started taking pictures. There was no problem until they pulled out the release forms for the students to sign and refused to say where the pictures were to be used."

"And Victoria quite properly refused to allow the students who were present to sign those forms," Dr. Hall finished for her.

"But the money, all that money, what about the building fund drive without that contribution?" Mr. Wellman had just begun when a second insistent ringing of the doorbell interrupted him.

"Just a moment, Clarence. It's my turn, I believe," said Dr. Hall, heading for the door.

"Ah, Mr. Merriweather, so good to see you." Dr. Hall greeted the newcomer and gestured for him to go ahead into the library.

Doffing his hat and coat, Merriweather joined the group by the fire. "Good evening, Dr. Hall, Mrs. Hall. I rather expected to find you here, Clarence," he said, acknowledging Wellman's presence with a curt nod.

Victoria stepped forward. "Welcome, Mr. Merriweather, may I take your things?" She favored him with a smile as she took his hat and coat. "Would you care for some refreshment?"

"Thank you, dear lady, but no refreshments right now," Merriweather said, turning to take a seat on the sofa. "Please sit down, everyone, I have news!"

"I know, I know," moaned Wellman. "We've lost the $250,000 Markham endowment. And all because of..."

"Mr. Wellman!" Dr. Hall began.

"Wait, wait," Mr. Merriweather broke in. "Dr. Hall, Clarence has gone off half-cocked as usual. I think I can straighten all of this out in just a few minutes. First and foremost, I just received a very interesting call from Claude Markham. As you know, I handled his contribution to the Ivy Building Fund, so he called me when this situation cropped up. It seems that his son-in-law, a fellow named Peters, who runs his advertising department called him tonight to ask him to stall on the endowment because the school wasn't cooperating in the ad campaign.

"Well," Merriweather continued, "Markham finally got the whole story out of Peters and is furious with him because the gift was always meant to be just that... a gift! There were never any strings attached, real or implied, and certainly never a requirement that the school should endorse or promote Zipcola in any way! Markham laid the law down to Peters and called me to make sure that the school was aware that there was no contingency involved in his gift to Ivy's building fund."

"But Peters said...and I gave approval...I was so sure...and Mrs. Hall was..." Mr. Wellman was almost stuttering in his confusion.

"And," Merriweather went on, "Mr. Markham wanted me to commend the cautious people at the school who refused to cooperate with Peters and his plans. He is glad that the standards he remembers are still in evidence at Ivy."

Dr. Hall stood up. "Thank you so much, Mr. Merriweather, for bringing order to this chaos. I am very glad to learn that Mr. Markham's gift was without such a contingency, for, if it were, ethically we should have had to refuse it."

Wellman stood, too. "Refuse it? Really, Dr. Hall, I'm still not sure I understand all of this. I guess there could have been the appearance of impropriety, but if the students were acting as individuals, how could that reflect badly on the college? And the college would have been assured of a substantial monetary gain."

The other three laughed and said in a fair approximation of unison. "Clarence, it's a matter of ethics."

Having shepherded a sheepish Mr. Wellman and a smiling Mr. Merriweather down the hall and out the door, Dr. Hall and Victoria finally sat curled together in the big armchair in front of the dying library fire.

"Toddy," Victoria said, "I understand why the building fund gift couldn't ethically be tied to the ad campaign, but I really don't understand exactly what I did that was so right. I never even thought of any ethical considerations. I was just uneasy about the students signing those release forms when we had been given no explanation about how the pictures were to be used."

"Vicky, my love," Dr. Hall said, "I understand your confusion. We actually had two ethical issues involved in all of this. The easiest to understand is the one that Clarence didn't see, although he should have: the concept that a gift or endowment cannot be encumbered with the expectation that the giver will be compensated in some monetary way and still be accepted by an organization such as Ivy.

"The greater issue, and the one you instinctively implemented, is the principle of 'in loco parentis' which holds that the institution, the school, acts 'in place of the parent' in providing guidance and protection to the students placed in its care. Protection of the students is the responsibility of all members of the faculty, administration, and other adults on the Ivy campus. Our students are ours to protect, to shield, but never to exploit or coerce. Thus it follows that we may never allow them to be exploited or coerced by others in the guise of serving the good of the school.

"Tonight, my love, you merely acted as any prudent parent would in to protect the young people under your charge from possible exploitation."

Victoria's eyes shone. "Thank you for being you, Toddy. I love you," she murmured as she snuggled closer to him.

"And I never cease being thankful that you have chosen to spend your life with me, Vicky," replied her husband.

———◆———

CAPTAIN MIDNIGHT

The Vanishing Ruby

by Stephen A. Kallis, Jr.

Charles J. Albright, world-renowned by his code name, Captain Midnight, re-turned the speed brake lever of his F-86 to neutral after the brakes had ex-tended fully and reached for the landing gear handle as the airspeed indicator neared 185 knots. As he flew the landing traffic pattern, he scanned the instrument panel, satisfied that all readings were well inside the limits. The speed he let ease to 160 knots, and then moved the wing flap lever to down.

Captain Midnight reflected that the F-86 was an excellent aircraft, although it was being phased out by its successor. While the Squadron was getting some of the newer F-100s, he still enjoyed flying the Sabre. As he began his partial flare at 140 knots, he smiled in recalling just how many different types of airplane he'd flown to and from Squadron Headquarters since the facility had been established near Grant City. He touched down on his mains, retarding his throttle to *start idle* using a smooth and unconsciously metered motion. Engaging the nosewheel steering as the rudder became sluggish, he cleared the active and taxied towards the hangar area.

Switching to ground control frequency, he transmitted, "SS-1 to ground, cleared the active."

"Roger, SS-1," the ground controller responded. "Taxi to Area Alpha."

He deplaned, leaving the Sabrejet to the capable hands of the Squadron crew, and headed toward his office. Although Captain Midnight was the head of the Secret Squad-ron, he made certain that he would assign himself occasional field operations, to ensure that he'd not send his agents into situations he'd not be able to handle himself. Although he was approaching the age of retirement, he was more than content to keep active.

With expected punctuality, Captain Midnight entered the Headquarters conference room some seven minutes before the meeting was scheduled to begin. He'd changed from his flight gear to the Secret Squadron uniform of midnight blue shirt, slacks, and tie; as an active pilot, he had the Secret Squadron winged-clock flight wings over his left shirt pocket. He walked to the conference room with a spring in his step that belied his years.

Within minutes, the others had arrived. All were wearing visitor's badges, and one was in the uniform of a commander in the US Navy. He was introduced as Commander Craig MacDonough, Jr. from the Office of Naval Research. The other two men were in civilian clothes. One was a gaunt man with thinning brown hair who was introduced as Dr. Ernest Lumin, a research scientist. The other was a muscular man with close-cropped hair who was introduced as John Subik, a security expert.

Captain Midnight noticed that a slide projector had been set up and a projection screen pulled down.

After everyone had been seated, Captain Midnight said, "Well, gentlemen, what do I owe this visit to?"

Commander MacDonough said, "The Secret Squadron has been involved in what's been characterized as more unconventional activities than the conventional security groups usually face. We've got a situation here that seems to fit right into your kind of mission."

Captain Midnight allowed himself a fleeting smile, recalling the first time he heard that observation. MacDonough hadn't even been born then.

"I think it's safe to say that since World War II ended, the development of technology has accelerated tremendously," MacDonough continued. "Things that were once considered science fiction are now fact. Artificial satellites, computers, and the like were once the stuff of dreams, yet all are present today. And to be sure, what's been going on in various laboratories throughout the world is even more amazing."

"I take it, then, that this involves some sort of new invention?" Captain Midnight asked.

MacDonough nodded. "You've heard of the laser?"

"There have been some stories about it in the newspapers," Captain Midnight said. "Some of it seemed a bit sensationalistic."

Dr. Lumin chuckled. "Some of it may *seem* sensational, Captain Midnight. But some might also be surprisingly real."

"How do you mean?"

"Our most powerful lasers at present are the pulsed ruby lasers. We are able to use a specially developed assembly made from a piece of ruby crystal to generate a pulse of light containing large amounts of coherent radiation at high peak powers. In the laboratory, we've been able to punch holes in sheets of metal using lasers." Dr. Lumin paused for a second, then added, "Rather like a science-fictional ray gun, one might say."

While Dr. Lumin was speaking, Subik pulled out an envelope and extracted a 35mm slide, which he placed in the projector. On the screen appeared a picture of a red cylinder of material, with polished ends.

"This is our latest development," Dr. Lumin said. "A laser rod made out of artificial ruby. Don't let the image fool you: it's small, with a diameter about that of a lead pencil. The precision in all aspects of developing took months. It is our hope that this can form the basis of a field defense against missiles."

Captain Midnight said, "Very impressive. And you're telling me this for what reason?"

"Because it's been stolen," Subik interjected. "The device was made in a high security area, and was supposed to be couriered to…a defense research facility in Nevada. Yet somehow the courier was intercepted and the ruby rod stolen. Although he was left for dead, the courier survived."

Commander MacDonough said, "And the reason we're asking for the Secret Squadron's assistance is because of what we've determined. All the evidence we've found indicates that the theft was the work of the Shark organization."

Captain Midnight understood immediately. Although his old foe, Ivan Shark, had died, his daughter Fury had taken over the organization. She wasn't quite the criminal genius her father was, but she was wickedly intelligent and equally ruthless, if not more. In the shifting power struggle in the international arena, the Shark organization had flourished.

"You want the Secret Squadron's help because of our familiarity with the Shark forces," Captain Midnight said. It wasn't a question.

MacDonough smiled. "We're not sitting on our hands, but the Secret Squadron has had more experience in dealing with Shark operations than the summed experience of all the rest of our agencies."

It took only a little while to work out the details; but the meeting ended with the Secret Squadron assuming the central role in the effort to recover the laser ruby. MacDonough, Lumin, and Subik indicated that they would send copies of whatever documents they had that would provide data concerning the ruby.

Over the next few days, Captain Midnight organized his forces to attack the problem. His old team of Ichabod Mudd, Chuck Ramsay, and Joyce Ryan wasn't as available as before. Although Joyce was still a Secret Squadron agent, her marriage some years previously and the fact she had two small children, a daughter and a son, restricted her activities. Her husband, Captain Roger Meriwell, an Air Force pilot, frequently accompanied her to the Squadron field at Headquarters, so that she could keep current as a pilot. However, much of her work was now administrative. Chuck Ramsay, now also married, was available, though he was just finishing off a case of his own. Ichabod Mudd, as reluctant to retire as Captain Midnight, was still Chief Mechanic, but now had a staff of nine subordinates, almost as skilled as he.

Captain Midnight knew that Fury Shark had learned well from her father. Shark had developed a powerful criminal organization by selling its services to the highest bidder. The Shark gang was completely apolitical. Further, there was neither reason nor logic for Fury Shark's people to steal the laser ruby for anything but cash or its equivalent. More important, once the laser was in her possession, she had to find a customer.

Rationally, Fury's agents would have to approach agents of foreign governments, possibly the only ones who would be interested in obtaining it and would have the capital to purchase it on her terms. Because of the nature of what she was selling, Fury Shark would have to move carefully and patiently.

The one difficulty was that the ruby rod was relatively small, and therefore fairly easy to conceal. The rod by itself was significantly smaller than the Code-O-Staff, and every Secret Squadron agent carried one of these successors to the last Code-O-Graph without attracting attention. And although the rod was used as the center to a larger assembly, everything except the ruby rod could be replicated anywhere.

He gave Ichabod Mudd a copy of the plans for the laser, and asked the mechanic if he could use the information to help locate the ruby. When Mudd asked him what he was suggesting, he replied, "I think that in order to work, the ruby needs certain supporting equipment. The...pumping light source, I think they called it, and the cooling system components. There may be some way to see if there have been suspicious purchases."

"I'll get on it, Cap'n," Mudd said.

Some days passed before the first lead was found. A media analyst in the Squadron's Crypto Section forwarded a classified advertisement that ran in the *Daily Courier's* "personals" section to Captain Midnight. The ad ran, "Ruby—I've never been so moved as by your plea for financial planning to assure security. You should try to contact anyone in our old group you can reach. The seven of us can help in many ways. Don't feel weak. Your true, dear friend, Eumenide." The analyst, Elizabeth Gaines, pointed out that after the first word, picking up every fifth resulted in the message, "*Ruby*—I've never been so *moved* as by your plea *for* financial planning to assure *security.* You should try to *contact* anyone in our old *group* you can reach. The *seven* of us can help *in* many ways. Don't feel *weak.* Your true, dear friend, *Eumenide.*" She pointed out that the Eumenides were another name for the classical Greek demigods, the Furies. "Naturally, 'weak' in this context means a period of seven days, rather than how it's spelled."

Captain Midnight asked Joyce to see what could be found on any Shark operation known as Group Seven. In less than a day, she had an answer.

"Geemanee," she said, "that took a lot of digging. But I've found three references to such a group in our recent files. It's active in the Seattle area."

Captain Midnight glanced at the calendar. "The *Courier* ad ran yesterday. That means that in four days, effectively, whomever the message was directed to will be contacting this Group Seven. We'll have to be in position by that time."

Less than a day later, Captain Midnight was in Seattle. He'd flown alone in his F-86 Sabre while Chuck and Ikky followed in one of the Squadron's still serviceable

DC-3s. Ikky had outfitted the older airplane as a "Flying Workshop," with a variety of different tools and instruments. After many years of inventing things for the Secret Squadron, Mudd decided to develop a means of having the maximum number of options. The DC-3 was one of the Squadron's older airplanes, and he had little difficulty convincing Captain Midnight to assign it to him. A jack-of-many-trades, Mudd put mechanical, chemical, and electronic devices in it.

Since Mudd wasn't a pilot, Chuck Ramsay flew the airplane. Though he was qualified in almost as many airplanes as Captain Midnight, the DC-3 was an especial favorite of Chuck's, since that model was one of the first he flew after getting a multi-engine rating.

Captain Midnight met them at the airfield, a smaller airport than the Seattle-Tacoma field. He brought Chuck and Ikky to a small office complex he'd rented for use as a temporary base. He'd waited for Mudd to arrive to install a security system, and the mechanic brought the requisite tools and supplies.

One of the first things Mudd set up after the security system was a shortwave radio with a crystal standard. He tuned to the Squadron Headquarters and received a message enciphered with the Code-O-Staff.

It appeared to be a large collection of random sets of five letter groups, but using the Code-O-Staff, the message soon came out.

"This is a vast improvement over the Code-O-Graph, Chuck," Captain Midnight pointed out. "The first two five-letter groups are 'zixgh ejzfg.' They decipher to, 'Group Seven.' Now with any of our Code-O-Graphs, the second and fourth characters—the es—would be the same number, whereas with the Code-O-Staff they'd almost always be different. There were 676 different letter-number combinations possible with the Code-O-Graph; with the Code-O-Staff, there are more than 5 trillion letter combinations. Much more secure."

The message was from Joyce. Deciphered, it said, "Group Seven member identified as Hugh Romani of Seattle." The description and address followed.

A quick check with the local authorities didn't pull up Romani's name, but a check with the local aerospace companies did. Romani was identified as a worker on the maintenance crew of a subcontractor to the leading manufacturer of the region.

"That's a typical Shark tactic," Captain Midnight remarked to Chuck. "Remember how Shark infiltrated his operatives into the Aerial Instrument Company at Grant City before the Second World War? By getting agents into the cleaning crew, the Shark group is in a position to gain a great deal of information."

"Cleaning crews generally work at night, Cap'n," said Ichabod Mudd. "That gives him time during the day for his Shark stuff."

So it was that the following evening, an ordinary-looking station wagon was parked about halfway down the street from the house Hugh Romani was renting. Captain Midnight, Ichabod Mudd, and Chuck Ramsay were in the car, staking out the place. In the car was a bulky assembly that was the latest highly directional microphone available. It was aimed squarely at the Romani residence.

Ichabod Mudd was wearing a single headphone, covering his left ear, so that he could monitor the noises of the house while still being able to converse in hushed tones with the others. Suddenly he said, "Cap'n, it sounds like he's at the front door."

Moments later, the front door swung wide, and Romani emerged, dressed in work clothes. Although there was a delay of about three-quarters of a second in Mudd's listening device from what they saw, the sounds corroborated that the Shark agent really was leaving to go to work. Soon, he'd left the area.

The trio waited for fifteen minutes before acting. There was always the possibility that Romani might return for a forgotten item, so by waiting, they assured themselves that they could work uninterrupted.

Mudd got them into the house easily, working open the back door carefully, and checking to make sure that Romani hadn't set a hair or piece of paper in the door jamb to indicate that it had been opened in his absence. Once he was assured that it was safe, he indicated to his companions that they could enter.

They'd not entered the house to gather evidence. It was evident that Romani wasn't guardian of the laser rod, since there were still two days before he was supposed to contact Group Seven of the Shark organization. Instead, the three of them did a search for places to plant bugs and tracking devices.

The Secret Squadron electronic laboratories had developed several miniature electronic devices based on the latest transistor technology. Within a few years, a government committee learned that there were miniaturized transmitters "as small as an olive in a Martini"; these were of the same breed. The Squadron technicians built the tracking units so that they would each "chirp" on a very high unique frequency for four days once activated. Two of these were planted in the heel of each right shoe of a pair of Romani's dressier shoes. They were confident that he would probably not wear his work shoes to a Shark Group meeting.

They also left an inductive tap and transmitter in his telephone. Although not connected directly to the telephone's wiring, it was able to pick up and transmit the voices on both sides of a conversation.

After departing the house with as much caution as when they had entered, it was a matter of waiting. Realizing that there was little value in keeping an empty house under surveillance, Midnight and Mudd returned to their temporary quarters and turned in.

The shoe transmitters did the trick. By late afternoon, Captain Midnight, Ichabod Mudd, and Chuck Ramsay were at the fence of an estate, surrounded by a huge yard that was bare of trees, bushes, or other cover. At one of the rear corners of the yard was a small clump of bushes where they concealed themselves. With a little special camouflage netting, they were able to be completely hidden.

The difficulty was that a lot of space lay between them and the house. Captain Midnight had a small telescope mounted on a miniature tripod. With it, he could see through the French doors that led from a terrace to the living room.

Inside were several people. The most striking was a woman Captain Midnight recognized instantly. "Ikky! Do you have the…device you got from the Agency?"

"Yes, Cap'n."

"We've hit paydirt. Fury Shark is there, but I'm not lip-reader enough to understand what she's saying."

"If this gadget works like that Agency man said, you'll hear her in just a little while," Mudd said. He popped open a case and assembled something that looked a little like an over/under rifle-shotgun with a telescopic sight.

The "gadget" was a prototype of a new eavesdropping device based on infrared technology. Using a telescopic sight more powerful than the one that Captain Midnight was using, Ichabod Mudd aimed the "barrel" at a shiny panel in the room. He activated a switch, then checked a meter on a panel atop the portable power supply. Deflection of its needle indicated that the unit was working.

"Cap'n! Take a listen!"

Captain Midnight reached for a headphone and plugged it into a jack. The sound was not the best quality, something like a movie soundtrack with a pronounced hiss. However, he was able to hear the unmistakable voice of Ivan Shark's daughter.

"So you understand that we have managed to find a validated customer," she was saying. "There was a…situation about two weeks ago that made me decide to move the ruby unit to this area. Someone working for one of our potential customers decided that it might be less expensive to relieve us of the item than to pay what we're asking."

One of the men asked, "Are you sure that this customer isn't going to try the same?"

"No," said Fury with a very satisfied tone. "Not since word spread among our clients as to what was done to the person who tried it."

The discussion went on for a while, both about the laser component and other items currently on the Shark organization's agenda. A third jack fed the sound to a compact tape recorder. Though there was no way that the Secret Squadron could conduct a raid in the circumstances with only three people, the information they were getting would enable them to counter many of the Shark organization's forthcoming activities.

More to the point, they learned of how the ruby was going to be transported. Although the item was small enough to be concealed easily, Fury was wary enough to contrive to keep the situation under control. She decided to find a place where both parties could make the exchange with a minimum possibility of double-crossing. She and her aide, Magnus von Krell, would fly a light plane to a flat field in the country with no cover for any ambushers. Her airplane and that of her buyer would rendezvous over an agreed-upon area, and the two would proceed to the field, where they would land. Any other aircraft in the area, and the deal would be off. And since both airplanes would be small single-engine aircraft, the possibility of concealing extra men was nil.

Captain Midnight formulated a plan. With a couple of days before the transfer was to be made, he could set up a good counter to the plans, possibly trapping Fury Shark in the process.

The following day, Captain Midnight was in his F-86 aircraft. He was flying a cloverleaf pattern at 20,000 feet, the AN/APX-6 IFF unit set to NORM, so any radar challenges would reveal he was a "friend." Beneath him was an area removed from the normal air routes, which made his job easier. Another thing that helped was that both Fury Shark's aircraft and that of her customer would be Piper Cubs.

He recalled with some nostalgia that the last time he flew a Piper Cub for Squadron work was in South America, during the later stages of World War II, when he was contending with Señor Schrecker and the "Rocket Plane," and mused that his engine-out best angle of glide was more than twice the Cub's top speed. He knew the J-3 Piper Cub well.

But the advantage of having his foes flying Piper Cubs was that W. T. Piper had his airplanes painted a bright Canary Yellow. His purpose was so that his airplanes would stand out against a blue sky, but they also stood out against virtually any terrain.

Captain Midnight's plan was to fly at an altitude where neither Fury nor her customer would be likely to look, and, when he spotted the two Pipers, follow them to their rendezvous field. As soon as he identified it, he'd radio Chuck Ramsay, who was at the controls of a Bell Model 47 helicopter, who, with Ichabod Mudd flying shotgun, would fly directly to the field.

In time, Captain Midnight spotted two Cubs, each flying from different directions towards a lake. The two airplanes rendezvoused, and one then took the lead, with the other following.

"SS-2, this is SS-1, over," Captain Midnight transmitted on the Secret Squadron's primary frequency.

"SS-1, this is SS-2, standing by, over," Chuck Ramsay responded.

"SS-2, take off now. Fly," and Captain Midnight glanced at his instrument panel and did a little mental arithmetic, "bearing 065. I'll give you a hack when I'm right overhead, over."

"SS-1, this is SS-2, airborne. Heading 065, over."

Captain Midnight studied the flight direction of the pair of Cubs, and had a pretty good idea where they would set down. "SS-2, this is SS-1. I'll give a hack over the field where I believe they'll land. I'll do a double roll over the field, over."

"SS-1, this is SS-2, Roger on that roll, out."

"SS-2, this is SS-1. Coming up on that field. Counting, three…two…one…hack! Out." With that, Captain Midnight executed a double roll, passing over the exact center of the field at the end of the first roll.

A glint of sunlight caught Chuck Ramsay's eye from overhead, and he turned his helicopter a few degrees to the right to alter course to the field. He noted the new course, and unconsciously compensated for wind drift.

The Bell 47 moved out at full throttle, speeding through the air at 125 miles per hour, more than 35% faster than the top speed of a Cub. Chuck glanced over at Ichabod Mudd, who was snapping a drum cylinder on a Thompson submachine gun.

"Looping loops!" Chuck had said when he first saw what Mudd had carried aboard the helicopter. "Where did you get *that?*"

Mudd had smiled, and had responded, "I've got me a friend in the FBI, and he gave me this a few years ago. I put it in the DC-3 for this mission. Good thing I did: the helicopter isn't armed."

Per arrangement, Fury Shark's airplane landed first, followed by the other Cub. They taxied to the center of the field, and stopped, separated by some fifty feet. Fury emerged first, dressed in slacks and long-sleeved sweater. She reached back into the Cub and withdrew a small briefcase.

A rather stocky man with Slavic features emerged from the other aircraft, also withdrawing a briefcase. He and Fury walked toward each other, while both pilots drew forth rifles and covered the two.

From the minute that the airplanes landed, Captain Midnight put his airplane into a descent. He knew it would take a few more minutes for the helicopter to arrive, and he had to make sure that neither Fury nor the other agent would get away. There was no way he could land in time, but there were actions he could take.

As his altitude decreased, his airspeed built up. He zoomed over the field some fifty feet above the surface, moving into a climbing turn as he zipped past where the Piper Cubs were.

Fury and her customer scarcely had any warning. The jet tore past them, generating such a wake as to flip the Cubs on their backs. As the pilots scrambled to extricate themselves, the helicopter arrived.

Fury's run from the clearing was stopped by a short burst from the machine gun Ichabod Mudd had brought along. Her customer was similarly halted.

Because of the small number of personnel on the mission, Captain Midnight had brought the FBI into the picture as soon as he knew the exchange plans. As soon as Chuck and Mudd arrived, the Secret Squadron leader shifted the frequency of his transmitter to a prearranged local Bureau frequency, and he provided the agents with the location of Fury Shark and her customer.

The helicopter, high enough to keep track of all four captives, kept them in control until the Federal men arrived. They were arrested "on suspicion" until they could be turned over to the Secret Squadron.

The following day, Captain Midnight, Ichabod Mudd, and Chuck Ramsay were at their base offices, wrapping up their operation. With Fury Shark in captivity, the laser element saved, and a foreign agent in custody, it was about as pleasant an atmosphere as one could hope for. In the afternoon, Captain Midnight, on the basis of encrypted instructions, knew where and how to deliver the laser element. Chuck and Mudd would finish removing Squadron equipment from their temporary base before dusk, and would fly it back to Squadron Headquarters.

But it was just after breakfast. The three of them had concluded their meal with a tall, cold glass of Ovaltine each. They were relaxing when Chuck brought up something.

"Sir, since we've gone through all this effort, would it be okay if we see this laser unit?"

Smiling, Captain Midnight said, "I see no reason why not."

The Secret Squadron leader extracted a smallish metal case from a briefcase. After donning thin rubber gloves, he opened the case, and they all regarded what was inside.

"Looping loops!" Chuck exclaimed. "It looks so...so...ordinary. Like a piece of dime-store red glass."

Mudd studied the rod closely. "The polishing looks very precise, Cap'n, but I gotta agree with Chuck. It don't look too special."

Captain Midnight nodded. "Looks can be deceiving. We know that it's special, but that isn't evident by its appearance. That's a good reminder for all of us: there may be all kinds of hidden potential in what look like very mundane items—or people."

As both Ichabod Mudd and Chuck Ramsay pondered the thought, Captain Midnight closed the case and repacked it. Soon, it would be where it belonged.

With a quick motion, the Secret Squadron leader snapped the briefcase shut. He chuckled, and said, "This case is closed."

$$\Longrightarrow\!\!\diamond\!\!\Longleftarrow$$

THE BICKERSONS

You've Got Me, John

by Ben Ohmart

B lanche had only been in an airplane once before in her life. She was ten years old, bundled off in the dead of November to visit an ailing aunt in Peru, Indiana. The memories were vague: why did she have to go by herself, sporting a wet paper sack full of chicken fat and creamed peach casserole in a glass pint container? But she remembered the so-called turbulence, and now clutched her forty-year-old fingernails so hard into the vaguely cushioned seats that she left little tinges of dime store red when she finally pulled them out.

But it was strange. She didn't remember there being so much *room* on a plane. And this non-stop flight to Syracuse, New York was supposed to have been booked as solid as the ice on the wings. Yet there was plenty of room in coach. Hardly anyone was around.

Blanche craned her mustard-oiled neck for a better view of nothing. No one waiting in line for the loo. She looked past the back row just behind her into the minuscule aisle that held the rolling drinks cabinet. A few eyes and faces poked out quickly and quietly, then hid away with care.

"Strange," she admitted.

John was snoring: labored, and gasping, and with rolling tongue clucking the inside of his bourbon-moistened mouth. The noise was incredible. Extraordinarily inhuman. And for some reason, it, mixed with the murky outside weather and constantly droning engines, never bothered Blanche for a moment. Maybe it all canceled each other out.

"John. John!"

"Mmmm?" John Bickerson didn't move.

"Wake up, John. There's nobody around."

"That's not a good enough reason. Go to sleep."

With professional somnolence, the husband with the thin mustache, wielded-shut eyes and thirty-five cents in his pocket tipped lightly on his side, began the rudiments of unbuckling his seatbelt, and began to roar a snore so vast it began edging over a full paper cup of water (complete with ice cubes) on a nearby tray via the suction.

"John!"

It usually took three "John's" to get him going, but she was cut off by the third announcement from the Captain in the last twenty minutes.

"LADIES AND GENTLEMEN. I REALLY MUST APOLOGIZE ONCE AGAIN FOR THIS. BUT WE STILL CAN'T LOCATE THE CAUSE OF THE NOISE. WE'RE HEADING DOWN TO 8500 FEET AND SHUTTING ONE ENGINE DOWN. AGAIN, THIS IS ONLY TEMPORARILY WHILE WE MAKE A SWEEP OF THE PLANE AND DO ANOTHER TECHNICAL CHECK. YOU MAY EXPERIENCE SOME TURBULENCE, BUT I PROMISE YOU, THERE'S ABSOLUTELY NO CAUSE FOR ALARM. AND AS ALWAYS, THANKS FOR FLYING VLUGE AIRLINES."

As soon as the cabin's intercom went dead, there was a generous *lurch* in the structure of the flying machine, sending ice aft and drunken people forward. Then, the engine on the left side of the plane sputtered and died. Blanche counted all thirteen seconds, as John snored, until the motor caught fire and continued again.

"LADIES AND GENTLEMEN, WE APPRECIATE YOUR PATIENCE. EVERYTHING *SEEMS* TO BE FINE, AND WE SHOULD BE LANDING IN SYRACUSE IN JUST UNDER THIRTY MINUTES…"

Blanche didn't hear the rest. There was a sickening moan from her handbag. Quickly eyeing her lethargic husband, Blanche tossed an unobtrusive hand to her seatbelt clip and leaned forward for her purse beneath the seat in front. She unclipped the chipped silver fastener. A small golden-coated cat yawned, and proceeded to make the most horrendous sounds imaginable as the airplane began its slow descent through clouds and passengers' popping ears.

"It's all right, Nature Boy. Just go back to sleep."

She fed him two more sleeping pills dipped in squid broth, made sure the holes she had cut throughout the purse were still unblocked by tissues, keys, peanuts and assorted feminine accessories, and refastened the bag once again.

Pushing it under her feet, she prodded poor husband John, again suffering an acute attack of Blaster's Reaction. "John!"

"Mmm…"

"John. John! You could sleep through the Chicago fire without missing a beat. I swear, you could sleep through the biggest disaster of the year and never hear a thing!"

"I hear you, Blanche."

"Is that supposed to be funny? Buckle up your bourbon belt, John, we're landing."

The constant, inane activity of the Syracuse airport was enough to keep John Bickerson awake to the conveyor belt to secure the one suitcase they owned in the world. But the motorized tread of the slow-moving baggage wasn't nearly enough to keep Bickerson from finally falling asleep, hands on the rails nearest the chute. People were beginning to talk, and laugh.

"John. John!"

He awoke instantly, grabbed the nearest bag and pulled! Unfortunately, the lady was rightly indignant and used her purple umbrella with all the zeal her seventy years could afford.

In the car from the Hotel Abbercroft, John nursed his head wound with some used tissues from Blanche's purse.

"Serves you right. You were lucky she was old, you know."

John was breathing lightly, pain sapping his remaining strength. "Well, she shouldn't keep the price tag on her dress. I thought it was the address label on our suitcase."

"She didn't look anything like our suitcase. Just admit it, John. You were zonked!"

"I was not zonked! I haven't had a *drop* all day!"

"I know. You had three full glasses!"

The driver blasted his radio volume up as high as it would go to a Duke Ellington concert and turned in to the Hotel Abbercroft, in the heart of Syracuse's downtown snowdrift.

Cars, cabs and buses—as far as the plows could see. Snowflakes tinkled in what dull sunlight managed to find its way through the intense cloud cover of New York state. Those few brave souls hungry enough to keep outside for tips were turning into snowmen quick. One of these frozen creatures was quick to open the door to the Bickerson car.

"Bags, ma'am?"

Blanche replied, "My husband will attend to the bags. Thank you." She tipped him anyway.

The hotel was at least warm and full of hundreds of bodies milling around, mostly between the front doors and the front desk. It was middle-class spectacle at its best. A lovely, plugged-in waterfall adorned the center of the large room, with too-yellow lights reflecting strange speckled patterns all around the contemporarily-styled lobby. Men in hats bartered with men in convention badges while porters loaded up whole sets of luggage into wheeled carriers.

Mrs. Bickerson pointed her husband in the right direction of the overpopulation and gave him a slight shove to get him started. Having a suitcase and seven large plastic bags to deal with was a blessing and a curse on his journey to the long check-in line. John fell asleep more times than he was prodded to move forward in line. The bags kept him vertical.

Over safely by the wall, between the popular telephones and the dying, potted tree a cat moaned as if on his third day of starvation.

"Oh...Nature Boy!"

Blanche opened her purse and instantly cursed her own thoughtlessness. *John had the cat food in one of the bags.*

It took 2.5 hours to get registered, get the key and find a free porter to escort them up to the 7th floor. They didn't need a porter, but it was hotel policy to get as many tips for the underprivileged subservients as possible.

All John Bickerson could see when the door opened was the bed.

Bed.

What a bed.

It shone like a springbox Promised Land. Like a picture in a brochure for only the best and most expensive vacations—this is what glistened in John's one-track mind as he mumbled and made his way to that cloud.

"Just go ahead and flop down, dear," Blanche calmly cooed. "I'll unpack everything."

He didn't need to hear that. He was dead out before his nose hit the pillow.

But he couldn't sleep. John Bickerson couldn't sleep. He couldn't get comfortable. It was too hard, too soft. His bloodshot eyes opened fervently, scouring a reason his perfection should be gunned down so expertly like this.

Then he remembered.

"Huh? Whadaya say, Blanche?"

"What?" She called from the little kitchenette, attached via sliding door to the bathroom. An odd bit of architecture indeed.

As John approached the partially opened door, he saw a...

"Blanche! What's that alley cat doing in our hotel room?"

"It's not an alley cat, silly. That's Nature Boy."

"Who's Nature Boy?" he fumed.

"The cat. *Our* cat. Why can't you ever remember his name?"

"Does he remember mine?"

The Thing, halfway through a tin of the best smoked salmon credit could secure, hissed at his breadwinner and proceeded to launch his back hair on end when the so-called Master of the House evilly approached.

"What's he doing here?"

Blanche turned pink with vague guilt. "I brought him, John."

"You what!"

"He looked so lonely when I was packing up the cat food, John, I couldn't leave him."

"Why were you packing up the cat food?"

"I thought we might want a snack on the plane. You know they only give you a little drink on the way, no meals."

"I'm not eatin' any cat food, Blanche."

"You don't have to now, John."

He couldn't win. At least by this time in his life though, John Bickerson was resigned to a life as a loser. He suffered through another half hour of her endlessly doltish chatter on the nutritional merits of animal food and why they were expecting a case of Milkbones upon their return.

Night fell. John grabbed a good forty-five minutes of sleep in the shower, and was relatively fresh to join the festivities that were to start at 7:30 that night.

Even on the slight walk to the elevator, the whooping of mad salesmen began. Blanche shook her head.

"I knew it would be like this. I knew I couldn't let you come to this convention by yourself," she sternly explained as a roll of toilet paper covered in lipstick was flung threw the closing elevator doors.

"These guys are just letting off steam, Blanche. Every man has a right to do it *sometime.*"

"They shouldn't get so steamed up in the first place. You said there wasn't going to be any of *this*, though. I *knew* you were lying."

"How was I to know what goes on in the heads of these jerks?"

"You're one of them."

"Now listen, Blanche…"

The doors parted, displaying an impressive paper banner of red and gold letters. 23RD ANNUAL BOWLING BALL SALESMAN CONVENTION.

The banquet hall was like a mad house. Half-nude women being chased through the laughing halls by middle-aged guts in tall hats, blowticklers honking from their grinning mouths; it was like the world's greatest Thorne Smith exhibition ever assembled.

The hall leading from the elevator was supported by beams, and around every one was either a man and woman in frenzied, whispered conversation, or balloons. There weren't many balloons.

Every man who entered the great and tall hall (the Stafford Room) was given a name badge and a pin. There was a helium tank near the roast beef table for blowing up all the black balloons that were constantly being assassinated with those pins.

John Bickerson knew that if he showed even one spark of interest in the surroundings that spoke to his heart, he'd never hear the end of it. He closed his eyes and tried not to hit any walls.

"Mr. and Mrs. Bickerson," he told the intoxicated man at the lead-in table.

"You brought your wife to a convention?"

He stared openly and open-mouthed at Bickerson who muttered something about ham sandwiches and banquets and snatched his little sticky BADGE and GUEST buttons from the gaping and now sober guard.

They ventured into the room, where things cooled immediately. As John and Blanche passed the pirates, each one in turn began to calm and retain more composure. As John eagerly, helplessly toured the room to lay eyes upon a friend to see him through the impossible night—or a shot of fire water so he would cease to care—everyone quickly caught the disease of respectability.

Somehow, they could all tell there was a married couple in the room.

The speeches slowed everyone up too. The proceedings were almost reputable. Except that Blanche kept feeling that John's eye was always being drawn to an incredibly attractive woman in blue with her red hair insinuated into a Veronica Lake pattern. By the time all the peach cobbler was passed out during the monologues, Blanche was seeing red as well.

John didn't learn a thing he didn't know before. Bruce Lox, President of the Winona Ball Plant, throughout his speech kept harping on the same tired subjects that even his boss yelled in John's first day on the job. "Know your bowling balls! Don't take NO for a door slam! Everyone likes to bowl! Everyone *loves* to bowl! And they *will* bowl, if only they have the proper equipment!"

Lox warmed to his theme, tempered by occasional drunken cheers from the audience.

"Show me a man who does not bowl, and I will not show you a pool player. I will not show you a fool. I will show you a man without a ball of his own. I will show you someone who has never bowled. Stock up on free coupons to give out to people. Or take the man out bowling if it's your last stop of the day! Make a meal out of it!"

John Bickerson was snoring by the time the last cheer died down. Garbled surprise began at the tables nearest, slowly working up to the front tables. Even Lox had to stop his winning rhythm and gape in awe. The sound of the snoring rattled the mock crystalware and vibrated a few choice pieces of cutlery to the floor.

When the shouting began to remove the traitor, Blanche hung her head in shame.

The room to the door opened and Paul Smith, one of the more popular porters, wheeled in the offending Bickerson. The dead-to-the-world body was still going strong, now burbling like a chicken under water, tempered by alternating breaths that sounded like a vacuum cleaner in outer space.

"Thanks, Paul."

Blanche handed him a whole buck and the hotel worker dumped his load on the floor and headed out.

"Don't tell anyone what room he's in, huh?"

"Are you kiddin'?"

The door half-slammed. Blanche climbed out of her expensive, spangley dress and winced at the strangled whining that now proceeded to dribble from her husband's fully open mouth.

"John—John, go in the bathroom, go on!"

The next sound the man emitted fairly shook the glass door leading to the terrace.

"Stop it, stop it, stop it!"

"Mmm, stop it, Blanche. Wassamatter…?"

"It's you! I can't stand it anymore, I'm going out of my mind!"

"If you're going out, get me some ice."

"That's the whole trouble right there. If you hadn't had those four bourbons with your chicken pot pie, you wouldn't've fallen asleep and ruined our whole night! Get up off the floor, go on!"

There was almost panic in his wife's pleading voice. Struggling, John forced himself off the very comfortable plush carpet and focused sixty percent of his eyes.

"What, what's the matter, Blanche?"

"Come on." She helped him up, but knew better than to sit him on the bed. The straight chair in front of the hard wooden desk might do.

When his posture was awake enough, she squatted to see his red-eyed face better.

"John, this simply can't go on. If your wild salesmen friends knew we were in this room—"

"I've never met one of them before tonight."

"You didn't meet them *tonight*. You can't be so incredibly tired, John. You slept on the whole plane trip over!"

"That ride only took two-and-a-half hours, Blanche."

"I'm counting the two hours we had to wait on the plane. You slept in the airport waiting area, and I've never been so embarrassed in my life."

"You should get out more."

"Are you trying to be funny, John Bickerson?"

"Not funny. Sleepy…"

The wooden chair strained at John's turning over on his side.

"No, you don't, John. We're going to have it out right now!"

"You have it out. I'm going to bed."

He turned over more, just enough. WHACK!

On the floor, wide awake, in a slight puddle, sat Bickerson.

"Good heavens! I'm on the floor, Blanche!"

"Serves you right for trying to sleep on a chair."

She started to help him up and stopped.

"John—it's wet! Are you all right, darling?"

From his pocket came the steady *drip drip* of a steady stream of fluid. John's face went pale.

"My life! It's draining away! Quick, get a towel, Blanche!"

Thinking he was wounded by the fall, Blanche dashed for a thin hotel towel— they were all thin—and only upon returning did she understand. There he was. Lapping up the spot with his tongue, his strong right hand around a broken, plastic flask, its broken tape strangely matching a piece of tape crudely showing from John's lower back.

"John!"

"Now don't start beefing, gimme that towel!"

The spot was mopped up quickly enough. Soon the towel was bloated with enough sauce to secure a few good squeezes. Blanche watched the towel squeezed, the liquor floating into that tired mouth. She was amazed—as usual.

"You had that bourbon taped to your person! Why didn't you just put it in your back pocket?"

John stared incredulously. "Are you kiddin'? After seeing the way these crazy men act around here? I'm lucky to have my pants after half a day in this loony bin."

The sniffles began. Blanche was on the verge of crying. "I hate this place. Why did you make me come?"

"I made you come! You didn't trust me to come to this stupid place by myself. I didn't want to come. It was my boss that—"

"All right, but we've got to get out of here. They all hate you. We'll be lucky if we survive the night."

Wearily, John rose and dropped what was left of his best friend into the tiny garbage can.

"What are you talking about, Blanche?"

"You fell asleep during the talk tonight. You started a riot. If I hadn't've found a porter with shoulders like a football player—"

"And a outstretched hand."

"—we wouldn't be here now."

Fuming in misery, John replied, "I hate that porter."

The halls outside were rumbling with discontent. Obviously, the trekkers didn't know where the Bickersons' room was, but the loud, loose talk that filtered in through the thin walls gave a clear picture of what the conventioneers would love to do if they had the right room number.

Blanche rose resolutely, and began quickly tossing folded clothes and the cat into the suitcase.

"We're not going, Blanche. I'll lose my job."

"You'll lose it anyway, once your boss hears what happened here today."

"I fall asleep at the table, and they hate me for life? It doesn't make sense!"

Working on finding the seams of a pair of pants that looked like the sail on a boat, Blanche absently replied, "It wasn't just sleeping. No. Every time you close your eyes, your mouth comes open like a Cupie Doll. It was rolling thunder in there for twenty solid minutes."

"It rained tonight?"

She couldn't stand it any longer. Throwing down some male shirts that could've doubled as a trampoline cover, Blanche whirled on him desperately.

"They were laughing at you, John! Once that stopped, the place was dark and silent. Every scowl was directed right at *you*. I'd never been so embarrassed in my whole life!"

"Yes you were, earlier tonight!"

Packing resumed.

"It can't go on this way, John. When we get home, you're having the operation."

"What operation?"

"I'm not spending the rest of my life with an oil rig. You're either getting your snoring fixed or I'm going home to mother!"

"Is she still alive?"

"John Bickerson, you know perfectly well that my mother had me when she was only sixteen!"

"Yeah, I know," he answered thoughtfully. "She's really lasted, hasn't she?"

"Why you—"

"All right, all right!"

John stepped over to his wife, and put his arms around her. They were close. She could never resist that smile, and the nearness to him.

He said, "You win. I guess I've given you a lifetime of trouble. The least I can do is have this foghorn seen to. As soon as we get back, honey."

He kissed her, and she smiled.

But a tinge of doubt creased Blanche's forehead the next moment.

"But first, we've got to get out of the hotel alive."

Blanche wasn't kidding about the hostility of the bowling ball salesmen now infiltrating the hotel. All brows were pointing south, all arms were folding, and the busy talk that once had been so loud and zany, screaming through the halls, was now rumbling and ominous.

Paul Smith knew his tip was bound to be big on this one, as he slowly steered the clothed dinner cart through the aggrieved hallways. The army-like population reminded Paul of a film he'd seen recently. *12 Angry Men*. With a much bigger cast.

Rolling the cart was slow, what with two people crouched underneath with a suitcase. Heavy. It was difficult for Paul to continue pushing without opening his mouth to breathe. He tried to hide his redness of face and the neck veins that popped out from the exertion. It was the most weight he'd moved in a long time.

Reaching the interior of the elevator was a milestone. But everyone's heart skipped a beat when a hand stopped the door from closing. Three dark men entered the tiny elevator, cloaked in grimaces. The first three floors were passed in silence. But as they drew nearer the lobby, one spoke, without turning his head.

"Amazing how it takes just one idiot to ruin a whole convention."

A pause of one floor.

"Yeah," admitted the other villain.

The doors parted on the first floor. A robust, five foot Mr. Shaw stood there. On his arm was a ravishingly beautiful creature with sparkling green eyes, red hair and a figure like an hour glass stuck at around 10:30 a.m.

That's when the power went out.

The elevator doors stayed open, while the entire hotel was flooded in darkness. There was a panic to get out of the tiny lift, lest it plunge a full floor to the bottom.

Paul knew it was no good waiting for the power to snap back on. It wasn't the first time such wonderment happened; it could take hours.

"I think you're safe now, Mr. Bickerson," Paul whispered. "Just take that door there, walk down a flight. Stairs lead right to the garage."

"We came by taxi!" Blanche shout-whispered.

"Come on," John groaned.

The blacklisted couple stood, creaking their knees in the safety of blackness. There was lots of shouting from various directions. Candles flickered, and flashlights beamed in the hands of running hotel employees. From somewhere nearby a bowling ball rolled its silent way along.

Unfortunately for John Bickerson he met up with the ball and the exquisite creature beside Mel Shaw all at once.

She was wearing a dress that had to be assembled—and climbed into – in layers. The speckles it flaunted must've been something in the daylight. It, and the body it hid, was a work of art.

Tumbling into the loose bowling ball, John defiled that work known as Gloria Gooseby, unconsciously weaving his tie, cuff links and loose shirt threads into her speckles and long, dangly earrings. The two bodies hit the floor as one.

The sound of running feet and insanity filled the small hallway, coming closer and closer. Mel Shaw quickly grabbed the lead light from a passing spooked bellhop and shone it at the right place. It was the wrong place for a Bickerson to be.

Six hours later in a cheap hotel room off an obscure piece of highway, half of the Bickersons had retired. Poor husband John slept soundly, lethargically suffering from an acute condition the baffled medical profession had labeled Hammer's Drawl. As the roaring snore began its suction through the mouth, the heavy curtain on the other side of the room twitched. When the air was expelled, the material sighed with relief.

But there was no relief in sight for Blanche. Her eyes were tossing, her pale eyelids were turning. The bags underneath them were packed tightly for a long voyage.

Suddenly she lumped up in bed, beauty treatment all over her face.

"It's like being married to a traffic accident..."

The bewailing began: moaning soft and low, and increasing steadily upwards, as if a large and unlucky sea bass had swallowed a willowy melodrama actress.

"Stop it, stop it, stop it!"

The last guttural groan was the worst—and most like Edna May Oliver.

"John! Wake up! I can't take it another night! My heart is racing, my mind is fluttering like a hummingbird, my eyes are so wild they can't shut up!"

"Shut up," her husband answered groggily.

"What was that?"

"W-h-at?"

"I said I haven't slept a wink since we escaped from that horrible place! I have no idea how you can just drift asleep the moment we find a terrible hotel."

From the other side of the paper thin wall came a pounding, and a truck driving voice which exclaimed, "There's some of us tryin' to get some sleep!"

"I'm with you, bud," and off John's busy nose went.

Blanche was about to try insanity again when the ringing phone caught her attention.

"John—answer the phone."

"Hello."

"Go to the *phone* and answer it."

"Oh…!"

The poor sleepy stumblebum got blindly from his bed, and crashed sleep shade first into the still unpacked bags. A howl of pained anguish flowed through the room.

"John, what happened?"

"I just won the Irish Sweepstakes," he grumbled.

"Hurry up or he'll hang up."

"I'd like to hang him up…" He moved more carefully to the evil instrument. "Hello?"

A husky, hopeful voice was at the other end of the line. "Daisy?"

"Huh?"

"Look, baby, it's no good. The old woman found out about us, so I don't think I can see ya anymore. She's nothing but suspicions, she's following me around day and night, never lets me eat, never lets me sleep, I'm never alone or happy for even one second in my life. I don't know what to do, what to live for. I just—I don't know what I should *do* with my life."

"DROP DEAD!!!"

He slammed the phone down on its base with such force the aging brown table on which it stood collapsed and broke into seventeen matchsticks.

"Commiserating at this time of night—!"

"John! What are you doing?"

"Packing. We're not staying another minute in this broken-down—"

"We've got two flat tires on our rent-a-car, and you know it."

"Don't be such a pessimist. We've got two good tires too."

Packing completed, as there was nothing to pack, he grabbed his wife's hand and led her to the door.

"We can't drive on the rims!"

"Then we'll walk home. It's just the next block."

"What?" Blanche staggered back to the support of the bed. "You mean we paid a good five dollars just to spend the night a block away?"

"I don't know if that five bucks was *good* or not. It came from your sister Clara."

"Just what do you mean by that? Clara and Barney are as honest as the day is long."

"Days are getting mighty short these days. Come on, Blanche."

"No! I want to know what you mean—"

"Look—Blanche! I've been up since two o'clock this morning. Nothing to eat, nothing to drink, the ankle strap on my bourbon bottle lost the paper clip! I just drove a hundred and seventy miles to get away from those crazy, grasping drunks, and it wasn't until the last nineteen miles that they stopped rolling bowling balls at us! All I want is a little sleep, a little peace, a little kindness. Is that too much to ask? Mmm?"

"They're your crazy friends, you know."

John Bickerson was wide awake now. "Friends! I've never seen any of those bums before in my life and you know it!"

"Then how did they all know your name?"

"What do you think this thing is—a price tag?!"

John hit the still-sticking nametag on his chest with all the force he had stored up. The self-swing knocked him so far back onto the bed, his head hit the wall and took a gladiola off the wallpaper.

"We're getting out of here, Blanche," he yelled angrily. The knocking on the neighbor's wall began again. "We're getting out! Do you hear me, Blanche?"

The neighbor pleaded with the woman from an undisclosed room. "Do you hear him, Blanche?"

"We will not. If you were foolish enough to get a room for five whole dollars, we're not going to waste it walking the night away towards home."

"Walking the night away!? It's the next block!!!"

As if he'd already drunk sixty-five cups of coffee, John's chest was thumping.

"Then why did you stop here, John?" She was climbing back into bed, seemingly auditioning Sleep.

It was inevitable. She always got what he wanted—uh, what she wanted. It was time to give up and crawl into bed.

"I was sleepy beyond words. I couldn't drive another inch. Sometimes you just have to give up. But when that stupid phone rang—"

The phone rang. John's battered eyes lit up like Satan's firestarters.

With incredible energy, Mr. Bickerson threw back his bedsheet so violently that static cling sparked. He marched over in bare feet, livid and fuming. Just as he reached the offending instrument, it stopped.

"Goodnight, John."

He turned his head, and saw a smiling wife beaming back. In her hand was a phone cord.

With true love and affection, John countered, "Goodnight, Blanche."

He was asleep before his frontal lobe hit the floor.

⎯⎯⎯⎯◆⎯⎯⎯⎯

MA PERKINS

The Letter From John

by John Leasure

Early morning in Rushville Center found the town's only mailman, George Evans, beginning his day with a sense of mission. The Letter had finally come and he had decided to change his route so as to start closer to the Perkins home. He would catch Ma Perkins before she left for the Perkins Lumber Yard on the opposite end of the small town. He knew how important this letter would be to the newest Gold Star Mother in Rushville Center. He knew because of his own personal pain.

His son Edgar, a bright boy in school, had been lost in the Pacific war a year ago. He knew the pain Ma, as everyone in town called the Perkins widow, was feeling. She had mentioned to him after the news had arrived that John always wrote on a regular schedule. Ma had calculated that there might be one or two last letters yet to come. A few weeks had passed and no letter. But sorting through today's mail, there it was.

Edgar had not been much of a letter writer, which always held a certain irony for the mailman. But he would have given much for one more letter; one last bit of Edgar's thoughts before...before what happened happened. So a little earlier start and a bit out of his way and Evans would feel better with The Letter out of his hands and with Ma Perkins.

He cut across the lawn, walking past the front porch of the Perkins house, taking note that the Blue Star Flag still hung in the window untouched. Well, everyone comes to the task in his own time.

A blue star on a rectangular flag was the symbol of a family member serving his country in this awful war. Families hung these themselves with pride and a sense of duty. There were stars denoting wounded and missing in action. It was the gold star that generally stopped everyone who saw it hanging. The gold star told all of the

119

greatest sacrifice made by the family behind the flag. It had taken his wife a few weeks before she sewed the gold star over the blue hanging in their own window. Yes, he knew what the Perkins family was going through.

This early he knew Ma, and maybe her daughter Fay, would be making breakfast before the start of their day. The large family kitchen was at the back of the house and Mr. Evans stopped a moment before approaching the back porch. It would do no good to have his own tears get in the way of his duty. He pulled his handkerchief from his back pocket, wiped his eyes and blew his nose. He couldn't offer Ma any of the platitudes offered him by well meaning friends. No, the pain didn't go away. And time, at least one year of time, had not made the boy's passing any easier. Evans and his wife were able to hide the grief better, but the feelings were still there, the hurt still palpable.

With a heavy sigh and a renewed sense of purpose Evans sprinted up the back porch steps. He smiled in spite of himself because the smell of fresh bread baking and possibly fresh sweet rolls came to his nostrils as he rapped his knuckles on the wooden screen door. There were benefits to starting with the Perkins home.

The knock at the door made Fay jump. She turned from taking the sweet rolls out of the oven and stared at the door. Who would be knocking at the back door this time of the morning? Fay looked up at the wall clock. It was still a little too early for Shuffle to stop by for a morning coffee with Ma. Anyway Shuffle would have just walked on in as would her sister Evey, or just about anyone else they knew. Everyone seemed to feel they were always welcome at the Perkins home and there was no need for such formalities. So the knock on the door probably was bad news.

Fay placed the baking dish of sweet rolls on the sink sideboard to cool a bit and slowly wiped her hands on her apron. What other bad news could there be? Wasn't the news of John enough? There was another incessant succession of raps on the door. Well, whoever it was wasn't going away. With a deep breath, and an even deeper sense of dread, Fay opened the back door.

"Mr. Evans?"

"Mornin' Fay, is Ma around?" The smell of fresh baked sweet rolls—and Evans had decided the smell of cinnamon meant sweet rolls—all but knocked him over as Fay propped open the wooden screen door with her shoulder.

"No, she's already gone," said Fay, looking a bit perplexed and worried. "They called from the dairy last night and wondered if we could return John's uniforms. Rationing seems to have hit everywhere and they needed the extras of John's. Can I help you?"

It seemed to Fay as if all the air let out of the mailman. His shoulders sagged and his shoulder bag dropped to the porch. Fay reached out to steady the man.

"Come on in and have a cup of coffee and a sweet roll, Mr. Evans. It's early yet."

The Perkins Lumber Yard dominated their end of town. It was a traditional lumber yard, but Ma had placed some household goods and hardware items along with camping and fishing equipment in the front of the store a while back. Diversification. She had read about it in a book and thought it a good idea.

Shuffle Shober had thought it silly but kept it to himself rather than make a big deal over it with his friend, Ma Perkins. Willie Fitz, however, had not been silent. He complained every time he had to dust the extra merchandise. But Ma ignored her son-in-law's comments and with the coming of war the extra goods and services instituted by Ma had been a good move. There was less and less need for building materials as the war wore on but people needed to repair and replace things. Coffee pots, fishing poles, hammers and nails had all helped to keep the family business open and even prosperous during these lean years. Shuffle laughed as he dusted the coffee pots this morning.

Yessiree. Ma Perkins knew her business all right. And it was all the more surprising since she had come to business late in her life. Pa's death had forced her to work the family business and continue to raise her family and provide for them.

There was Evey, John and Fay. All three were the pride of Ma Perkins, surely. But as surely they could also try the patience of Job. The three of them could fight like the dickens and say the most hurtful things. But Shuffle never heard Ma complain, or even raise her voice in anger. He knew that even though the three children were now adults, there were still problems from time to time.

The news about John had been particularly hard for Ma and those closest to her. How do you console someone over the loss of a child? Regardless of the age of the child, a mother shouldn't have to bury her young. And even that wasn't possible for Ma. John's body was buried somewhere in Europe, unknown and unmarked. There had been a fine memorial service and a headstone in the family burial plot bore John's name. But somehow it didn't feel finished even to Shuffle, and he wasn't family.

The jangling bell over the front door brought Shuffle back to himself. He glanced at the clock. It was still early.

"Is that you, Willie?"

"Who else would it be this early, Shuffle?" came the slow, world-weary voice of Willie Fitz. "Fay called over to the house and Evey insisted I get right on over here. I haven't even had a proper breakfast yet, Shuffle."

"Well, Sweet Jerusalem, Willie. What's all so important to get you over here so early?" asked Shuffle, a bit worried now. "Ma's okay, ain't she?"

"Ma's fine, but she may not be when she hears the news," Willie took a long draw of coffee before finishing his sentence, much to Shuffle's exasperation.

"What news, Willie? Ya said Fay called, so it ain't her. Did Ma leave the house already?"

"Yeah. Ma took John's extra uniforms over to the dairy. They called last night wantin' 'em."

Shuffle waited for the young man to go on and had to resist reaching over and shaking the news out of him. Shuffle knew Willie had to tell the story in his own way and time. The older man poured himself another coffee as Willie settled into Ma's desk chair, putting his feet up on the desk to tell what he knew.

"Mr. Evans shows up at Ma's practically before dawn. Scared Fay half to death. She was sure it was bad news bangin' at the back door." Willie drained his cup and with a satisfied 'ah' sat it down on the desk.

"And was it, Willie?" asked Shuffle.

"Was what?"

"Bad news. Was it bad news? Tarnation, Willie, finish the dang story."

"Okay, okay. Mr. Evans had a letter from John. Said Ma had told 'em she was expectin' one last letter. He brought it over first thing."

Shuffle heaved a big sigh. "That shore was nice of him. Ma was grateful and she's gonna be late today. Is that why you rushed over here so early?"

"No, Shuffle. Didn't ya hear me?" asked a somewhat put-out Willie. "I said Ma took John's uniforms over to the dairy. She wasn't home when Mr. Evans got there. Evey sent me over here to tell Ma that the letter is comin' so she don't miss Mr. Evans over here."

Both men looked up at the clock. When would Ma Perkins arrive at the lumber yard and how would she take the news of the letter?

On a normal and concentrated walk, you could cross the whole of Rushville Center in twenty minutes. But on his mail route it took George Evans nearly all day to walk the town. The Perkins Lumber Yard was usually last on his route. That was why he had started early in trying to deliver John's letter to Ma first. But circumstances had conspired against him and he had missed Ma at the Perkins home.

Fay had been kind enough to give him one or two of her fresh-baked sweet rolls and she wouldn't take the letter either. She was firm that Ma be the one to receive it and read it first. Fay was honest enough to tell Evans she wasn't sure she could refrain from opening the letter herself. She even understood why he had to start his regular route and surely it would be in the afternoon before he reached the lumber yard.

Evans stopped a moment and sorted through his shoulder bag. He was approaching the Pendleton home and he knew better than to wait until he got in front of the house to gather their mail. No one in town took as many magazines as the Pendletons. And no one received as much mail as them either. Augustus Pendleton was the town's banker, which placed his wife, Matilda, and their snooty daughter at the top of Rushville Center's social ladder, making them equally as important, at least to hear them tell it.

He sorted through his satchel and realized the four magazines and little package meant he was going to have to knock on their door rather than leave the mail in the box on the post outside the picket fence which surrounded the large house and yard. He sighed as he opened the gate. There would be no kind invitations here.

Evans had hardly stepped one foot on the porch when the front door flew open and Matilda Pendleton, in a bathrobe and with curlers in her hair, came flying out of the house. The shocked mailman knew the woman was talking but was so taken aback by the sight of her that it took a moment for it to sink in a bit.

"Evey Fitz called and told me about the letter. Augustus says Ma Perkins is at the bank now and wanted me to tell you to hold on until he gets here."

The mailman handed Matilda Pendleton her mail in shocked silence as he heard tires screeching behind him. There was the Pendleton Packard suddenly pulled up in front of the house. Augustus bolted out of the car shouting to the mailman, but still it wasn't sinking in to Evans what was going on. Why were the Pendletons involved and what had this to do with Ma Perkins? The he saw her.

"Good morning, Mr. Evans," came the calm, sweet voice of Ma Perkins as she made her way from the car to the porch. "Banker Pendleton tells me you have something for me that can't wait."

"Yes, well, when Matilda called the bank and there was Ma Perkins picking up the day's cash box for the lumber yard, it seemed silly to have her wait until this afternoon when you got around delivering to there," blustered the breathless and self-satisfied banker.

Evans suddenly didn't care why Matilda Pendleton was hovering so over his shoulder. He dug in his satchel and pulled out the much-discussed letter.

"I came by your house early this mornin' to deliver this letter to you, Ma," began the mailman, "I knew you were waitin' for it."

"Well, land sakes, Mr. Evans, it must be important to have you come out of your way like that," Ma said as she took the letter from the shaking mailman. It was then she recognized the handwriting and she looked into the eyes of George Evans. "Thank you so very much."

"I—I thought it was somthin' you needed to get as soon as possible," said Matilda, pushing the mailman aside.

"No, no thanks, please. Just doing what we can to help others in their time of need," offered Augustus.

"And I appreciate all of you doin' what you done. I really do," said Ma as she put the letter, unopened, into her purse. "Did Fay give you some of her sweet rolls, Mr. Evans?"

"She sure did, Ma," smiled Evans as he noted the disappointed looks on both Pendleton faces.

"Well, aren't ya going to open and read the letter?" asked a bold Matilda.

"Not right now, dear. I want to read it with the family tonight after dinner. I think that's only right, don't you, Augustus?"

"Of course it is, Ma. Of course it is. Well, let me take you on out to the lumber yard," offered the banker.

"If you don't mind, I'd rather walk to the lumber yard. It's such a pretty mornin', ain't it, Mr. Evans?'

"That it is, Ma. That it is. We can at least walk to end of the block together."

"I'd like that, Mr. Evans. I'd like that very much."

Both of the Pendletons stood and watched the two make their way down the street. "You'd better call Evey and tell her, Matilda."

"Tell her what? She's gonna know what's in the letter before I do!" Matilda turned with a swirl of her bathrobe, leaving her husband alone on his own doorstep.

Shuffle tapped the last of the old tobacco out of his pipe on the railing of the Perkins front porch. He could still hear Evey Fitz rattle on from the kitchen about how disappointed Matilda Pendleton was *she* didn't hear the letter first. The woman's laugh was enough to set a man's teeth on edge as she stated with delight that she just might keep the contents of John's letter secret until the next meeting of the Jolly Seventeen, the young woman's social club presided over by Matilda Pendleton with Evey as the Vice-President.

"What do you think is in the letter, Shuffle?" asked Willie for the umpteenth time that day.

The family friend scooped a bit of fresh tobacco from his pouch, tamped it down with his thumb, lit a match and took a long draw on the pipe before answering, "I don't know, Willie. Probably nothing more than is usual for a letter home."

"Mebbe. But it is still a bit creepy and all," offered Ma Perkins' son-in-law. "Coming after his being killed and all."

Shuffle was just about to give Willie a caution about saying something like that in front of Ma when Fay appeared at the front door, "Wash up you two, dinner is just about ready."

The old friend smiled at Fay, a pretty young woman, who many in town called "the sweet one" behind Evey's back. Still, Shuffle knew how headstrong Fay could be about any number of things. He also knew she had experience with loss and death. Fay's husband, Paul Henderson, had died a few years ago, leaving the young widow to raise their child, Paulette, alone.

Though Fay was financially secure, it was Shuffle's opinion that Fay was looking too hard for happiness in the person of a husband and father for the little girl. Fay's trust and love had not been placed in the right man yet. Still, he knew the young woman had the strength to take most anything life could hand her, since she was the daughter of the strongest, as well as the kindest, of women, Ma Perkins herself.

"You comin', Shuffle? Or are you just gonna sit there starin' into nothin'?" prodded Willie.

"I was just thinkin' there, Willie," Shuffle said as he knocked the ash from his pipe. "I was thinkin' how good that chicken smells in there."

Ma Perkins said the prayer after all present had taken their places around the dining room table. Shuffle noted the good dinnerware reserved for Thanksgiving, Christmas, weddings or funerals. It didn't pass Evey's notice either.

"Well, aren't we bein' fancy tonight with the good china and all," observed Evey, holding up the silver fork of her place setting.

"Oh, I don't think of it as bein' fancy, Evey. Just a special evening among friends and family," Ma said, ending all discussion of the table setting. "Mr. Evans said he enjoyed your sweet rolls this morning, Fay."

Fay blushed and told the story how frightened the knock on the door made her and then how strangely Mr. Evans had acted when he heard Ma wasn't home. When the conversation lagged a bit Ma asked Evey about the Jolly Seventeen's new community project. Infused by the question and a captive audience, Evey regaled the family and Shuffle with talk of their plans for the coming year.

Ma looked about the table, satisfied that the most important people in her life were with her and would be present to hear John's letter. It had not been an effort not to read the letter. In fact Ma was aware that all of this, the dinner and such, was a way to delay the reading.

Ma rose as Fay and Evey began to gather the dishes and clear the table.

"Why don't we all go into the livin' room," Ma said as brightly as she could. "We'll all be more comfortable in there."

"What about the dishes, Ma?" asked Evey.

"They'll be there afterwards, child," Ma said as she herself went into the living room.

Evey and Fay looked at each other, shrugged their shoulders and followed the rest of the group into the large, but cozy, front room of the Perkins home. Ma was sitting in her rocking chair. She reached into her sewing basket on the floor beside her and took the letter in hand. She adjusted her glasses and carefully opened the envelope.

"Dear Ma," began the letter.

"What's the date, Ma?" asked Evey, as Fay shushed her.

"It's been blacked out, Evey, so you can't read the date," Ma said as she searched the letter briefly for some other date. "There's some other places blacked out along the letter too."

"You mean someone else has read this letter?" asked an incredulous Evey.

"It's war, Evey," said Willie. "You know, 'Loose lips sink ships.'"

"But Johnny wasn't on a ship," said a somewhat bewildered Evey.

"Why don't I just read the letter and mebbe we can piece together dates and places later," Ma said as she smoothed the letter and began again.

> "Dear Ma:
>   How are things in Rushville Center? I never ever thought I would miss my hometown as much as I do. I even miss Fay, but you don't need to tell her that."

There was the titter of nervous laughter as everyone remembered the huge fights John and Fay would have over just about everything. Fay tried to dab at her eyes without drawing too much attention to herself.

> "I cannot believe I am where I am sometimes. I have seen and been in places that I only knew from Mrs. Adkins' geography class.

But I have seen none of the grandeur she talked about. I have seen rubble and all but total destruction everywhere. Between both sides, there will be little left of the Old World, as Mrs. Adkins called it. Perhaps we of the new world will be able to help the old rebuild and replenish once this war is over.

And it will be over, Ma. I don't think very soon, but I cannot imagine the other side being able to stand..."

"Land sakes, there is a whole section here blacked out." Ma squinted a bit and could not read through the black. She continued, "We are pressing further and further....' And more black oh, here is more of the letter..." And Ma continued:

"But what keeps us going, what makes this all worthwhile is that whenever we come into a city or village the people cheer as they realize it is Americans and the Allies. Sometimes the only English word they know is freedom and they say it with tears in their eyes. At the end of a terrible battle when there is nothing but the smell of death and dying in the air, it is that one word of English that can keep us going. Freedom.

Please give Paulette and Junior a hug and a kiss for me. I see the children here no older than them and I understand that I am here to prevent this kind of destruction at home. I am here to make sure my niece and nephew and maybe my own children will not have to experience this terrible pain called war. I pray that this is what they call the last great war, the war to end all wars. I cannot imagine the world surviving this again.

I need you to understand, Ma, that I know why I need to be here. I understand and have no regrets regardless what may happen. Also know that you raised me well and I work hard everyday to make you, Evey and Fay and the rest of the family proud of me. I hope to be able to hug you and give you a big kiss when I get home. But if that is not to be, know that my love for all of you will be undying and forever.

Love to one all,
John

P.S. Tell Shuffle I've become quite good at poker and I have one or two things to show him when I get home."

Both Evey and Fay went over to their mother and knelt and hugged her at the same time. "It's a good letter, Ma," Fay offered.

"And it sounds just like him," Evey said. "I swear I could almost hear his voice while you were reading it."

"Yes, it sounds just like John. But I may have to talk to Shuffle about corrupting the young man with poker." Ma gave her friend a sly grin.

"Now, Ma…" began Shuffle.

"I can tell you for certain, Ma, that it was John more times than not who won at cards," said Willie.

"Oh? And how would you know, Willie Fitz?" asked Evey, with hands on her hips and trying not to laugh.

"Ya done it now, Willie," said Shuffle with a guffaw, causing everyone in the room to laugh.

Laughter, they say, is healing. If that is true, then the family and friends of Ma Perkins healed themselves that evening as they shared memories of John Perkins in ways they hadn't been able to since the news of his death. Finally the laughter died down and Fay saw the clock on the wall.

"Well, we still have a table full of dishes to do in there, Evey."

"Why don't Willie and me give you a hand there, ladies?" said Shuffle, making his way to the kitchen.

"I swear, Shuffle, we do this now and they'll jest expect it all the time," whined Willie.

"It wouldn't hurt you to help in the kitchen once in a blue moon, Willie Fitz," snapped Evey.

"We'll consider this a blue moon tonight, Willie," offered Fay as she pushed her reluctant brother-in-law through the kitchen door.

Ma could hear the laughter and good-natured ribbing coming from the kitchen and it made her smile. Yes, John, this is the kind of an evening you died to protect and we are all grateful for it. But we'll miss you, son.

She folded the letter and placed it in her sewing basket. There under the letter was a swatch of yellow cloth. Ma hesitated for a moment, then took it and carried it with her to the front window behind her chair. On her tip-toes she unhooked the Blue Star Flag, folded it and carried it to her chair.

Slowly rocking back and forth, Ma stitched the yellow fabric, cut into a star, over the blue star on the flag. This was a job long overdue, but easier to do tonight than before.

"Yes," Ma Perkins said to herself, "We'll miss you, son."

THE BLACK MUSEUM

The Ticket Stub

by Michael Leannah

Dear Reader:
*   By the time you read the following pages, the events herein de-*
scribed will have long passed. I am sealing these papers today in a stout
envelope and placing it in the care of a trusted nephew who has been
directed not to reveal the contents until the year 2002, when I will
most likely—and comfortably—be in my grave.
*   Some stories need to be told this way.*
*   Signed on this day, October 22, 1952*

With the heavy tolling of the tower bells, all of London seems to shiver and quake. Even here in the cavernous Black Museum, below the streets, deep under the ground beneath Scotland Yard, one can hear them, faintly. One can feel them shaking the dampness of the cold stone walls.

But our story this evening does not involve the iron bells tolling on the streets of London. No, tonight we are more concerned with quieter items, the items on display here in the Black Museum, Scotland Yard's warehouse of homicide.

Some of the artifacts presented here were not always quiet. Take, for instance, this common hammer. Quite a ruckus it made during the long career of carpenter Henry Watkins of Devonshire. Its last blow was delivered by Henry's wife, Madeline. The last blow silenced Henry himself. Forever. And delivered Madeline to prison for the rest of her unhappy life.

And here is a steel-plated coach's whistle, once in the possession of John Drucker, director of athletics at the Frampton Gymnasium in Kensington. Once loud, now silent. The poison applied to the mouthpiece of the whistle did its job. The young man who applied it, Lloyd Sterling, Drucker's rival for the affection of one Marlene Case, hung at the gallows in Wormwood.

These and countless other artifacts are presented here now in the Black Museum, where silence reigns supreme. The clip of my footstep and the drone of my voice, sounds heard but briefly during my weekly visits to these rooms, are the only sounds these walls are accustomed to hearing. Which is a shame, as each of these common household objects displayed on these tables, perched on the shelves of these cabinets, could tell an engrossing, even hair-raising, story.

Let's see. A shoe that once belonged to a man found decomposing in the mud under London Bridge. Police found the shoe on the floor of a car in Redcliffe. The owner of the car was later found in Pentonville Prison, where he was executed on a cold night in May.

Here is a length of wire, ten inches, frayed on one end. The little white card beside it says it was used to electrocute a small child, a child who had the misfortune of witnessing a crime of passion and who needed to be silenced. Electrocution will do that.

Ah, here we are. The ticket stub. Torn with a twist and a pull, at top the numbers read "-348" and at bottom, the letters "-eum." By all accounts an ordinary piece of litter one normally finds at the bottom of a coat pocket. The ticket is not dated, and heaven only knows the fate of its other half.

In the beginning, when the ticket was crisp and new, it belonged to a man named Albert Trumble. Trumble had been out walking the streets of London by himself on the day the ticket was used.

Albert Trumble was a mild-mannered postal clerk, an unassuming, gentle man who generally kept to himself. Pushing fifty, he had been alone now for thirteen years. His wife, Pauline, had passed away in her thirty-third year. Consumption. The two had had no children.

Albert was small and wiry. A good stiff wind was capable of blowing him down. His eyes were bad; without his glasses he couldn't have seen his own hand in front of his face. He kept his graying hair plastered down with a cheap tonic he bought by the half-liter. The features of his face were sharp, as if chiseled with well-cared-for sculpting instruments.

Albert Trumble passed the time on weekends walking the streets, taking in the sights. It was better than staying home and dwelling on his loneliness.

On Saturday, October 3, he took a bus into the heart of the city and disembarked at Waterloo Way, then proceeded to walk west to the banks of the Thames. He trudged across the Hungerford Foot Bridge, observed a man and his grandchildren feeding a flock of gulls, then crossed to the Ox and Plow for a steaming bowl of stew. Next, he meandered southward and met a man who asked if he was interested in receiving free admission to a peculiar exhibition. The ticket that Albert Trumble accepted is now on the table here in the Black Museum.

Albert Trumble presented the ticket at the given address and enjoyed himself immensely. After a stay of approximately ninety minutes, he resumed his walking. He did not know he was being followed.

It was late in the day and the skies were growing dim. Albert trudged his way to his bus stop, boarded, and sank into a seat near the front, behind the driver. A man followed him onto the bus, positioning himself near the rear on the side opposite Albert. The man rode in silence, glancing calmly from time to time at the folded newspaper in his lap.

Albert Trumble got off the bus at Aylesbury and headed for home, stopping first at the Billy Goat Pub to slake an ever-increasing thirst. It was his usual practice to call upon a bottle of dark stout to perform this task. Today was no different.

"Keep your money, bub," the bartender growled when Albert pushed a note forward on the bar as he rose to leave. "Your friend there has already paid for you."

Albert followed the bartender's glance and his wondering gaze was met by the raised eyebrow of a man sitting at the end of the bar, an overweight man who smiled kindly as he stirred the drink in front of him.

"I thank you," Albert said, taking an uncertain step toward the man. "Do I know you?"

"I should think you do. Don't you remember? I ran into you earlier. You were walking down by the Thames this afternoon. Do you remember saying hello?"

"Oh, yes. Yes. How thoughtless of me. Of course I remember you." Albert didn't want to appear unobservant or impolite so he did not question the man further. He did not recognize the man.

"Our paths meet for the second time in a day," the large man said kindly. "Destiny is telling us something."

"I should say so," Albert Trumble agreed, though with a twinge of uneasiness.

"What say we have dinner?" the man at the dark end of the tavern suggested. "For quite some time now my stomach's been telling me to get some dinner. No sense in ignoring it any longer. And no sense in eating alone." Albert peered at the man through the smoky haze.

"The name's Peter—Peter Fripp," the man said as he absently checked the contents of his billfold. "And?"

"Uh—Albert. Albert Trumble." Albert stepped forward and stuck out his hand for a shake but Peter Fripp's full attention was now on his wallet and he didn't see the proffered hand. Albert discreetly let his arm fall into place at his side.

Albert's doubts were quieted by Peter's calm and easy manner. The ice of suspicion melted into trust.

Albert noticed the large gold rings Peter wore prominently on four of his short, thick fingers. This was a man of means, generous and friendly to boot. Why deny an opportunity to get to know someone of society? Perhaps this meeting would lead to further engagements and who knows how many acquaintances.

"Do you live far from here?" Peter asked in a genial tone as he rose and draped his cloak over his arm, pulling on loose, thin leather gloves.

"No," Albert replied. "Just up the street."

The two men strolled along Hudson Street with the Cheshire House Inn their destination. Peter suddenly realized he needed to make an important telephone call—a business agreement that had slipped his mind.

"You can use the telephone in my flat," Albert offered.

"I hate to impose," Peter said.

"No imposition at all," Albert insisted. "Besides, it will give me a chance to change my shirt before dinner."

Peter accepted the invitation and the two men walked to Albert's abode in a vine-covered brick apartment building. Albert was halfway up the staircase when he saw Peter hesitate.

"You go on up," Peter said. "I've forgotten that I'm out of cigarettes. There was a shop up the street. I'll be just a minute. Is that your door? Number nine? I'll be right back."

Albert watched as the man shuffled off. Odd sort of character, Albert thought. But a friendly chap nonetheless.

Peter walked with a determined stride to a newsstand where he purchased cigarettes. Then he walked two doors further and entered Wooler's Butcher Shop.

"Hello," Peter said to the stout clerk behind the counter. "I've come for the parcel I left here yesterday. You'll find it in the freezer with my name—Fripp—on it."

Minutes later, Peter rang the bell at number nine, and a jovial Albert greeted him.

"What have you there?" he asked, looking at the cardboard box in his friend's hands.

"It's something I just picked up," Peter said. "Let me put it on the kitchen table here and I'll show it to you."

The box was misshapen, taped shut, and slightly damp.

"Have you a scissors?"

"Of course." Albert rummaged through a drawer by the window and produced a pair. "They're on the small side. You may have to remove your gloves." Peter managed to snip the tape. He opened the flaps and pulled a plastic bag from within.

"What in the world?" Albert said with a bewildered smile that twisted his brow comically.

Peter lifted the bag and set it on the table. The contents clunked. Albert peered over Peter's busy hands as the bag was opened.

"What is it? Ice?"

"Yes, it is ice," Peter said. "A very large cube of it. But look carefully." With his gloved hands he held it up to the light. "There is something in the ice."

"It looks like a...a brick," Albert said.

"Yes, it is a brick. But look even closer."

Peter held the ice block up higher. Albert squinted, straining his eyes to see.

And Peter, taking the ice in both hands suddenly, brought it down full force on Albert's head.

Albert's glasses clattered to the linoleum. He cried out but his cry was weak and pathetic. He stumbled backward into the wall, his eyes wide with wonder and fear. Peter raised the ice block again and bashed it into the top of Albert's head.

Albert fell like a loose sack of bones. He opened his mouth to say something, but Peter didn't give him the chance. This time he threw the ice at Albert. Blood spattered the floor.

The ice slid beneath the table. With his foot, Peter nudged it to the side of Albert's lifeless face.

Peter casually opened a cupboard, then shut it. He nosed about in the pantry and opened a closet and several more cupboards before finding what he was looking for: a glass pitcher. This he raised high and threw with great force to the floor next to the ice block, the ice block that was now quickly melting.

Peter gathered the cardboard box and the plastic bag. He examined the scene. He had left no footprints. Only a small amount of blood had splattered onto his jacket. When he got home, he would dispose of the jacket, along with the box, and the bag, and the rest of his clothes.

And his disguise.

As the curator of the Black Museum, I have been well acquainted with the ins and outs, the why and wherefore, of murder. And it is my belief that when one is employed in the duty of crime detection or in the study of crime, it is only natural to venture into the realm of crime. To test the water, so to speak.

I, your host tonight, was the murderer of Albert Trumble.

Trumble was pointed out to me one day by an acquaintance of an acquaintance. It wasn't at all difficult to dig a bit into his life and find out his habits, his idiosyncrasies. He was a nice chap, harmless, uninspiring. Very predictable. That was his downfall.

I observed him from afar for several weeks. I followed him on his rounds, on his weekend bus rides into the city, as he poked around in the shops, biding his time until evening came when he could once again return home.

I saw the many times he unsuccessfully initiated conversations with the people he met on his travels. His shyness, his poor self-image, did him in in the end, for he was an easy target when I approached him with an invitation to enter the Black Museum.

"The Black Museum?" he said. "I've never heard of it."

I gave him a ticket, a "complimentary pass" is how I phrased it, as if I gave them out frequently to promote the museum. Just as I expected, he wasted no time in using the ticket. Indeed, he followed me and presented the ticket immediately. I tore the ticket and gave him the stub. He pushed it into his pants pocket.

I think he enjoyed his visit to the Black Museum. He made inquiries over several of the items, once even going so far as to say, "Hard to believe someone could do such things to another human being."

"Yes," I said in response.

When he left, I quickly donned my disguise. Within minutes, I found him again, sitting on a bench gazing out on the Thames. I followed him onto his bus and later into the Billy Goat Pub.

The day before, I had left the package with the butcher, paying a small fee to have him keep it in his freezer. Using ice as a murder weapon was an idea that had occurred to me quite some time ago. Indeed, the ice idea was the seed for my entire plot.

I froze a common brick in a block of ice and used the ice to deliver the fatal blows. As Mr. Trumble was alone in the world and had few friends, it wasn't likely his murder would be investigated before the ice was entirely melted. The police would assume that the brick was the murder weapon, and that the puddle on the floor left by the melted ice was the result of the pitcher, supposedly filled with drinking water, being smashed in the struggle.

Of course, the medical examiners would find wounds not consistent with the shape of the brick, which would bring confusion. This was exactly what I wanted. The ticket stub in Trumble's pocket, too, was a false lead. The police would search for a match but they would not find one. I printed the thing myself; it was one-of-a-kind.

The police scoured the apartment for fingerprints, but, alas, I was wearing gloves throughout the crime. And besides, melted ice carries no prints.

It was quite amusing to hear the talk at Scotland Yard in the days that followed. The final conclusion after months of frustration was that the brick found at the scene was not the murder weapon, that the instrument used in the killing must have been removed from the premises.

When I asked the head inspector for the ticket stub, he seemed a trifle puzzled.

"I thought the Black Museum dealt only with crimes that had been solved," he said. I told him we sometimes make exceptions. Now when I give tours and people inquire about the stub, I tell them the whole story, leaving out particular details, as you can imagine.

Ah, the bells of London are ringing again. I can feel their tremor. But the tolling never lasts long. In just a moment all will be silent again. Just as I will be silent again in a moment or two, as my story is now finished. And by the time this is read, I will have begun my long silence, the longest of all silences.

One request. Please see that this account is properly placed next to the ticket stub, in the Black Museum.

HONEST HAROLD

Attack of the Crawling Things From Outer Space

by Justin Felix

The alarm rang precisely at seven. Honest Harold Hemp, always slow to awaken, peered past his ruffled pillows and tried to make out the time as the clock shuddered on his nightstand. "Zoink," he said as he rolled his large frame toward the side of the bed, grateful that his prissy boss Stanley Peabody no longer required him to do the 6 a.m. weather report at KHJP. During the previous week, he never could seem to get himself into the office by six (it was difficult enough to get there by eight); though no one ever called in to complain. Apparently no one listened to the weather that early in the little town of Melrose Springs. Harold could hear his mother down in the kitchen already, humming and dutifully preparing breakfast and a sack lunch for him. He was grateful for those comforting sounds as he arose and plodded his way to the bathroom for a quick shower and shave.

Harold was just about finishing when his mother called to him. "Harold, your oatmeal is ready."

"Coming, Mother." He wiped his cheeks with a towel, got into a tight shirt that must have shrunk at the cleaners, and grabbed a tie before making his way to the kitchen table.

"Have you heard the news, Harold? It's in today's paper."

"Seeing as I've just got up, probably not. What is it?"

"Melrose Springs is going to have a movie premiere tonight. It's the first time this film has been shown anywhere." Mother poured herself some orange juice and sat down opposite Harold. She pointed at the bottle with a questioning glance, but Harold shook his head no. He was happy enough with just milk.

135

"Really? How wonderful! It's about time something happened in this one-horse town. How is it that I haven't heard about this before? I'll bet it's something that'll be fun to see. What is it? A new Marilyn Monroe picture?"

"Well, no…"

"I'll bet it's one of those musicals! Remember the one that played here last year? What was its name? It had that great number."

Harold was about to burst into song when his mother cut him off. "No, I don't think it's a musical. It's…"

"Does it have any stars? Boy, would I love to see Humphrey Bogart again!"

Harold took a deep breath to prepare his best Bogart impression when Mother cut him off again. "No, Harold. By the title of the film, I don't think anyone of Bogart's stature is going to be in it."

"Oh? What is the title?"

Mother checked the article briefly. "The paper says *Attack of the Crawling Things From Outer Space*. It's one of those new science fiction films that the kids are all crazy about these days."

"*Attack of the…*" Harold felt beside himself. "Not one of those pictures! Bug-eyed monsters indeed! It's bad enough television is keeping kids indoors after school with inane programming rather than outside where they belong. But now this has to invade our nice town?" Harold flung his spoon into his barely-touched bowl of oatmeal and slammed his right fist onto the table, causing his milk to teeter in its cup. "I won't put up for it! We have to keep in mind the best interests of the children of Melrose Springs. By golly, if I can convince the citizens of this fine town to fund police officers to man the crosswalks when the schools let out, I'll certainly convince them that empty-headed stories about alien invasions are not appropriate material for our families!"

"But, Harold, don't you think you're overreacting again? I mean, these movies aren't that bad. Why, I went to one of them with the Sunny Side of Seventy Club. It was rather fun, I thought. It had this alien wearing a helmet who was from the Planet X, and he…"

"Mother! I can't believe what I'm hearing! Planet X! Ssss! I will not be a party to such trivial conversation." Harold stood up, tossing his napkin beside his unfinished oatmeal.

"Where are you going, Harold? You still have some time, and you've barely touched your breakfast."

"I have to prepare some comments for my show today, Mother. Stanley Peabody never sold the sponsor time for the last fifteen minutes, so I'll use it to editorialize against the movie to my faithful listeners. I'll see to it that no self-respecting citizen will patronize this kind of film." With that, Harold grabbed his hat and coat and stepped out of the house, the door slamming shut behind him.

"Dear oh dear," Mother said, conscious that she had developed the peculiar habit of talking to herself. "I wonder what made Harold wake up on the wrong side of the bed this morning. He didn't even take his lunch with him." She stood and began clearing the table. Placing the dishes in the sink, she smiled a little. "Of course, Harold switched to his woolen underwear last night."

The office phone buzzed. "Good morning. Radio station KHJP," Gloria, the radio station's young secretary chirped. "Just a second. I'll connect you." She transferred the call to its appropriate destination as Honest Harold entered.

Harold usually greeted the girl cheerfully, but he was in no mood to dally with her today. "Gloria, is Stanley in?"

"What's wrong, Harold? No 'hello' or 'how are you today?' That's not like you."

She leaned forward on her desk and smacked her chewing gum. Gloria was unusually adept at her gum chewing, as it never hindered her phone voice and was never apparent in her mouth when Stanley, their boss, was near her station. He sighed before asking the obligatory "How are you today?"

"Oh, I'm very well." She giggled the type of giggle Harold expected to hear at an elementary school's playground and not a business office.

"That's good. Now, I need to talk to Stanley. Is he free?"

"Aren't you going to ask me why I'm doing so well?" She now bit her lip as if she were about to burst with good news. Harold was about to inquire when the dam gave way and she answered the question she expected him to ask before he could ask it. "I'm going on a date tonight."

If Harold could have rolled his eyes without Gloria noticing, he would have. That was not news. Gloria almost always was dating someone new. "He's going to take me to that new science fiction movie playing at the Bijou tonight."

"Oh no. Not you too!"

"Wha—?" Gloria had the habit of not pronouncing the "t" at the end of words.

"That's just what I wanted to talk to Stanley about. Things that crawl from outer space. Hah! What nonsense!"

"Oh, I don't know. I think it'll be kind of fun." Gloria looked like she was about to giggle again, but she noticed that Harold was upset. As was often the case when he was in one of these moods, she thought a joke might cheer him up, so she decided to tell him the one she had heard from her new beau.

"What do you call a spaceship that leaks water instead of oil?"

"Gloria, ask yourself this question. Do you really think I care to hear the punch line?"

"A crying saucer," she replied anyway.

Harold did not laugh.

"That was a little joke, Mr. Hemp, " she said smiling and leaning back on her chair.

"Yes, very little! Look, I need to talk to Stanley."

Her smile dissipated after Harold's stern response. Harold was always a person of emotional extremes, and she could tell that Harold really meant business today. "Go ahead in. He's not seeing anybody."

"Thank you," he said, emphasizing each word in a disciplinarian manner. Gloria wondered what had gotten Harold fired up this morning as he knocked on Stanley Peabody's office door.

"Come in," Stanley could be heard saying through the heavy oak door. Harold stormed in.

"Oh, it's you." Stanley's typical response to Harold was disappointment every time he visited to discuss business. To say that they did not get along was an understatement. Their animosity had its roots back when they both were courting Doc Yancey's young daughter. They never really made amends even though she had left Melrose Springs a couple months ago. "What do you want?" he sighed, finishing the yogurt he had been eating.

"I want to talk to you about the final fifteen minutes of my show."

"Oh, I'm glad you mentioned that," he said, licking his spoon clean. "You're going to be so happy with your station manager today."

"I doubt that," Harold said under his breath. He had found that he could get away with half-whispered retorts as Stanley was hard of hearing.

"I found a sponsor for the final segment of your show."

"You did? But I was planning an editorial piece."

"Well you can plan it for some other time. Your listeners don't want to hear a blowhard like you babble about some inconsequential matter anyway." Harold was about to take offense but Stanley continued before he could get a word in edgewise. "Independent International wants to sell its new movie, *Attack of the Crawling Things From Outer Space*, not only during the children's shows this afternoon but also on yours."

Without missing a beat, Harold replied, "I will not sell that dumb movie on my show."

"Believe me, Harold. For once, I agree with you. I don't think these fantastical movies should be shown in our little town. This Flash Gordon stuff is too fanciful for the adolescent mind, yours included, Harold. But money is money, and theirs is just as green as anyone else's."

"I refuse."

"Hemp, I was hoping you would say that. I've been itching to find a justifiable reason to have you sacked. You can't just refuse another sponsor like you did with Grandma Llewellyn's Liquid Lather Shampoo. If you refuse this new sponsor, I'll fire you. I mean it this time."

Harold's frustration sprayed in so many directions he was getting dizzy. First, this unsavory movie, he learned, was set to open at the Bijou. And now Prissy-Pants Stanley Peabody was threatening his job again. He detested Stanley not only for his position but also his familial connections. His uncle owned both the radio station Stanley operated and the town's only newspaper. This meant that Stanley could throw his weight around, often unchecked, in the day-to-day operations of KHJP.

"And you better sound like you mean it when you praise this picture to your audience, Hemp!" Harold also did not care for Stanley's habit of calling him by his last name, which he frequently did with an unmistakable air of contempt.

Harold stood. He didn't speak. He didn't breathe. He couldn't lose his job. The pay wasn't great, but performing on the radio was his true passion. Since KHJP was such a small station in a small market, he was generally given free reins to do what he wished in his allotted time. He knew on principle he should be beseeching his listeners to not go to the movie, but he also knew that it wasn't worth losing his job over. Besides, he didn't have only himself to support. Mother counted on him as well.

"Well? Say something, Hemp."

"I think I can't wait to tell my listeners what a great picture is opening tonight. Goodbye." Harold knew when he was licked.

The afternoon sun was waning when Harold completed his workload for the day at KHJP. A briskness in the air signaled that soon it would be time for the holidays. He walked through downtown Melrose Springs, avoiding eye contact with the Bijou theatre where the science fiction film would be playing that night. Like his mother, Harold had the habit of talking to himself when alone. "Just because I plugged the film today as a spokesperson for the radio station doesn't mean I can't lodge a complaint about it as a concerned upstanding citizen." He came near the police station before realizing that it was the destination he had really set out upon in the first place. He walked in to file a complaint.

Marshall Pete greeted him as he entered. "Why, hello there, boy," he drawled. "What brings you here today?"

"Pete, I want to lodge a complaint."

"Okay. Let me get the appropriate paperwork." Pete had to be the most inefficient officer in the history of crime prevention. Almost immediately, Harold regretted stepping in to the station that also served as the county jail. Pete began shuffling through a mountain of forms on his desk. "What kind of complaint do you want to file?"

"A complaint about a movie that crosses the line of community standards."

Pete's fingers flipped through a folder. He stopped and squinted at one of the pages within. "This form should do. What's the complaint?"

"Pete, there's a movie opening at the Bijou called *Attack of the Crawling Things From Outer Space*. I believe that this film has the moral equivalency of garbage. Just like those awful Universal monster films they used to show last decade. I think that…"

"Wait." Pete grabbed a pencil. "Let me write that down. Where did you say this crime was being committed at?"

"It's not really a crime. But they're showing this movie at the Bijou called…"

"The Bijou. Let me write that down." Harold had filed papers with Pete before. He should have remembered that Pete took longer to fill out a form than the dumbest pupil in class took to finish his homework. For starters, the old duff did not write in cursive, instead relying on block letters that he crafted with slow, deliberate strokes in pencil.

"Now, what's being shown there?"

"*Attack of the Crawling Things From Outer Space.*"

Pete looked at Harold for a brief moment through his coke-bottle glasses. "Let me write that down." He began scratching again on the form, mouthing the words as he wrote them. "*Attack...of...the...*" He stopped as if in thought. "What is this movie about?"

"It's about Elliot Ness and a crime ring," Harold quipped impatiently. "Pete, what do you think it's about?"

"Now ain't that a doozy," Pete replied. "I think I'll have to do something about that." He scratched his head in thought.

"You mean that you'll help me protest this movie due to its content?" Harold thought that at last he had found a sympathetic ear.

"No, I'll have to see it."

"Oh for Pete's sake!" The uselessness of going to Marshall Pete about this matter was making itself steadily transparent.

"No. I'm Pete. It'll be for the sake of the prisoners." He leaned over to Harold conspiratorially. "They don't get to see many pictures."

"You don't say. I wonder why," Harold deadpanned.

"They don't get out much," Pete replied matter-of-factly.

"Oh brother!" Harold wondered if Pete was really being dense or just having fun at his expense.

"Yes, and they don't mind that I act out some of the parts of the film. In fact, you could say that I have a captive audience." Pete laughed at his joke. He had been waiting two days to find an opportunity to spring it.

"At least someone is finding your jokes amusing," Harold said, with the same sternness he had used with Gloria earlier in the day.

"Oh, come on, Harold. Lighten up." Pete looked at the form he had begun. "Do you really want me to fill this out?"

"No! I should've had my head examined for thinking I could get something accomplished visiting you."

"Why, thank you, Harold. That really means a lot to me." It was at moments like this that Harold suspected Pete purposefully behaved as if he were a few pennies short of a dollar. It probably meant less work for him.

"Goodbye!" Harold left in disgust. Marshall Pete wasn't such a bad guy; indeed, Harold counted him as one of his friends. The elderly peacekeeper, though, really knew how to get under his skin.

After a half hour's walk around town, letting the approaching evening calm his spirits a little, Harold stepped up to the door of Theodora's Dance Studio. He wasn't sure if his girlfriend had finished her last class for the day. After talking with Marshall Pete, though, he wanted to find someone who would share his views. If anyone were to agree with him about the inappropriateness of such a film as the one premiering in a few hours, it was his true-blue girlfriend. He rang the doorbell and it chimed to the beat of the rumba. He wondered where he could find such a unique bell as he waited for a response.

"Is that my Haroldy Waroldy come to see his dancing instructor?" Theodora teasingly cooed from behind the door.

Harold loved the young woman's playfulness. He deepened his voice and replied, "No! It's the Big Bad Wolf looking for Little Red Riding Hood. Let me in or I'll blow this door down."

The door opened. Theodora looked as lovely as ever, Harold thought. She smiled. "Oh goody. I like playing with wolves." Harold chuckled at this double entendre. "Why don't you come in?"

The dance hall was empty of students at the moment. Harold felt fortunate for while he was still hot under the collar about the movie issue (though not so much as he had been during the day), he didn't want to create a scene.

"Did you come here to ask your beautiful dance instructor out tonight?" Theodora turned and sashayed, leaning her back against Harold's robust figure.

"Well, no," Harold replied, trying to keep his focus, which was not an easy thing to do when it came to Theodora.

"Harold, I have a wonderful idea for tonight!" She wrapped his arms around her and held his hands.

"You do?" he said, somewhat surprised by her early advance. "Well, that's great, but I really came here to talk about…"

"Why don't you take me to that scary movie that's premiering tonight at our theater?"

"Huh?"

"You know, the one with the crawling things from outer space that was mentioned in the paper." She moved slowly in his arms.

"But…"

"You know how much I like scary pictures."

"Yes, but…"

"Remember when you took me to that movie about the murderer who hummed when he killed those women?"

He did indeed remember the picture. He took Theodora to see it a couple weeks after they had first met. They had had a nice supper beforehand as well. It was his first formal date since Doc Yancey's daughter moved away. "Yes, I do remember that, but…"

"Remember how you had to hold me tight because I got so scared?"

Harold grinned. He did remember that. He held her a lot during the film.

"And you walked me home afterward. I was so afraid that I leaned up against you all the way."

"Say, that's right." Harold chuckled at the memory. When they had finally reached her home, after what seemed like a heavenly eternity, she kissed him goodnight. What a kiss!

"Of course, if you take me to that movie tonight, I'll need some reassurance that I'm safe." She turned to face Harold, smiling. He still held her. "You'll have to walk me home afterward. And I'll be so grateful." She ran her fingers slowly down Harold's cheek. "Do you know what I mean, Harold?"

"Heeeeee," he responded. It was his habit to issue such a response when he felt overwhelmed. "I sure do. Theodora, let me give you some reassurance right now." He leaned in to kiss her but she pulled away.

"Does this mean you'll take me to the movie?"

"You bet!" he said, the memory of the day's event seeming as distant as his childhood. "Now, pucker up, Theodora."

——◆——

DIMENSION X

Willoughby Goes and Gets It

by Joe Bevilacqua and Robert J. Cirasa

It was natural enough to be curious, but they were more than that. Boarders become a lot like a family, especially when they take their dinner together, and over the years, the reclusive professor's failure to join the others became an obsessive mystery to them, especially since his door was so visible from the dinner table, exactly centered within the frames of the successive archways at the passage from the vestibule to the parlor and then from the parlor to the dining room. By now, it had all become a kind of grace, a nightly litany of speculation that began every meal.

"Why do we always have to discuss that poor man's affairs?" scolded Miss Dawson. "Why, you've cast him in more parts than Shakespeare has characters. What does it matter to you what he's doing in there? He's a scientist. That's good enough for me."

"He's a Communist! And you're a dupe if you don't think he's up to something no good."

Frank was a bus driver, and so naturally, he was more skeptical of other people than a schoolmarm. In the five years since his discharge from the Army, he'd traveled the 48 line and seen so many people sitting suspiciously at park benches and standing around public trash cans that he just knew the senator was right about all of those spies and their microfilm drop sites. And it was starting to have an effect on America. Every day, more people passed slugs into the fare box—too many to be just common dishonesty. It was an insidious assault upon free enterprise itself.

143

Miss Dawson, on the other hand, was an idealist, even in the depths of her middle age, and with more than a handful of generations under her pedagogical belt. No amount of classroom unruliness—or political agitation—could dim the prospects in her mind for human improvement through learning, especially science. It was a certainty to her that the world was steadily becoming a better and better place, thanks to people like the Professor, who she was just sure was a benevolent genius.

Jeremiah Butler, on the other hand, knew the dark side of science and its monstrous inventions, having given up his legs to a spray from a German machine gun as he went over the top of a trench in the Ardennes during the first war to end all wars. No one could convince him that science was good for anything other than a disability check from the Veterans Administration every month for the past 516, as regular as the wheel gears of his chair. Not even the still comely Miss Dawson, who although just four years his elder, looked easily twenty years his junior, thanks mostly to Jeremiah's last thirty years of relentlessly bitter self-pity and dissolute lethargy. He filled his days with little more than the smoke from his cigarettes and a smoldering resentment of the able-bodied, weight-lifting young Frank, the fortunate Frank, who had managed to escape entirely unscathed from his three years of World War II service as a general's chauffeur on the dangerous roads in and around the basic training camp at Fort Dix, New Jersey, where they prepared unfortunate men like Jeremiah to go somewhere and be maimed or die.

"Scientist…Communist…*murderer*—I'm telling you, he's a murderer," insisted Jeremiah.

Mrs. Way grumped with exasperation. She could almost abide a murderer more than a self-pitying do-nothing.

A widow for nearly twenty years, Mrs. Way had been a pretty woman in her younger days but was now showing the effects of the seventy-four years upon her, a condition for which she expected no pity. She simply defeated it with cosmetic art, shaving the bristly remains of her eyebrows completely off and drawing in perfect replacements a youthful eighth of an inch higher over her eyes; applying a sultry sky blue shadow to her eyelids, a baby rose pink blush to her cheeks, and a lusty hot red lipstick to her lips; then dusting the whole of her face with a powder that made her smell like a delicious cotton candy. She might have been a wooden arcade gypsy in some penny fortune-vending machine but with a volatile and chiefly sour temperament, accented with a Tourette's-like quirk of her voice that laced everything she said with a growling "errrruhhh" at periodic points of punctuation. Pitched low within her throaty but not unwomanly voice, it accented her usual irritation; pitched high, her occasional pleasure. Even as she listened to others or mused to herself, she would erupt every so often with the ornery or, more rarely, delighted sounds of her disposition.

"Murderer! Errrruhhh… That's a thing to say about someone, isn't it?" she barked at Jeremiah. "Why don't you run to the district attorney and tell him, eh? Bring all your evidence and testimony. Errrruhhh… At least he pays his rent on time, which is more than I can say for you."

"Mrs. Way! Please! I hardly think that's an appropriate thing to say, even sarcastically, to a man in Jeremiah's position! He gave his legs for you!"

"And I gave him his wheels, didn't I? I'm a taxpayer, same as you, Miss Dawson. And I'll thank you for not making yourself the *Emily Post* of this boarding house. I don't need to be tutored by your courtesy how to humor a delusional vet like Jeremiah, who lost any sense of responsibility not too many years after his legs, if you ask me. Errrruhhh…"

"Ya see? This is what the Communists do. It's class warfare, I tell you! He's slowly indoctrinating us, 'raising our consciousness' with his atheistic ways! Pretty soon, each one of us will stop coming down to dinner, just like him! Just like all the Communists! They won't take a meal together because they don't believe in saying grace! We should've gone to the FBI a long time ago!"

Frank was off on his fixation again and eager for an argument, but both Miss Dawson and Mrs. Way had long ago learned to ignore his outbursts and just roll their eyes, each in their respective fashion, Miss Dawson with patrician disdain and Mrs. Way with carnival mockery. But Jeremiah hadn't learned anything in a long time. Taking aim with squinting eyes directly at Frank's chewing chin across the table, he set about saying the one new thing that had ever been said at dinner for the past five years of their collective cohabitation.

"The FBI don't want none of this business. It's for the police," he barked with a jerking nod of his head in emphatic punctuation. Then screwing his brow into even greater concentration, he leaned over his plate and whispered in confidence to his dinner mates in a sweep from left to right, "Did you ever notice that no one ever goes into his rooms, but every once in a while, someone comes out? Some stranger you've never seen and never will see again in the neighborhood?"

"Well, they must be zombies, then, I suppose—him being a murderer and all," replied Mrs. Way sarcastically. "Errruhhh!"

"Don't tell me. I'm the only one who lives here on the ground floor here with him. I'm in the parlor most of the day. I see who comes and who goes."

To Jeremiah, the point was incontrovertible. No one knew the ground floor of Mrs. Way's boarding house as he did. With the scrutiny of a detective inspecting the scene of a crime, the mentally housebound amputee spent day after day tracing and retracing the plan and pathways of the floor, which were of typical Victorian design. The front door opened onto a vestibule with the stairs along the left wall leading to the second floor. Immediately to the right was an archway to a parlor. To the left of the parlor, toward the rear of the house was a dining room separated from the parlor by another archway. Behind a door at the right of the staircase was the kitchen, which was also separated from the dining room by a swinging door. Most of the boarders resided on the second floor—with the exception of Jeremiah, who occupied only one small room, formerly a large walk-in pantry on the right side of the house next to the kitchen, and the Professor, who occupied the entire left side of the first floor with a door immediately at the bottom of the stairs and opposite the archways of the parlor and dining room. But through that door, Jeremiah had never passed, however much he might have imagined doing so as he studied it day after day.

It was out of this door exactly at that moment that Professor Hudibras exploded and bolted across the vestibule and parlor into his always-empty seat at the dining room table.

The startling speed of his arrival was an odd effect for a person of his physically sluggish type. He was a small egg-shaped man of an indeterminate middle age. His hair was thinning not only on his head but his facial cheeks as well, which puffed out like a poorly bearded blowfish's when he spoke. Even his large and ham-like hands seemed ill suited to motion of any kind, yet jutting them out awkwardly from the arms of his wrinkled white lab coat, he grabbed onto the edge of the tabletop with the snapping efficiency of a lobster and pulled his chair up to the table to announce with breathless urgency that a guest of his would be arriving momentarily.

The table fell into a stunned silence until Mrs. Way managed to recover her hostess wits.

"Errrruhhh…" she growled quizzically. "A guest?"

"Yes. A young gentleman. And one of considerable appetite. Might you have an extra chop—or two—to spare?" he asked anxiously.

"Why, errruhhh…I suppose he can have the rest of mine," said the taken-aback landlady with the confused blend of sarcasm and odd but authentic congeniality she reserved only for the Professor in their individual dealings, which really comprised just monthly exchanges of rent and receipt but somehow in her mind amounted to something more, something doting.

The response to her offer came immediately, but from a different quarter of the room.

"Oh, boy—lamb chops! Where do I sit?!"

In one simultaneous glance, all of the diners looked up to see a just barely prepubescent blonde tousle-headed cherub-faced boy dressed in denim blue jeans, red-and-white tattersall shirt, and black-and-white sneakers. He could have been any older brother's pest of a younger brother—all eagerness and no restraint.

Filled with maternal impulses at the sight, Miss Dawson was the first to recover her speech and invite the boy to occupy the space next to her—which he did almost simultaneously to forking up the lone lamb chop from the serving plate at the table's center, as the Professor looked on in apparent amazement. As the boy cut and chewed with eyes as big as an empty stomach, Miss Dawson gazed at him admiringly. Although she adored children, she had never married nor borne any offspring herself, not for lack of suitors, but because she never found one "suitable" and instead chose to devote her life to the children of her classroom.

The other diners looked at Willoughby in a different kind of stupefaction—with the exception of Jeremiah, who thrilled visibly with what he considered plain vindication of his theoretical fears. Looking at the bus driver with his left eye and closing his right eye as a signal, he addressed a question to the boy.

"Welcome, boy. Visiting your uncle, are you?"

Interrupting his chewing with the suddenness of spiritual insight, the boy responded gleefully, "Naw. But I was one once! Hey, you got any lemonade? Kids love lemonade, ya know."

"Perhaps I should explain," interjected the Professor, rising from his seat and pocketing his ham hands into his lab coat. "This young man is no relation of mine. He is from a place much farther away than anywhere my family dwell. His name is…" and then he paused to ponder the boy's aspect for a second before finishing his identification. "His name is…Willoughby."

Looking up at the Professor, the boy shrugged with agreeable indifference and returned his attention to his chop.

"Willoughby, is it?" responded Mrs. Way with a discernable note of fretful skepticism. "I see."

"That's a Russian name, isn't it?" challenged Frank.

"Well, it's *some*body's name," corrected Jeremiah.

"It's a perfectly nice name, Willoughby," interjected Miss Dawson protectively. "And you seem like a perfectly nice—and hungry—boy! Mrs. Way, don't you have another helping for him? He seems famished!"

"Yeah! I want some more chops!"

"Shouldn't you be leaving now, Willoughby?" inquired the Professor in a fatherly tone. "It's getting rather late."

"Aw, that's okay. I can stay here forever! I got permission. We can play a game! A parlor game! You guys know 'Go and Get It?'"

"Master Willoughby, please. We are not children," pleaded Professor Hudibras. "And dinnertime, I believe, is over. Isn't it, Mrs. Way?"

"I think it's safe to say the kitchen is closed, but the parlor is certainly open. I'd be curious to see what sort of parlor games your young friend likes to play. Why don't you teach us the rules, now, 'Master' Willoughby? And please go slow for the benefit of Frank and Jeremiah here. They're not very good students, as I'm sure Miss Dawson can testify. Errruhhh."

The two men glowered back at Mrs. Way with resentment similar to that which they expressed each Saturday night—TV night at the boarding house—when their request for *Gorgeous George* was always vetoed by the landlady's insistence on *Sid Caesar*.

Willoughby simply ignored their dispositions and excitedly explained, "Well, basically, you each take a turn thinking up something for me to go and get for you from the future! And then I go get it! Of course, the advanced version of the game gets really complicated, but we can stick with the beginner's version until you guys get the hang of things."

"The future, eh?" responded the bus driver with a mocking sneer. "Hear that, Jeremiah? He goes and gets stuff from the future."

"You'd have to have a future to get something from it," the crippled soldier scowled.

"Now that's enough of your sourness, both of you. I think Willoughby's game sounds like a lot of fun, and I think we all ought to play it with him. Don't you, boys?" the schoolmarm challenged as she frowned with teacherly intimidation.

"Please, Miss Dawson. The future is not a game," pleaded a now sweating Professor.

"Sure it is! You'll see. How about you, lady? What do you want me to get?" Willoughby asked, pointing to Mrs. Way.

"Errrruhhh…All right," she said, taking up his challenge with perverse delight. "Go get the man of my future—my soul mate."

"Right. I'll be right back."

And off the boy went, out through the archway and into the vestibule; up the stairs, down the stairs, and into the kitchen; into the cellar, up from the cellar, and into the bath; into and out of the Professor's rooms; and back into the dining room. Then standing next to the Professor himself, he proudly announced, "Here he is!" Both Mrs. Way and the Professor blushed in embarrassment as the others broke into an uproar of laughter, even the dour Jeremiah, who seemed to leap off his wheelchair with delight at the boy's cleverness.

"Why you rascal!" exclaimed the veteran, sure in his conviction that the boy had no real contact with the future. "That's quite a con you've got! But let's see what you can do with this bit of fetch. Go and get me what the cripples will be using a hundred years from now. And it better not look anything like this wheelbarrow of mine. Got it?"

"Right! I'll be right back."

And off the boy went, out through the archway and into the vestibule; up the stairs, down the stairs, and into the kitchen; into the cellar, up from the cellar, and into the bath; into and out of the Professor's rooms; and back into the dining room, but emerging from the Professor's quarters this time entirely in the air, hovering three feet off the floor in a magnetically levitating personal transportation vehicle of supremely futuristic technology and style as he zipped around the dinner table, over the serving plate at its center, and then positioned himself directly over the veteran's head, laughing in unison with the vehicle's hum. This time, Willoughby was the only one laughing. Amazed, the others simply ogled the spectacle of the floating boy and the nearly traumatized man beneath him who was experiencing a fear of aerial assault he had not felt since the trenches of the Ardennes.

"Willoughby!" scolded the Professor. "You're frightening Jeremiah! He suffers from shell shock! Lower yourself to his level immediately."

The boy complied gleefully, parked the device precisely level with Jeremiah's wheel chair, and jumped out of its cockpit with a flourish as he encouraged the frightened invalid to take the helm himself.

"There ya' go! All yours. And it's a beauty. It'll zig and jump any way you can zag and jive!"

Everyone was dumbfounded. All, that is, but the Professor. Frank and Miss Dawson stepped closer to examine the contraption while the skeptical Mrs. Way remained aloof in her seat and poor Jeremiah turned his head away in fear.

Although it took the utmost of Willoughby's continued prodding and instructions and the eventual supportive emergence of the others' own enthusiasm for the gadget, the veteran managed to overcome his trepidation, transfer himself into the new vessel, and float about the room and soon the entire household: up the stairs and down the stairs, into the rooms and out of the rooms, and back over the dinner table, growing ever more childlike with each sweep of the space about him, much to the delight of Willoughby and the foreboding of the Professor, until he became a positive nuisance to the others, who had to duck as he grew bolder in his motions and began to fear for their safety as well as grow impatient for their own turns at Willoughby's astonishing game.

"That's enough, you old fool!" complained Frank. "Settle down. This ain't an air field." But none of their pleas had any effect. It was only when Jeremiah dizzied himself with a particularly sharp crazy-8 figure that he finally landed and Willoughby regathered his purpose.

"Okay, I'm ready for another one!" announced Willoughby, turning to Frank and Miss Dawson. "Try to make it a hard one, this time, will ya?" But before either one could respond, Professor Hudibras objected with utmost seriousness as he straightened up from crouching under the table.

"That's quite enough, Willoughby! You're a menace! You know very well the chaos you may be creating with all of this shuttling! God knows what you've done to the moments from which you've taken these things. Now you've had your meal, and it's time to leave. I won't allow you to extort me any further. I don't care how you make things appear. You don't belong here!"

"Professor! Your manners!" exclaimed Miss Dawson at the Professor's apparent rudeness, an alarm not at all shared by the others. Jeremiah could only marvel at his hovercraft and think of a flying carpet, while Mrs. Way couldn't help but perk up with worried curiosity at the Professor's enigmatic reference to a more complicated relationship with the boy than she thought was proper for a bachelor residing in her house. Only Frank responded with similar urgency, leaping up from his chair and taking the crouching stance of a professional wrestler to thwart what he perceived of as the Professor's threat to his own chance for a bit of his future.

"Now wait a minute here, Professor. This boy's not going anywhere. I believe it's my turn to play fetch, isn't it, Willoughby my boy?" Then straightening himself and smiling with satisfaction at his own ingenuity of conception and delightedly expectant with a curiosity about both the future and the limits of the boy's magical resourcefulness, he posed the boy his challenge. "Now you're a clever boy, aren't ya? Playing jokes on the lovebirds here and pulling a gadget out of the Professor's closet for the cripple. But what sort of short-order work can you do with the fate of the world? Hmmm? Can you go and get me..." he said before pausing for dramatic effect and then continuing, "the end of the Cold War?"

"Sure!" beamed the boy. And once again, he scampered off through the archway and into the vestibule; up the stairs, down the stairs, and into the kitchen; into the cellar, up from the cellar, and into the bath; into and out of the Professor's rooms; and back into the dining room, this time with a newsboy's sling hanging across his chest from his shoulder to his hip and hawking in classic newsboy fashion as he pulled paper after paper out of his sack and slapped them down in front of Frank's face: "Extra! Extrie! Read all about it! Polish electrician boots out Commies! Extra! Extrie! Iron Curtain opens! Berlin Wall crumbles! Sold as souvenirs! Extra! Extrie! Soviet Union shuts down! Russians elect president! Extra! Extrie!"

As each paper plopped in front of his widening eyes, Frank breathlessly scanned their headlines and dates, barely able to catch the years of one issue before another supplanted it: 1989, 1990, 1991. And then on top of the entire pile, Willoughby slapped down an illuminated tablet about the size of Frank's hand. Upon its face appeared a miniature image of the front page upon which it sat, the last issue of newspaper dealt out to Frank.

"'Course I couldn't carry three whole years," the boy anxiously explained as he resumed his normal speaking voice, "so you can read the rest of the issues electronically on this hand-held. You turn the pages with the stylus on the side. It's real easy to do, but it's a little hard on your eyes. If you want, I can get you microfilm instead."

"Microfilm" was the only thing Frank was able to fully comprehend from the entire exchange. He knew that Russian spies used microfilm to steal secrets, and so despite his general bafflement, he found it reasonable to accept everything Willoughby had just presented as somehow truly evidentiary. Looking open-mouthed in astonishment at the boy, he swallowed to regain his voice and asked, "What kind of prophet are you, kid?"

"I assure you, he is not a prophet," interjected Professor Hudibras. "Nor is he a boy in the usual sense of the term. He is a simple mischief maker who should be returning to his proper place before something goes horribly wrong."

"Now, now, Professor. I don't see what harm our young guest has done," reacted Miss Dawson. Like the others, she could not help but be impressed by Willoughby's feats, and whetting by them to satisfy her own curiosity about the future, she hastened to disarm the Professor's growing hostility. "I think it's fair to say," she continued, "that we are all quite delighted with Master Willoughby's extraordinary game, and I at least would certainly like to continue with another round, as I think everyone else would as well." Glancing about her at the others, she found a nearly solid expression of support from their faces, which joined in looks of defensive reproach aimed at the Professor. The one exception was Mrs. Way, who continued to "errrruhhh" under her breath, furrow her brow, and squint her eyes in suspicious examination of the boy, who stood in his perpetually impish way amidst them with beaming expectation at his next task.

Fearing that any argument would simply fuel further inquiry into the nature of the boy and the circumstances of his arrival, the Professor simply exhaled with resignation and took his seat with folded arms. It was a major feat for him. Retired a few years earlier, he had wielded an iron fist as chairman of the Science and Technology Department at Wilton University and was not used to relinquishing control, especially not to a child.

"Be my guest, Miss. Dawson. Play ahead," he said through a forced smile and clenched teeth.

Rising from her seat as the Professor sat down grumpily in his, Miss Dawson instinctively took on the demeanor of her profession, towering over the other adults, who were all seated now, and the diminutive boy, who alone stood with the school teacher like a favorite pupil singled out of the class for special, almost maternal attention.

"Thank you, Professor," Miss Dawson bothered to reply, acknowledging the man's deference with a nod of her slightly cocked head before straightening her posture and addressing Willoughby with academic propriety.

"Well, Master Willoughby. You are certainly quite a prodigy. I have had several thousand students over these past years of my career, chiefly eighth graders (such as I am guessing you are yourself); many of them very gifted; some dozen or so positively precocious. And I have nurtured them all with every expectation that each and every one would go on into adulthood to achieve the utmost of his or her potential as a knowledgeable thinker and a responsible citizen. Rarely, however, have I had the satisfaction of witnessing their blossoming. They all seem to move away, many first to college or the service, then to the myriad and scattered career opportunities so abundant throughout this modern America of ours."

So dignified seemed her remarks and her bearing that everyone about her, including the Professor, could not help but provide her with their full attention. They had been utterly transformed into good students, and sensing her command of them, she continued with her peroration.

"Then also, even the oldest of my pupils remain still too young for their greatest undertakings and the public report to come with them. Understanding this incontrovertible aspect of time and human development, I had always accepted the deferment of my ultimate satisfaction at their accomplishments and my influence on them to the later chronology of my career. But now..." and she halted with a serene and doting look down directly into the eyes of the beaming and utterly rapt Willoughby, then continued. "Now I find the urge to know the fruits of my labor an insuppressible one." And then with solemn composure, with a deadly seriousness, she commanded the genie-boy before her.

"Bring me, young man, my most successful student ever at the height of his accomplishment."

So enthralled were they all by the sublimity of her address that even Willoughby lost a beat of his impulsive enthusiasm and stood silent for many seconds before coming back to his usual life, as though out of a catatonic seizure, with the disciplined response of a soldier.

"Yes, Ma'am."

And off he went, walking this time backwards out of the room with his eyes still focused upon the woman's head, then breaking off in the vestibule, and instead of speeding up and down the usual steps, turning directly towards the Professor's apartment door and entering it with a most deliberate gravity.

The group he left behind remained motionless, a tableau of enthrallment with all that had come upon them: the simple surprise of the boy, the wonder of his marvelous retrievals, the intensity of their own satisfactions and the longings they revealed. Jeremiah hovering still, Frank agape over the news, Miss Dawson erect in expectancy—and Mrs. Way fixed in staring askance at the Professor, and the Professor abashed, simply abashed. Assembled about their table, here in their home, they found themselves parts of a great unfolding. And they remained as though they had always been so.

Until after longer than before, the boy again opened the door, and staggered in under the burden of a corpse across his shoulders, her legs like an unstrung puppet's, her head like a flower, the back of its skull blasted open and peeled away into petal-like shards, and its pigment the pigment of blood, which colored her dangling arms, his clasping hands, and every step he took across the floor.

The gruesomeness jolted apart the boarders, as they each gasped and grunted and moved back from the center of the boy's approach, like identical poles of magnets, until Willoughby dumped the body face down upon the floor, and the Professor stepped forward in angry reproach. "My God! How could you?! A horror like this! For a game?! And through my rooms?!"

The boy stood unflapped in the gore smeared upon him and responded unapologetically, "It's what she told me to get." Then turning directly to Miss Dawson, he continued, "You told me to get your most successful student ever at the height of his accomplishment. And I got him. Only he ain't a he. He's a she."

The hint of logic in Willoughby's deflection of responsibility was just enough to draw everyone's horrified eyes to Miss Dawson, who desperately responded to their instinctive incrimination of her with a stammering effort to understand and to absolve herself somehow in the grisly business.

"I? How do you mean I? What *I* asked for? *I* asked for a murder? I never asked for this! What do you mean? Why did you do this? Who is this?"

"She's the President," answered Willoughby.

"The President?!" exclaimed Miss Dawson.

"Yeah. The President. Some guy just shot her. I'll bet you're pretty proud, huh?"

"Proud?! I'm horrified! To think I've brought some child of mine to such a violent fate! I don't even want to know who she is. I never want to know who she is! I will not see a slaughtered corpse among my students!!" And then unable to contain her distress any longer with language, she broke into an enormous inarticulate sob and buried her face whimpering into the palms of her hands.

A blanket of speechless compassion settled upon the entire group, with the odd exception of Willoughby, who with an almost perverse impertinence observed, "She was a pretty good president. And an even better one now."

The remark roused the Professor to gallantry, and broke the respectful averting of his eyes away from the woman's discomposure and toward the littered and askew tablecloth, which he saw for the first time was finely embroidered ivory linen; he stepped resolutely forward toward the boy and the corpse at his feet.

"Now that really is enough," he said commandingly. "I cannot permit you to go any further." Then addressing the group, he held himself to account. "I must apologize to you all. I have abused the hospitality of this household and its occupants. Desperate to protect the privacy of my scientific work, which as you now know concerns the navigation of time and space, I surrendered to the threats of this teleportal stowaway from another realm, and in order to avoid his raising an alarm about the propriety of a boy found within my quarters, I humored the boy's seemingly innocent demand to satisfy his hunger and acquaint himself with some inhabitants of this world. But I never expected him to wreak such havoc with you all as he has."

"Errrruhhh," groused Mrs. Way. "You can't expect anything else from a boy in a boarding house. That's why I don't allow them!"

Willoughby giggled with impish pride at her antipathy, as the Professor sought to correct her.

"But he is not really a boy at all, Mrs. Way, however he appears."

"But I was one once!" interrupted Willoughby.

"Please, Willoughby! Haven't you confounded them all enough already?!" reproached the Professor. Then turning in exasperation back to Mrs. Way, he blurted out the incredible truth as the boy stood by growing almost transfigured, almost radiant with it.

"He is a very old—and *deceased*—old man! His youth is assumed, the trappings of a customized afterlife devised by the spiritual technology of a place far, far in the future and far, far from this world—a place he is trying to flee!"

Although such an announcement ought to have estranged its audience with the extraordinary degree of its fantasticality, it settled mystically upon the other three boarders with the rapturous enlightenment of the Paraclete. With magical effect, Miss Dawson ceased her crying and lifted her face in a slowly forming expression of transporting serenity. Frank widened his eyes with the breaking insight of an epiphany. And Jeremiah grinned with the contented recognition of a providential rectification underway. Only Mrs. Way maintained a reserve, the skeptical reserve of her compulsive cockeyed squint and breathless growling. But she was nothing to the others now. They knew only a forthcoming spirit.

Jeremiah was first to the rescue, his war memories making him especially sensitive to the plight of refugees. Engaging the humming flotational mechanisms of his hovercraft, he elevated himself to eye-level with the Professor and said, "You send that boy back and you might as well murder him. Don't you know anything about sacrifice? Ain't you been payin' attention?" Then lowering himself to eye-level with Willoughby, he offered the boy personal asylum. "You can stay with me, kid. I got room for a cot." And then the others joined in with their own support.

"Hey, sure," said Frank. "Stick around, kid. And I'll pick up your board so ya can eat with us. You got good lowdown on the Commies, and we could blow a lotta whistles."

And then Miss Dawson, renewed now fully to the dignity of her professionally erect posture, added promptly, "And I shall enroll you into the eighth-grade forthwith. You have an extraordinary aptitude for history, Master Willoughby, and many lessons await to be learned. I expect you will join my fourth period, the gifted class."

They all seemed like swell ideas to the agreeable Willoughby, who replied simply "Okay" to each of them, to the consternation of the Professor. Frustrated by this spontaneous adoption of a being he himself had considered purely an ontological nuisance and alarmed by the disorder to his science that it threatened, the Professor interjected one dire caution after another in a desperate attempt to neutralize their sympathies. But it was useless. The boy had been virtually apotheosized as the innocent of innocents in their minds. And finally seeing it was so—and beginning to understand from the inscrutable smile of the boy *how* it was so—he ceased all resistance and insisted instead that the boy would share his own quarters, where his impulses could be controlled and talents with time could be constructively employed toward a nobler end than parlor games and the plumbing of his fellow boarders' souls.

"You see," he explained to them all, "I have a plan to cure the world of all its ills." It was the true perfect project to capture a boy's imagination, and Willoughby could not help but boyishly exclaim "Oh, boy!"

"Come, Willoughby. Dinner is done," the Professor instructed. "We have some science to do before retiring. And bring the president along. She must be returned. Your other party favors can stay."

Eager to obey, Willoughby gathered up the corpse and hoisted it back upon his shoulders, then turned with the Professor to retrace their steps out of the dining room, through the parlor, and back through the door from whence they both had emerged so surprisingly for dinner an hour ago. They seemed a son trailing his father to the others.

Except, of course, to Way, who could only think of clearing away the table and cleaning up the bloody mess. And wresting away the other things that Willoughby had gone to get.

———◆———

LUM & ABNER

A Pine Ridge Christmas Carol

by Donnie Pitchford

And now, let's see what's going on down in Pine Ridge. Well, Christmas is but a few days away, and the townsfolk of the little community are engaged in preparation for the event. It is evening, and a crisp breeze is twisting around the houses and trees. The snow has stopped falling, and the smooth, white surface of the winter street of downtown Pine Ridge is being broken by footprints, as a number of warmly bundled citizens travel toward the schoolhouse. Some are singing Christmas carols, others are discussing the events of the day. The children are sliding in the snow and ice, scrambling to fashion snowballs to hurl at each other, while their parents scold them to stop, reminding them of Santa Claus' uncanny ability to see exactly who is being good or bad! A few parents merely pretend not to notice. After all, it is the "season to be jolly," and they were "younguns" themselves once.

Old Doc Miller is discussing the approaching event at the schoolhouse as he walks alongside the Blevins family. "Yes sir," he says, "it's a mighty fine thing these folks are doin' to raise money for our poor folks. Those nine families might nigh lost everything in that flood. Most of 'em didn't have their places insured proper, and now the banks are tryin' to foreclose."

Charlie Redfield overhears Doc, and asks, "Did old Squire Skimp own any o' them mortgages, Doc?"

"No, Charlie, he didn't."

"Well, it's a durn good thang he didn't, Doc. I hear tell ole Squire ain't got the patience them banks is got."

"Well, now, before you jedge Squire too harsh, Charlie, remember he is purty

155

involved in this play tonight. He's givin' a lot of his time to help out."

"Yeah, Doc, you may be right. What is this little thang we're gonna see? Is it a buncha Christmas songs?"

"No, Charlie, it's a play called 'A Christmas Carol.' I hear tell Lum Eddards wrote it from a book by Charles Dickens."

"Figgers. I never knowed Lum to ever write nothin' hisself. Jist like him to copy it outta a book."

The schoolhouse is beautifully decorated in red and green, and Sister Simpson is still on the job, tacking up shiny silver garland, while Will Spencer makes a final inspection of his impressive signs. Lum Edwards enters the small foyer of the schoolhouse, reading the poster Will has just touched up, which rests on a makeshift easel: "The Pine Ridge Players Present, 'A Christmas Carol,' by Charles Dickens, adopted...er, I mean adapted by L. Eddards, playwriter. Tickets two dollars per adult, one dollar per youngun."

"How's that, Lum?" asks Will.

"Grannies, Will," answers a beaming Lum, "that's the outcappinest bunch o' signs you ever did."

A chuckling Abner says, "I doggies, Will, as long as a sign's got 'Lum Eddards' writ on it summers, Lum'll be happy!"

Seated at a rugged old oak table is Cedric Weehunt, wearing his Sunday suit, which threatens to pop its buttons (Cedric's mama wants to wait until she is certain her boy has stopped growing before he buys a new suit). On his lapel is a large badge that reads, "Official Ticket Taker," and by his side is Ed Beckley, whose job is to handle the money.

"Mr. Lum," asks Cedric, "how much money do we hafta raise tonight ta help all them flood folks keep their places?"

"Well, Cedric," says Lum, "added to all the money raised by box lunch sociables and sech, we gotta come up with another 'leven hunnerd dollars to pay up the mortgages and help folks finish re-buildin'."

"I guess that's why this play is so awful ex-pensive fer tickets, huh, Mr. Lum?"

"Yessir, Cedric. But don't fergit, these folks ain't gonna have much of a Christmas. It's up to us more fortunate folks ta give what we kin ta see they have a place ta live an' food ta eat."

"Yes mum. I done donated a jar o' my favorite kinda peanut butter to the food drive fer 'em. It was chunk style."

"You're a good boy, Cedric."

In the small cloakroom, behind the chalkboard in the rear of the schoolhouse, the actors are busily dressing and applying makeup. Mousey Gray is over in a corner, rehearsing his lines as Bob Cratchit, with his wife Gussie (portraying Mrs. Cratchit, of course) providing her usual "destructive" criticism. Little Doody Bates runs frantically back and forth, using the crutch he will hobble on as Tiny Tim as a stick-horse. Brother Riggins, the circuit-rider, is warming up his vibrant vibrato, as he voices the ghostly Jacob Marley. Entering the cramped "backstage" area is Dick Huddleston, leading citizen of Pine Ridge, cutting a fine figure in black suit and tie.

"Well," he chuckles, "how's the star of the show getting along?"

Replying is none other than Squire Skimp, garbed in the costume of Ebenezer Scrooge! "Well, Dick," the Squire exclaims, "it's good to see you! I don't mind admitting I'm just a tad nervous. It's been a few seasons since I trod the old boards, you know!"

"Oh, you'll do just fine, Squire. By jacks, you sure look the part of Scrooge!"

"Abner, what time is it?" Lum asks nervously.

"Lum," Abner says in a bedraggled tone, "it's one minute later than when you asked me before."

"Yeah... Grannies, Cedric, here comes some more folks! Thank goodness...maybe we'll have a full house after all! Howdy, Frank! Miz Barton."

"Lum," reminds Abner, "don't fergit, we're gonna have two shows, so maybe more folks'll come to the late show."

The interior of the school house is buzzing with conversation, interrupted by applause as Miss Emaline Platt walks briskly out to the old upright piano. Gingerly, she sits and begins playing a medley of bright Christmas tunes. Lum's smiling face can be seen through the foyer door. Head usher Grandpappy Spears, thinking someone left the door ajar, attempts to slam it to keep out the "pigeon-toed" cold air. Only the back rows hear Lum's yelp, as he tries to extract his mustache from the closed door. Hearing the commotion, Grandpap opens the door, asking Lum, "Hepya find a seat, mister? Oh, dad blame it, Lum, I thought you was somebody."

Ernest McMillan brings down the "house lights," and flips on the spotlight he has built for this occasion. The familiar figure of Dick Huddleston strides to center stage amid friendly applause. He speaks: "Ladies and gentlemen, allow me to welcome you to the Pine Ridge Players' presentation of 'A Christmas Carol,' written as a play and directed by our good friend, Lum Edwards. The stars are all Pine Ridge folks. The real stars are you fine folks, however. The tickets you bought will buy a brighter Christmas for a number of our good people who are less fortunate than we are. Let us not forget that Christmas is a time of giving gifts, and we are celebrating the receiving of the greatest gift God ever gave His children: our Lord, Jesus Christ. Let us pray..."

As Dick prays, all heads bow. Some tears are shed softly, and menfolk murmur "amen" frequently. How like this little community to unite in such a spirit of love! A deep, resonant "amen" is spoken by Dick, and Miss Emaline's piano ushers in the mood of the play. Squire Skimp enters pompously, playing his role to the hilt. In the opening scene, a trembling Bob (Mousey Gray) Cratchit timidly asks Squire Scrooge for Christmas Day off.

A nervous Lum paces the length of the foyer during the performance, until an exasperated Abner says, "Fer goodness sakes, Lum, why don't you go around behind the schoolhouse and walk the floor in the cloakroom? You're about ta drive us stark ravin' mad crazy!!"

"Abner, I'm jist so narvous! I can't hardly stand ta watch the play! And so much de-pends on it. Iffen these folks don't like it, they'll blab it ta the folks who wanna come to the late show, and..."

"Doggies, Lum, I jist peeked in thar and it 'peers ta be goin' awful good!"

The applause at the end of the first performance is thundering, as a smiling Dick Huddleston assists Abner in locating the trembling playwright Lum Edwards and dragging him to the stage. "Let's hear it for our director!" shouts Dick, "This was all his idea!" Lum is speechless as the crowd jumps to its feet in ovation. The Pine Ridge Players march back onstage to take a final bow, before the patchwork curtain draws shut. Making his way stage right, Lum nearly bumps into Miss Emaline, who drops her prim and proper schoolmarm pose for a moment, embracing Lum and kissing him on the cheek, cooing, "Lum, the play was wonderful!" Blushing, Lum is still unable to speak!

There is only a half hour before the final performance. "Lum," reports Ed Beckley with a sigh, "We brought in four hunnerd and fourteen dollars."

"Grannies! That's purty good!"

"But Lum, we still gotta raise another seven hunnerd or so tonight, or it ain't gonna be enough."

"Ah, don't 'worry, Ed! With the kinda re-ception I got...er, I mean WE got on the first show, they's bound ta be folks comin' in from the county seat, and all over! Why, I bet folks is jist spreadin' the word like wildfire about how great this show is!"

It is growing ever more cold as the folks arrive for the second and final show. As Dick walks into the foyer to help Lum and Abner greet the people, Lum pulls him aside and asks, "Dick, what are we gonna do if we can't git enough folks to come to this show ta raise the rest of the money?"

"Oh, Lum, don' t worry about that now!"

"But, Dick, I'm afeered the banks ain't gonna give us no more time!"

"We'll work it out somehow, Lum. Why, Squire was just saying how he had connections with the banks and might be able to..."

"Grannies, Dick, you know the kind of reputation ole Squire has. I'm afeered we're sunk."

"Now, Lum," says Mousey backstage, "I'm sure everything will work out. This play is so wonderful, it can't help but raise the money. Why, this play is so grand, that it's..."

"Yeah, I know, Mousey, it's jist like a mother to ya, right?"

"Well, no sir, I was gonna say it's better than the movie I saw of 'A Christmas Carol.'"

"Oh…"

"Lum," asks Abner as the second show gets underway, "have you figgered out how much money we're bringin' in this time?"

"Well, Abner, the house ain't near as full this time. I…I jist…" At that moment, a commotion on the front porch of the schoolhouse captures the old fellows' attention. They look up at the front door just in time to see a frazzled Snake Hogan, angrily brushing new-fallen snow from his coat as he enters, followed by his long-suffering wife and two of their youngest children. "Dad blame yer ornery hide, Eddards! You would hafta go puttin' on some consarn play-actin' show on a night like this!"

Lum approaches the snarling town tough guy warily, saying, "N-Now, Snake… uh… W-W-We can't con-trol the weather!"

"Oh, shet yer big fat mouth, ya eediot! Gimme some tickets to this pig-slop play, so this naggin' wife o' mine'll be satisfied!!"

Cedric speaks up with, "Yes mum, Mr. Snake! That thar'll be two dollars fer you and yer womern fer earn of ya, and a dollar fer each o' both of yer two younguns! Both! I think…"

Turning rudely to Cedric, Snake barks, "You big overgrowed goof, I ain't payin' cash fer nothin'! You jes' put that waste-o-money amount on my Jot' Em Down Store account!!!"

"Mum?"

"Now, hold on here, Snake!" Lum says bravely, "You can't git away with this! You fork over the cash, or go on home! This is fer charity, ta help them poor folks who lost their homes!!"

"Why, Eddards, you boney furry-lipped varmint, you can't talk to me like that!!!"

"Oh, yes I can, Snake! Me an' Abner and ever'body else is done had enough of yer bullyin'!! And if you ever talk to Cedric like that ag'in, I'll bust you up good!!!!"

There is fire in Lum's eyes; fire from a good cause. Snake realizes Lum means business, and for once in his life, backs down. "Uh… see here, now, Eddards, thar ain't no need ta act like a coupla scrappin' younguns over this! Okay, here's the money, Cedric!! Dad blame it…"

Onstage, Squire Scrooge is wringing emotion from the audience with his performance. It seems to them that the Squire is truly living the role! He is just now enacting the scene in which Scrooge encounters the third and final spirit, that of Christmas Future. The spirit is silent and ominous, pointing to a grave marker that bears the name "Ebenezer Scrooge." The Squire is clutching dramatically at the spirit's robes, pleading, "I will honor Christmas in my heart, and try to keep it all the year. I will live in the Past, Present, and the Future. The spirits of all three shall strive within me. I will not shut out the lessons that they teach. Oh, tell me I may sponge away the writing on this stone!"

The spirit answers, "Okay." It is Ulysses S. Quincy under those robes, and fortunately, the crowd is so enraptured by Squire Scrooge's moving lines, they are only barely aware that the spirit has blown his part!

The final performance ends with yet another thundering ovation, after which Dick Huddleston calls Lum to the stage to present him with an engraved plaque, showing the appreciation of the community for his efforts. This precious moment seems to persist as a rosy haze in Lum's eyes until Abner shakes his partner by the shoulders: "Lum! Whatza matter with you? The play's been over might nigh thirty minutes! Come out here to the box office and help Cedric count up the money! Ed Beckley had ta go back to the drug store to git some stuff for Doc Miller ta doctor Grandmaw Masters' flu!"

"Huh? Oh, yeah…sorry, Abner…"

"Weellll, gentlemen, gentlemen, gentlemen!" greets an exuberant Squire Skimp, entering the "box office" foyer of the schoolhouse. "A most enjoyable evening! Yes, indeed, what a thrill it was to perform in front of an audience again!"

"Uh-huh," mumbles a dejected Lum.

"Why, what's the matter, Lum? You should be ecstatic! Just look at that huge box of cash!"

"The actual truth is, Squire, we got a lotta money here, but it ain't enough."

"Oh? Is that so?"

Abner says, "Squire, we only brought in a little over six hunnerd dollars, all tolled. We're close ta five hunnerd dollars short."

"I got fifty-nine cents left, Mr. Abner!" Cedric adds.

"That's nice," Lum reacts softly.

"Well, gentleman," the Squire says with a twinkle, "I wouldn't worry too much. Maybe there'll be a miracle!!" Chuckling merrily, the Squire bids them good night, and saunters out the door.

"Grannies, fellers," says Lum, his voice quivering, "I'm gonna take a walk out in the snow and…think. Abner, you and Cedric guard the money."

"Poor old Lum," Abner says sympathetically. "Cedric, you stay here with the money while I go into the schoolhouse ta use Miss Emaline's phone. Got ta call Lizabeth an' tell her I'm on my way so she can warm me up some cocoa."

"Yes mum."

It's about ten minutes later, as Lum reenters, his handlebar mustache and eyebrows flecked with snow, his nose and cheeks red from the cold. "Cedric," he says, "let's git this money back to the store and git it locked up!"

"Yes mum."

Abner returns: "Doggies, men, I'm sorry that phone call took so long."

Suddenly, Lum's eyes brighten as he looks into the money box. "Oh my good-ness!!!"

"What is it, Lum?" Abner asks.

"Cedric...Abner...did any of y'all notice anybody payin' us in fifty and hunnerd dollar bills?"

"No mum!"

"Why, no!"

"Well, Cedric...Abner...did Ed Beckley swap us any big bills fer small change ta use in his drug store?"

"No mum, Mr. Lum."

Shaking the snow off his face, Lum looks closer into the box, and says, "Men, somehow, we have got us some big bills here! Look!!"

Abner, wiping his glasses, peers into the box. "Well, I do know!"

"Wonderful world!" shouts Cedric. "Boy!!"

"Hold it, fellers," says Lum, "we gotta count ever bitta this money ag'in!!"

"Men," Lum announces, "I can't ex-plain it, but we now have got exactly 'leven hunnerd and fifteen dollars and fifty-nine cents!!"

"Fer the land sakes!" exclaims Abner, "How in the world did that happen?"

"I don't know, Abner, I jist don't know. Nobody coulda came in here and put it in, with y'all here watchin' after it, right, Cedric?"

"Mum?"

"I said, nobody didn't come in here after me and Abner left, did they?"

"Oh, yes mum, Mr. Lum, I seen Mr. Squire come back!"

Both Lum and Abner leap to their feet, and Lum shouts, "What? Squire Skimp? Did he give you any money? What did he do? What did he say?!"

Thinking a few seconds, Cedric recalls, "Mr. Squire came in here right after you fellers walked out, and he said he had ta go back in the cloakroom and git some stuff he fergot."

"Doggies," says Abner, "I was back yonder by Miss Emaline's desk, but I don't re-collect nobody walkin' inta the cloakroom!"

"Think, Cedric," pleads Lum, "did he say anything about this exter five hunnerd dollars in here?"

"No, mum. He jist asked me ta pick up his hat fer him when he drapped it on the floor yonder."

"Yeah?" asks Lum frantically. "What didja do?"

"Well, I reckon I jist bent over thar and got it fer him, I reckon. I think."

"I doggies, Lum," Abner says, "are you a-thinkin' what I'm a-thinkin'??"

"I shore am, Abner...I shore am!"

"Mum? What do y'all mean, Mr. Lum?"

"Doncha see, Cedric? Abner means that while you bent over thar ta git Squire Skimp's hat, he musta slipped that five hunnerd dollars inta the money box!"

"Who did, Mr. Lum, you mean Mr. Abner did? Gosh, he must be rich!!"

"Fer goodness sakes, Cedric," says Lum, "I mean that Squire Skimp put that money in the box!"

"Oh," says Cedric. "Well, I'll be doggone."

The trio is silent a few moments while the impact of Squire "Scrooge" Skimp's newfound generosity takes effect. It is Abner who breaks the silence: "Squire Skimp. Doggies. Bless his heart. Ba-less his little heart!!"

"Yes sir," Lum says warmly, "God bless him."

Cedric adds, "Yes mum. God bless us, ever' one!"

FRONTIER GENTLEMAN

One Card Draw

by Michael Giorgio

The first person I met upon leaving the stage in Poker, Wyoming Territory was as dirty and dusty and withered as the town. He was a slight man, maybe five-two and nine or ten stone with his boots on. Bits of breakfast biscuit trapped in his scraggly beard complemented the egg yolk and bacon grease on his tattered vest. "Whatcha want here, mister?" His tone left no doubt that any answer I supplied would be automatically suspect. "Ain't no steady work available 'round these parts right now lessen you wanna shovel out stables. We got more'n enough businesses competin' for what little gold's to be spent, so don't figger on settin' up shop here 'less you're honest. If you're smart, you'll be on your way next time the stage passes through. We ain't had no mail delivery in a month and when the Wells Fargo does finally stop here, we get you instead of the US Mail." He spat a stream of tobacco juice, leaving a dark blotch on the hard-packed road. "Now, tell me, whatcha doin' in Poker? And I ain't plannin' on asking a third time." With his high-pitched voice, his implied threat sounded more ridiculous than intimidating.

"If you are quite through, I'll tell you," I answered, allowing a hint of irritation to settle in my voice. "When the stage pulled in, Poker struck me as an interesting little—"

"Driftin', huh?" His hand moved to the butt of his gun and suddenly it seemed prudent to take him seriously. "We don't take none too kindly to drifters in Poker."

I put my hands up in front of me. "Rest assured, I am hardly a drifter, Mr.—"

"Dilworth. Sheriff Rex Dilworth." For the first time, I noticed the point of a silver badge poking out from under his vest. "And now that you know who I am, why don'tcha tell me who you are. Make everything nice and even like."

163

"Kendall. J.B. Kendall."

He ignored my outstretched hand. "What's your business, Kendall? With that fancy way of talkin' you got, you a salesman? Gambler mebbe?"

"Neither, Sheriff. I'm a reporter for the *London Times*. I—"

Three shots rang out and Sheriff Dilworth lost all interest in me. He took off, running as fast as his short legs and advancing years could manage.

I trotted after him, catching up two buildings away. "It sounded like the shooting occurred at the end of the block."

Dilworth slowed to a walk. "I'm sure it did," he said, scowling. "Over to Juicy Lucy's place, like as not. I'd bet my wife's good corset it's Ace Farrell and Jackson Burke gettin' into another scrape over Lucy's new gal." He took a much-needed breath. "Melody Rose Labeaux is a looker, I'll give'r that much. But this fightin' over her's gotta stop."

"Melody Rose Labeaux? I take it Miss Labeaux is the new girl at Juicy Lucy's."

Dilworth spat again. "You take it correct, Kendall. And she's been a burr under my saddle ever since she showed up here. It ain't entirely her fault, I suppose. Woman can't help her looks none. She's just usin' what the good Lord give'r. But she's got Farrell and Burke wrapped 'round her little finger. Fools act like they ain't never seen a woman a'fore. I'm tellin' ya, I never thought I'd see the day them two'd go all loco over a woman," he concluded when we reached the swinging doors of Juicy Lucy's Saloon. When I stepped inside, the odor of old beer and bad cigars overwhelmed me momentarily and I paused just inside the swinging doors. Luckily, as it turned out, for a bullet whizzed in front of me inches from the end of my nose.

"Oh, now look what you done did," Sheriff Dilworth complained to a burly man who still brandished a smoking revolver in his beefy hand. "You nearly kilt Mr. Kendall there and he ain't done nothin' to you."

"Neither have I, Ace Farrell," came a voice from behind the piano. "And you know it."

"I don't know no such a thing, Jackson Burke. You asked Melody Rose to marry ya even though you know I done already planned to ask her to marry me sometime."

A man with an impressive handlebar moustache poked his head around the side of the piano. "You haven't asked her though, have you? Therefore, she's fair game."

Farrell brought his hand to his holster. "Don't be referrin' to my woman as no game."

"I wouldn't do it, Farrell," the sheriff warned ineffectually as Jackson Burke ducked back to safety.

For a few seconds, no one moved. Farrell's hand was inches from his gun, with Sheriff Dilworth paused to draw if Farrell did. Burke remained out of sight. I stayed in the doorway, afraid that if I moved the spell would be broken and bloodshed would quickly follow.

Suddenly, a shot rang out from above us. Like trained animals heeding the command of their handlers, the men assumed non-hostile positions. Guns remained in holsters and Jackson Burke warily slunk out from his protective barrier. I looked up to see who the man's savior was.

She was a large woman in every direction, her dimensions accented by strategically cut slits in her crushed velvet ensemble. When she spoke, her voice paralleled her appearance-voluminous, seductive, and in total control. "If I told you once, I've told you a thousand times. Take this arguing out of my place. You want to brawl, take it to Culpepper's Saloon." Ace Farrell started to protest, but one withering glare from Lucy Curtis stopped him posthaste.

Juicy Lucy descended the stairs one graceful step at a time. Two steps from the bottom, she stopped, took in both Ace Farrell and Jackson Burke in one glance, and shook her head. "You two are pathetic. Do you realize that? Our town banker and largest ranch owner and here you are with nothing better to do than fight over a wisp of a saloon girl. It's a spectacle; that's what it is. A disgraceful spectacle."

Lucy Curtis moved down the last steps and crossed to the bar. "Excuse me, Bart," she said as she passed the young bartender.

"Bert," he corrected.

"Bert, Bart. Stick around long enough, I'll get it straight."

The bartender smiled and resumed wiping out glasses. Mrs. Curtis sashayed to a bell pull, giving the rope four vigorous yanks. After half a minute, she repeated the procedure, an irritated look on her face.

The second floor door opened and a beautiful woman stepped out. Chestnut hair framed high cheekbones, a small upturned nose, and classical blue eyes. Melody Rose. If ever a name fit a woman, she was definitely that woman. One look and it was clear how two lifelong bachelors could become smitten. If I were destined to stay in Poker, there very easily would have been three swains vying for her attentions.

The lady smiled at her two suitors, then turned toward her employer. "You summoned me, Mrs. Curtis?"

"I did. Your gentlemen friends have been fighting again—"

"Oh dear." Miss Labeaux brought her hand to her face, an exaggerated, calculated motion. "What do you suggest I do?"

If the men were interested bystanders, they would have seen this for the preconceived plot it obviously was. Lucy Curtis' reply confirmed my hypothesis. "As we've discussed, the time has come for a resolution. Gentlemen, step over to my table, please. Melody Rose, Sheriff Dilworth, please join us."

I surreptitiously moved to the bar so I could follow the unfolding drama. Once everyone was seated, Lucy signaled Bert. The bartender immediately began pouring drinks.

"Gentlemen," Mrs. Curtis started, "the time has come to stop this foolishness once and for all. Before Melody Rose's arrival, you two never caused any problems in here."

"Mrs. Curtis—"

"Now, now, Melody Rose, no one's blaming you. After all, I don't hire unattractive ladies. I leave the homely ones for Culpepper's."

Sheriff Dilworth shifted slightly. "I met my wife at Culpepper's," he said to no one in particular.

Lucy Curtis flashed a small smile at the sheriff before returning her attention to Farrell and Burke. "The two of you are financially comfortable enough to give Melody Rose a very nice life. She tells me that she loves you both and can't choose between you. Well, I have a solution, if the two of you are willing to abide by it."

The bartender brought a tray of drinks to the table. Melody Rose's "thank you, Bertram," was the only acknowledgment of his efforts. I couldn't help but think that the bartender and the saloon girl would have made a handsome couple. It was clear, however, that she had her sights set on more than a hired man. Judging by the curt nod he gave her in reply, Bert knew it too.

Mrs. Curtis sipped her cordial. "My idea is this. You each put up five thousand dollars—"

"Five thousand?" Jackson Burke spat. "For what?"

"For a dowry," Juicy Lucy answered. "A proper young lady has to have a dowry." Miss Labeaux blushed slightly. "The winner gets his five thousand back, five thousand more, and Melody Rose's hand in marriage. The loser gets the privilege of being best man at the ceremony, just to prove there's no hard feelings."

"No hard feelings except in the pocketbook," Burke grumbled.

"Well, if you're so sure you're going to lose Melody Rose to Mr. Farrell, we could just call the contest off," Mrs. Curtis cooed.

The banker shook his head in quick denial. "It's not that. It's just that…well…five thousand dollars is a lot of money to gamble when it's not clear what the bet is."

"It's not a wager. It's a contest. Each of you spends one evening courting and proposing to the lovely Melody Rose, properly chaperoned of course. Afterward, Melody Rose decides whose proposal to accept. Plain and simple." She sounded like she was giving instructions at a quilting bee rather than arranging a marriage.

"Sounds easy enough," Farrell said. "When do we get started?"

"Tomorrow. After you bring the money, of course. Mr. Farrell will have tomorrow evening, Mr. Burke the next."

"That ain't fair," the rancher complained. "He gets an extra day."

Lucy Curtis rolled her eyes. "Reverse it then. That is, unless Mr. Burke has any objections."

"None whatsoever."

"Good. Now, Bart will hold the money. There's a strongbox under the bar."

"Who's going to be this chaperone? You?"

Lucy shook her head. "Not a chance. I thought the sheriff could do it."

Rex Dilworth nearly toppled out of his chair. "Me?" he sputtered. "I…can't. I gotta be on duty tomorrow. But I know a fella that can. My new friend Mr. Kendall." He shot me an apologetic look. "He's a newspaper fella all the way from London. This oughta be right up his alley, bein' British and proper and all hisself."

Mrs. Curtis looked at me. "What do you say, Mr. Crandall? Are you game?"

I joined the quintet at the table. "Kendall. J.B. Kendall. And I'd be delighted." The sheriff and Mrs. Curtis looked relieved. "The stage won't be back for a few days yet anyway."

"Then everything's set. Melody Rose, you go on upstairs and prepare for the night's trade. Gentlemen, shake on the bet and get out of here. I'd like to enjoy one evening without your bickering."

Everyone quickly scattered, leaving me alone with Juicy Lucy Curtis. "Tell me, Mr. Kendall, what brings a British newspaper reporter to a nothing hole like Poker, Wyoming? And please don't say Wells Fargo. I've heard that one a thousand times and it's never been funny."

"Then I'll refrain from the obvious joke. My newspaper gives me free reign to travel the American west and send back colorful stories of the people settling this territory."

"And you're going to write about this marriage farce?"

"I might."

"Well, if you do, make sure they spell my name right." Mrs. Curtis laughed. "That's if you decide I'm important enough to merit mention."

"Important enough? This whole proposal contest was your idea."

"Not entirely. Melody Rose came up with the idea. I just helped her refine it. After all, with my experience, I'm smart enough to know she's at the best time of life to latch onto a good man and settle down. Before it's too late."

I looked at Mrs. Curtis. Not as Juicy Lucy Curtis, saloon owner, but as the bright-eyed innocent young dreamer she must have once been. She must have seen too much of herself in the beautiful Melody Rose. Maybe in leading Miss Labeaux to respectability, she hoped to validate her own life in some way. As far as I was concerned, she already had.

Promptly at five o'clock the next evening, Miss Labeaux and I started off in Lucy Curtis' buggy. Our destination was the largest home in Poker, the ostentatious house belonging to banker Jackson Burke. My passenger sat primly, her hands folded neatly. My attempts at conversation were met with monosyllabic answers, so I gave up. When we pulled up in front of Burke's house, Melody Rose came to life, flashing a coy smile when her first beau strolled up to meet us. "Good evening, Miss Labeaux," he said as he assisted Melody Rose. "Evening, Kendall," he added as an afterthought.

The Burke front parlor rivaled many London homes. A varied collection of crystal and ceramics dominated every available surface, giving the room a cluttered yet somehow regal appearance. "This is a most impressive display, Mr. Burke," I said.

"It is something to behold," Melody Rose said.

The banker's chest and ample stomach swelled with pride. "I'm glad you like the room, Miss Labeaux. I've collected pieces from around the world, both in my travels and through purchases from other collectors. All in preparation for the day when I would find the perfect lady with which to share them. And now that day has come."

"Oh Mr. Burke, you're going to make me blush." With one dainty finger, she absently traced the intricate pattern of a delicate porcelain figurine. "I don't have many nice things, but those I have will—"

"Yes, well, you'll be able to arrange your trinkets any way you want in your boudoir." Burke turned away. "Caldwell has dinner ready. The dining room is right this way."

Burke led Miss Labeaux and me to a heavy oak table draped with a delicate ivory lace. Two place settings were across from each other at one end of the table. The third was on the opposite end, an elaborate floral centerpiece in between. This, I gathered, was where I was to dine. It was an ingenious arrangement.

The banker pulled out a chair. With a flourish, Burke motioned for Melody Rose to be seated. "Such courtesy," she said as he pushed in her chair. "You're going to spoil me, Mr. Burke. Honestly you are."

"That's my plan," he answered as he settled in. I took my place without invitation. From my seat, I could see Melody Rose gazing across the table at Burke.

I heard a bell tinkle and assumed Burke rang for the meal to be served. "What's for supper?" Melody Rose asked.

"Dinner this evening will be glazed lamb medallions, roasted potatoes, a mixed vegetable medley, and fresh baked bread. Following a fresh fruit cup appetizer, of course." He paused and though I couldn't see him, I knew Burke was flashing his fullest smile. "Normally, Caldwell selects the menu, but I oversaw tonight's preparations personally. After we wed, that will be your job, along with acting as hostess whenever we have company."

Melody Rose's gaze dropped. "I'm afraid I don't know anything about formal affairs."

"You'll learn. Don't worry about that."

"I don't know. I—"

"You'll learn." I wasn't sure if it was a prediction or a command. "Luckily, such things come naturally to the fair sex."

Miss Labeaux smiled weakly and turned her attention to the crystal bowl of fruit in front of her. She picked fitfully at the fruit as Jackson Burke described his banking operation in great detail. It was obvious to me that Melody Rose didn't comprehend everything and that she wasn't particularly interested. The banker, however, was oblivious to her boredom, prattling on and eating his appetizer with equal relish.

When the main course was placed before her, Melody Rose paused, a puzzled look on her face. She looked in my direction and nodded every so slightly toward the table. Glancing down, I saw her gently tapping her gold flatware.

It took a moment, but I determined the source of her quandary. The array of gleaming utensils was staggering and I knew she was uncertain as to which pieces to use. I held up the proper knife and fork and smiled what I hoped was a reassuring smile.

For the remainder of the meal, Burke attempted to impress Melody Rose with stories of his lineage, education, and self-proclaimed 'pioneer spirit.' It was this spirit that led young Jackson Burke to leave Providence with nothing more than several thousand of his father's dollars and the drive to establish a bank of his own.

For her part, Melody Rose nodded in all the right places and appeared sufficiently enthralled with the banker's many boasts. As Caldwell removed the dinner plates, Burke finally offered Melody Rose the opportunity to share her story.

"There's not much to tell really. I was raised on a farm in Illinois, the seventh of thirteen kids. Middle of the pack, you might say. I was bossed around by the older ones and had to cook and clean for the younger ones. When I turned sixteen, I was either going to get out of Illinois or marry a farmer and have a bunch of kids like Mama did. I didn't want that. Coming out west looked like a lot better choice."

"And now you're ready to settle down," Burke said.

Miss Labeaux didn't answer immediately. Before she did, she flashed that man-melting smile of hers. "As much as I can."

"Glad to hear it. After we're married, we'll have several children—"

"But—"

"A little, close-knit family of our own. And I'll have heirs to take over the reins of the bank. Perfect," Burke decided.

Caldwell slipped back in with three helpings of frosting-heavy cake. With only one fork remaining, Miss Labeaux finally knew which utensil to use and dug into the cake at once. She grimaced upon taking a bite and, in a most unladylike manner, spat the entire mouthful onto her plate.

Jackson Burke was on his feet at once. "Miss Labeaux, I am so sorry. You didn't give me a chance to tell you. I had your engagement ring baked into the cake. A sweet surprise for the sweetest woman I know." He rushed to her side and awkwardly got down on one knee. "Will you do me the honor of becoming Mrs. Jackson Burke?"

Melody Rose pushed a finger around in the sodden heap of chocolate, fishing out the diamond. "You'll have to wait, Mr. Burke, until Mr. Farrell's had his chance." After using her napkin to wipe it clean, she slipped the ring into her bag and kissed the banker goodnight.

Ace Farrell's ranch house was, in appearance and location, far removed from Jackson Burke's home. The living room was sparse; the furniture, utilitarian. Still, there was something quite comfortable about the hardwoods and adobe. But it was decidedly a man's home, with no hint of that special feminine influence.

"We're gonna eat out on the back porch tonight, Miss Melody Rose, Mr. Kendall," Ace Farrell said after showing us inside. "It's a mite cooler there and the only cookin' I know how to do is over a fire."

We followed him to the back of the house. "You do all your own cooking, Mr. Farrell?"

"When I don't go into town. I generally eat at the Poker Cafe, or Juicy Lucy's, of course. Once we get hitched, though, you'll be doin' all the cookin' for me and the boys."

"You and the boys?"

"Sure. At least on the nights we men folk don't head into town. On them nights, you'll just have yourself to cook for." Farrell lifted a large slab of beef from the fire, plopping it on a plate and shoving it in front of his intended.

Miss Labeaux pushed her steak around with her fork, stabbing at several burnt spots on the meat. "I don't know how to cook for one, Mr. Farrell, let alone for a group of hungry men who've been working hard all day. I'm accustomed to eating at Mrs. Curtis' myself."

"Heck, then I'll hire us a cook. I been lookin' for another one ever since the boys talked about gettin' up a lynchin' party for old Ed Clark after he overcooked their beans one too many nights. Clark ran outta this place like he had a wolf nippin' at his hind region. We ain't never seen him since." Farrell laughed, thrust a steak at me and turned back to the fire.

Melody Rose set her fork down. "Hiring a cook would be an excellent idea, Mr. Farrell."

He laughed again, a hearty robust man's laugh that made Miss Labeaux flinch. "Guess I ain't much of a chef for such a dainty lady," Farrell said as he joined us at the table. "But I was hopin' to impress you by at least tryin'. Hey," he said suddenly. "I forgot all about givin' you the beans and biscuits I done made. Let me go get 'em." He started to stand.

"That's okay, Mr. Farrell. A girl's got to watch her figure."

"How 'bout you, Kendall? Beans and biscuits?"

I shook my head. "I'm fine, thank you."

Farrell sliced off a large chunk of beef and shoved it in his mouth. "So Kendall," he said around chews, "what does this newspaper of yours pay you to do anyhow?"

Directing an apologetic look at Miss Labeaux, I quickly described how I currently earned my living. My explanation led to more questions, which I answered as curtly as possible without being rude. Unfortunately, the rancher didn't take the hint. He continued to talk to me, ignoring Melody Rose's attempts to enter the conversation.

Only after swallowing his last mouthful did Ace Farrell direct his attention to Miss Labeaux. "Melody Rose, why don'tcha bring these things into the kitchen while me and Kendall sit and have us a smoke. After that, I guess it'll be about time for me to pop the question."

Miss Labeaux was a good sport. She not only cleared the table, but washed the dishes as well. While she worked, Ace Farrell attempted to enthrall me with the facts and figures about his A-Bar-F Ranch. I let him prattle on, not having the heart to tell him I'd seen bigger and better in my travels.

After three-quarters of an hour, Farrell moved the party to his front room. There he led Melody Rose to the chair of honor: a mahogany with the only cushions in the room. He knelt before her and quickly whisked off his hat. "Miss Melody Rose," he began solemnly. "I've been alone for a mite longer than is natural for a normal, healthy man. I gotta have a woman in my life for good and I know from the past few weeks that you are the woman for me." He took a deep breath. "Miss Labeaux, will you do me the honor of marryin' me?"

"Well -"

Farrell held up his large right hand. "Hang on." He patted the pockets of his shirt and jeans. From a front pocket, he extracted a glittering object. "Almost forgot Granny Farrell's ring." He held up the diamond triumphantly. "Well? Will ya?"

Melody Rose smiled at him as she opened her small purse. Taking the ring, she dropped it inside, where it presumably joined Jackson Burke's offering. "Come to Mrs. Curtis' tomorrow afternoon. I'll let you and Mr. Burke know my plans then."

After a buggy ride during which I learned nothing from Miss Labeaux about which suitor was the forerunner, I retired to my room for a fitful night's sleep. The morning passed slowly as I explored Poker in detail. The cafe, a few saloons, the bank, a mercantile, and a livery stable comprised the business district. There was a church and a schoolhouse, but neither looked as prosperous as the street level drinking establishments or the businesses operating above them. No matter which beau Miss Labeaux selected, she'd be one of the wealthiest women in Poker. As I wandered about, I wondered just how impressive a claim to fame that would be.

I arrived at Juicy Lucy's at half-past twelve, thirty minutes before the prearranged time Miss Labeaux's suitors would learn their fates. Not surprisingly, Jackson Burke and Ace Farrell were already there. As on my first visit, the two men were the only patrons in evidence. The bartender, Bert, calmly wiped glasses and pointedly ignored both of them.

The would-be bridegrooms were seated on opposite sides of the saloon, their eyes trained on the second floor landing. I took a seat at the bar. "They're here early, aren't they?"

The bartender rolled his eyes. "Those two have been here all morning. Mrs. Curtis unlocked the doors at nine this morning especially for them." He shook his head and disappeared into a back room.

I turned on my barstool and studied the two contestants. Jackson Burke leaned forward in his chair, poised to spring the moment Melody Rose appeared. In contrast, Ace Farrell sat stock straight. When the door at the top of the stairs opened, both men twitched but held their positions. Their disappointment was audible when Lucy Curtis, and not Melody Rose Labeaux, appeared in the doorway. "Gentlemen, please join me at my table." She descended the stairs and glided to her place.

Burke and Farrell looked at each other for a moment, then returned their attention to the second floor. "Gentlemen. My table. You too, Mr. Kendall."

The subtle shift in Mrs. Curtis' tone propelled the two men to move to her round table at the foot of the stairs. As they relocated, neither man took his eyes from the landing. "You might just as well quit your gawking," she told them. "Melody Rose isn't coming down until she's told to do so."

"Until she's told?" Burke sputtered. "Why?"

"Yeah. What's going on around here?" Farrell chimed in.

"Melody Rose asked me to talk with you. It seems that she's having difficulty choosing between the two of you, though God only knows why she'd even want to try." It was obvious that Mrs. Curtis enjoyed the reaction her jibe caused.

"So what do we do?" Burke asked.

"I'll tell you exactly what we're going to do. We're going to sit at this table until the two of you come up with an acceptable resolution to this problem. As you can see, Burt has already left a bottle and four glasses. By the time the bottle's empty, an answer better be forthcoming or Melody Rose will let both of you go."

Farrell helped himself to a drink. "Seems to me there's no reason that we can't both go on courtin' Miss Melody Rose. She's gotta make a decision eventually. I can wait until she figures out the right choice."

"And when she does select me, will you bow out gracefully?"

"You watch what you're sayin', banker man." Ace Farrell's hand moved to his holster.

"Enough!" Lucy Curtis glared at the rancher until his gun hand was once again on the table.

Half a bottle of whiskey disappeared without a word being said. "I've got an idea," I said at last. "That is, if you're willing to gamble."

"Count me in," Farrell said quickly.

"Me too," Burke said, though his face betrayed his forced enthusiasm.

"Okay, then. My idea's simple. Each of you draws one card from the deck. High card wins the hand of the fair Miss Labeaux."

Burke shook his head. "I'm not gambling on the rest of my life, Kendall. It's ridiculous."

Mrs. Curtis held up the whiskey. "It's getting kind of low, Mr. Burke. I think Kendall's idea is good. His way, you've got a fifty-fifty chance. Otherwise, you lose altogether."

"There's still plenty in that bottle. We'll come up with a better plan."

The saloon owner stood, bottle in hand. She made a show of emptying the contents on the saloon floor. "Whiskey's gone, Mr. Burke. What's it going to be? Mr. Kendall's one card draw or does Mr. Farrell win by default?"

The banker scowled. "You play dirty pool, Lucy. You know that."

Mrs. Curtis smiled wide. "Dirty pool's my best game."

Jackson Burke exhaled heavily. "Get the cards."

Lucy Curtis walked to the nearest gambling table. "Here's a fresh deck. Who draws first?" she asked as she rejoined us.

"Well," I said. "Since Mr. Burke had the first evening, perhaps Mr. Farrell should."

Ace Farrell quickly reached for a card. Mrs. Curtis spread the cards before him.

"Keep it face down," she said once he drew.

"Sight unseen, I'll pay you five thousand dollars for that card," Burke said suddenly. Farrell shook his head. "No deal."

"Ten thousand."

"Nope."

"Fifteen."

The rancher hesitated. "Let me look at it first."

Burke nodded. "Go ahead. Turn it over so we can all see."

His hand trembling slightly, Farrell reached for the card. "Eight of diamonds."

Mrs. Curtis smiled. "Middle of the pack. Six numbers lower, six higher. Fifty-fifty chance versus fifteen thousand dollars, Mr. Farrell."

He shook his head. "I'll risk it. And don't try to raise the stakes, Burke. I don't need the money."

Jackson Burke reached for his card. "Wait," Mrs. Curtis said. "Melody Rose should be here for this." She reached for the bell pull and yanked twice.

Instantly, two sets of eyes looked upward. There was no sign of life from the second floor. Mrs. Curtis tried again, and again there was no answer. "Bart!" she called. "Run upstairs and fetch Melody Rose!"

I looked toward the bar. Bert was not there, but the strongbox was in the middle of the bar. Standing, I went for the box. Not surprisingly, it wasn't locked. "Mrs. Curtis?" I held up the single sheet of paper it contained.

Lucy Curtis rushed to my side, grabbed the paper from my hand and quickly scanned it. "Gentlemen. It seems that all bets are off." Farrell and Burke moved over to the bar. "It's a wanted poster," she told them, holding it up for their inspection.

WANTED
Melody Rose Labeaux
and
Bertram Labeaux
CON ARTISTS!
Reward offered for their arrest!

The small print went on to describe their pattern of crime. Apparently, the twosome traveled throughout Wyoming and the surrounding territories, pitting wealthy gentlemen against each other for the hand of the lovely Melody Rose. Once the men were smitten, a bet was made similar to that made by Burke and Farrell.

Mrs. Curtis stopped reading the details when she realized neither man was listening. As we watched, they shook hands and walked out of the bar together.

"I can't believe they took me in," Lucy Curtis complained. "As long as I've been in this business, I've always been able to spot con artists. But those two fooled me completely. I hope Mr. Farrell and Mr. Burke don't hold it against me. I need their trade." She retreated to her upstairs lair.

All alone in the saloon, I sat and sipped at my drink. Sheriff Dilworth burst into the room just as I drained the last of the whiskey. "Hey, Kendall!" he said through puffs of breath. "You seen Lucy, Ace or Burke around? We finally got mail and guess what come for me."

"A wanted poster for Mr. and Mrs. Bertram Labeaux?"

The sheriff looked confused. "How'd you—"

"They're gone, sheriff. You're a little late, but you might still be able to trail them. As for me, I'm going to take your advice and get out of Poker the next time the stage arrives. Who knows? Maybe I'll run into the Labeauxs again sometime in my travels." Before I left Juicy Lucy's, I turned over Jackson Burke's card. Eight of clubs. A tie, with no winner.

———⟫◆⟪———

PAT NOVAK, FOR HIRE

A Poole Of Blood

by Stephen Jansen

That's what the sign outside my office says—"Pat Novak, For Hire." I rent boats and do a few other odd jobs. Whatever it takes to keep a roof over my head, and some joe in the pot. I try not to ask too many questions about some of those "odd jobs"... once I wipe off the filth, the money's just as green as what's in your wallet.

It was a rotten night, a rainy Wednesday, where the damp wind kept shoving against the door like some rude mother-in-law, insisting you open up. I was just settling down next to the Philco, tuning to *I Love A Mystery* when a tall, gorgeous knockout of a dame let herself in.

"Are you...Pat Novak?" she gasped, out of breath.

"That's what the sign outside the office says, right?" I said.

"It also says...you're for hire. Would you like...to make...two hundred dollars... right now?" she panted.

"Only if Jack, Doc, and Reggie don't mind."

"Pardon me?" she breathed.

"Never mind. Sure, I'm interested. Doesn't mean I'm accepting, though. Why don't you take a minute or two and catch your breath before you explain what kind of job you have in mind? Shut the door."

So she shut the door and took a few minutes to catch her breath. I took a few minutes and watched. Kind of a shame when she was done.

"My name is Veronica Poole, Mister Novak."

Her voice was like butter. Hot, melted butter that runs down the side of your hand and into your cuff, but you don't really care, because it feels so nice. She ran her

175

slender fingers through her wet wavy blonde hair, pulling the stray curls away from her face, and continued.

"I want you to know that I don't usually frequent areas like this."

"Of course not," I said.

"This…waterfront is not what I would consider the best place to procure a hired hand."

"And yet here you are."

"Yes, well…" She wiped the front of her dress as she spoke, like somehow the air in my office had got it dirty, and continued. "Sometimes one has no choice. I don't believe that any of my acquaintances would take me up on this offer. And I overheard that you might be of some help."

"Where did you 'overhear' anything about me? You don't look as though you hang out at any of the places that people talk about me." I spat.

"I heard of you in a club called Limberger's on Madison and 45th. There was some older fellow I spoke to, the words spilled out of him just as fast as he poured liquor in. He spoke somewhat flowery, but he couldn't say enough nice things about you… Couldn't seem to get enough to drink, either."

It sounded like my old friend Jocko Madigan. Good old Jocko. He used to be a doctor in his younger days, until he switched from giving shots in the office to getting them at the local saloon. He was a good friend, but he did tend to run on at the mouth…like the Mississippi. And he always did enjoy that 'theatrical' crowd that hung out at Limberger's. I always felt kind of uncomfortable around them. I'm not sure why.

"I hope you at least bought him a drink for the information," I said.

"I had to buy him six."

It was definitely Jocko.

"Let's cut to the chase. What do you have in mind, Miss Poole?"

"I just want you to follow a friend of mine for a few hours and tell me where he goes."

Sounded like a pretty easy two hundred bucks.

"Too easy," I said.

"Pardon me?"

"Nothing. But it'll cost you three hundred clams." I didn't really expect her to accept the amount so quickly.

"That would be fine," she said.

"I'll have to have the two hundred up front."

"Of course."

And she had the two hundred up front. She took two freshly manicured nail-polished fingers and slid them inside the front of her damp silk blouse. They came out with a couple of warm centuries. I'd swear that both Ben Franklins were grinning a bit. Withdrawals at the First National were never as pleasant as this.

"His name is Jack Webster. He'll be at Danny's Diner on Liberty and 23rd in about an hour. You'll know who he is by his wandering eye. Don't let him know you're watching him, though. You'll need to follow him for about two hours, and keep track of where he goes and whom he meets. Then I'll meet with you tomorrow for the details."

"And the other hundred bucks."

"And the other hundred. That's all there is to it. Good night, Mister Novak."

I didn't even have time to say good night back, she shot out of there so fast. I inhaled deeply, trying to get the last hint of her perfume, before it mixed with the stale smoke and mustiness of my office. Very nice.

I wasn't fool enough to believe that this 'job' was going to be as easy as she made it out to be. None of them are. But I was pretty hungry, and had plenty of fresh spending money now. So I shut off the radio, grabbed my hat, and headed toward Liberty and 23rd. I figured that walking there in the rain would probably help me blend in with the other hooch-hounds that were wandering around town looking for a bite around midnight. The more scruffy, the less noticeable. The less noticeable, the better.

Danny's Diner was nowhere near as nice as the name made it sound. Calling it a greasy spoon would be too big of a compliment. Like calling a Bacon-Lettuce-and-Tomato sandwich a three-course meal.

I sat myself down in the corner, where I could watch for this Jack Webster fellow to come in the door. A few other people were in the place. Some were resentfully finishing their gruel, some had evidently forgotten that they had ordered any food, and were taking little drunken catnaps over their cold meals. A burly guy with a stubbled bald head, a couple of armsful of tattoos, and a food-stained apron came over to my table.

"What can I getcha, Mac?"

"How about a menu? Or don't you have any menus in this place?" I asked.

He snorted, "Right up there, Mac, above the counter. Everything we got is up on the chalkboard."

The 'Special' of the day was looking pretty good, until I noticed much of it sticking to the front of baldy's apron. My appetite left me for someone else.

"I'll just start with coffee," I said.

"Comin' right up."

"I'm sure it will."

The coffee wasn't as bad as you might think. It was worse. But it was hot, which I figured would kill anything in it that I didn't want to think about.

About ten minutes later, Jack Webster came in. I could tell it was him, because when he sat down at the counter and looked up at the blackboard menu, he looked at the empty seat next to him at the same time. Plus, when baldy came over to take his order, he couldn't tell which eye to look at, which one to talk to. He got so flustered and embarrassed, pretending not to notice, that he spilled a whole shaker of salt all over the counter.

As baldy scuttled off to the kitchen to cook his order, I watched Mister Webster carefully. He fiddled with his fingernails a bit, using the butter knife from inside his paper napkin to pick at them. Then he looked at his watch, and glanced nervously outside, staring intently down the street as if he expected something to appear out of the rain. But nothing did.

Baldy returned with a plate of steak and eggs. I wasn't sure, but it looked to me as though the steak was shoe-shaped. A size nine "Redwing" T-bone, medium-rare, if you please. I wouldn't have eaten it even if he had cut it with a different knife. He slathered the food with catsup and began to shovel it in.

He must have been keeping one goofy eye on the street, because all of a sudden, he jumped up, tossed some money on the counter, and leapt to the door. Once he was outside, he gazed down the intersection, staring down both streets at the same time. Then he hurried down 23rd like there was no tomorrow.

I left two bits on the table, and tried to hurry out without looking like I was hurrying. I caught a glimpse of Webster almost two blocks away. I'd have to hustle to catch up, the man was fast on his feet, even in the rain.

I splashed down the two blocks like a duck on fire, but I'd lost sight of him. I stopped and listened. I could hear his harried footsteps in a nearby alley. I sat tight and kept listening. I was close enough now, that I couldn't possibly lose him.

When I heard three or four other pairs of footsteps come out of nowhere and meet up with Webster's in that alley, I figured I might as well take a closer look. Now, some people pay good money to watch a knock-down drag-out fight. I got a front row ticket to this one for free. Webster held his own for about a minute, until two of the mugs got hold of his arms, and pinned him like a dried butterfly so the other two could get in their punches good and solid. The sound of knuckles pounding flesh blended in strangely with the rain and the city noises.

Webster got knocked out soon after his front teeth did, but the four toughs kept it up. They were really giving him the Broderick. I thought for a second that I might jump in and try to stop them, but I wised up quick - these guys looked like professionals. An amateur like me would be no use to anybody. So I kept back, out of their sight until they were done.

It must be a lot of effort, working someone over so thoroughly. The four men just let Webster drop to the ground when they got tired, took out their handkerchiefs and wiped the blood off their hands, and shuffled on down the alleyway.

When I was sure that they were gone, I moved closer to Webster. He was laying in a pool of blood. His face looked a lot like the rare steak and eggs with catsup that he'd had for his last meal. And when I say "last meal..." well, you know just what I mean. There wasn't anything that anybody could do for him, now. He was dead.

I wondered why they'd done this to him. That wandering eye of his couldn't have been the only reason. I thought of that Edgar Allen Poe story they made us read in middle school: "The Telltale Heart." There was an old man in that story whose queer eye had made his houseguest go nuts and murder him. Cut him into pieces and buried him under the floorboards. I couldn't remember if that story was actually true or not. It looked true enough right here in front of me, though.

I gritted my teeth and got a little closer to him. Maybe I could get some answers from his personal belongings. The four thugs were certainly gentlemen: they left his wallet and watch. Other than his comb, I didn't find anything else. So I started through the wallet. The usual fare. Some receipts, his driver's license, lodge card, some cheesecake poses clipped from *Titter* or some other men's magazine, and a photograph of a dog: "Grover, 1938." No snaps of any girlfriends here. That wandering eye probably kept them away in droves. Kind of a shame that—

"Hey," someone said.

I looked up in time to see a blur attached to a huge goon's arm. I stared in mute fascination as the blur became bigger, a big blurry fist, moving toward my face so fast, it looked slow. I could almost count the hairs on the knuckles of this mug's paw, but I still wasn't able to move out of the way. Kind of funny, the way that works.

Sock. Right in my eye. Then the garbage-filled street flew up and hit me hard, on the chin. I got that familiar metallic-salty sort of flavor in my nostrils and throat after I finished collapsing. Never really did like the taste of a fight. Well, the taste of losing a fight, anyway.

I felt a tug on my lapels.

"Come on, youse. Get up. I didn't hit ya that hard."

I struggled to my feet, kinda tipped against the slimy wall of the alley. The guy sure wasn't helping: he kept hold of my lapels, and kept shoving me around so I couldn't really keep my balance.

"Why you foolin' around with this guy here?" he asked.

"I dunno. I just saw him layin' there…" I played stupid. With the way my head was reeling, I didn't have to do that much acting. Then he called for his pals.

"Hey, youse guys! Get back over here! I told ya I thought I hoid somethin'!"

Great. It was one of the four thugs. I tried to pull away. I knew that these four were capable of murder. I really tried to pull away. But my arms were old rubber bands, and my legs were yesterday's mashed potatoes, and that doesn't add up to too much of a struggle in anyone's book.

I just hoped that they were still tired from Webster's beating. They weren't too tired to make some wisecracks, though. I kept my mouth shut as they all hammed it up.

"Look, he was going though his wallet."

"You were rollin' this guy?!? What kinda lowlife are you?"

"Yeah…dis town just ain't safe fer anybody, anymore."

"Gimme that wallet…I'll make sure that it gets to the…authorities."

"I think that maybe this fella needs to be taught a lesson, don't you guys?"

"Yeah."

"Sure."

In some parts of the city, it rained cats and dogs. In this cramped, filthy alleyway, it rained fists and feet. All over me.

When I came to, I saw a pair of shoes right next to my face, and flinched, expecting to be kicked again.

"Don't worry, Novak, I'm not going to kick you. Besides, it doesn't look like there's anything left to kick out of you."

It was Police Inspector Hellman.

"You're right," I mumbled, cautiously rubbing my jaw to see just how bad off I was. "There's not much left."

"Enough to take downtown, though!" he bellowed right in my swollen face. "Here you are, once again, found unconscious right next to a murder victim."

"You need to get to work finding the four guys that did it. Plus, they probably ended the promising career of some genius optometrist."

"Don't act so smart, Novak."

It seemed as if Hellman had always been on my case. Well, ever since I decided not to marry his sister, anyway. Okay, she decided not to marry me, after she noticed some lipstick showing up in places that her lips had never been. So I probably deserved some gaff from her. But her brother, the Inspector, just hasn't let up on me yet. And it's been almost four years now. Jerk.

"Come on, Hellman… What do you think—I killed this fella I never met before, then worked myself over?!? Or maybe I just finished a really rough game of football and took a quick nap? It just happened to be next to this dead guy, but I was so tired I didn't notice him. Yeah, that's probably it."

"Keep mouthing off, Novak. It's sure to get you places. I guess you don't realize that this is number twenty-eight?"

"Number twenty-eight. What's that supposed to mean?"

"It means that this has happened to you twenty-seven times before!"

"You're full of beans," I said. But I started to realize that maybe Hellman wasn't out to get me—I did end up in some tight spots like this pretty often. This wasn't really number twenty eight… Well, I didn't think it was really that high already.

"But 'who's counting,' right? Well, I am," Hellman hissed. He could pitch a mighty menacing whisper when he wanted to.

"Oh, get over yourself, Hellman. You know I didn't have anything to do with this guy's death."

"Then how 'bout you start spilling about how you just happened to be right in the vicinity? And don't you dare say 'beginner's luck,' because I know that you're an old hand at this 'eyewitness to murder' bit."

"All right, relax. About ten or eleven o'clock last night, this knockout skirt came in to my office, and hired me to keep tabs on a friend of hers."

"This zotzed guy here?"

"Yeah. Name's Jack Webster. At least that's what she told me. I think his driver's license had the same name, too."

"No wallet there for us to ID him," Hellman said.

"The four horsemen took it."

"Horsemen?!?"

"The four toughs that beat Webster to death! Cheez! How'd you ever make it to Inspector?!?" I exclaimed.

"The last one died mysteriously, and I was next in line. Go on."

"Yeah, well, I started watching him over at Danny's Diner—at Liberty and 23rd."

"I know the place. I hadda drop the Health Inspector off there the other day."

"Good. That joint oughtta be closed down."

"Nah. He likes their chili."

I could see that it was gonna be a long night.

I had to go over the details of the entire night several times, until Hellman understood what I was saying, marked down what bits he thought were important, and believed most of what I was telling him. After about two hours, he let me go home, including his usual:

"Don't leave town, Novak."

"Right."

"I'll be keeping an eye on you."

"Right."

"And be sure to check in with me if that dame does show up for the 'details' about her friend Webster."

"Right."

"Remember, I'm watching you."

"Right."

Yeah, right.

I didn't really feel like going home yet. I wasn't tired, since I was forced to take that nap in the alley, so I decided to drop by Limberger's for a nightcap. I shuffled along the empty streets feeling a pain in my side with each breath, a twinge in my knee with each step. A drink or three would be just the thing.

Coming up the last couple of blocks to the nightclub, I just happened to put my hand in my jacket pocket. My fingers touched something cold and metallic. I pulled it out, and there it was… Webster's watch!

I hadn't even remembered about it to tell Hellman. The four thugs must have missed it when they took his wallet and stuff. Or maybe I had the forethought to hide it right away when I heard the first guy's voice:

"Hey."

"Huh? Wha—what?" I flinched.

"Are you going inside, or am I holding this door for nothing?"

"Oh. Yeah. Thanks."

I was already at Limberger's.

I stuffed the watch back into my pocket, and wandered up to the bar, sticking out a fin to draw the bartender over. Then I heard a familiar voice:

"Patsy! My dear boy, are you all right? You look like you took an hour-long fall down an 'up' escalator." Good old Jocko.

"Hello, Jocko. I might look pretty bad, but I'll live," I sighed.

"What are you doing in here? I thought that you preferred the seedier types of establishments to these upper crust ones."

"There's plenty of seeds in this crust. Anyway, it's all the same stuff in the glasses, right? Bartender, get me a scotch. A double. On the double."

"Patsy, I think you've got the right idea, but the wrong drink. Why not try something a little different? How about a Pink Lady?"

"Does a Pink Lady have more of a kick than a double scotch?!?" I snapped.

"No, but it would make a more—"

"Then shut up, Jocko! I've got more on my mind than trying drinks with stupid names, or blending in, or making new friends. I just about got killed tonight, and I need to get a little hammered—the quicker, the faster."

"The quicker, the better."

"That's what I said."

"You know, Patsy, you've got quite the attitude," Jocko began on his typical tirade. "A person in your shoes, falling into as much trouble as you do, it seems should be able to take a few extra chances, be a little more adventurous. Just because a drink has an unusual name, and might take a few more to get one just as drunk as the common variety swill that you're used to gulping down, doesn't mean that it's bad. It could end up being very good. 'Variety is the spice of life,' I believe the saying is. And what a wonderful saying. It works for food, for drink, for all of life's marvelous experiences! And yet you still continue to follow the same path, the same continuous circle, the same hideously drab rut, getting deeper and further entrenched every day—never improving yourself, forever falling upon the same problems that have always plagued you. And it's all due to your intolerance of change. You, Patsy, are a creature of habit. And the shame of it is, it's a dirty, filthy habit that you seem absolutely unwilling to change."

I angrily gulped down the last of my 'common variety swill,' and wiped my fat lip with my torn sleeve.

"Are you finished, Jocko?"

"Yes, I believe that I am."

"Good." I dug into my jacket pocket. "You still pals with that pawn shop fella? The one that had contacts all over the city?"

"Benny? Benny the Bookworm? Why, yes, of course. He and I still talk every now and then. Quite an amiable association."

"Great." I handed Jocko the watch. "See what he can dig up about this."

"My, quite an elegant watch," he said, fondling it gently.

"That's what I thought. A little too elegant to be attached to the owner's arm."

"Won't the owner miss it?" Jocko asked.

"Not at all. He's dead."

"I see. I'm sure that as usual, you had nothing to do with his demise?"

"Nothing at all."

"You never do. Any idea who 'Ronnie' is?"

"What do you mean?" I asked.

"There's a faint inscription on the back, here. It says. 'Here's to teamwork, Ronnie,'" Jocko squinted as he read the back of the watch aloud. "Was the owner's name Ronnie?"

"Nope. It was Jack."

"Then maybe the watch was a gift from someone named Ronnie," Jocko theorized.

"Or maybe Jackie-boy lifted it from someone named Ronnie. Just see what you can find out about that watch, okay? Any previous owners, any strange history, anything at all."

"Anything for you, my dear Patsy."

"Thanks a lot, Jocko. I really appreciate it."

"My pleasure."

"All right, I've gotta go saw some wood, Jocko. I'm beat, in more ways than one. G'night."

"Good night, lover!"

Jocko would often shout that out as I left. I never liked it. Some jokers would even look up at me queerly. Sometimes I'd glare back at them hard, and they'd get real interested in their drinks again. I didn't have the strength in me tonight to do any glaring. I just left Limberger's and limped back to my office.

I woke up to a vague silhouette outlined in foul morning sunlight, corrupted from streaming through my filthy office window. The shadowy figure shook me roughly. It spoke in a rough voice, too:

"Come on, wake up, ya bum!"

It was Hellman.

"Aw, come on, ma—I don't feel like going to school today…" I tried to joke.

"Get up. Quit fooling around."

I felt like I'd had the tar beaten out of me. Wait. I did have the tar beaten out of me, just last night. Or rather, a couple of hours ago. No wonder I felt this bad - I hadn't only dreamt it.

"Alright…I'm up. I'm up. You start any coffee?" I asked hopefully.

"Make your own coffee, Novak. I'm not your secretary."

"That's right, Hellman. You'd have to learn how to type to get that position. Besides, you don't have the type of figure that I usually hire."

I started a pot and rinsed out my cup in the sink while Hellman nosed around my office, either looking for 'clues,' or just plain meddling.

"Here's the scoop, Novak."

"Hold on," I said. I lit a cigarette and sat down. "Okay."

"Comfy now?"

"As comfortable as I can be, with your ugly mug stuck right in front of me, first thing in the morning."

"Girl get in touch with you yet?" Hellman ignored my insult.

"Did you find a note from her while you were snooping around out here?"

"No."

"Then I guess I haven't heard from her yet," I said. "I've been out like a light since I got back here."

"Well, I figured I wouldn't just wait around for you to let me know when she contacted you. So I'll just stick around with you until she shows up."

"Okay. That sounds like a lot of fun. I hope my cleaning lady doesn't mind having to vacuum around you and your huge flat feet."

"Can it, Novak. This is a murder investigation, and I'm going to check out every single lead that I can. Of course, you are the biggest lead out of the entire teaspoon-ful, and I don't plan on letting you take it on the lam."

"I don't plan on taking it on the lam."

"Good. Because I don't plan on letting you take it on the—"

"You want a cup of joe or not?" I cut him off sharply.

"Yeah, sure. Why not?"

I started pouring Hellman some coffee into a cup which I didn't bother to rinse out, when I caught a glimpse of Miss Poole on her way down Pier 23, beelining for my office.

"You better decide whether you want to be seen or not," I shot to Hellman in a hushed tone. "Because my gorgeous client is on her way in, right now."

"I'd hide in the closet, here, if I didn't expect a dead body to fall out right on top of me..."

"Then get in. I haven't picked out number twenty-nine yet."

"Funny, Novak. Funny." Hellman wedged himself into the closet, leaving the door open a crack so he could check out whatever happened out here.

She didn't even bother to knock when she got to my door. Just stepped right in, like she felt right at home, and closed the door behind her.

"Mister Novak. How are you this morning?" she asked, very matter-of-fact, with a too-proper, tight-lipped smile. Like some knowing librarian who knows that she knows way more than you'll ever know. You know?

"Not too bad. You?"

"I've been better. I assume that you followed Mister Webster last evening?"

"Sure did. For about an hour or so."

"Well? Did you keep track of the who's and the where's?"

"All in good time, sister. Did you bring that last hundred simolians?"

"Yes, of course." She opened her purse, took out a hundred dollar bill, and handed it to me. "You look disappointed—is something wrong?"

This bill was cool and dry. Coming out of that safe, boring purse Ben sure looked a little disappointed to me.

"Nah. This will buy as much as any other hundred." I folded it in two and shoved it into my front pocket. I figured I might as well start asking some questions, since I already had my money, and plenty of time to listen. "So, you and Mister Webster were friends, Miss Poole?"

"That's right."

"Was he a good type of fellow?"

"Well, yes, I guess so."

"Just how close were you?" I asked.

"I don't see how this concerns you, Mister Novak. I would just like your report from last night. Where did he go, and whom did he see?"

"I don't know exactly why, but I have a nasty feeling in the pit of my stomach that you already know the answer to that question."

"Whatever are you talking about?" she asked indignantly.

"Well, for one thing, when you hired me last night, I was no where near this beaten up. But then, when you waltz in here this morning, not a single word about this fat lip, this shiner, or the blood on my shirt."

"Or the smell. I'm polite, Mister Novak." Polite like a car accident. She continued: "I know that some men enjoy fighting. I simply assumed that you were one of those types of men. And that even though you might revel in it, it doesn't mean you happen to be any good at it."

I pictured Hellman stifling a laugh in the closet. He loved it when dames got mouthy with me. I went on with my hunch.

"And for another thing, I've been talking about Webster in the past tense, and you've been joining right in. Like you already know he's gone 'past tense.'"

"What—what are you telling me, Mister Novak? That Jack is…is…dead?"

"Oh, come on sister! You're not that good of an actress. I'm convinced now. You already know he's dead, don't you?"

"I'm… sure I don't understand what you mean, Mister Novak."

"You obviously know. And it only happened a few hours ago. No time for the papers to print the story, no coppers willing to discuss a fresh murder case…"

"Murder! Jack has been…murdered?!?" She tried her best to look shocked, but like I said, she wasn't that good of an actress.

"Yeah, yeah, he's been murdered! And I think that the only way you could know already, was if you had something to do with it."

She stared down at the floor for a minute, then gazed at me. I'll never forget that look. Kind of a mix of weary hatred and sultry passion all at once. After a pause that seemed to last for nine months, she spoke.

"You're right, Patsy," she said. "You're much brighter than I'd given you credit for."

She slid up close to me, and her heady perfume filled my nostrils.

"You're also much more handsome than I thought at first, last night."

She kissed me. Her lips were smooth, moist rose petals. But I knew I'd have to watch out for thorns.

"Tell me why you had him killed," I whispered hard into her ear.

"The money, Patsy, the money! Where do you think I keep getting these hundred dollar bills? Men in love tend to throw their cash around quite a bit. And that cockeyed dope had a million-dollar life insurance policy on top of all his money."

"I guess that figures. But where do I fit into the picture? Why did you hire me?"

"Frankly, to make sure that the job actually got done. You never know if a hit's actually going to come off, if the mark is a friend of the hit man's. Jack was sort of a lowlife, and had plenty of pals in the crime world. I couldn't be on hand for the actual event—I had to make sure that I was seen quite a bit in several very public places, so no one could place me at the scene."

"So you were having a grand night out on the town, creating your alibi."

"That's right, Patsy. A girl's got to do what's necessary. Now, tell me that Spike and his pals really did do him in." She sidled up close to me.

"Yeah. They did him in all right. He's being fitted for a Chicago overcoat right now. You just need to choose what type of wood," I said through gritted teeth.

"Oh, come on, Patsy. Don't be mad at me. I'll have more than enough money to share, soon enough. You do like money, don't you?" She wiggled against the hundred I had put away. "And you do like me, don't you?"

"Well, I like your face, and your figure, and that expensive perfume… but I don't think I'll be able to afford all of the bus fare to and from the state penitentiary."

"What are you saying? You'd give this up? Are you crazy?"

"People have been telling me I am for years now."

"Then what am I wasting my time for? You're obviously too stupid to know good thing—a great thing—when it comes along! I was so right about you last night. Idiot! What a foolish—"

"Oh, close your head! You're the crazy one. You had a man murdered. You hired me to watch the hit. You think I'd want to spend time with you, a remorseless murderer? You confess right in front of me, and then call me stupid! Sounds to me like you should have been eating more fish when you were growing up."

She glowered, shooting daggers at me with her eyes.

"Fine. You go ahead and try to convince the police that I had anything to do with this. You're the disreputable cuss who gets involved with murders left and right. I'm a fine, upstanding member of high society, who never heard of you, or Jack Webster, or Spike Lupo and his gang. I've made sure that I left no physical evidence of a liaison between Webster and I. It's going to end up being your word against mine. Who do you think they're going to believe?"

I was unsuccessfully trying to come up with some reasons why they'd believe me rather than her, when there was a knock at the door. It was Jocko.

"Patsy, my boy! How are you? It's morning, I hope that you have something to help a body start the day…"

"Yeah. There's coffee right over there, Jocko," I said.

"Don't be silly. How would that possibly help? It could inadvertently sober me up. Where's the bottle now?" He started opening drawers and peeking inside. "You really ought to stop moving it around. You know that I'll find it anyway. Like a bloodhound. An alcohol bloodhound. I thought we were friends, Patsy. Why would you want to hide your liquor from your friends?"

"With friends like you, who needs a sponge?" I said. I reached into the space between the desk and the wall and pulled out the bottle of scotch, and handed it to Jocko. Good old Jocko accepted it happily.

"Who's your beautiful pal, Patsy?" Jocko asked, as he poured himself an eye-opener.

"Miss Poole is no pal of mine. What's up, Jocko?"

"I've got the information on this watch." He set Webster's watch on the desk in front of him. Miss Poole's eyes got as big as saucers, and the color drained from her cheeks. "I didn't have much hope originally, but Bennie actually did remember who picked it up, even though it was about two months ago. He said it was some unbelievably gorgeous blonde. A tall drink of water...probably about this young lady's height." He motioned toward Miss Poole with his glass of scotch. "Benny said she ordered the engraving on the back. Paid for it with a hundred dollar bill, and let him keep the change."

"Benny remembers the good tippers, huh?" I said.

"Benny remembers the prettiest woman he'd ever seen. He told me he still couldn't get her face out of his mind," Jocko said, finishing his drink.

"What was that she had engraved on it? 'Here's to teamwork, Ronnie?'"

"That's right, Patsy." Jocko pulled the cork out of the bottle for another drink.

"Well, Miss Poole, I wonder what that engraving meant? I mean, who could Ronnie be? I just don't know." I turned to Jocko. "Jocko, aren't you going to offer the lady a drink? I think that Veronica here looks like she could really use a stiff one. Veronica looks a little parched. Veronica, can I get you a chair? Veronica, I must admit that I'm getting a little parched calling you by your full name. Do you mind if I call you Ronnie for short?"

"You give me that watch. Spike and his group were supposed to grab all of Webster's belongings, and get rid of them." Veronica lunged toward the desk. "You give me that watch!"

Jocko took a big step backwards, his mouth agape. I wrestled with Ronnie, keeping her away from the watch. She was a wildcat. Kicking and spitting and cussing like nobody's business, I had a hard time holding onto her at all. My injuries from last night didn't help. Neither did Jocko.

"Come on, Jocko! Give me a hand, here...I can't...Look out!"

She made one last-ditch effort to slip out of my grip, and it worked. I just couldn't hold on to her. She leapt past me, and onto the desk where the watch was. A tempest of files, letters, and old bills erupted across the floor. But she didn't jump up and bolt for the door like I figured she would.

She just laid on top of the desk, spread-eagle, not moving at all.

"This doesn't look very good from this angle, Patsy," Jocko said.

I stumbled closer to her, then reached down and turned her over so she was face up. There was a puddle of crimson spreading right over her heart, like a liquid field of poppies, with my letter opener stuck right in the middle. She whispered faintly:

"Now...no one...gets...the money...Or me...Stupid..." She exhaled one last time. Jocko came closer and took a look, held her wrist for a moment.

"She is one with the doornails, now, Patsy. Nothing we can do." He sighed.

I was startled by a voice from behind me.

"I guess this is number twenty-nine, Novak."

Hellman always did show up at the end of all the action.

"Where the heck were you?!? She confessed five minutes ago. Then Jocko comes in with physical evidence and word of a witness. You should have come out earlier!" I exclaimed.

"Did he just come out of the closet?" Jocko asked. Good old Jocko. Always on top of things.

"Just be glad that I'm here now, so you have a credible witness to this accident. So people won't think that you just murdered this dame."

"Well, at least tell me that you heard her confess," I said.

"I heard everything. Her plan was some big trap—I assume that she pretended to be in love with Webster, gave him that nice watch, and probably some other really nice things. Then she got Spike Lupo's gang to off him, getting his cash, and that million dollars of life insurance. We'll check with the insurance company, I expect that her name is on the policy. Yup. Some big trap."

"She should have kept her big trap shut," I said.

"I'll need that watch to enter into evidence, and the name and address of this Bennie fellow, to see if he can identify this woman. I gotta call the morgue, and have them pick up the body." Hellman sounded mighty efficient, now that I had done all of his work for him. He went to the phone and started making his calls.

I looked over at Jocko. He was standing back a bit, his eyes a bit misty. I sometimes forget that he was a doctor, that it was his job to save lives. Miss Poole might have been one more that he could have saved, but it just didn't work out that way. I walked on over to console him a bit.

"Hey, Jocko. There was nothing you could do. It all happened too fast."

"It's tragic, Patsy. Simply tragic," he sobbed.

"Come on, Jocko. Think of it as 'fate.' Really, I don't think that she's worth getting too worked up over…"

"It was just so…unnecessary. If only I were a little quicker, if my reflexes weren't so shabby…I could have saved it…"

Saved it? Then I saw where Jocko was actually looking, with such melancholic agony. Right past Veronica Poole's body, at the bottle of scotch that had tipped over and emptied itself over the floor full of papers. Good old Jocko.

———◦◦◦———

YOURS TRULY, JOHNNY DOLLAR

The Paddy Rose Matter

by Patrick W. Picciarelli

I was on my way out of the door when the phone rang. Reluctantly, I picked it up. "Johnny Dollar."

"Pat McCracken, Johnny. Universal Adjustment Bureau."

"Pat, how're you doing?" I adjusted the shoulder strap on the tackle box I was lugging.

"Not bad, Johnny, not bad. Listen," he said, "I've got a case that needs your immediate attention. There's this— "

"Whoa, Pat. You caught me walking out the door. I'm on my way to catch up on my fishing. It's been—-"

"…Paddy Rose. Ever hear of him, Johnny? Owns a bunch of restaurants in Manhattan."

"Well, no, Pat, I haven't, but I'm catching a plane in an hour for Lake Mojave. Give me break, will you?" Pat went right on jabbering like he hadn't heard a word I said.

"Today's paper, Johnny, you got it?"

"I haven't got the paper, Pat. Fish don't read. I— "

"Page three. This guy Rose holds a $500,000 life insurance policy through Limited Liability and Trust out of New York. He turned up dead last night at the bottom of a steep embankment by the West Side Highway. Up around 103rd Street. He was taking his daily bike ride, made a turn off the embankment." He was quiet for a moment. "Johnny, you there?"

I sighed, put the tackle box down. "Yeah, Pat, I'm here. Murder?"

"Broken neck. Official cause of death is suicide."

I was confused. "So? Insurance doesn't pay off in the event of a suicide."

"The policy's three years old."

"Oh," I said. It's a little-known fact that insurance companies will pay off on a suicide if the policy has been in effect for over two years. "Who's the beneficiary?"

"His wife, Johnny. The former Pie Parker of Nashville, Tennessee. She—"

"Did you say Pie, Pat? What kind of a name is Pie?"

"When you see her you'll see that the name fits. Good enough to eat. She's a knockout, Johnny, and thirty years younger than her husband."

"You think she killed him?"

"Why else would I be calling you? Insurable interest, Johnny, my boy. We prove she bumped him, the insurance company saves themselves a half mil. You interested?"

"My usual expenses?"

"Johnny, you pin this on the wife, you can put your fishing trip on the expense account." I heard him snort. "Hell, you'll probably do that anyway."

"You know me too well, Pat. I'm on my way."

EXPENSE ACCOUNT SUBMITTED BY SPECIAL INVESTIGATOR JOHNNY DOLLAR TO PAT McCRACKEN, UNIVERSAL ADJUSTMENT BUREAU.

The following is a list of expenses incurred during my investigation of the Paddy Rose Matter.

Item #1: $50 deposit on a rental car.

I drove from my Connecticut home, arriving in midtown Manhattan a little after noon.

Item #2: $100 in advance for four days at the Empire Hotel off Columbus Circle.

Next stop: Lieutenant Charlie Walters, first whip of the 24th Precinct's detective squad. It was a nice spring day so I decided to walk the forty blocks uptown to the West Harlem location of the station house.

Item #3: 25¢ for a hot dog with the works and a Coke from a street vendor on Broadway. I'm going easy on you, Pat, I could have eaten at the Copa.

Charlie Walters was a career cop who had seen too much and compensated for it by stuffing his face with free meals from the numerous restaurants which dotted the Upper West Side. Charlie's motto was, "A good cop never gets hungry, thirsty, or wet." Words to live by. I'd known Charlie for years and liked him.

We exchanged pleasantries for a few minutes after he ushered me into his tiny office. I sat on an uncomfortable metal folding chair while he parked himself in an over-stuffed leather throne he'd probably liberated from a bookie's wire room.

"So what brings you to my fair city, Johnny?" His ample girth tortured the buttons on his shirt.

"Didn't know you owned New York, Charlie."

"Cops run this town, Johnny. We just let the politicians think they do. Spill."

"Paddy Rose."

"Yeah, so? Suicide. Drove his bicycle off a mini-cliff in Riverside Park by the West Side Highway. Why would you guys care about a suicide?"

After I explained the two-year clause to him, I asked about the bike.

"This guy Rose was a health nut. Sixty-seven years old and he thought he was thirty. Guess he was trying to keep up with his wife. You oughta see this dame." He gave me a thumbs up.

"I heard. Get to the bike."

"Oh, yeah. Every morning around seven he does a few miles in the park." He tossed me a picture of the crumpled bike, one of those 3-speed English jobs just becoming popular in this country. "You could set your watch by the guy. Anyway, he's tooling up the path next to the highway when he suddenly cuts the wheel sharp to the left and over he goes. About a forty-foot drop. DOA." He threw up his hands. "Case closed."

"The guy was insured for 500k, Charlie. Doesn't that raise a flag?"

"You mean the wife? Sure, of course. But we got us a witness. Saw the whole thing. From the time Rose rounded a curve on 102nd Street until he did the Brody at 103rd Street." He lit a cigarette and offered me one. I shook my head. "Give up?" he asked.

I nodded. "Someday we'll find out that cigarettes can kill you. Just want to beat the devil."

Walters looked at the smoke curling lazily toward the ceiling. "Yeah, sure, and milk is bad for you, too, right?"

I shrugged. "You never know. Was Rose despondent?"

"His wife says he was. Coupla restaurants going under. His only son killed six months ago in Korea. Coulda put him over the edge."

"Anyone else say he was suicidal?"

"We spoke to a bunch of his employees. They said he was quiet, kept pretty much to himself."

"Relatives?" I asked.

Walters shook his head. "Just the wife."

"Soon to be a very rich widow."

"That don't make her a killer, Johnny."

"Sure gives her incentive, though."

Walters scribbled something on a piece of paper and tossed it across the desk to me. "Witness's name and the address where he'll be while in my fair city. He's a visiting college professor from Pennsylvania."

Professor Danton Marrilu. My next stop.

Item #4: $1.00 cab fare with tip to Ambassador Hotel, West End Avenue and 116th Street.

The Ambassador Hotel was favored by higher-education types because of its close proximity to Columbia University. It had seen better days, but I'm sure the rates were better than the Waldorf's. The desk clerk directed me to room 338, third floor, rear. The ancient elevator operator told me that it was one of the last steam-powered elevators in the city. I could have crawled backwards up the stairs quicker.

I was about to knock on the door to room 338 when it swung open. A thin man in his early thirties, balding, wearing a three-piece suit, wire-frame glasses, and holding a briefcase stopped short.

"Yes?"

"Professor Danton Marrilu?"

He gave me the once-over. "Yes."

I handed him my card.

"Johnny Dollar, Special Investigator?" He licked his lips. "Is this about that poor man in the park? The one on the bicycle?"

"Yes, sir. I'm an insurance investigator. The deceased was heavily insured. Just like to ask you a few questions. May I come in?"

"Oh, dear. Well, I was just going out. I'm on my way to the library on 42nd Street. Research on an upcoming paper." He looked over his shoulder into his sparsely-furnished room. "I suppose I can spare a few minutes."

We went inside. I sat on a threadbare sofa while the professor stood by a window.

"What do you teach, Professor?"

"English literature. I'm in town for a few days before I journey to London." He looked in the direction of a hot plate perched next to a rusting sink. "I'd offer you something, Mr. Dollar, but as you can see, this is just a temporary domicile. A place to hang one's hat, so to speak." He smiled thinly.

"I don't want to waste your time, Professor. If you can tell me what you saw that day, I'll be on my way."

"Oh, surely. Of course."

He told me pretty much the same thing Charlie Walters had recounted. He was talking a morning stroll in the park ("I miss the rural quality of Pennsylvania, Mr. Dollar. Riverside Park isn't exactly the Laurel Mountains, but at least it's got trees."). As he neared 103rd Street he spotted the late Paddy Rose cruising down the path at a great rate of speed.

"He was moving quite rapidly, Mr. Dollar. He had a crazed expression on his face, like he was building up courage to do something."

"Uh-huh. Tell me about the exact moment he went over the edge."

"Well, he looked me right in the eye, Mr. Dollar, turned the wheel sharply to the left," Marrilu wrenched his arms sharply, "and disappeared down the hill." He removed a starched handkerchief from his breast pocket and gently mopped his forehead. "Sorry, Mr. Dollar. I'm not used to things like this where I come from."

"Sure, Professor. What did you do then?"

"I looked down the embankment. He...he wasn't moving. It was quite a steep grade. There was really no discernible way I could safely navigate the hill. I ran out of the park and dialed the operator for the police from a phone booth on Broadway. Then I went back to the scene to await their arrival."

"Yes. Very civic-minded of you. I was wondering, Professor, could you give me your address in Pennsylvania...you know, just in case we have to reach you in the future."

"I won't be home for quite a while, sir."

"How long's quite a while?"

"Up to two months, depending on how involved I become with my research project."

"These things," I said, "sometimes take a long time to settle."

"You mean the insurance?"

"I mean the insurance."

"Oh, well, yes, of course." He scribbled his address and phone number on a piece of paper and got up. After handing it to me he said, "Excuse me, Mr. Dollar...I really must be going."

I rose. "Certainly." As I walked past the end table by the bed I noticed a framed picture of two young boys. "Yours?"

He beamed. "My sons, Peter and Max." He held up the picture. "Max is the oldest. Hard to tell them apart, isn't it, Mr. Dollar?"

I held the photograph for a few moments before handing it back. "Indeed it is. Your only two children?"

Marrilu seemed puzzled. "Why, yes. Why?"

"No reason. Just like kids."

Item #5: 10¢ for a phone call to the home of the late Paddy Rose.

A woman answered. "Hello." She had the sweetest southern drawl I'd ever heard. It poured from her like fresh maple syrup.

"Mrs. Rose?"

"Correct." It sounded like a three-syllable word the way she said it.

I told her who I was and why I needed to see her.

"Certainly, Mr. Dollar. Are you familiar with Queens?"

I told her that I was and she gave me directions to her house that sounded as if she were reading poetry. "I'll be there in an hour."

"Looking forward to it," she said breathlessly.

She wasn't the only one.

Item #6: $1.50 for a quick lunch with tip at an Irish pub on Amsterdam Avenue.

I picked up the rental car from in front of my hotel and made it to Pie Rose's house—"mansion" was a more apt description, with five minutes to spare.

To say that Paddy Rose's widow was pretty was like calling the Mona Lisa a picture. She was absolutely stunning. Her shoulder-length blond hair was carefully disarranged in what was supposed to look naturally windblown, but which must have taken her a while to put together. It worked for me. I put her at about five-eight, but she appeared even taller due to her lithe frame. She had the creamiest complexion I'd ever seen on a woman, with gleaming white teeth behind red lipstick. She was wearing pleated white pants and a pale blue silk blouse. She was beautiful enough to make a rabbi go to church.

She swung the door wide. "Mr. Dollar? Do come in."

I followed her into a sunken living room. I would have followed her anywhere. She glided onto a sofa and patted the cushion next to her. "Please sit."

I sat.

We stared at each other for a few seconds until she broke the ice. "You had some questions, Mr. Dollar?"

"Oh, yes, questions. Uh, your late husband, Mrs. Rose…"

"Please, Mr. Dollar, call me Pie."

I'd call her Frank if she wanted me to. "Yes, of course. Well…Pie, could you tell me where you were when your husband was…died?"

She let out a throaty laugh; her eyes gleamed. "You get right to the point, Mr. Dollar, don't you?"

"Just doing my job."

"First of all, aren't we talking about a suicide here, Mr. Dollar?"

"That's what I'm paid to find out, ma'am…Pie."

She crossed her legs and settled back into the couch. "Okay, I'll play. I was here, Mr. Dollar. Alone. Paddy went to his Broadway restaurant every morning. That's where he kept the bicycle. He'd ride for a while first thing every day."

"Forgive me for saying this, Pie, but you don't seem very broken up over your husband's death."

She wasn't visibly put off by my remark. "You aren't from the south, are you, Mr. Dollar?"

"Southern part of Bridgeport, Connecticut. That count?"

She smiled. Teeth everywhere. "Not where I come from, sir. I've been taught to contain my emotions in public."

"An old southern tradition?"

"An old Parker tradition. I loved my husband, Mr. Dollar. He was older, but that didn't make him any less a good husband, if you know what I mean."

"Uh, yes, I know what you mean."

She got up and walked to a mahogany bar that took up one side of the room. "Drink, Mr. Dollar?"

"Bourbon would be nice," I said.

She gave me one of those dazzling smiles again. "You must have some southern blood in you." She poured my drink. None for her. She told me that she never drank. Offering me one was just southern hospitality. I made a mental note to move to Tennessee when I retired.

"Let's assume that your husband's death wasn't a suicide," I said, the hundred-proof bourbon coursing through my veins like molten lava. "Do you know anyone who would want your husband dead?"

"You mean other than me?" Another killer smile.

"Yes, Pie, other than you."

"My husband's partner Alvin Karpis stood to gain. They had survivor's insurance. If either one of them died the partner would inherit the business."

"You mean you don't get the restaurants?"

"Correct."

I loved the way she said that word. Okay, she was out of the restaurants, but she still came away with five hundred grand. If that wasn't a motive for murder nothing was.

Pie Rose gave me Karpis' address. We parted at the door with a handshake. Her hand was as soft as her voice. She held onto it as she said, "If my husband was murdered, Mr. Dollar, the killer had better hope you find him before I do." Then her eyes got cold.

"Southern hospitality?"

The smile returned. "Southern justice. Another old family tradition. Good day, Mr. Dollar." She turned on her pretty heels and shut the door. I just stood there for a few seconds. I mentally smoked a cigarette. I needed it.

I visited the scene of the suicide, accident, murder, whatever it was. Riverside Park stretched from 72nd Street several miles uptown. Parts of it were deserted, as was the path where Paddy Rose met his end. The path he rode his bike on was just about wide enough for the bike. Maintaining any significant speed and being able to control the bicycle would have been difficult. Did he swerve to avoid something? I looked down the hill at the exact spot where Paddy took his flyer. A yellow NYPD crime scene tape was stretched between two trees. Quite a fall. Not many would have survived it.

Item #7: $1.85 for a long distance phone call to the Sommerset, Pennsylvania police department where I confirmed that Professor Danton Marrilu did in fact reside in the town and was on an educational sabbatical. He had two sons, named Peter and Max. The professor's physical description fit, too. Hey, you never know. I'm paid to cover all bases. Still, something was nagging me about Marrilu.

Item #8: 25¢ toll for the George Washington Bridge.

Alvin Karpis lived in an upscale neighborhood in Fort Lee, New Jersey. I parked my rental car in a gravel driveway, went to the door of the well-cared-for English Tudor and knocked. There was no answer, but I distinctly heard the metallic sound of a lawnmower in motion coming from the rear of the house. I walked back there through heavily-leafed maple trees.

A well-built man in his thirties, wearing shorts and stripped to the waist, was pushing the mower up a slight grade. I cleared my throat and he turned.

"Can I help you?" He ran a muscled forearm across his brow.

I identified myself. "Like to ask you some questions about your partner's death."

"Well, let's go in the house, then. Give me an excuse to goof off."

We sat in the kitchen, sunlight streaming through spotless windows. He offered me a drink and I settled for ice water.

"Now what can I do for you, Mr. Dollar?"

"We're trying to determine cause of death from Mr. Rose. Thought you might be able to help."

"Cause of death? I thought the police ruled it a suicide."

"They did. We didn't."

"Oh."

I went through the same questions I asked Pie Parker, got basically the same answers. He and Rose had been in business together for ten years.

"Get along?" I asked.

He shrugged. "As well as any partners. He had his life outside the restaurants, I had mine."

I looked around. "Married?"

"Divorced."

"How well do you know Mrs. Rose?" I took a sip of my water but watched his reaction over the rim of the glass. There's other motives for murder besides money.

"Not well, really. She'd come down to our Chambers Street restaurant occasionally." He shrugged. "Other than seeing her there, I couldn't say that I knew her well."

"You own the empire now, is that right?"

His eyes became steely. "And you're implying what, Mr. Dollar?"

"No implications, just asking a question."

He got up. "A question you already know the answer to, Mr. Dollar, I'm sure. I resent this line of questioning. Let's cut to the chase, shall we? I did not kill my partner. This interview is over."

Item #9: $66.00 for an English racing bike similar to the one Paddy Rose was riding when he went over the embankment to his death.

I rode the bike into Central Park, which was located just across the street from my hotel. It was a sunny day, a little warm for spring, but the nice weather had brought throngs of people into the park. I found a fairly unpopulated asphalt roadway and conducted an experiment. After a few bumps and bruises I believed I had my killer.

I waited over three hours for Professor Danton Marrilu to emerge from his hotel. It was a little after 8 p.m. and the sun had just dipped below the New Jersey horizon.

Marrilu had abandoned his school teacher costume for a light windbreaker, chinos and a dirty pair of Keds.

He walked briskly to the Broadway subway station with me a respectable distance behind. Marrilu took the downtown express to Grand Central Station and the #7 train to Roosevelt Avenue in Queens. I could have blindfolded myself after that and knew exactly where he was going: to the home of Pie Rose, grieving widow.

I waited behind a mailbox down the street from the Rose house. It was dark by this time, but I could see the shadowy figure of Marrilu standing at the front door. It opened shortly and Pie Rose stood silhouetted in light imitating from the interior of the house. Even at this distance she looked statuesque and regal. She was wearing the same white skirt without a slip, and the penetrating light gave me a clear view of her legs.

It looked like I had my conspirators. I felt as if the air had been knocked out of me. For the brief time I'd been in her presence, I'd become almost infatuated with Pie Rose. I didn't want her to be involved in the killing of her husband. I drew my Smith & Wesson revolver and sighed. I had my job to do.

I walked down the street with the pistol at my side. Just before I got to the house I slipped down a neighbor's driveway and inched my way along the building line until I was at the side of the Rose house. Pie's new home would be less accommodating.

I crouched and duck-walked to the living room window. The widow and Marrilu were inches apart, the professor's back to me. Pie had a solemn expression on her lovely face. Whacking up five hundred grand can be serious business.

I made my way to the rear of the house and entered through the open kitchen door. I heard muffled voices from the living room. As quietly as I could I pushed the kitchen door open an inch. I was able to see Pie, but Marrilu was obscured. She glanced past him, saw me and her eyes went wide. It was now or never.

I crouched low and barged into the living room. Marrilu whirled, gun in hand. "Freeze!" I hollered.

Marrilu leveled the pistol at me and I fired. Pie Rose screamed. The professor clutched his stomach and went down. I jumped to him and kicked the gun away. While I held my pistol on Pie Rose I felt for a pulse on Danton Marrilu. He was dead.

"Johnny," Pie said, "please put the gun down."

"Not a chance, sweetheart. You're going to jail for the murder of your husband." I holstered my pistol.

Her eyes were pleading. "Johnny, you're wrong."

"Oh, I am, am I? What was Marrilu doing here?"

From behind me I heard a voice say, "He came here to kill her, Dollar."

I turned to see Alvin Karpis emerge from the kitchen. He had a .45 Colt automatic in his hand.

In addition to being scared I was confused. "What?"

"You followed Marrilu, I followed you. Simple. Take your gun out of its holster and drop it on the floor."

I complied. "You and Marrilu?"

"Me and Jim Weimann. Marrilu's dead, Dollar. We lured him here because him and Weimann could pass for brothers. Jim was an unemployed actor with visions of grandeur. For a partnership in the restaurants he took out my partner."

"What about her?" I gestured toward the widow.

"She's a smart broad, Dollar. Couldn't afford to have her around. House robbery gone bad. It woulda worked."

Pie Rose turned to Karpis. "You killed my husband."

Karpis snorted. "He found out I'd been skimming. Threatened to sue me for my end of the business. He had to go." He cocked the hammer on the big automatic. "Now it's your turn."

A shot smashed through the living room window. Karpis' head snapped back and he went down like a week-old soufflé. Pie screamed.

The front door, blown in off its hinges by a sledgehammer, splintered across the living room rug. Charlie Walters marched in like Patton crossing the Rhine.

"What kept you?" I said.

"I came here looking for the dame. I had to get it straight before I acted."

"Hey, Charlie," I said, "another fraction of a second, we would've been DOA."

He rolled his eyes. "Trust me. Never woulda happened."

Pie Rose stared at me. "You set this thing up?"

"Yeah, he set it up," Charlie said, "but he thought you were the killer. In cahoots with this phony professor here." He pointed to corpse number one.

Pie looked at me with the moist, alluring eyes. "Is that true, Johnny?"

"Hey, look," Walters said, "you two work out the particulars, I'm gonna call the meat wagon. Excuse me. Where's the phone?"

Pie directed him to the kitchen.

We stared at each other for at least a minute.

"Okay," I said, "let's get out of this room." We went into the den.

I told her that something was nagging me about the professor. While I was interviewing him in his room he had pointed to one of his children in a picture and described him as being the oldest.

"That told you something?" We were on a thick leather couch, only this time our thighs were touching. I could talk like this all night.

"Pie, the man was supposed to be a professor of English literature. He spoke well, or at least gave the impression that language was important to him. But he said 'oldest.' If you have two kids, one is older, not oldest. Grammar school English. If he had more kids, oldest would have been right. But I asked. He said he only had the two kids. A little mistake, but I filed it.

"Then I experimented with a bike. If you're riding a bike and turn the handlebars sharply to the left, the bike will go in the opposite direction. In other words, it'll go right. The opposite applies if you go the other way."

"That makes little sense."

"Little sense or not, it's true. So the way the professor described the incident had to be false, which means he killed him. Probably broke his neck and staged the accident."

Pie lowered her eyes. "All over the restaurants."

"It's money, Pie."

Charlie Walters came back into the living room. "They're on their way."

I nodded and looked at the door. He took the hint. "Uh, I'll wait outside."

Pie said. "You thought I hired this killer?"

I looked her in the eyes. "Yes. I'm sorry. Forgive me?"

She smiled wanly, but it was a forgiving smile. "Yes, of course."

We talked a while longer, the morgue attendants arrived. I suggested to Pie that she might want to stay at a friend's house for the night. "I'll stay here. Can I call you, Johnny?"

"You certainly can."

"I'm not one to run away from things, Johnny."

"Southern tradition?"

"Correct."

Expense account total, including hotel, food, and rental car: $314.85.

I spoke to Pie Rose yesterday. She's up for dinner with me, but it'll have to wait a year. Another fine southern tradition.

Yours truly,
   Johnny Dollar

ROGUE'S GALLERY

The Case of the Missing Bandleader

by Bryan Powell

Two men sit in a white cargo van, parked at a curb of a deserted city street. Each is dressed in black. The man in the passenger seat is smoking a cigarette.

"Are you sure he's in there?" the passenger asks.

"Shut up, Willy," the other man replies. "And put out that smoke."

"You've had too much of this Yank coffee, Mueller. It's given you an irritation," the man answers, snuffing the butt in the ashtray.

"My irritation is you," the driver answers, his eyes fixed on the rear view mirror, which affords him a clear line of sight to the double doors of a nearby building.

Without warning, one of the warehouse doors swings open. A well-built man steps out. He wears a white Panama hat and a cream colored suit. He carries a brown satchel in his right hand and a heavy chain with a padlock in his left.

"Get down, Willy. Here he comes," the man in the driver's seat says in a commanding tone.

They slide down in their seats, watching as the man puts down his satchel, chains the door handles together, puts the lock in place and closes the lock. He picks up his satchel and turns to walk down the sidewalk in the direction of the van, which is no more than ten yards away. As he walks past the van, the man named Willy steps out, takes three quick steps toward him and hits him behind the right ear with a sap. The man falls to his knees, his back arched in pain. Willy hits him again, twice, in rapid succession. With the last blow, the sap catches the man along the cheekbone. His face appears to explode in blood. The man collapses, satchel falling to the sidewalk beneath him.

The other man, Mueller, emerges quickly from the van. He rolls the stricken man with his foot, pulls the satchel from beneath his weight, unlatches it and inspects the contents. Willy lifts the limp form of the man from the sidewalk, throws him over his shoulder like a sack of flour, opens the back doors of the van and tosses him in.

The men get into the van, gun the motor and speed away.

Rogue speaking. Richard Rogue. I'm a private detective, a shamus, a gumshoe. If the price is right, and if you don't want me to kill anyone or break too many laws, I just might help you solve your problems.

It's late August, and far too hot for comfort in our fair city, but then that's August for you. If you don't like it, move to Maine and hope for the best.

It's nearly five o'clock, end of another busy day at the office. I'm at my desk, surveying my work-in-progress. A produce wholesaler named McGee has me on retainer to find out who's helping themselves to the lettuce, so to speak. There is a septuagenarian on Seventh Street whose husband ran off with his stenographer. The wife wants him back. Why? Couldn't say. Sometimes people would rather live with it than live without it, even if it's not worth having.

I could be working either of these cases, or one or two others, but I feel as vigorous as a fat lizard on a hot rock. On a table across from my desk, I have a small fan blowing across a large tray of what once was ice, and is now merely cool water. Small comfort. Both windows are open. The cross-breeze is as refreshing as a panhandler's breath.

More than once today, I've pried my white shirt from my brown leather swivel chair. I've oiled the squeaky parts of the chair. I've siphoned a couple inches off of my desk bottle of rock and rye.

I scan today's racing form, pick up the phone, make a call and bet a fin across the board—ten races at five per—all to win. I'm flush, so I can stand it.

I decide to close my office, my heart set on a cold lime phosphate and a quick sandwich at the lunch counter on the next block. I'm reaching for the door when it opens and a young woman enters.

She stands five and a half feet tall, give or take an inch. She has large hazel eyes and dark auburn hair that falls gently onto her shoulders. She is *gorgeous*. She has the kind of face that might make a preacher give up religion, or make a sinner believe. It's a face you hope you'll remember when you're old and senile, sitting in a metal chair in a retirement home somewhere, waiting for your daily dose of glazed plums.

She wears a gold-and-black print bolero jacket, a sheer white blouse, a black skirt that hugs her like a V-8 Ford hugs the highway, and black pumps with low heels. She carries a small purse that matches the jacket. She also has a small manila envelope in her hand. She looks as if she doesn't sweat, or perspire, either. She is probably wearing makeup, but I can't say for sure. She doesn't appear to need it.

If you know me, you know that I spend much of my free time, particularly after sundown, in the company of one Betty Callahan, who at this very moment is visiting her family up the coast a few hundred miles. Betty is every bit of five feet tall, an Irish flame with reddish brown hair and green eyes. She's a reporter, a good one, as spunky and fearless as any man in the job, but far more kissable. When she's sitting across from me in our booth at Brown Derby, all is right with the world. She's light and breezy and good clean fun…well, she suits me, that's all I can say.

But, I'm not thinking about any of that right now. Betty seems very far away indeed. Funny how that works.

"Are you Richard Rogue?" the woman asks.

With considerable effort, I successfully ratchet my sagging lower jaw back into gear.

"That's what it says on the door, last time I looked," I answer. Witty, I am. She lets that pass, and waits.

"Please have a seat," I say, motioning to the straight-backed chair across from my desk. "How may I help you, Miss…?"

"My name is Moore. April Moore. I need to hire you, Mr. Rogue," she says. Her tone is as taut and efficient as her hips, but there is something else, too. Something urgent, intense, passionate.

"Tell me about it," I say.

"I'm the personal assistant and secretary to Earle Jameson."

"Earle 'Kid' Jameson? The famous horn player and bandleader?" I ask.

"The same," she says. "Mr. Jameson…is missing."

"I've heard his work. I like it. Caught his remote a couple of weeks ago from the Midnight Club. Still, Miss Moore, missing persons cases are a matter for the police. I can give you the number for Lieutenant Irvin. He's as charming as a mongoose, but he does good work."

She swats away my suggestion like a fly.

"No, Mr. Rogue, I need help *now*. The police want me to wait 48 hours. By then it might be too late."

"Miss Moore, you know better than I that musicians can be…unreliable," I say. "Maybe your Earle is buttoned up in a tourist camp somewhere, on a bender. Or maybe he's met someone who sings his tune. Or—"

"First of all, Mr. Rogue, he's not 'my' Earle, nor am I his. He's my employer, and a good one. I respect what he does. And, all that aside, I need my job."

"I'll make a note of that," I say. Willful, and perhaps available. Noted.

"Mr. Jameson was at a recording studio last night, the C-Note, over on Cypress," she says. "He was finishing the master recording on his V-Disc session. I was supposed to pick up the master this morning, for shipment to New Jersey. Camden, to be exact, so it could be pressed and shipped overseas. It's unusual to do it this way. Typically, the army handles all of this, but this is a set of recordings that Earle—Mr. Jameson—helped put together himself. But when I called him this morning, there was no answer. I talked to his doorman. He never came home. I talked with the engineer he's working with, Captain Scott. He's in the army—part of the V-Disc program. Captain Scott said he left Mr. Jameson alone at the studio late last night. Well, early this morning. Mr. Jameson was going to lock up when he'd finished. That's not unusual. My boss is a perfectionist."

I put on my best detached expression while I study the barely perceptible curve of her perfectly white teeth. I should know better.

"So you want me to find him, or find out what happened to him?" I ask.

"Yes. Didn't I say that?"

"OK, Miss Moore. I charge twenty-five bucks a day plus expenses. I need one hundred dollars up front as a retainer. Cash."

"I anticipated as much," she says. She reaches into the purse and retrieves five charming green photos of Andrew Jackson, one of my favorite dead presidents. She also hands me the envelope. "Here's a promo photo of Mr. Jameson, and several phone numbers," she says. "You'll find the studio number there. Here's how to reach Captain Scott. And, here's my card. My apartment phone number—my private number—is on the back."

"OK. I'll let you know what I find out."

She rises, shakes my hand, turns and walks to the door. Before she opens it, she turns.

"Mr. Rogue, this is important to me. Is it important to you as well?"

"Yes. Absolutely," I reply. What else could I say?

After the lovely Miss April Moore leaves, I take a deep breath, pour myself one more short one from the desk bottle and call Lieutenant Irvin.

"Whatcha got, Roguey?"

"A missing person. Earle Jameson, the big-time bandleader, last seen at C-Note Recording Studio on Cypress late last night. Any traffic that way today?"

"Nothin'. But I'd have to check with the street patrol sergeant to verify."

"Can you do that? I'll call in later."

"What am I, Roguey, your secretary?"

"Love you, too, Lieu." I hang up the phone before he has the chance.

I go downstairs, exchange pleasantries with Herb Hyde, who runs the cigar stand in the lobby. I go to the garage and retrieve my jalopy. The sandwich will have to wait. It's at least twenty minutes to Cypress, and after all, the lady said it was important to her. And thus to me, and to the Andrew Jackson family.

The studio is dark and padlocked. Perhaps my clock is not set to musician's time. The exterior of the building is a gray-green corrugated sheet metal, increasingly littered, as you walk farther from the padlocked double doors, with cigarette butts, crumpled brown paper bags, newspapers, an occasional wine bottle...the usual debris.

I round the corner of the building, looking for a side entrance, and step on a soft, brown leather shoe. There's a foot in it, and a leg attached to the foot, and under a blanket of newspapers is the rest of a man who's seen better days.

"Hey! Move on!" he says in a sleepy growl.

I kick the foot once or twice, just hard enough to get his attention.

"Hey, buddy, get up. Rise 'n' shine time, compadre."

The crumpled newspapers part to yield an equally crumpled man.

"What do you want? Can't a guy get some sleep around here?"

"I need to ask you about last night, pal. Where you around here?"

"Can't hear ya," he says, dismissing me with a wave of one filthy palm.

I retrieve my money clip from my pants pocket and peel off two pictures of another dead president. Washington. Not my favorite, but handy at times such as these.

"Last night. Hear me now?"

His leathery hand swallows the bills like a python inhaling a bullfrog. "What do you want?"

"Last night, late, where you here?" I ask.

"Sure. I'm always here. Where'd you think I'd be, takin' tea and crumpets with the Queen?"

"Did you see anything unusual? Did you see this man?" Rogue holds Jameson's photo in front of the man's face. The bum focuses, with apparent effort.

"No," he says, flatly, "but you might check with Lefty."

"Lefty?"

"Yep. Drives the Times truck, drops the early morning newspaper bundles, about a block over. More people on foot over there. There's a newsstand."

"OK. Thanks, rummy. Go back to sleep. You look as though you could use it."

"Nuts to you, and the horse you rode in on," he replies, rolling away from me.

I get back in the beater. It's getting dark, and a newspaper's night delivery man might be on the clock by now. The Times distribution center isn't more than a couple of miles from here—Betty and I have been in the place once or twice—so I point my wheels in that direction.

"Nawp. Never seen him," Lefty Carter answers when I flash Jameson's picture. Carter is a big man with red hair and a streetwise manner. He is "Lefty," no doubt, because his right arm is missing. A metal prosthesis, complete with hook-shaped pincers, is in its place. A war injury, perhaps, but it's not my place to ask, and he offers no explanation.

"It would have been about two a.m.," I say, hoping to prompt a memory.

"I'd remember that," he says, "because I was almost run off the road by some fool drunks about that time. Ran a red light, swerved in front of me makin' a left turn. Coulda killed me. Must have been about two fifteen."

I take out my handkerchief and mop my forehead and the back of my neck. It's still hotter than a fry skillet during the breakfast rush. I continue. "This car—what can you tell me about it?"

"Not a car. A van. A white job. Writin' on the back doors. 'Lock-a-Bye Locksmith Services.' And a phone number. Didn't get the number, but I remember the name. If I ever met 'em face to face, I'd put a lock on some fingers, give 'em a nice turn," he says, holding up the hook, which seems more formidable in tandem with his malevolent expression.

"Get a license plate?"

"You're kiddin', right?" he answers.

I bid Lefty adieu, hoping we never shake hands in a dark alley. On the drive back to the office, I stop at Blake's, a slightly disreputable billiard room of my liking, for a shot and a beer and a bowl of stew, in that order. Then I go to the pay phone and call Lieutenant Irvin.

"Hiya, sweetheart. Got anything on a white van, Lock-a-Bye Locksmith Services painted on the rear doors?"

"Rogue, it may surprise you to know, but I work for the city, and we actually have a case or two——"

Rogue tries to cut him off.

"Lieutenant——"

"——of our own here," Irvin continues. "Got a murder-suicide, husband shot his wife, had a grocery store robbery on... Wait a minute, did you say 'Lock-a-Bye'?"

"Right. Got somethin'?"

"Let me pull the sheet."

I wait on the pay phone, wishing I hadn't eaten the stew, which continues to simmer in my gut. Or maybe it's the brown whiskey continuing the aging process.

"Still there, Rogue?"

"Just chalkin' my cue stick, Lieutenant."

"Just got this. Found the van over on Pier 19. Radio car just called it in. And Roguey...there's blood inside. I'm heading that way now. Something I should know?"

"When I know, you'll know," I answer. What's the harm in a little white lie? "Thanks, Irvin. Call me when it's time to buy tickets to the next policeman's charity ball."

I hang up. I take Miss April Moore's card from my wallet, put another nickel in the phone and begin to dial. Now, why am I calling her? What do I have to report? Or, do I just want to hear the sound of her voice, to imagine her mouth close to the phone? 'Get a grip, Rogue.' I push down the receiver hook to disconnect the call, and listen as the coin falls to the return. I collect it and head for the docks.

I arrived at the boardwalk at Pier 19 just in time to meet Irvin. The air is damp with the smell of wet wood, burnt engine oil and spoiled fish. A nice place to visit, but I wouldn't want to die there.

"It was reported stolen last night," Irvin says, pointing to the van. "According to the night watchman, it wasn't here two hours ago. He took a look inside, because it was left open, got suspicious, and gave us a call."

"What else can you tell me?" I ask.

"There's blood inside, on the floorboard, enough to know that the person it came from didn't walk out. Looks like he, or she, got dragged from the back here. From there, I dunno. Got a man going over the van, and three uniforms checking these warehouses."

"I'm going to look around, myself," I say.

"Careful. And shout if you find something," Irvin answers. He turns his attention back to the vehicle.

If that blood belongs to Earle Jameson, it can't be good. And whoever carried off the bleeding person, or the bloody corpse, couldn't have gone far.

The uniform boys are inside the two adjacent buildings, so I retrieve my flashlight and my gun from the glove box of my car and step around the corner to check the next building. As I do I notice a decrepit shack at the end of a narrow pier, over the water, some fifty feet from the main buildings. Anyone walking to that building would probably park right where that van was parked. There's no better way to get there, except by boat.

The pier creeks like an old porch swing. I make my way as quietly as possible out to the shack. There's no lock on the door. I ease it open and step inside, gun in my right hand, flashlight in my left. I hear a scuffing sound. I recognize it, only too late. It's the sound of shoe leather on floorboard. I turn, but I don't see anything except a flash of white light behind my eyes. I've been hit from behind, hard, and the floor is rising up to meet me.

Next thing I know, I'm swimming. Breaststroke, to be precise, swimming not through water but through air, air so stale and pungent that my eyes burn and my nostrils flare. I turn upward, swimming, pushing toward – what? – and then the air becomes clear, fresh and blue and layered with clouds. My strokes become more powerful, as if the air is lighter, as if I'm being lifted or pulled in support of each stroke. The clouds pass quickly, until I see that ol' familiar Cloud Eight and my ol' alter ego, Eugor.

"You oughta know better, Roguey!" cackles my elfish friend, stroking his beard and grinning like he has nothing to lose. Which, of course, he doesn't.

"Know better about what?" I ask. The euphoria of my swim is replaced by a ringing in my ears and the profound fear that my noggin is going to burst like a child's birthday piñata at any moment.

"The girl. You lost your edge, your good sense, because of the girl. That's why you're here on Cloud Eight, isn't it?"

"Oh, shut up, Eugor. It's important to her. Sometimes, you do something for someone just because it's right."

"Don't think I just fell off the ol' turnip truck, Roguey. I'm not buying. You want her to want you, and that's what's in your sniffer, nothing else."

It must be nice to have this on-high point of view, I think to myself.

"Now, you've gotta get out of here," Eugor continues. "You've got a job. Find the bandleader. Find the recording. It's not supposed to be about the girl."

"Easy for you to say. Did you see her?" I ask.

"Of course I did, Roguey. She's apple pie, m'boy, the stuff that men go to war for. She's the girl you take home to mother, marry in a big church wedding, take dancing on Saturday nights and spend Sunday mornings reading the paper with. Do you think for a minute you'll ever live that kind of life?"

"Who are you to say?" I reply.

"Look, Roguey, she came to you as a private detective to do a job. Do right by her. Do your job. Where is Earle Jameson?"

"Eugor, I—"

"Bye, Roguey," he says. As if a blanket were pulled out from me, I roll off of the cloud and free-fall back into the stench as the floor of the shack hits me right in the eye.

More smells. Sawdust. Lantern oil. Rum. Sweat. I open my eyes, one at a time, slowly, and I'm looking right into the eyes of Earle Jameson, lying on the floor just inches from my nose. I hope my eyes don't look like his—dim, fixed, vacant. He's been beaten so badly that his jaw appears disconnected from his face. His skin is torn at the cheekbone as if someone were trying to peel his face like a fat, ripe orange.

Earle 'Kid' Jameson has called his last tune.

I push away from the floor and shake my head to clear the cobwebs. Big mistake. The cobwebs become shards of broken glass careening within my cranium. I must stop getting my head split open. Sooner or later, I might not be able to put Humpty Dumpty together again.

I sit up on the floor of the shack, trying not to look at Earle Jameson's battered remains. The killer, or killers, were just here. Why? It didn't make sense. Why stay with the evidence? Unless there was something they wanted from Jameson, and they were trying to beat it out of him and something or someone interrupted them. Or perhaps they just enjoyed it. I try not to think about that. They left in such a hurry that they left me alive, even left my gun on the floor. Where did they go?

I pull myself up amid the wretched melange of dull and sharp pains circulating in my head. I slowly take apart the room. On the floor under a small table I find a scrap of paper, of very recent vintage, on which is scrawled, "Fl 157 Gate 10, 7 a.m." I slip the paper into my wallet. I want to look more, but I can't think. I need air, now. I push open the door and walk back down the pier to the boardwalk, where I distinctly remember falling flat on my face.

I awake in a bed. Not a hospital bed, and surely not my own bed. It's a woman's bed, soft and frilly and forgiving, a four-poster with canopy. The first glimpse of dawn is peeking through the window to my right. April Moore is sitting on the edge of the bed to my left, leaning over me.

"You're awake," she says.

"Am I alive, or is this Heaven?" I ask, never at a loss for a cornball line.

"You're in my apartment," she answers. "You've been here for about four hours. That's a nasty blow you took on your head."

"How did I get here?"

"Your friend Lieutenant Irvin found my card in your shirt pocket. He said he tried to reach someone named Betty, but she's out of town. He wondered if I was a friend, too. He wanted to take you to the hospital, but you refused. Do you remember that?"

"No."

"You were apparently conscious, more or less, for a few minutes after they found you."

"Well, I—wait a minute…if you talked to Irvin, then you know about Earle."

"Yes, they found him. They told me."

"I'm sorry."

"Me, too. He shouldn't have died that way. Who did it, Mr. Rogue? And why?"

"I don't know. We'll find out. I promise you that."

She excuses herself while I get up, wash my face, brush my teeth and inspect my cuts, bruises and bandages. I climb into the same weary threads that I'd spent the last 24 hours in. April had brushed my jacket and pants and hung them up—I assume she'd undressed me, as well—and as I put on my belt, grab my wallet and keys, I remember the slip of paper from the floor of the shack. It's still in my wallet.

"April?" I call out. I try to yell a little louder, but the reverberation inside my skull sounds like land mines detonating in a deep well. The effect is not pleasant.

In a moment she's there.

"Yes, Mr. Rogue?"

"Please call me Richard," I answer. "April, when you were to pick up Earle's master recording this morning, where were you going to take it?"

"To the airport, to put it on a cargo flight to New York. There's a whole shipment of V-Disc masters on that flight, everything from Frank and Bing to Spike Jones to Duke Ellington. Extraordinary, one-of-a-kind performances. These recordings can never be released to the public. They're only for our troops overseas, for boosting their morale. When the plane arrives in New York, a military envoy will pick up the masters and deliver them to the pressing plant in New Jersey," she says. "Wait, I've got the information right here. Flight 157, gate—"

"Ten," I say, finishing her sentence. "Gate ten. Can you drive?"

"Of course. But how did you know—"

I grab the phone and call Lieutenant Irvin. He answers on the first ring. Thankfully, the man never sleeps.

"Glad to hear you're alive," Irvin says when he answers. "We ran the prints from the van and the shack. We're looking at two Nazi spies, Richard. Hans Mueller and Willy Schmidt, if those are their real names."

"Describe them."

"Well, neither one has a swastika tattooed on his forehead, or anything like that," Irvin says. "Mueller's about six-two, wiry but muscular, Schmidt about five-ten and stocky. Both have blond hair. Schmidt has an ugly crescent-shaped scar on his right cheek, just below the corner of his eye. You can't miss it if you see him."

"OK," I reply. "Irvin, something's happening at the airport this morning. A seven o'clock flight to New York. I found a note in the shack. I, um, wasn't presentable to share it with you before now. I need you to meet me there. There's no time to explain. Gate ten. Bring some muscle, and plenty of it."

"Done." We hang up.

April is waiting at the door. "Time to go now," I tell her.

I probably could have driven, brain damage or no, but I needed the time to think.

I tell April about the Nazis who killed her employer.

"Why?" she asks. "For his recording?"

"No, they tortured him to get the information about the flight. They want all the recordings."

"What will they do?" she asks. "Destroy them? Burn the plane? Put a bomb onboard?"

I wondered, too.

"April, we haven't found Earle's master. His last recording. Maybe they dropped it in the bay or smashed it on the roadside, but my bet is that they want the recordings. Nazis are ruthless *and* greedy. They want it all…all the power, all the land, all the toys. They want to steal our national treasures. They want to deprive our fighting men of the lift those recordings would provide. It's not going to happen."

"How would they steal the masters?" she asks. Her eyes are wide with concern, but she's calm, focused, resolute. My attention shifts, if only for a moment, from the task at hand to the effect of the breeze in her hair.

I blink slowly and answer. "They'd take them before they're loaded onto the plane, and divert them to another plane," I say. "That's a guess, of course, but that's the only way I can see it happening."

We beat Irvin to the airport, leave the car at the curb and run inside. We find our way to the baggage handling area for gates nine through sixteen.

"April, I need you to wait here. Make sure Irvin finds us when he gets here."

"OK, Richard. Be careful."

I try the door marked, "No Admittance." It's open. There is no guard in sight. When I step through the door, I see the guard, motionless, crumpled on the floor in an alcove to my right. I step to him and check his pulse. Nothing.

The baggage area is just short of cavernous, with conveyor belts, forklifts and carts and bins filled with boxes and luggage of all size and description. I pass the loading area for gate nine and am moving toward gate ten when I see Mueller and Schmidt walking toward me. Irvin was right about the scar. Each man is wearing a blue jumpsuit, zippered front, with the airline logo, standard attire for cargo workers. Mueller's suit is loosely zipped in front, with a telltale bulge under his left arm. Gun. Schmidt, who no doubt is also armed, is pushing a six-wheeled cart that carries two wooden crates. Each crate is roughly a foot-and-a-half in height and width and perhaps three feet long. Neither man appears to recognize or even notice me. They were in a hurry back at the pier, too much of a hurry to look at my face, a fact that will play in my favor.

We're closing fast. Before they notice me, I duck behind a cargo bin. After they've past, I pull my revolver from its holster, step out, raise it with both hands, point it at Mueller's back and shout.

"*Achtung!*"

Mueller spins reflexively at my call to attention, sees the gun and reaches for his. It's in his hand, coming out from under his jumpsuit.

"Drop it! Now!" I shout.

The gun keeps coming. I fire two shots. One hits him in the chest, the other rips through his throat. Subconsciously, I register the sound of the bullet thudding into a luggage bin behind him. He's dead before he hits the ground.

Auf wiedersehen, baby.

I turn to Schmidt, who probably could have shot me dead by now if he'd had the wits to do so. Instead, he's abandoned the cart, ducking behind a towering bin of packages and luggage. I'm ten feet away, or less, moving with my back against the bin closest to his.

Suddenly, I see the bin in front of me tumble over. The big moose has dumped it almost right on top of me. Suitcases and boxes hit my head and shoulders, knocking me to the ground. My gun clatters on the concrete floor, sounding like a toy.

I gather myself and my gun in time to see Schmidt running for the exit door. There's no way I can stop him, but it doesn't matter, because Irvin and his boys have just stepped through the door. Schmidt reaches into his suit for his weapon and the cops unload. Schmidt does a passable impression of the St. Vitus dance and hits the floor, shot full of more holes than Dillinger.

Flight 157 will leave on time, V-Disc masters and all.

I find April outside the baggage area. Someone has already told her what happened. Tears are streaming down her face. She throws her arms around my neck tightly and sobs into my shoulder.

"Thank you, Richard," she whispers through the tears. "That disc was all I had left of him. His last words to me, and you've saved them. Thank you."

I hold her while she cries, and take a deep breath. So she loved him. It's happened before. I'll get over it, I suppose, but not today. I doubt she ever will.

It's been three weeks since that morning at the airport. The heat wave has broken and the relief of autumn is imminent.

I'm in my office, sorting through my mail, when I come upon a package from Captain Scott, who'd helped produce Jameson's last recording.

I cut the string on the parcel and its packaging with my Barlow pocket knife. I unwrap a twelve-inch recording disc in a paper sleeve, with a red, white and blue label that reads only, "V-Disc," and beneath it, "April, in Love. The Earle Jameson Five." A handwritten note from Capt. Scott reads, "You're not supposed to have this, according to the army and Petrillo, but I think you're entitled. Keep it under your fedora. Sincerely, Russell Scott, Captain, U.S. Army."

I stare at the note for a long time, and then at the recording. Do I want to hear it? For Jameson's sake, if not for my own, I decide that I do. I don't have a record player at the office, but I do have one at home, so I rewrap the bundle, lock the office, and I go there.

When I get to my apartment, I turn on the player. While it warms up, I pour a tall one. Then I place the record carefully on the turntable, turn it on and ease the needle arm down onto the outside groove.

What follows is a gorgeous, spare ballad, with piano, guitar, double bass and drums underpinning Jameson's vocals. The tune builds gracefully as Jameson plaintively makes his case, in words that he'd written himself:

"When the darkness that surrounds you fades

And you cast aside your masquerades

Skies once stormy now are clear

And before you stands all you hold dear

To once again believe in Spring

And all the joy that true love brings

This is why each day I sing

To April, in love, my April, with love."

After the last verse, Jameson moves boldly into a saxophone solo. A master of several different horns, for this tune he chose an alto sax, an instrument that he imbued with a light, silky resonance. Late in the solo, he holds one note, which arcs downward before rising in a glorious testimony that is worthy of the woman who inspired it.

Somewhere, angels are weeping. I might even shed a tear myself.

Inner Sanctum Mysteries

Concerto in Death Major

by Christopher Conlon

The door creaked as Mary opened it. Somehow she'd known it would, though it was decades later and her old friend from the days of radio was now living in much-reduced circumstances, suffering from frail health and mostly forgotten by a world of satellite TV and Internet links. But even now, here, in this dilapidated old brownstone apartment building, his door would creak. Of course.

And of course it would be dim when she entered. Sepulchral. And of course he would be sitting in the shadows, a dark blanket wrapped around him like a shroud. And of course the first thing she would hear would be his chuckle, gleeful yet subtly menacing, and his deep, whispery voice—rather hoarse now, obviously older, but still instantly recognizable—welcoming her: "Good evening, Mary... Come in out of the cold."

"It's wonderful to see you," she replied, genuinely moved. How long had it been? Forty years? Fifty? She was elderly now herself, and it was difficult to get around anymore. In fact, she rarely went out. But when she'd learned he was here, so very close to her home, she knew she had to come, to spend one last evening with him, share one last cup of tea, hear one final story. "How are you?" she asked.

His eyes, which were all she could see clearly of him, seemed to glow in the darkness. "I remember a poem," he said quietly. "Emily Dickinson. 'Because I could not stop for Death, he kindly stopped for me.' Well...he hasn't quite stopped for me. But I fear he may be just up the street." He chuckled softly, in the old way.

She was about to reply *No, don't say that,* but she checked herself. It would be an insult. It was true; true for both of them. There was no reason to lie.

"And you?" he asked.

"I? Oh, I can't complain. I just became a great-grandmother, you know." She could still hardly believe the words as she spoke them, could barely comprehend she had lived so long that they could possibly apply to her: *Great-grandmother. I am someone's great-grandmother.*

"That's marvelous, Mary," he said from the dark corner. "Congratulations. Please, sit down. You'll pardon me if I don't stand to take your coat. It can be...difficult. Now."

"It's quite all right." She removed her coat and sat near him. She noticed that there was, incongruously in this sparse, ancient room, a microwave oven on a shelf in the corner. There was an old-fashioned tea service on top of it. "Would you like me to make us some tea?" she asked. "I...brought some along."

"Lipton, of course," he said, and she heard the smile in his voice.

She nodded, returning the smile. "Lipton. You remember. 'The tea with the...'"

"...brisk flavor,' " he finished. "Of course, I'd love some. Water is there, in the pitcher next to the tea service."

They were silent as she prepared the tea. In the dimness she could make out only a simple table with two chairs on one side of the room along with book-lined shelves covering the walls. The ceiling seemed oppressively low and she noticed small brown water stains in places. Heavy curtains hid the windows; the carpet under her feet was thin and worn. Near her friend there was an old radio, she saw, and a door which probably led to the kitchen and bathroom. There was also a fireplace, unlit but ready with logs and kindling.

"Would you like me to start a fire?" she asked.

"That would be lovely," he agreed. "I rarely use the fireplace. But your visit is a special occasion."

She lit the fire with matches she found on the mantel and then fetched their tea. She set her friend's on the table beside him; she noticed how his hands shook as he lifted the cup.

"Delicious," he said, as Mary sat down again. She stared into her own cup, then into the blossoming fire.

"Those crackling flames," he said quietly, "remind me of a story."

She smiled. "Everything reminds you of a story."

"Ah, but this is a real barn-burner. Just the thing to warm us on this winter's night. Would you like to hear it?"

God, she was a young woman again, a *girl.* She could close her eyes and it was 1944, 1945. "You know I would," she said.

"Very well," he said. "This is about a man named David Boren. A musician, a concert pianist with a flair for the dramatic...But by the end of this tale, the only piece of music that will be appropriate for him will be the *Funeral March.*" He chuckled. "I call it: 'Concerto in Death Major'..."

"'...Burned beyond recognition.'" The burly detective looked up from the report, straight into Esther's eyes. "Nothin' but a ring on one finger. You're a lucky lady, Miss Toomey, to have escaped that blaze."

"Yes," she agreed after a moment, keeping her eyes averted from the white light glaring in her face.

"It's quite a loss for you," he said, his voice noticeably unsympathetic. "A loss for the world, I guess. I understand that your fiancé was a concert pianist. That's what they tell me, anyway. David Boren. Can't say I've heard the name."

"He was a great artist," Esther said quietly. She'd been here so long; she was so tired…

"Mm." The detective flipped through the report again, almost angrily, as if searching for something that eluded him. "Miss Toomey, I want you to go over it one more time."

"But I've already…"

"I know it's hard," he said. "But something doesn't work here. I can't put my finger on it. Maybe if you tell me again I'll see how all the pieces fit."

Esther sighed, exhausted. "Can't I at least have a cup of coffee?"

"Later."

"But I've told you," she said wearily. "David came to my home past midnight. I was alone. He looked…crazy. He was wild-eyed. His hair was every which way. He was covered in scratches and…"

"And what?"

She closed her eyes. "Blood. He was covered in blood. There was blood on his shirt and on his shoes. He said that *they* were after him. He wanted me to run away with him, to an old shack on the bayou."

"Now, stop right there," the detective said grumpily. "How does a concert pianist know about shacks on the damn bayou?"

She sighed again. "He owns—*owned* the property. A caretaker used to live there, years ago, but he died and David just let the land go."

"So you went with him. Why? Why didn't you call the police?"

"I thought I could reason with him. I thought I could calm him down. David was never violent. He never raised a hand to me. I wasn't scared of him. I was scared *for* him."

"Mm. All right. So what happened once you got there?"

"Well, he *did* calm down. For a while. We were there for two days and nights. We had a little food. Sometimes I thought he was all right. At night he wrote a great deal. I didn't know what it was, then. But it seemed to be good for him to write. So I didn't say anything. But he was always looking outside, convinced *they* were coming for him. Even then, I thought I could…bring him around, make him see reason. But on the second night he heard the sirens. I heard them, too… They sounded like mad dogs howling in the night." She shivered. "He panicked. He shoved the papers into my hand and said he couldn't go on, that I should run, that *they* would shoot him down. He pushed me out of the cabin and locked the door. When I smelled the smoke I screamed for him to let me in, for him to come out, anything. He'd set fire to the shack. I tried to get in through a window, but the flames were too close.

Finally I just sat down and wept. That's when your men arrived. With their sirens."

The detective looked at her for a long time.

"Okay," he said. "Let's go over your fiancé's statement again. This...*essay* of his." He reached to the desk, pulled up a haphazard stack of paper. Some of it was crumpled, some creased and ripped. He drew a heavy breath and exhaled, his face a mask of disgust. "Do you want to read it, or shall I?"

She frowned. "You do it."

STATEMENT OF DAVID BOREN

Life has been such a phantasm of late that I barely know myself or what's happened. Sometimes I wonder what I remember, if I remember anything at all. What do I remember?

I remember the orphanage. I remember learning to play the piano there, from Mrs. Balfour. I remember the scholarship to music school when I was sixteen. And I remember Esther, meeting her there; I remember that we would play pieces as we sat together, she with her left hand and I with my right. I remember her sweet odor, her soft laughing voice...

Those are things I will never forget.

But what else? The car, cracked-up? Waking up next to it, having no memory of how the old sedan managed to plow into the oak tree on that mountain road, right at the edge of a cliff? Trying to walk down the hill, stumbling, finally seeing headlights behind me and feeling grateful that a police car was pulling up slowly next to me?

"Mister!" the voice shouted at me from the car. "That your car back there? You okay?"

"Yes," I remember saying. "Yes, I think so."

"Well, let's have a look at you." The policeman stopped the car and got out, flashed a light in my eyes. "Wanna tell me what happened?" I noticed his heavy Irish brogue.

"I...don't know," I said. "I can't remember."

"What's your name?"

"David Boren."

"Address?"

"I..." I shook my head. "I don't know."

"You don't know? Whaddya mean, you don't know?"

"I mean I don't remember."

"Huh. You drunk? What're you doin' out on this road at this time o' night?"

"I told you, I don't remember."

"What d'you do for a livin', Mr. Boren?"

"I—don't know." I looked at my hands. I knew I did something with them. "Music," I said slowly. "That's it. I play music."

"Oh, musician, eh? What instrument?"

"Piano." I was childishly delighted to feel this come back to me.

"Hey, a piano man, what d'you know about that! My cousin Pete plays piano in a honky-tonk on the East side. Maybe you know him."

"No, I…Not that kind of music."

Just then his police radio crackled into life. *"All units be on the lookout for a man driving a brown sedan."* The voice gave the license number, then: *"Man's name is David Boren. Twenty-seven years old, five feet eight inches tall, one hundred forty-five pounds, blonde hair, blue eyes. Wanted in connection with the murder of Casper Thorne, age twenty-six, found dead this evening at…"*

I didn't hear the rest. The policeman glared at me and his right hand quickly pulled the gun out from his holster.

"Put your hands up, Mr. Boren," he said, his voice steely. "Can't remember, eh? You don't *wanna* remember, that's more like it. C'mon, I'm takin' you in!"

I don't know what happened. All I know is that the name *Casper Thorne* had shot through me like a burning spear. I was breathing raggedly and sweating. I didn't know why, but I knew I couldn't allow myself to be arrested. I knew it as surely as someone would know in a nightmare not to walk down a dark street, as surely as someone might feel that there were terrible forces lying in wait for him somewhere in that darkness.

I didn't know why, but the policeman's gun didn't frighten me nearly as much as that name: Casper Thorne.

I didn't think. I just moved. I grabbed the gun and danced sideways, pulling the policeman past me. I ripped the gun loose from his hand as he fell and was just lifting it to aim at him when, with a sickening scream, he vanished.

He had tumbled off the cliff.

It was a very long drop.

I stood there stupidly, frozen to the spot. I tried to think. Why had I been on this road? Where had I come from? Who was Casper Thorne?

I knew only one thing—that I had to get away. The name Casper Thorne seemed to repeat itself again and again in my mind. The policeman was dead and when the first car came down from the hills the driver would see me and I would be arrested…and Casper Thorne…

I ran. Something was wrong, horribly wrong. I felt as if I'd stepped into a dream. I knew who I was: I was David Boren. I was a well-known concert pianist. Yes, I remembered! I tried to piece my memories together as I charged down the hill. Had I been playing somewhere? A concert? A recital? What had I played, and where? It was all a blank…

At last I came across a roadside diner. I decided to stop and wash up, maybe have a cup of coffee, gather my thoughts. I stood just outside the door and slowed my breathing. At the last moment before walking in I realized I still had the policeman's gun in my hand. I deposited it in the waistband of my trousers.

I splashed water on my face in the washroom. It seemed to help. Finally I went to the counter and had the waitress bring coffee.

The place was mostly deserted. One lone woman sat at the other end of the counter and two guys were in a booth in the corner, sharing a newspaper.

"Pal," the waitress said, "you look like you been through a war."

"Oh, yeah—got a little lost out there."

She scowled. "What are you doin' walkin' around out there at this time of night?"

"I…" I felt my breath coming fast again. "No, it's nothing, just my…my car ran out of gas."

"Oh." She nodded, but looked suspicious. "Well, look, the owner here, Jake, could probably put a gallon in a can and drive you to where you left your car."

"Uh—yes, that's…that would be very nice."

She walked off. I knew I couldn't get in any vehicle with any owner of any diner. Impossible. I had to get away.

Just then I noticed the two guys in the booth looking at me. They were glancing from the newspaper to me and then back again. There was a copy of that same newspaper sitting on the counter beside me and I picked it up and looked.

CITY-WIDE MANHUNT FOR MUSICIAN-MURDERER DAVID BOREN.

David Boren, 27, rising young star on the classical music scene, is being urgently sought by the police in connection to the murder of local man Casper Thorne…

It hit me like a blinding light in a black room, like a staggering blow to the head. Casper Thorne, Casper Thorne! I backed away from the newspaper in terror and then fled out into the darkness. I heard the waitress call from behind me: "Mister, you ain't paid for that coffee…!"

I don't know what I did then. Somehow I got off the mountain and found myself walking, utterly exhausted, down a dim street. There was only one thing to do: I had to get to Esther. I knew that if I could just reach her, everything would be all right. Esther. Twenty-two years old. I pictured her big dark eyes and her brunette hair that flowed to her shoulders. I remembered how her long slender pianist's fingers looked entwined with my own. We were to be married soon, I knew—that much I remembered. If only I could get to Esther, this nightmare would end.

I finally got my bearings and realized that I was only a few blocks from where she lived. The quickest way to the house was through the city cemetery; I didn't hesitate. I hopped over the fence and started winding my way through.

There was a full moon that night and blue light seemed to glow on the old tombstones. I was halfway across when I heard a sound—a sound, in the middle of a cemetery, in the middle of the night!

Someone was whistling. An aimless, unmelodic tune.

I stood still, leaning forward in the darkness, trying to see amongst the shadows of stones and ancient trees where the sound came from. Finally I did. It was an old man, lying on his back next to a newly-dug grave. He was using an old jacket for a pillow and drinking from a flask.

"Evenin', mister!" he called to me.

I moved slowly toward him. "Good evening."

"Beautiful night," he said complacently. He raised the flask toward me. "Have a nip?"

"No...No, thank you. What are you doing out here?"

He gave me a sour look, as if I'd overlooked the obvious. I noticed his crooked teeth and the beard stubble peppering his face. "I'm the gravedigger, young man. This here's my latest masterpiece." He giggled drunkenly and patted the side of the open, empty grave.

"Gravediggers don't normally work past midnight," I pointed out.

"Aw, I got me a place just up the street," he said, gesturing vaguely. "But it's nice here. Peaceful, like. Sometimes I come here just to unwind, think my thoughts."

And, in that moment, I saw what he meant. It may have been macabre, but it *was* peaceful in the cemetery. A light breeze swept through the trees; everything was motionless and calm. That was what I needed, more than anything else: calm. I sat down next to the old man and said, "You know, I think I *will* have a taste, if you don't mind."

"Sure!" he said eagerly, offering me the flask. "Don't often get company out here this time of night." I thought he would ask me why I was there, but he didn't. It didn't matter to him.

The contents of the flask hit me like a freight train. I gasped and shook my head. The gravedigger chuckled.

"Powerful stuff," I said.

"Make it myself," he said proudly. "Right in my own bathtub. Better'n what you get in the store."

I smiled, handing the flask back to him. "It sure is."

We sat there in silence for a few minutes. I felt I wanted to stay here forever. Finally I looked at the big open pit and asked, "Who's this for?"

"Aw, who knows. They tell me to dig 'em, I dig 'em. I don't ask questions. Except...come to think of it, I do remember somethin'...this fella was murdered."

My blood froze in my veins. "Murdered?"

"Yeah." He looked at me, scowling. "Murdered. Fella name of...Aw, it's on the tip of my tongue..."

I knew what he was going to say before he said it. And I knew that I couldn't *bear* to hear it, not again, not here. And I saw, implanted in the mound of dirt next to the grave, the spade he had used in digging the hole. It would be better than the gun. Quieter.

I stood and moved toward it.

"Now, consarn it...it was just in the papers...Fella name of...Boren? No, that's the fella they're lookin' for, the one that done it. You know, you look a little like him, like the picture I saw in the paper."

I lifted the spade. I was behind him, partially obscured by the mound of dirt. He couldn't see me.

"Yeah, ain't that funny. You do look like him. But the fella what was murdered...Dorn, Horn...what was that name...?"

I moved toward him.

"Thorne!" he cried triumphantly. "His name was *Casper Thorne!"*

I brought the spade down onto his head once, twice. Again! Again!

I ran then. Esther, I had to get to Esther—she was the only one who could save me, who could make sense of all this madness. I jumped the fence at the far end of the cemetery and charged wildly through the deserted night streets. The name *Casper Thorne* seemed to reverberate mockingly inside my skull. I heard it a dozen times, a hundred, a thousand, and every time I heard it I answered inside my mind with: *My name is David Boren, I am a well-known concert pianist, my fiancée's name is Esther.*

Esther lived in a large old house, nearly a mansion, at the end of a street of such opulent homes. I stumbled as I ran up to the door and fell partly against it, slamming my fists against it and crying, "Esther! Esther!"

The door opened after what seemed an eternity. Esther stood there in her nightdress, her face a mask of fear. "David! What happened to you?" she cried.

I nearly fell into the house. She closed the door and followed me hurriedly into the sitting room, which was elaborately done in whites and grays and in the middle of which was a shining ebony baby grand piano. I collapsed exhaustedly onto the piano bench. She ran to the kitchen and brought back a wet cloth, stroking my forehead with it gently. Finally she sat down next to me on the bench.

"David, what *is* it?"

I told her. I told her about the accident and the policeman and the newspaper in the diner and the gravedigger. I told her everything.

At the end of it all she said, "We must call the police, David."

"No!' I cried. "Don't you see? That's the one thing I *can't* do!"

I turned then, impulsively, to the keyboard, intending to play a bit of something calm, soothing—a Chopin nocturne, maybe. Anything to slow my thundering heartbeat, soothe my shattered nerves. But as I raised my fingers to the keys I noticed something I'd not seen before. I was wearing a ring, a gold ring I had no memory of. I studied it closely.

"This isn't mine," I said, terror seeping through every fiber of my being. "Is it?"

"I don't know." Esther leaned forward to see the ring. "David," she said, "there's an inscription, or something. Letters. They're very small. Wait, I can just make them out. Yes, two letters. Initials. *C. T.*"

His ring! I was wearing Casper Thorne's ring! I tried frantically to pull it off, but it was too tight. It seemed melded to me, singed into me like a brand.

"David," she said, her arms around me, "do you really not remember Casper Thorne?"

"I've never heard of Casper Thorne!"

"Oh, David," she said, "I think you've done something awful."

"No! No!"

Music had always saved me. I turned to the keyboard again and decided to play. Chopin, yes. "Help me, Esther," I said desperately. "You play the left hand, I'll play the right. The way we used to." But as my hand descended to the keys I abruptly realized that I had no idea how to play.

It was as if I'd never taken a piano lesson in my life.

"Esther, what…what are the notes…the Nocturne, the one we always played…?"

Just then there was a loud knocking on the front door. "Police!" a voice shouted. "Open up!"

We looked at each other. "David, give yourself up," she whispered.

"No, not until I get to the bottom of this. I have to get away. I need someplace I can think. Do you remember that land I own, out on the bayou? There's an old shack there. We can escape out the back way."

"David…"

"Please, Esther!"

Her eyes revealed her decision. "All right. I'll come." She grabbed a change of clothes and we fled out the rear entrance, the rapping on the door continuing, loud enough to wake the dead.

And that brings us to this lonely shack on the bayou.

This is where I, David Boren, shall die.

I know now that it is quite hopeless. Esther has talked to me, told me patiently about Casper Thorne. She's told me that he was a local rich boy who wanted Esther for himself, and he was not accustomed to taking "No" for an answer. She's told me how he showered her with gifts, with letters, and how, after she and I had had an argument, she accepted his invitation to go to a dance. She had just wanted to show me, she said. She'd not meant anything more by it than that. She'd wanted to make me jealous, to force me to appreciate her more. I spotted them there, she said. But she had known the instant she saw my face that this would prove to be more than just a high-schoolish game, a prank, a cheap trick.

"You had murder in your eyes," she told me.

And so I guess I did murder Casper Thorne. Apparently that was what I was doing in the sedan, driving around the mountain in the middle of the night. It seems I was disposing of the body.

I have no memory of any of this. The accident wiped it all away.

It seems strange, to be guilty of a crime I cannot remember. On the other hand, there is the policeman as well, and the gravedigger. Those I remember all too well.

I am guilty.

Soon I will fold up these papers and give them to Esther, tell her to go far away from here. Then I will do what anyone who has committed the deeds I have should do.

I will burn.

I hear sirens now, far away…the time has come.

Farewell.

Signed,

DAVID BOREN

The burly detective dropped the papers onto his desk with a look of disgust and leaned close to Esther.

"Now," he said very quietly, "why don't you tell me what *really* happened."

Listening to the document again had made Esther go numb. Her brain seemed frozen. The light in her eyes was so intense, so blinding. "Happened?" she asked distantly. "Happened…?"

"This ain't jelling," he said. "Why does a famous pianist suddenly go nuts because his girl dances with somebody? Why does he murder? Why does he put on his victim's ring? Why does he lose his memory? And this *newspaper* he says he saw. He didn't see no such thing, 'cause it don't exist. There's no headline about any murder of Casper Thorne. Casper Thorne is alive and well, as far as anybody knows. The boys are out lookin' for him now. So you tell me, young lady. You *tell* me."

She had been here for so many hours that she no longer knew if it was morning or night. It seemed as if there was no world but this little gray room with the bright light in her eyes, and this huge man before her demanding information. She remembered, long ago…she'd been a student, a brilliant one, she had a rare gift for music…everyone said so…then there was David…and there was Casper…oh, if only they would let her sleep…just sleep…What was this wetness dripping onto her hands?…Tears…She was weeping, weeping…

"All right!" she cried suddenly. "All right, I'll tell you! It wasn't David! It was Casper!"

Somehow out of the corner of her eye she saw the detective gesture at an unseen assistant. This other man came close to her, pencil and paper in hand, writing down in shorthand everything she said.

"What?" the detective demanded gruffly. "What do you mean?"

"The man in the shack! Burned beyond recognition! It's not David! It's Casper!"

"How is it Casper?"

"We planned it," she said, staring at the flat plane of the desk before her, head throbbing with pain. "Your men who are looking for Casper won't find him. He was in the shack. It was Casper who lit the fire, Casper who…burned up."

"That explains the ring," the detective said. "Now tell me the story."

Esther sighed as deeply as she ever had. "Casper and I were lovers," she said quietly. "I was engaged to David, but I was never in love with him. I'd known him since I was a child, but it was his imagination that said we had been in love all that time. From the start he was a better pianist than I. The marriage would have been good for my career. We could have performed duets, that kind of thing. But I never liked him, not really, and when we started dating I realized I couldn't stand him *touching* me…I met Casper. He was no rich boy. He worked as a waiter. He had no money. But he loved me. Or I…thought he did. One night when I was with David he showed me how he had made a will leaving everything to me. David had no other family, and with his career taking off as it had he had quite a sizable estate. So Casper would kill David and I would inherit David's money. With that Casper and I could live comfortably for a long time, and I could build my music career as the widow of the fabled David Boren…" She fell silent.

"So Thorne killed Boren."

She nodded wearily. "He took the sedan up the mountain road that night and got rid of the…the body. Have your men go search that mountaintop. David's there." She shivered. "The rest I had to piece together when Casper came to me that night, frantic and covered with blood. The accident had done something to him. His…guilt, I guess. I don't know. I'm not a psychiatrist. But it had been *my* idea, all my idea…the killing, the…He loved me so much, Casper did, that he would have done anything for me. But it drove him mad. He came off the mountain convinced that *he* was David Boren."

The detective inhaled thoughtfully and leaned back. The greater part of the confession completed, he could afford now to go easier on the girl.

"What did he say when you called him Casper?"

"He wouldn't hear it," Esther said, shuddering at the memory. "He simply didn't hear it. He heard me calling him 'David.' He heard me telling him that story about the dance, too, where he was David and he saw me dancing in Casper's arms. I never said any of that. But he heard it…in his mind."

"That explains the newspaper," the detective nodded. "There was no photo, no story. But he *saw* it that way. And what he heard on the car radio, too."

Esther nodded. Her cheeks felt sticky with tears and she rubbed them with her palms. "It was all in his imagination," she whispered.

The detective looked at her for a long time. Finally he reached behind him and turned out the bright light. Cool darkness filled the room. "Not quite all," he said grimly, reaching for a cigarette and lighting it.

"What?"

"It wasn't quite all in his imagination. There's Boren, who you say we'll find on that mountain. And there's the cop he shoved over the cliff. And the gravedigger. That ain't no imagination."

"No," Esther whispered.

"All right," the detective said tiredly. "Time to stand up, young lady. You've got an appointment with a jail cell."

The fire had died down to embers and Mary sat silently for a moment, reflecting on the story.

"I feel sorry for poor Mr. Boren," she said. "The *real* Mr. Boren. But then again, I feel sorry for all of them."

"Oh, I don't know, Mary," her host said quietly. "Though it's a shame the real Boren didn't commit those murders. Then he and Esther could have gotten together to play a fine game of musical chairs. Musical...*electric* chairs." He chuckled.

Mary smiled, but realized that it had grown late.

"I'm afraid it's time for me to go," she said. "My granddaughter is coming over tonight. She's bringing her child, my great-granddaughter."

She could not see his face in the darkness but somehow felt that he was smiling.

"Yes, well," he said. "Let me see you to the door."

"You needn't do that," she protested, as she pulled on her coat. "I'm quite all right."

But he stood. He was stooped-over now; still, anyone could see what a tall man he was—tall and very slender. He wrapped the blanket carefully around himself and reached to a heavy cane next to the chair. He used it to help his progress to the door.

"It's been so wonderful to see you again," Mary said awkwardly. "It's a shame that I was the only one to hear the story. Years ago..."

"Yes," he said quietly. "But there are always more stories. As long as there is even one person left to listen."

She smiled. "Of course."

He opened the door. "Goodnight, Mary."

She looked at him closely for a long moment, then leaned forward and kissed him gently on his withered cheek.

"Goodnight," she whispered, her voice catching suddenly in her throat.

As she stepped quickly out she heard the words she knew she would hear.

"Pleasant dreams..." he said, chuckling a final time.

Behind her, the door creaked quietly closed.

The Authors

JOE BEVILACQUA is a veteran award-winning radio producer, writer and actor who has worked for National Public Radio stations for more than 20 years. He has written and produced over 100 radio plays, including the comedy series; *The Misadventures of Sherlock Holmes, Old-Time Radio Parodies*, and the humorous science fiction serial, *The Whithering of Willoughby and the Professor*, in which he performs all the characters himself. His has also produced radio documentaries, including *We Take You Now to Grover's Mill: The Making of the "War of the Worlds" Broadcast* and *Lady Bird Johnson: Legacy of a First Lady*. Examples of his work are available at www.comedyorama.com.

ROBERT J. CIRASA is a Professor and Chairman of the English Department at Kean University. He earned his Ph.D. from New York University and is the author of *The Lost Works of William Carlos Williams* and other criticism on modern poetry and science fiction. Together with Joe Bevilacqua, he has co-authored more than 20 radio plays which have been broadcast over National Public Radio, including a series of stories featuring the characters of Willoughby and the Professor.

CHRISTOPHER CONLON'S poems, stories, and articles have appeared in such varied publications as *America Magazine, Washington Post, Filmfax, Poet Lore,* and the *Tennessee Williams Annual Review*. His numerous tales for *The Long Story* literary journal are collected in *Saying Secrets: American Stories* (iUniverse), and he is the author of a poetry chapbook, *What There Is* (Argonne House Press). His first full-length book of poetry, *Gilbert and Garbo in Love,* is scheduled for publication in 2003 by The WordWorks in Washington, DC. A former Peace Corps Volunteer, Conlon now lives and works in Silver Spring, Maryland. His website can be accessed at www.christopherconlon.com.

JUSTIN FELIX published an essay about science fiction concept rock albums in the Winter 2000 issue of the academic journal *Extrapolation*. He has also written many movie reviews for various Internet periodicals. He lives in Bowling Green, Ohio, and is working on a doctorate in English. The story in this book is his first published piece of fiction. His interests include old time radio, science fiction and horror, film, composition, and education.

JACK FRENCH is a former Navy officer and retired FBI Agent who has been research-ing OTR since 1975. He formerly edited *Nara News* and currently edits *Radio Recall*. Jack has over 1,400 shows in his personal collection and has written exten-sively about juvenile westerns, lady detectives, RCMP heroes, and aviators. He received the 1993 Allen Rockford Award at the FOTR Convention for his contri-butions in OTR research. Jack has lectured on OTR subjects at the Smithsonian, the Newseum, and the National Press Club. He is a past president of the Metro Washington OTR Club and resides with his wife in Fairfax, Virginia.

MARTIN GRAMS, JR. is the author and co-author of numerous books and magazine articles, including *Suspense: Twenty Years Of Thrills And Chills* (1998), *The His-tory of The Cavalcade of America* (1998), *The CBS Radio Mystery Theater: An Episode Guide and Handbook* (1999), *Radio Drama: An American Chronicle* (1999), *The Have Gun-Will Travel Companion* (2000), *The Alfred Hitchcock Pre-sents Companion* (2001), *Invitation To Learning* (2002), *The Sound Of Detection: Ellery Queen's Adventures In Radio* (2002), and author of two authorized publi-cations: *Inner Sanctum Mysteries: Behind The Creaking Door* and *I Love A Mys-tery* (both due for a 2003 release). He has also written articles for SPERDVAC's *Radiogram, Scarlet Street, OTR Digest*, and *Filmfax*. Martin has contributed chap-ters for Midnight Marquee's *Vincent Price* (1998) and *The Alfred Hitchcock Story* (1999). Martin is the recipient of the 1999 Ray Stanich Award.

MICHAEL GIORGIO was the first winner of the Friends of Old Time Radio's annual scriptwriting contest for his script "The Whistler: Promoted to Death." Since then, he has had radio plays produced by Shoestring Radio Theatre (San Fran-cisco), Thirty Minutes to Curtain (Northridge, California), WCRS RadioStage (Akron, Ohio), and Don't Touch That Dial! (Johnson City, Tennessee). His short stories have appeared in *The Mammoth Book of Road Stories, The Strand, Mystery Time*, and others. Michael lives in Waukesha, Wisconsin with his wife and fellow writer, Kathie, stepchildren Christopher, Andy, and Katie, daughter Olivia, and a menagerie of animals. He is an advertising agency accountant by trade.

JIM HARMON (James Judson Harmon) was born April 21, 1933 in Mount Carmel, Illinois, a small town that had also been home to radio's Lone Ranger, Brace Beemer, a distant relative, he's told. He grew up getting virtually every sickness around except polio, and becoming a fat kid. He listened to the radio, and read science fiction magazines. In his teens he began writing SF and by his twenties, was selling it. He wrote a lot of space and time travel stories, many anthologized. His first SF book all his own should be out in 2002 or early 2003, *Harmon's Galaxy*, from Cosmos Press. But he has written a lot of other things: several paperback novels like *The Man Who Made Maniacs* and a number of movie scripts, only one actually produced (and available on video), *The Lemon Grove Kids Meet the Monsters*. Of course, for several decades he has been writing books about old time radio like *The Great Radio Heroes* (1967, and a revised edition in 2000). He and his wife, Barbara, a microbiologist, live in Burbank where Jim continues to write and produce radio programs. He also works out at the gym, and is trimmer now than he was in his childhood years.

STEPHEN JANSEN has had a love affair with audio since he first heard "Strawberry Fields Forever." His father introduced him to OTR in the late 1970's, recording *CBS Radio Mystery Theater* at night for daytime listening. He has been a staff member of the North American Radio Archives for several years, writing articles for the magazine *NARA News*, and recording it for the sight-impaired members. He heads an OTR performance group, "Theatre of the Mindless." He writes, records, and produces new audio drama, albeit at a snail's pace. He can be reached at ilamfan@att.net.

STEPHEN A. KALLIS, JR., a Life Member of the Society of Motion Picture and Television Engineers, developed a way to generate control tapes for film laboratories' additive color printers. His articles have appeared in the *American Rocket Society Journal, SMPTE Journal, Cryptologia*, and *General Aviation News*. His book, *Radio's Captain Midnight: The Wartime Biography*, chronicled the Ovaltine adventures through 1945.

MICHAEL LEANNAH is an elementary school teacher and a writer of fiction. Though he focuses primarily on children's literature, he has also written a collection of short stories and a novel. His original radio scripts have won national awards.

JOHN LEASURE worked in the entertainment industry for eleven years in a myriad of positions, duties and responsibilities. A freelance television writer in primetime (*Knots Landing*) and an amazingly short stint in daytime (*Loving*), he settled in as Manager of Labor Relations at Lorimar Production which, through mergers and buy-outs, became Warner Bros. Television. Currently Mr. Leasure is Manager of Human Resources for a social service agency in his home town of Portsmouth, Ohio where he also teaches part-time at a small university.

BOB MARTIN is an old-time radio enthusiast and collector. His interest in radio and voice-over work date back to his early childhood years. His first voice-over experience at the microphone was in an elementary school play where he portrayed the voice of the American flag. He remembers being inspired early on by Vincent Price's phenomenal reading of Edgar Allen Poe's "The Tell-Tale Heart" on television. In the early 1970's, Martin attended the Mel Blanc School of Commercials, headed by Blanc and his son, Noel. In college, he participated in theater productions and was a member of the Long Beach Community Playhouse. In the years 1990 through 1996 Martin was producer and host of KUOP 91.3 FM's popular Old-Time Radio Show in northern California. Although his busy schedule as deputy director for a multi-county organization and part-time writer doesn't permit him to participate in radio work today, he continues to enjoy collecting old-time radio programs.

JIM NIXON was born and raised in Minneapolis, Minnesota. He holds graduate and undergraduate degrees from the University of Minnesota and spent twenty years in aviation management before moving to the Boston area, where he spent another fifteen years in aviation consulting before returning to Minnesota in 2001. He began writing in 1983 with a novel set in the rapidly-changing airline industry. His radio play based on *The Lone Ranger* won a Friends of Old-Time Radio script contest in 1996. His novel, *Champion of Justice*, published in 1997 under the name of Fredric James, was based on his interest in old-time radio and is available at Amazon.com. He now divides his time between working for H&R Block, writing and working on model railroads. He considers the WXYZ radio dramas his favorites among the great radio programs of the past.

BEN OHMART was born in Albany, Georgia and now lives in Boalsburg, Pennsylvania. He has written for the stage, screen and radio, and currently reviews CDs for several on-line and print publications. His current book projects include biographies on Paul Frees, Daws Butler, Don Ameche, The Bickersons, and Philip Rapp. Ben runs BearManor Media, a small publishing company dedicated to old radio, old movies and whatever else takes his old fancy.

PATRICK PICCIARELLI is a retired NYPD Lt., licensed private investigator, and adjunct professor of writing in the graduate school at Seton Hill University. He is the author of four published fiction and non-fiction books and has sold a screenplay. His first book, *Jimmy the Wags: Street Stories of a Private Eye* is being made into a TV movie by Danny DeVito. His latest book: *Mala Femina: The Life of a Daughter of a Don* will be released by Barricade books next year.

DONNIE PITCHFORD, a native of East Texas, is married to the former Laura Pearson. Both are Christians and educators. The National Lum and Abner Society was founded in 1984. Donnie serves as its President, contributing audiovisual support, art, articles and character voices, working with Vice-President Sam Brown and Executive Secretary Tim Hollis. Since 1985, Donnie has taught broadcast journalism (CHS-TV) at Carthage High School (Texas) where Mr. P's students produced an eight-hour OTR marathon (on cable TV) entitled *The Golden Age of Radio!* For more NLAS information, check out http://home.inu.net/stemple/index.html. To learn more about CHS-TV, look for their link at http://www.carthage.esc7.net/.

BRYAN POWELL (no relation to Dick Powell) is a freelance journalist and musician based in Lawrenceville, Georgia, near Atlanta. He holds a Master's degree in Mass Communication, print journalism concentration, from Georgia State University. He has written more than a thousand articles for various magazines and newspapers, primarily covering blues and jazz music. Bryan is married, with two daughters, and is the happy owner of several thousand hours of old-time radio programming. This is his first published work of fiction.

CLAIR SCHULZ has been a teacher, librarian, museum archivist, and a bookseller specializing in literary first editions and continues to be a mossback by choice of lifestyle. He has written articles which have appeared in a variety of periodicals including *Nostalgia Digest, Mad About Movies, English Journal, Old Time Radio Digest, Firsts*, and *Today's Collector*. His primary goal now is to reach the same level of contented fogeyism achieved by Richard Peavey, the venerable fuddy-duddy on *The Great Gildersleeve*.

ROGER SMITH, a Texan, was born in Tyler, and graduated from Waco High School. At various times, he attended Texas Tech as a theatre major. At 21, after recovering from a lion attack, he went to work for Clyde Beatty for the season of 1964 as his assistant trainer. Beatty died the next July, and Smith went to the old Jungleland, in Thousand Oaks, California, to continue his apprenticeship as a wild animal trainer under the master trainers there. He enjoyed a long and fulfilling circus career, and is now returning to his educational theatre training to renew his career as a writer and actor. Roger has four children, and his tenth grandchild is due in December.

CAROL TIFFANY is a retired RN, now living in Palm Bay, Florida. She grew up listening to the radio in Indiana and Ohio during the 1940s and 1950's. She rediscovered Old Time Radio while living in the San Francisco Bay Area during the late 1960's and began what has become quite an extensive tape collection during the 1970's. After moving to Colorado in 1980, Carol became involved with local radio in Greeley. A member of RHAC (Radio Historical Association of Colorado) since 1986, she currently edits the club's newsletter *Return With Us Now*. This is her first fiction story.

THE BICKERSONS SCRIPTS
VOLUME 1

by Philip Rapp   Edited by Ben Ohmart
ISBN: 0-9714570-1-8 $15.95

And now, here are Don Ameche and Frances Langford
in Philip Rapp's humorous creation...
The Bickersons!

The Bickersons was one of radio's most popular and funniest comedy teams. Now for the first time ever - you can read these never before published scripts. Included are full scripts from The Old Gold Show, the 1951 Bickersons series and other rarities. With an introduction by Phil Rapp himself!

Read just what the actors read!

____ YES, please send me ____ copies of *The Bickersons Scripts* for just $15.95 each.

____ YES, I'm interested in buying _____ copies of *The Bickersons Scripts* in bulk for my radio club, organization or store. Please send details.

____ YES, I would like more information about your other publications.

Add $4 postage for up to 5 books. For non-US orders, please add $4 per book for airmail, in US funds. Payment must accompany all orders. Or buy online with Paypal at bearmanormedia.com.

My check or money order for $_____ is enclosed. Thank you.

NAME_____

ADDRESS_____

CITY/STATE/ZIP _____

EMAIL _____

Checks payable to: Ben Ohmart * P O Box 750 * Boalsburg, PA 16827
ben@musicdish.com

THE GREAT GILDERSLEEVE

by Charles Stumpf and Ben Ohmart
ISBN: 0-9714570-0-X $18.95

"*The Great Gildersleeve* by Charles Stumpf and Ben
Ohmart ranks as one of the best books on a radio
program, if not the best."

— *Classic Images*

"Very comprehensive. A wonderful book!"

— Shirley Mitchell

"It really takes me back to those delightful days on the show."

— Gloria Peary

Give the gift of old time radio

___ YES, please send me ___ copies of *The Great Gildersleeve* for just $18.95 each.

___ YES, I'm interested in buying ____ copies of *The Great Gildersleeve* in bulk for my radio club, organization or store. Please send details.

___ YES, I would like more information about your other publications.

Add $4 postage for up to 5 books. For non-US orders, please add $4 per book for airmail, in US funds. Payment must accompany all orders. Or buy online with Paypal at bearmanormedia.com.

My check or money order for $_____ is enclosed. Thank you.

NAME_____

ADDRESS_____

CITY/STATE/ZIP _____

EMAIL _____

Checks payable to: Ben Ohmart * P O Box 750 * Boalsburg, PA 16827
ben@musicdish.com